SPRING IMPERIAL

Evelyn Hart was working for the Resident in Kashmir
when she met her husband who was serving in the Indian
Army. In SPRING IMPERIAL she has written an outstanding saga set in twentieth-century India, where she
spent much of her early married life.

Spanning almost fifty years and two continents,
SPRING IMPERIAL is the dramatic love story of Carissa
Thornton and Lance Gardner who meet one fateful day
in September 1938. Cara is captivated by the romantic
story of Lance's ancestors and the crumbling palace,
Spring Imperial, in the Ganges Basin which he has
inherited and hopes one day to restore.

Rich in drama and history, SPRING IMPERIAL is the
compulsive chronicle of a love that spans two continents
and defies time, place, and convention.

'HER PORTRAIT OF QUETTA DURING THE WAR
YEARS IS SPLENDIDLY LIFELIKE AND START-
LINGLY CORRECT'

M. M. Kaye

SPRING IMPERIAL

Evelyn Hart

CORGI BOOKS

SPRING IMPERIAL
A CORGI BOOK 0 552 13438 4
Originally published in Great Britain by Century Hutchinson Ltd

PRINTING HISTORY
Century Hutchinson edition published 1988
Corgi edition published 1989

This book is set in 10/11pt Sabon by Goodfellow & Egan Ltd,
Cambridge.
Corgi Books are published by Transworld Publishers Ltd., 61-63
Uxbridge Road, Ealing, London W5 5SA, in Australia by Transworld
Publishers (Australia) Pty. Ltd., 15-23 Helles Avenue, Moorebank,
NSW 2170, and in New Zealand by Transworld Publishers (N.Z.) Ltd.,
Cnr. Moselle and Waipareira Avenues, Henderson, Auckland.
Printed and bound in Great Britain by
Cox & Wyman Ltd, Reading

To
*All those who served in and loved India, and especially
those who were fortunate enough to live in Quetta
during the war years.*

CONTENTS

OVERTURE

I knew the letters would be there. My mother had told me I would find them in the bottom drawer of her Sheraton escritoire, the only piece of furniture which, for sentimental reasons, I am keeping. Once it stood in the Wick House drawing-room.

She had been a tidy woman. As a child, I found that a great bore: always made to put my toys away when I was still in the midst of playing. Why not make as much mess as one liked and then have a big clear-up at the end of the day, or better still, at the end of the week, or even one mammoth yearly spring cleaning! That is how I choose to live in the comfortable chaos of my mews apartment. Yet, having gone through all my mother's belongings on the Wick Bungalow Estate, I feel glad of the order that has undoubtedly made my task easier.

An attractive and smiling woman right into her older days, my mother had always been generous hearted to me an only child without being overbearing; she was good company in spite of years of strain, the active party of our _ménage à trois_, the one who took me out for breezy walks with our black labrador, Bugler, onto Hengistbury Head; the one who played tennis with me and taught me to sail. She made friends easily, and had several 'very great friends' whom I have never met and never particularly want to meet, absorbed and inviolate as I am in my own life and work.

I remember my mother once making a tentative opening about one of these 'great friends'. She said with some hesitancy that she thought she ought to tell me, that she felt I really should know. I do not quite understand why, but my

9

reaction then to this attempt to tell me something that I took to be private, was swift and defensive. I said I did not *wish* to know. I pretty well told her: please to shut up! Thinking about it later I suppose I did not want anything to interfere with the satisfactory relationship we had developed in my adulthood. After the intimacies and dependencies of childhood, we were now equals. We each went our own ways without interference or probing. She was proud of my work, and I was proud of the way she took off and made a new life for herself instead of moping as she could so easily have done in her straitened circumstances.

After my beloved father's death twenty years ago in 1960, my childhood home became more of a brief stopping place to my mother than anything else; she was hardly ever there! In the sixties, when the world had been opened up by inexpensive air fares to those who lived on small incomes, she had taken advantage of cheap travel in a big way, wintering abroad regularly, summers often spent in Scotland. Even though I had only seen my mother at lengthy intervals after my father's death, I missed her and now regretted that I had not shown more interest in what she was doing.

Because of her lengthy absences, I no longer had a wailing wall to rush to when something went wrong in my life, nor a shoulder on which to cry for sympathy! Not that I needed her for that. I had long grown out of that attitude, together with the rebellion of my teenage years, which, had I stopped to think, was unnecessary. My parents never criticized my wish for independence, nor did they try to restrict me. It was my life, they said. It was up to me to get on with it in the way I wished. Selfishly, and very satisfactorily, I did just that.

I am now an established career woman of thirty-nine with Oxford Greats, but no stultifying marriage or amorous interludes to get in the way of my work. After years spent laboriously learning the job, I have become manager of a literary magazine. The challenge is tremendously exciting and monopolizes my life to the extent that I have become as much of a workaholic as my father was!

The news of my mother's recent death came as a considerable shock. Though of pensionable age, she was not old, and had been, as far as I knew, in excellent health. The cable came from a lawyer's office in Delhi: 'It is with deep regret we have to inform . . . your mother passed on suddenly and peacefully in garden. Funeral taken place. Letter following.'

I felt more bereft and left out after reading the cable than I believed possible. Due to my own attitude I did not even know with whom she was staying.

Our family lawyer in Christchurch (now Dorset but I still think of it as Hampshire) showed me my mother's will. She left everything in England to me. Knowing that she had no money or property *outside* the UK, I wondered at the rather strange way of putting it, but the thought went out of my mind in the ensuing business of clearing out the bungalow. Finally only the letters were left to be dealt with.

I took a quick look at the bundles (and the diaries I found with them) in the drawer. It was my mother's wish that I should read the letters after which I was to take one of two courses: either burn them, or return them to the originator. Once again it was up to me. My mother had said years ago, when she first told me about the packets, that on more than one occasion she had wanted to destroy them herself, but that when it came to the point she did not have the heart to do so. The letters, she had said, were about what every woman should experience once in a lifetime – even her feet-on-the-level Geraldine! Everyone should know the glory of being in love, should give time to bask in its warmth, and through it grow in character and understanding – and at the same time learn to love oneself a little.

To me it all sounded like a lot of codswallop, and on that day in the near-empty bungalow I pretty well made up my mind to burn the letters after doing my duty by skimming through them.

I found several batches tied with red ribbon written from India, starting in the autumn of 1938, to Miss Carissa D.

Thornton at Wick House, the family home since pulled down to make way for the bungalow estate where I was brought up. Some 'by hand' notes with other letters lay loose. For the ease of the reader the letters were numbered – bless my mother again. The diaries appeared to be war-time ones, written in a place called Ambala, another in Quetta. The last diary gave an account of a journey home, continued briefly in England, and stopped altogether except for, years later, a minutely subscripted piece at the end which seemed to have been written in the year of my father's death and would need a magnifying glass to decipher it. All the diaries were very finely written in 'a line a day' leather books of small space. I did not attempt to read them in the bungalow.

However, after opening one or two envelopes at random I became intrigued to read more. Was the writer dead? 1938 was a long time ago. I remembered my mother telling me when I was attaining puberty that in her day 'sex' was a word never used, and girls of her upbringing were told little more about 'the facts of life' than they had been in Victorian times. Most girls, she said, kept to the straight and narrow path out of fear of having an illegitimate baby. She then proceeded to tell me all.

But, to come back to the present, was the writer dead? Hardly! My mother had said either to burn the letters or return them *personally*. In her thoughtful way she would surely have inserted a note to say he had since died, were he no longer living. Who was this completely unknown to me pen-man who patently adored my mother? Was he the 'special friend' she had attempted once to tell me about? The pages my eye had scanned were enough for me to recognize the considerable potential of the story therein. But not only that. One of the letters I happened to glance at touched me so deeply that I felt the prick of tears in my eyes. *Me* of all people. Was it because they were written to my own mother that I was so affected? Because the moment was soon after her death? On balance I did not think so. The author wrote in unusual form for an Englishman – and presumably he was English as they had met in England on his leave. He wrote emotionally, often poetically, the words at times as if caressed, but just when the letters were on the verge of becoming over-sentimental, a deft nuance or subtle turn of phrase allowed a buoyant humour to bubble through and make me chuckle. I wanted to meet the writer!

Whoever he was, he was quite unlike the stiff upper lip type of few words and dry wit of my father's army set. This man was not ashamed to pour out his innermost thoughts and feelings, which in the last of the pre-war letters orchestrated into a crescendo of desperation and ended with a stark question sent by cable. What had my mother's answer been?

The only way to find out was to read the letters through from the beginning in chronological order, picking up the diaries in the gaps where the letters left off. I looked at my watch. The house was cold, and it was getting late. I would read on in the comfort of my London home.

Putting the letters and diaries into a suitcase I had brought for the purpose, with a last look round the bungalow of so many happy childhood memories, I stepped outside and closed and locked the front door for the last time. For me it was the end of an era.

On the drive up to London at a goodly speed in my Jaguar, I went on puzzling over the whole bizarre story that had leapt out from the pages into my unsuspecting mind. It was all news to me. Well, naturally, my mother would not tell me about a love affair of long ago. But that had not been the end of it. Would I be correct in putting two and two together? Those coincidences; those Indian connotations; those travels all over the world; and then on top of it her recent death abroad? My meticulous mother had never disappeared into the blue. She had always made certain I had an address care of a box number to write to or a number to ring in case of emergency. I had never needed to.

Although my parents had often talked of India during my childhood, it was only recently that I had come to realize my mother was exceptionally well informed about the country. What was the attraction for her? She could not have been

13

more English-looking herself, with her rose complexion, her lovely hair that had no more than a few strands of grey right up to the time I last saw her, and no touching up either! Her beauty was as natural as her character: without guile or subterfuge. I simply could not imagine her in the role of dramatic heroine of intrigues, sighs and tears – and passion. But then of course offspring can seldom imagine passion in their parents, perhaps because they do not want to, and me particularly, disliking the very thought of romantic notions as I do. Though I loved my mother, it was my father who had the greatest influence on me. No man has ever matched up to him in my eyes. Now that I am touching forty I know I shall never marry. I prefer it that way. Even so, after reading one or two of the letters, I developed an uneasy feeling that I had personally missed out on something somewhere. However, I quickly dismissed the sentiment as rubbish!

Of one thing I am rock certain, and that is that my parents' marriage was a happy one. There had been a great deal of give and take between them, a great deal of affection in the carefree days of my childhood and youth. Though my father was not a demonstrative man, and though he suffered much, I was aware from an early age of his love for my mother, revealed in the way his eyes lit up when she came into the room even after only the shortest of absences. And I knew by the way she cared for him and brightened his life that she held him dear too. Whatever tale unfolds in the letters, I know nothing can alter the truth of my parents' relationship, the truth of their trust, or the truth of my father's love for me and my devotion to him which came near to idolization for his intellect. I will never forget the pride I felt on the day when he allowed that my brain worked like that of a man!

On return to London, I garaged the Jag in the mews; let myself into my ground floor apartment; made coffee; lit a cigarette; and curled up on the sofa to read . . .

PART I

Wick Water

CHAPTER 1

Brigadier-General Charles Dunbar Thornton, CBE, DSO and bar, MC (retired), tipped his panama hat over his eyes and sank further down in the deck-chair to ease his leg. The fat labrador Bugler slumbering beside him cocked an eye to look at his master, thumped a tail, and went to sleep again. The leg was throbbing. God knew why in high summer when it was usually worse in winter. Shrapnel on the Somme. They'd extracted bits, but more continued to surface cheekily twenty-two years later! Bloody awful war, not like the Frontier wars or Mesopotamia where a soldier could fight as he was trained: use cunning. Instead, stuck in trenches. Gas. Brave men screaming like trapped rabbits on the wire. Blindness. Maiming. Nerves shattered. Lives ruined. He'd been lucky, even so the nightmare lived on, colouring his life. Both his children had been born during the war. Roberta and Carissa, bless 'em (he'd have a squint into the sun at them playing on the grass tennis court before the house), both the result of sick leave impregnations!

Good shot! Carissa had hit a fair smash from the net onto the back line of the court, chalk rising. Brother and sister were playing together against Captain Brownlow (recently come to the Gunner Barracks which housed a Medium Battery and an Experimental Bridging Establishment) and a school friend of Carissa's, Susan Langley, who wanted her to share a flat in London. Damned stupid idea to exchange a healthy outdoor life with all mod cons thrown in for cramped quarters in smog-bound Town. Young gals should stay at home till married. Useful having the Barracks near for her. Nice for him too. Kept him in touch with the Army – invited to guest nights, sports, watch manoeuvres, that sort of thing. Interesting experiments on the bridging. Secret. Preparing for war, cuss it.

He was proud of his two. Robert (the women called him 'Bobby') had passed top out of Cranwell. Sword of honour. Mad on aeroplanes since a kid when he spent all his pocket money and spare time making models out of matchsticks. Still did. Beautiful. Couldn't imagine how he did it. Neat fingered. Artistic like his mother. Carissa was his girl. Open. Had never sulked, though she could lose her temper like himself! Took what he said about this ridiculous business of a flat without whining. Couldn't stand querulous women. Doreen had tried to wheedle him in the early days. He'd soon put a stopper on that! Carissa took after him in colouring, only now he was more sandy than copper – Titian they called it in girls – red-blotched of face and hand: scabbed from cancer of the skin caused by years in the tropics. Doctor Walker of Square House had told him to keep out of the sun; bit late for that when all his working life had been spent *in* it. He must go and see him again for some more stuff. Itchy. And the wheezing. Chest hurt. Bloody war. He'd given up having baths. Washed under the armpits and in the crotch – good enough. Ford would tell him if he began to smell like Tom!

He missed sitting in the sun. India. He'd had a long spell there with his British regiment. Marvellous life for a young man. Pig-sticking. Polo. Big game shootin'. Funny people though. Arrogant. Best not to mix socially. Keep the blood-stream clear was as applicable to the natives as to the whites. *They* didn't want blue blood diluting their rich red! Why not keep the races pure? Save endless trouble. That ranting Hitler had a point there, as had the Jews. India was a good place as long as a man didn't marry young. Ruined many a career. In the old days the CO put the kibosh on that. Not any more. They'd lost control! *He* hadn't married until he was fifty. Met her in Bangalore, his Doreen. Daughter of that mad Irishman Major-General O'Rourke who had broken his neck riding to hounds in Ooty. Succulent girl she'd been. Horribly impractical though. House always in a terrible mess until he'd had enough and ran it himself with military precision.

Another war on the horizon? God! Damned Austrian house-painter grabbing large bits of Europe. 'The war to end all wars' – huh! His bowels turned to water at the memory. Bowels and leaky bladder, wife no bloody use. Pity, when you still had the urge. Have to stand up to the Hun. Why didn't the PM do something about it? Wishy-washy man if ever there was one. Now if it were that cavalry officer Winston Churchill . . . Instead they were turning out gas-masks and proposing to dig up parks and make slit trenches as a palliative to public opinion. Fat lot of use! Would a letter to *The Times* be a good idea? Couldn't be bothered. Clapped-out old general.

They were threatening to send a load of snotty urchins from the East End to be billeted. He'd show 'em! Do his bit in another war by licking 'em into some sort of shape – he and Ford between them. Liven things up, it would. Discipline. That's what the young of today needed to keep their noses dry. The lower classes no longer 'knew their place', and as for those fascists of Oswald Mosley's who were permitted to demonstrate when they should be hung, drawn and quartered on Tower Hill . . . Hot summer this . . . September 1938 . . . news topsy-turvy from Central Europe. Serious one moment; then Hitler takes the steam out by one of his over-dramatized speeches, shrieking that Germany's not ready for war; but next day, the wretched little demigod puts the heat on again! War scare as bad as it could be . . . heat off today, but it would be on again tomorrow. He was sweating, stiff . . . ah, hot weather! Better have a little snooze.

Brigadier-General Thornton's mouth fell open and he snored gently in the shade of the great copper beech

19

under which in spring was carpeted a mass of white and mauve crocuses. In cotton dress and floppy battered garden hat, Doreen came out through the conservatory, an empty trug on her arm, secateurs in hand. She came over on exaggerated tiptoe to peek at her husband, and seeing he slept did not disturb him, but waved vaguely at the tennis players who took no notice of her. She had not expected them to. She was a non-person in the household.

She sometimes wondered if anyone would notice if she left for good. She had contemplated walking out in the early days after the war, but her love for her children kept her; and now she had nowhere to go. Because her 'muddled way of living' had infuriated her husband, he had taken over the housekeeping, even down to ordering the meals. She still felt humiliated about not being able to go into her own kitchen and sit on the scrubbed table and have a cosy chat with the cook about the menus. (The latter was summoned every morning by Ford into the 'Brigadier's' study.)

When they first came to Christchurch she used to drive the car into Bournemouth for painting classes and to concerts at The Pavilion, but every time she returned with a scrape on the Wolseley there was a row. Her feeling was, what did it matter if she *had* bumped into something as long as no one was hurt and the car still ran? After a while Charles had refused to let her drive. He did not permit her to have a small second-hand car of her own, and her licence lapsed.

All that was in the past. She had become accustomed to the situation, and in many ways it was a relief not to have to bother with the feeding and the stores. She had been happiest when the children were young. Charles had never been able to accuse her of being a bad mother. In those days she practically lived in the nursery, playing games with them or reading aloud. And she took them out rain or shine: to picnics on Mudeford beach, to paddle and bathe and make sandcastles to their hearts' content; for boat trips, to the fun-fairs, to the circus, children's parties, to Sunday School at the Priory. Ford drove them when it was too far to walk. She had never had a nanny, not since the children were babies. Charles may have denied her everything else, but he had not been able to deny her her motherhood.

Now that the children were grown up they didn't need her any more. It was she that had the need . . . but she was content enough pottering about with her sketching pads, her gardening baskets and her needle-work, and popping over on the ferry to buy her water-colours and meet her friends at the Garraways Coffee House by the Priory. She never asked her painting friends to the house. Charles did not approve of them, particularly the men who wore sandals and grew their hair down their necks. Both peculiarities were ana-thema to him, as were women who displayed hairy legs. She sometimes thought how it must be a terrible burden to have so many abominations. Life was much more relaxed in Ireland where she had been brought up in freedom to run wild. Her family liked to call them-selves bog Irish in spite of which her daredevil father had risen in the service to a higher rank than Charles. But it was no use harping back. The family estate in Kilkenny had been broken up after her twin brother had been murdered in the 'troubles'. She had no Irish home to escape to.

She had achieved a certain contentment, so long as Bobby came back for weekends and leaves, so long as Carissa lived at home. If there was one instance that she was glad of, it was over Charles laying down the law on the flat-sharing with Susan. Without Carissa in the house she really would vanish into total invisibility. It was quite frightening being looked through as though you were a plate-glass window . . .

Doreen gave her typical little sigh, and made her way to the immaculately kept walled garden, where, with the garden boy holding her basket, she proceeded to pick a large quantity of sweet peas, which depredations nevertheless

21

made no impression on the long, expertly staked and neatly tied, row.

Christchurch was where Brigadier Thornton's roots lay. Wick House (the word was originally 'Week') was a rambling brick edifice built in early Victorian days by his grandfather, said to have made his pile smuggling. From the house they looked out to the famous old stone Priory set on a slight rise, the ruins of a castle prominent behind it, the Yacht Club below, the mill stream flowing between. To get to the town by car required a drive down Wick Lane and over green-painted Tuckton Bridge. Cut off as they were by the river, it was nearer to shop in Southbourne, unless one used the ferry. All that consisted of was a flat leaky boat with rowlocks tied on by string, a pair of chipped oars, plus a bailer. If the boat was on the other side, those wishing to embark rang a ship's bell on the bank, and sooner or later someone rowed over.

With his brothers the Brigadier had been brought up 'messing about in boats' on the Stour and Avon, which rivers converged into a harbour treacherous with mud banks and bounded on one side by a high-cliffed spit of land, Hengistbury Head. Often, when standing on the wooden 'bridge' of the Yacht Club, over which strained in the wind the navy-blue triangular burgee with its white shield containing three red diamond shapes, the Brigadier's keen eye perceived a yachtsman on a mudbank, which stranded sight produced a guffaw that the man was in for the discomfort of a six-hour wait until the tide turned. The channels had to be constantly re-marked due to the mudbanks shifting as the sandspit formed at Mudeford. It grew in length, barring the sea and making a river channel as far down as the base of Highcliffe. Every ten years or so, during an exceptionally high tide combined with a violent winter storm, the waters in the harbour rushing down broke the spit at Mudeford, thus greatly shortening the hazardous passage out to sea.

The Brigadier's elder brother had joined the Royal

Navy and been lost in the Battle of Jutland. He himself, born belligerent, was determined to be seen as no mere follower in line, and he had joined the Army. His brother had no offspring, and on his death Charles came into the property. But the war had had a more adverse effect on his health than Charles Thornton would admit even to himself, and after a spell in the twenties at the War Office, he had been more than ready to retire and bring back the house and garden to the precision that a succession of neglectful tenants had eroded. In his will he expressed the desire to be buried in the family vault in the Priory. Often he wished he were already there.

There was one other member of the family left in Christchurch, a younger brother of the name of Thomas, who having failed to pass into the Navy 'proper', had joined the Merchant Service.

By doing so the older generation considered Tom had let the family down, and his brother, the Brigadier, still did. Tom lived on a tiny pension in a clap-board shack on the Mudeford estuary where at high tide the water lapped the steps up to his door, and at low tide the mud flats made seaman's boots imperative. Perpetually puffing at a curling brown pipe containing foul tobacco, Tom's habitual wear was a yachting cap worn aslant over his grizzled head, a high-necked sweater that had once been white, and a pair of faded blue duck trousers tucked into the inevitable boots. His long-sighted blue eyes viewed with amused dislike his lofty brother's disapproval.

In the days soon after their arrival at Wick House, Doreen had invited her brother-in-law to dinner to meet the then new canon of the Priory who came smartly dressed in purple velvet jacket. Tom was unable to find the dinner jacket he had once possessed – in any case it would scarcely have fitted. He 'did' for himself and lived on chunks of bread, grilled mackerel and Heinz baked beans, all of which, combined with quantities of beer, had greatly increased his waistline. Instead he wore his one and only black suit kept for funerals. Black tie as well as suit were mildewed and food spotted. He rose to the occasion — as he thought — by wearing shoes, but unfortunately he forgot to wash his feet. The canon's lady to one side of him at table was quite put off her food and was seen to use her napkin a great deal more than was necessary. To add to his brother's disgust, Tom, plied by Ford, became heavy with drink, his 'bloomings' punctuating every other word.

Dinner that night was not a success despite an excellent meal and smooth waiting at table carried out by the pretty parlourmaid Rosie aided by Ford in white gloves to hide the callouses on his hands. Tom was never invited to the house again which suited both sides admirably.

However, he could not be completely ousted. He regarded Wick House as much his home as his brother Charles's, and he dropped in for a snack in the kitchen to scoff Cook's excellent pies and cakes whenever he felt like it, and as frequently for a drink with Ford, known to him as 'Fred'. The only other person who called Ford 'Fred' was Cook, and the only reason — according to Rosie, who was inclined to get fits of the giggles over it — that Cook (a widow) stayed on in the mad household was because she was crazy about Ford, who was a misogynist, a word she had learned from the gardener, Mr Field. Ford lived on his own above the garage block which used to be the old stables, but Mr Field had the lodge by the gate where he lived with his wife who came in daily to clean and wash up. With them lived the garden boy, a harmless middle-aged person of mongoloid appearance and drooling mouth who had a 'way with flowers'.

The trouble was that, with all these domestics at Wick House, Carissa — Cara for short to most except for her father — was not allowed to put anything she had learnt into practice. Cook would not permit her into the kitchen, not even 'to boil an egg', as Cara grumbled to her friend Susan. When it was Cook's day off Rosie and Ford took over. At the age of twelve, by which time Bobby was at Marlborough, Cara had been sent to boarding school in Parkstone. No particular pressure was put upon her to study, in spite of which she passed her school certificate in three subjects. What she put more energy into was games. She played lacrosse and tennis for the school, had golfing lessons at Highcliffe in the holidays, and at the age of sixteen won the junior tennis championships at Brocken-hurst.

After leaving school she took a domestic course where she learnt to starch and iron men's shirts (future husband's presumably), but as with the cooking, the skill was no use to her at Wick House. The soiled household linen was taken away weekly in large wicker baskets to be returned washed, starched and folded in layers of blue tissue paper far more expertly than she ever could. She managed to persuade her father (not by wheedling, that was fatal!) to let her take a typing course in Bourne-mouth, and though he would not budge an inch over her doing a full-time secretarial course in London with Susan, he was so pleased with the neat business letters she turned out for him that as a reward he allowed her to take the wheel of the Wolseley.

In subsequent years Cara often wondered if she would have been so tidy minded if she had not had such a hopelessly disorganized mother. For something to do in Wick House she found herself endlessly clearing up in the footsteps of her parent.

With the freedom now to drive into Bournemouth and browse round the shops, Cara developed an eye for fashion, and learnt how to get the best out of her modest dress allowance. Every autumn fashion changed slightly, not much, but in the tilt of a hat, the length of a skirt, the set of shoulders, the pinch of a waist, and the height of a heel, all dictated by Paris, the fountain of fashion. There was nothing smarter than a black coat and skirt with a coloured silk blouse, little hat, handbag, gloves and shoes to match, the sheerest of pale silk stockings carefully rolled up so that the rib lay absolutely straight at the back. Cara was, without being in the slightest bit vain, conscious of the fact that black for 'best' suited her fair skin and dark red hair.

Indeed by the summer of 1938 when she was twenty, whether she was dressed in her town black, in tennis skirt, or slacks for sailing, she was quite lovely. With her slender figure and arresting colouring men turned to look at her again as she passed, and at first glance, because of the natural grace of her walk, she appeared to be the epitome of sophistication, though her mother and Bobby would have told anyone who cared to ask that this was by no means the case.

She had little self-confidence, and she was particularly shy of men, dodging enounters with them rather than encouraging them. As a result she had no boyfriends. The ones who wanted to be friends at the ice rink where she went skating were mostly young men learning the floor business at one of the large Bournemouth stores, men she was afraid to bring home for the shame of her father asking which public school they had been to when they hadn't. Even more shy was she with the 'county' lot who lived in big houses in the New Forest and whom she met at private dances. *They* may have gone down all right with her father, but they intimidated her with their loud nasal talk of hunting, and of charity balls, their eyes flickering over her disdainfully when she confessed she had not been presented at Court.

She hated the word 'class' that her father constantly used. She was not sure what 'they are not *our* class' was supposed to stand for. Did her father think they themselves were 'lower upper', 'upper middle', plain 'middle', or even 'lower middle', which could well be the case with neither parent having private means and living on pension. What did it matter anyway? It was all so stupid. If she classed herself with anyone it was with the Christchurch Barracks subalterns, who were jolly fellows, either Gunners or Sappers. Bobby's friends were better still, a new brand mixed bunch. These her father admired, regardless of what school they had been to, for their RFC exploits in the war.

The summers were good fun at Wick House when Bobby brought his friends home and Susan came to stay, and they sailed and played tennis, skated, rode in the New Forest on horses hired from a livery stable, danced to the gramophone in the drawing-room after the parents retired to bed, and played snooker till the early hours on the billiard table in the basement, but the winter days, with their long evenings dragging on and on when she was alone with her parents, were boring in the extreme.

The last winter, that of 1937-38, had been dreadful. Horrible events had taken place in Europe; there were annexations and rumours of impending war, her father's speculation on events punctuating the political talks on radio. When she and her mother wanted to listen to music, the wireless was switched relentlessly to the news. Why the news again when he had already heard it at six?

Night after night Cara sat before the drawing-room fire as it crackled damp logs from the old apple tree that had fallen in the orchard. Her parents sat on either side of her, hedging her in. Circumscribed as any Victorian spinster-daughter, she dutifully knitted away at a cardigan for Father who felt the cold in the chilly house, which had a sort of central heating from a hot air grid in the hall, but no radiators. Cara knitted, as rapidly and as neatly as she typed, jerseys for herself and her mother and cricket pullovers for Bobby. In between it was always grey woollen socks for Uncle Tom, or mittens for her father's hands, which had turned blue.

Cara got through pounds and pounds of wool from 'Beales' in the winters, while her mother silently plied her blunt needle through her tapestry, and the wireless blared Hitler. There were evenings when Cara felt like screaming him down.

Though she had several times faced her father on the subject of her future, it had got her nowhere. He had never lifted a hand to her or Bobby, but his authority in

27

the household was absolute from 'he who knows best for your good' as he was always telling her. She knew perfectly well it was *not* for her good. It was for *their* good. And because she loved them she was trapped. They even used blackmail, her mother's, 'Your father is coming to the end of his life; it won't be long now, dearie. Give us a few more years, that's all I ask,' said with her sigh and her sorrowful look. Her father's, 'Stuff and nonsense,' when she suggested that if he wouldn't let her do a secretarial course he might at least allow her to go to the hospital in Boscombe and learn to nurse. 'You have no idea what you are talking about, *what* you'd be letting yourself in for, *what* men's bodies look like when mutilated. No, no, no, not right for a gal. Bad for you.'

'I could nurse women,' Cara had tried again. 'If there's war there'll be bombings and civilian casualties—'

'That is enough of that, Carissa! *I will not hear of it,*' Charles Thornton thumped the table beside him with a fist so that the wireless leapt.

Cara knew that if she waited another year until she was twenty-one she would be within the law to take off, and her father would not be able to bring her back. The notion was not an attractive one. She knew herself to be thoroughly unequipped for life outside the family, particularly a war-torn world, and she could see herself in no time, with her allowance cut off and she half-starving, crawling back and asking for forgiveness! Red-heads were said to have passionate natures and fiery tempers. She did not think she was the least bit passionate, and though as a child she had rages, now she did not – indeed she was the one who kept her father's temper within bounds.

The truth was she could not endure the thought of another winter in Wick House, and at the same time she could not leave. She knew how her mother's innocuous ways irritated her father beyond endurance and led to his perpetual bullying of her, which over the years had reduced her to a spineless nonentity with no mind of her own. She saw when her father's chest was hurting, and knew that if she gave the slightest sign of sympathy he would roughly brush it off. Only Ford was allowed into his dressing-room when he was forced to stay in bed (it was years since her parents had shared the big bedroom). Ford *knew*. Ford had been in the trenches. But it was *she* who kept the peace simmering controllably between her parents, jumping in to turn down the heat before the angry boiling over, keeping quiet when her father thumped the table and made the wireless leap.

'I'm trapped,' Cara said to Bobby in September at the end of that summer of 1938 when the news from the Continent could scarcely be worse. 'I feel like running away but I can't leave them.'

'Things are hotting up.' Bobby ignored the plea for sympathy he had heard before. 'Squadron's off to Egypt!'

'Oh Bobby, you lucky, lucky thing! It's not fair. It's so easy for you . . .'

'For my embarkation leave,' Bobby interrupted, 'Susan and I plan to go down to her people in Exeter and see the agricultural exhibition. Coming with us?'

'Really? Oh *rather*!'

'Should be K.O. Towards the end of the month. My advice actually, Cara old thing,' Bobby eyed his sister speculatively, 'is to hang on. One hell of a lot is going to happen. Events will take over, parents or no parents. Anyway I'll lay a wager you'll fall in love, and that will be that!'

CHAPTER 2

He stood on the Club 'bridge'. His figure was outlined by the arched French window leading out from the 'deck' where Cara sat at a table directly in line with the door. Bobby and Uncle Tom were with her in a crowd of others standing or sitting, or perched at the bar situated across a corner of the room. A series of commodores looked severely out from black picture frames at the noisy gathering.

The decibels were decidedly high, chattering voices and laughter loud as groups exchanged notes on who had been dismasted, whose sail torn, who had gone-about at the wrong moment and crashed into another yachtsman to furious imprecations, who had been left high and not so dry on a mudflat. The beers and gins and tonics fairly flowed. It was the end of a perfect racing day.

Bobby brought over refills of beer for Tom and himself and another glass of squash for Cara. His complexion was nicely rubicund, his brown curly head tousled. He and Cara had raced in the dinghy, and though they had not won the cup they had done well to come in fifth in their class. It had been a breezy day, and her face glowed with the sun and the wind, arms and legs tanned golden in her grey aertex shirt and white shorts. She sipped at her second squash, her thirst already slackened by the first, and only half-listened to Bobby and Tom's talk about lobster pots. Her eyes wandered out again to the figure, seen in shadowy tones, on the bridge against the blazing background, the evening sun a ball of fire low on the horizon. To her he appeared captured like an old-fashioned black and white silhouette portrait brought vividly to colour by the red sunset.

He was talking to a girl Cara remembered having met in the first round of a handicap tennis tournament in Brockenhurst. Her opponent had not been particularly agile at tennis, and in spite of conceding her a good many handicap points, Cara had beaten her easily and gone on to become runner-up. She remembered her as a photographic model, the daughter of wealthy parents, the father a tea, jute and timber exporter. He was reputed to have, as well as a lodge in Angus where he repaired every summer for the shooting, built a house on the outskirts of Brockenhurst that contained every possible modern gadget, thus conjuring up much gossipy speculation in the village. As well, Mr Tinling kept a yacht at Lymington that he periodically sailed to their holiday home in Jersey. Sometimes he sailed into Christchurch harbour where he was an honorary member of the Club, but Cara had not seen his daughter there. She knew the father by sight in his white ducks and smart yachting cap. He was the very reverse to her dear old uncle sitting across the table from her.

She was a handsome girl, older than she, made too tall, Cara thought, by the very high heels she wore, which emphasized the thinness of her stockinged legs below a short tight skirt with kick-pleat, or she could scarcely have walked in it. Cara looked down at her own long bare legs stretched out before her, which ended in an extremely scruffy pair of plimsoles. She shoved her feet under the table. Altogether, with dark hair cut short and in a fringe, with the padded shoulders of her startling, jazzy, long-sleeved shirt, the Tinling girl had the extreme boyish flat looks of the thirties that were the envy of many. Cara, who, since she had left boarding school and had lost her puppy fat, was as slim as any girl could wish, had given up rueing the fact that, with her naturally wavy

31

hair, her small breasts that were by no means flat, and her little waist that curved out into undeniable hips, she could never develop the ultra-modern look.

At first sight the man outside appeared the perfect counterpart to the fashion plate of his female companion as they stood facing each other in the doorway, each holding a whisky, he topping her by a good few inches, which must make him six foot three at the least, Cara thought. The Tinling girl (she couldn't for the life of her remember her Christian name; *a, b, c, d, e, f, g, h, i, j . . . J . . .* Joan? Jane? Janet – that was it, Janet Tinling) looked distinctly out of place in the friendly Yacht Club that was not used to wealthy customers, and where everyone was dressed in shorts, trousers and soiled plimsoles like hers and Bobby's, or like her uncle, in oiled sweaters, yacht caps and sea boots.

But on glancing at the tall man again, Cara saw that he was more casually dressed than she had at first supposed. She could not see his face though she could clearly see the outline of his profile against the fiery sunset: side parting, hair brushed straight across sloping forehead, rather long jutting nose, clean-shaven, strong chin, soft white collar with striped tie unpinned, the divided ends flying out loosely in the breeze, crumpled tweed jacket over grey flannel trousers. No, he was no fashion plate gent, and Cara supposed what must have caused her to think so at first glance was something indefinable about his loose-knit stance that suggested easy arrogance.

She watched him put down his glass on a table near the door, and take out from jacket pocket a flat cardboard box of cigarettes. He opened it for his girl-friend. Taking one out himself he tapped it on the lid before replacing the packet in his pocket, and, flicking a lighter, cupped it out to hers and then held it to his. Briefly, the tiny flame lit up straight dark hair and a deep tan. No one achieved that sort of tan in England. He must be from the tropics.

The tall man stepped aside to allow a woman to pass through the doorway, and in doing so looked up and caught Cara's eye where she sat sipping her drink and speculating on him. His eyes flickered lazily over her, and quickly Cara looked away. With a half-smile he turned his back on the doorway, and, picking up his whisky, went to the railings and looked out over the river with its boats bobbing at their moorings in the fading sunset and Hengistbury Head bathed in the last of the evening light. He stood there for a moment on his own, smoking. His companion followed, and Cara, looking up again, saw her tweak his jacket in a familiar way and then place an inviting hand on his arm.

A pang of envy for the situation came over her. The couple could have been married but she did not think so or she would have noticed the announcement in The *Times* and *New Forest News*. They were probably newly engaged – divinely happy. Well done, Janet, whose legs were too spindly to play tennis well! Well done, because it had come to her, Cara, with startling clarity when she had first seen him in the doorway, that this type, class, call it what you like, was the *sort* of man she would like to marry.

Still watching overtly, she saw him finish his drink, throw his half-smoked cigarette into the river, and come towards the French window, Janet leading. Cara cupped her cheeks in her hands, elbows on the table, and pretended to listen intently to what Bobby and Tom were saying because she did not want to have to greet Janet or meet the man she was with. Janet might not remember her if she jumped up to stop her in her tracks, which could be embarrassing; or maybe she *would* remember her but with dislike for having been roundly thrashed at tennis, which would be worse. And, desperately, *she did not want to meet* the man who belonged to Janet. To her short-lived relief Janet seemed to be passing her table without noticing.

'Why, if it isn't Carissa Thornton.' She heard the Tinling girl's voice, and looked up to see her turning back on a high heel. 'I'd forgotten you lived here.'

'Hello, Janet, we don't often see you at the Club,' Cara replied, thinking, *Oh blast*. At the same time she thanked her lucky stars she had resurrected the girl's name in time by using the old method of alphabet recall until something clicked.

'That's right, I hate the water. Makes me sea-sick to look at it!'

Janet Tinling could perfectly easily have passed by the table without stopping. But she did not. She could just as easily have moved on with only a nod of recognition to Carissa, a girl she had once met, sitting at the table chin cupped in hands and listening intently to two men, one young, one old. But she did not. She even could have moved on after saying, 'Hello, how are you?' not expecting more than a brief acknowledgement. But once again she did not. She stopped and stayed for a fatal few moments and thereby set in motion a chain of events which could be said in retrospect to have ruined her life.

Instead of moving on out of the room after the first short interchange, during which Cara remained seated, Janet tarried. Why? Did she want to show her arresting-looking friend off in that room full of people she had no common interest with? He was certainly worth showing off, would go down there better than she, was certainly dressed more in keeping with the Christchurch Yacht Club set than she. Probably she stopped because she loved him and wanted to please him in his hobby. Whatever the reason, she stood at Cara's side and added the fateful words, 'Lance wants to do some fishing; we've come here to investigate,' and proceeded to introduce him:

'Lance, meet Carissa Thornton. Carissa, this is Lance Gardner.'

Cara stood up shyly and held out a hot hand to the person who was smiling down at her with half-closed eyes, the sort she thought she might like to marry. And in her turn she introduced Bobby to them and then her uncle who remained firmly slumped and did not proffer a hand but barely nodded while biting the stem of his pipe, his cap at an acute angle over bleary eye.

'Join us for a drink,' Bobby invited.

'Thanks but we've got to get going. Early morning start for me,' Janet declined.

'So must we get going, Bobby.' Cara glanced at her watch. 'People coming to dinner. Better not be late!' She touched her uncle affectionately on the shoulder as she left, and made her way with Janet towards the steps at the main entrance to the Yacht Club away from the river.

'If there's anythin' yer wants to know about fishin', get in touch with me,' Tom pronounced gruffly behind her.

'That's very kind of you. Where can I find you?' she heard a deep well-enunciated voice reply.

'In me bloomin' shack, No. 1 Mudeford flats; or in pub.'

'What pub, sir?'

'There's only one fisherman's pub worth anythin' round these parts. The Old Ship Inn. On quay. You can't miss it.'

'Great. I'll be there tomorrow.'

'Come on, Lance,' Janet called from the top of the steps down which Bobby and Cara had run ahead hoping to escape, but out of politeness waited for Janet at the bottom. Lance followed imperturbably at his own pace.

'Can we give you a lift?' he asked as they walked over the small bridge by the mill stream, and on past the water-wheel with cobweb-draped mill-house towards the parking spaces on the green by the bandstand. Only one car stood there, a dark red Lancia di Lamda with hood up.

'No thanks,' Bobby said, 'quicker for us over the ferry. Come on, old girl. Cheerio, you two.' Brother and sister set off together. They broke into a run, Cara's hair bouncing, Bobby tying the sleeves of his sweater round his neck as he went.

'Outdoor types hardly out of the nest,' Janet said disparagingly though secretly she wished she was athletic herself so that she could give Lance a better game of tennis and be able to hit a golf ball adequately instead of having to walk round the course watching.

'I wouldn't say they're as young as all that. Same generation as us,' he replied, dark eyes following the two figures. 'Refreshingly unspoilt. Unusual name, Carissa,' he added more to himself than to his companion.

He went round to the nearside door of the car and opened it.

'Thank you, darling,' Janet said possessively, and swung gracefully into the deep leather seat.

Bobby and Cara had disappeared from sight in their sprint. They were already rowing across in the ferry by the time Lance had reversed the car and begun the slow drive up the narrow rise of the slip-road towards Christchurch.

He did not know why, but he drove away from the scene of the Yacht Club with its burgee, the lovely peaceful harbour, and the beautiful old Priory sentinel above, almost reluctantly.

'If yer wants to go fishin' with me yer'll have to get up in the dark. Be on our way by dawn.' Twenty-four hours later Tom was slurping down beer in the Old Ship Inn on Mudeford Quay where Lance found him. The air was fetid in the tiny bar, tobacco smoke thick, and at first he had difficulty in locating the old sea-dog in the murk. He was sitting on his own on one of the hard benches fixed against the wall.

'Suits me fine, sir. What bait do you use?'

'Bloomin' herrin's mostly. Yer job'll be to cut 'em up. Sniffy business.' Tom puffed at his pipe.

'What'll you 'ave, love?' the landlord's buxom wife Jess asked. She had earlier that afternoon shown Lance up the narrow stairs to a small room off the landing on which he had had to double up for fear of cracking his brains out.

'Best malt whisky in stock, Jess, with a splash of water.'

The room upstairs, Lance had been relieved to find, was high enough in the centre for him to stand upright. It had a patch of ragged carpet over creaking boards, a sagging iron bedstead, and one tiny square window which looked away from the race of river out to sea to the quiet of harbour. The view was of duck, dabchicks and herons bobbing and feeding in reed beds. A pair of stately white swans glided by followed by their nondescript cygnets; white and grey houses, some high and narrow, some low and long, lined the mudflats. There was a basin and jug in one corner of the room, a rickety hanging cupboard in another, a marble-topped chest of drawers, and a side table which Lance saw contained a blessed chamber-pot to save the lodger from a tedious creep down in the dark to the one and only outside 'bog'.

'Perfect,' Lance had said, 'suits me perfectly.'

'How long do you expect to stay, sir?' Jess had started off formally.

'About a week, I'm coming to the end of my leave.'

'Oh sir,' she looked at him with added interest, 'you might be called up. Terrible news dinner-time. They say Mr Chamberlain is to fly to Berlin to see Mr 'itler. Wonderful of 'im, isn't it! I think that's real romantic to go by air.'

'Yes, a great gesture if the PM can pull it off. I shan't be recalled, though. I'm not in the regular forces.'

'Not?' Jess promptly dropped the 'sir'. 'I could've sworn you was a military man with them shoulders. What then, love?' she was inquisitive.

'A box-wallah,' Lance had said succinctly, effectively shutting her up, and leaving her no wiser.

'Sexy hussy, watch yer step.' Now Tom glowered when Jess had dumped down a whisky in front of Lance and left with a pronounced bottom wobble.

'I believe I can look after myself.' Lance's eyes crinkled. 'For one thing the bed upstairs would collapse with Jess and my combined weight! Thank God it's large enough to lie diagonally across it without having to screw up my toes.'

'For another, yer'd be out on yer ear before yer could

37

bloomin' count jackknife! Our Tim Baker's a jealous husband. I can see yer has problems with that height of yers. Wouldn't fit into a bunk. And yer can stop sirrin' me. Tom Thornton's the name.'

'Your brother lives in Christchurch?'

'In the family home. Stuffy old bugger. I'm the black sheep; ran away to sea and a damned good thing too. But they can't turf me out, not altogether. The batman's a pal of mine. Call him "Fred", sonny, if yer gets asked to the place,' Tom said with a mischievous look incomprehensible to Lance. 'Not that yer will be asked, the bloomin' bastard—' Tom stopped full sentence to size Lance up. He looked at the slim elegant bony hands, one holding his glass, the other a cigarette. 'Yer from India?'

'Right first time.'

'Know it well. Ship often called into Bombay. On round to Madras and Calcutta. Treacherous devils the Hooghly sandbanks. Couldn't navigate that river without a native pilot. Have to learn the channels here if yer don't want to get stuck. For mackerel fishin' yer'll bait the lines with herrin' while I take yer out to sea in me motor-boat. Short passage since the channel burst the spit last winter. Good sailor, I hope? Choppy out there. Bad swell where the shoals lie. I'll tell yer . . .' Tom was well away with how and when and where the baited lines were trawled, together with the complications of wind and channel and getting back up the race before the tide turned.

The evening passed pleasantly with a further whisky from Jess and a plate of fresh grilled salmon caught locally up the Avon, and Lance turned in early after having dumped his black trunk at the bottom of the bed and unpacked his leather suitcase. He slept fitfully across the Inn's sagging bed and thought of the luxurious sprung mattress in the guest-room of the Tinlings' New Forest home, and wondered why he hesitated.

His alarm clock woke him in the dark to an exhilarating morning out to sea, the Needles on the Isle of Wight showing up like white wraiths in the early light. The haul was satisfactory, and that night Lance slept deeply, his lungs full of fresh sea air, his tanned face washed by clean salt spray, unnecessary trappings fast clearing away, enabling him to think unencumbered through the biggest decision he had to make of his life. He was glad that he had pulled out for a week or so and had not gone back just yet to join the shooting party. He would do that after he had made up his mind.

He knew he had done the sensible thing in coming fishing. He enjoyed any fishing, and had often in Dundee in his school holidays gone out to sea though not after mackerel. In India he had fished on several rivers for *mahseer* or brown trout. There was no better way to resolve a problem than to dissect it while casting! The movement of rod and line came automatically; the quiet of nature left thought undisturbed by man-made noise and hustle. His decision could no longer be put off. Last leave he had been too green at twenty-two to know how to cope with the situation when Janet, older than he, had become smitten. He had ducked out, though he had felt her attraction and was flattered. Now on this visit he had at first been too involved on a business attachment course in Dundee, headquarters of the jute industry in Scotland. Then, during the ensuing leave, he discovered Janet's feelings towards him had not changed in the four-year interval, and in the event he was surprised at himself that he held back until this late hour with so sensible, so advantageous and happy a step waiting for him to take. Why had he not jumped at the opportunity when he liked Janet, admired her?

The only person he had been able to talk it over with was his mother in Dundee, who was conveniently near to his course for him to live in the semi-detached childhood home. After listening to him quietly, the tall angular woman who wore her grey hair in the same style she had all her adult life, namely drawn back from her high forehead into a bun at the nape of her neck, said that on the face of it it sounded a good match on both sides. Naturally she was biased in *his* favour! On his side it would increase opportunities in his career to be Mr Tinling's son-in-law. But in the end, his mother said, it boiled down to personalities. The attraction must be there or the material benefits would turn sour. Only he could decide that for himself.

Lance esteemed his mother's advice. She was a Scottish schoolteacher of the old class with strict principles and considerable intellectual ability. As a young woman she had gone out to India to teach at St Andrew's Mission School for Orphans in Solah, and had become far too busy and involved with the children to think of marriage. However, she had consequently met Alistair Gardner, an elderly man some thirty-five years her senior, and had been attracted by his bearing. Alistair Gardner, the youngest child of James Gardner of nearby Kootgunge, who had died in 1845 when Alistair was a few months old, had been too proud to do a stroke of work in his life. He had lived on in growing poverty in the decaying splendour of his father's house, which, by the time of his mother's death, was heavily mortgaged to a *shroff*. Alistair's Scottish wife had taken him back to her home in Dundee where their children were born, Alistair dying within a few years. Mrs Gardner was left with a small daughter and two sons, teaching her only means of livelihood.

As soon as he had started to earn his living, Lance had helped his mother financially. He had at the age of eighteen joined the jute firm in Calcutta recommended by Mr Tinling, who was one of the directors in Dundee. He earned a good salary and led a good life at the Club. He enjoyed golf (which he played to four), tennis, swimming, fishing and shooting. The latter two pastimes he could never have afforded in Scotland. The firm on both his leaves paid for his fare home and back. On this trip he had bought his mother various things she needed for the house, had advanced all his savings towards his younger brother's fees at university, and had paid £105 for the second-hand Lancia on a turn-in guaranteed buy-back basis when he left the country. It had been a wise step, advised by his boss in Calcutta, Johnny MacCreath, a man who was as keen a Jute-wallah weekend soldier as himself. Without the expected return of £55 he'd have been stony broke and had to have asked for an advance of pay. Surely he would be mad not to seize the chance dangled in front of him? Janet, with her looks, her model's figure, was unlikely to be hanging around for another four years!

On his third night in the Old Ship Inn's sagging bed, Lance Delhmir Gardner dismissed his nagging thoughts about living with Janet's money, and decided he would be a bloody fool not to ask Mr Tinling in the time-honoured way for his daughter's hand in marriage. He would do so the moment he went up to Scotland. They would become engaged and she would either come out to India to marry him this winter, or Mr Tinling would have to wangle him an extension of his leave straight away. Simple!

Janet's answer was a foregone conclusion.

CHAPTER 3

There was a blue Wolseley car parked outside No. 1 Mudflats when Lance called to join Tom for their next lobster run. By now Lance was quite at home in Tom's shack. At this time of day he usually found him downstairs mending the faulty pots.

As he walked over the plank, pleased to have settled his future so pleasantly in his mind, Lance whistled a pipe skirl, a tune his Jute-wallah Battery played. He was a most lucky fellow to be going to have a sophisticated woman like Janet for a wife. He ducked into the threshold where before him lay a series of small dark rooms of dank smell. His 'cabins', Tom called them, a neatly made-up bunk in one where clothes were folded over a chair, stacked lobster pots in another. The old sea-dog appeared not to be down there.

Lance ducked out and clumped in his boots up the covered outside wooden steps which led to Tom's 'deck', a large room taking up the whole of the top floor. It had a series of panes of glass forming an uneven window which ran the full length. On the small balcony looking out to the harbour, proudly fluttered the Red Ensign.

The room was stuffed with memorabilia of sea-faring days including pictures of Tom's ships on the walls – one anchored by Shanghai bund, another sailing through the 'Straits', another in Hong Kong harbour. There was a green-tarnished brass ship's bell attached to the wall by a brass plate on which was engraved the caption that it had been taken from a pirate ship in the China seas. Tattered old charts, maps and books were stacked in dusty heaps

42

on the floor, and on a large heavy table were laid out empty tins, tools, fishing tackle, instruments, parallel-rulers, india-rubbers, piles of paper and stubs of carefully sharpened pencils. Tom may have found difficulty in washing or dusting, but he was an orderly man, as neat as most seamen. Everything was in its place for when he wanted it.

In pride of place facing the window was a telescope positioned to scrutinize any boat that sailed into the harbour. On fine nights Tom would sometimes sit up behind the telescope until dawn studying the planets and stars. In one corner of this sea-faring museum, cap on at its rakish angle, sat the owner cross-legged on a pile of cushions darning a pair of socks. Lance found him thus plying his needle and was diverted to see that it was possible to contort oneself into such a position while wearing boots, but then the old boy would die with his boots on, God willing . . .

'I wash them, he darns them,' a voice said from the other end of the room, and Lance looked across to see Cara up to her elbows in soapsuds bending over a sink.

'Yer knows my niece.' Tom waved the sock in her direction. 'Comes in to make me ship-shape.'

'I enjoy it. It's my tidy mind.' Cara let the water flow out in a loud gurgle, and proceeded to turn the tap full on for a rinse. 'Uncle Tom darns beautifully. Have a look.' She watched Janet's tall friend discard the sou'wester he was carrying.

Lance did as he was bid, and did indeed find the sock beautifully darned, the stitches woven threadwise so that the heel was rebuilt stronger than new.

'Her knitting 'em makes 'em worth mending; not like some of these new-fangled factory-made socks that don't last a week.'

'That's the story of my life,' said Cara from the sink where she was rinsing a shirt up and down, 'knitting socks. I might as well be a hundred.'

'Bloomin' rot and yer knows it, me dear. Besides being

the best small boat skipper I knows, she plays a stronger game of tennis than many a man.'

'Do you play?' Cara gave Lance a sideways glance from across the room where she was now wringing out the shirt. She hadn't really taken in his face in the Club, only his figure. The room was bathed in light from the long window and she could see she had not been mistaken. He was a devastatingly attractive male with deep-set brown eyes when he cared to open them, as now when he was looking over at her. More often they were hooded, and when he smiled they crinkled up into shining slits. His hair and skin were certainly very dark, and he had deep furrows on his forehead. His nose was handsome in an aristocratic way, thin-bridged and longish. His mouth worried her: a strange mouth when in repose. Was it sensitive, defensive, or plain cruel? Whatever, it quivered up on the instant into humour when he smiled. Though sitting nonchalantly in her uncle's chair by the telescope with his long legs stretched out in his boots before him, hands thrust deep in his pockets, he yet exuded vitality.

For once she did not feel shy. He was so completely at ease, self-assured, so – so undemanding. Somehow she was made to feel that it did not matter that he caught her in old shirt and trousers and up to her elbows in soapsuds, most of her lipstick eaten off, the freckles on the bridge of her nose uncovered by a dab of powder. That he did not mind, made *her* not mind if she did or said something quite outrageous! He was the sort of relaxed person who would go on sitting there, smiling to himself and enjoying her uncle's company, or whatever came next; take it all in. He was like a stranger to the land enjoying a new experience with the natives, interested and totally uncritical.

Uncritical. That hit the nail on the head. The very opposite of her father. That was probably why, Cara analysed at the sink when giving the shirt a final wring, she did not feel awkward with him in the room. She did not in the least mind that this stranger was seeing her uncle's awful shack. Now if it had been Janet, she would have been covered in shame!

'Yes, I play tennis.' Lance gave his lazy smile.

'Well,' Cara said briskly, hanging up the shirt on a string in the cubby-hole beyond the sink that went for the 'galley'. She placed a basin under it to collect the drips. 'Well, Mr Gardner, Bobby and I are stuck for a man tomorrow. The one from the Barracks who was coming, rang to say he couldn't. Too busy working for an army exam or something. Susan, that's Bobby's and my friend, is arriving later this afternoon to stay a few days before we all go off together to Devon for Bobby's embarkation leave. He's in the RAF; going to Egypt – that is, if there isn't a war to blow everything. I've rung round everyone I can think of who isn't a complete rabbit, but they're all away on holiday or booked up. Would you make up the four?'

'*Faute de mieux*.' Lance threw back his head in a laugh which transformed his face, showed excellent teeth, and produced a crease that was mightily like a dimple down one cheek. 'Certainly. Delighted to oblige. Only hope I come up to scratch!'

'I didn't mean it like that . . .' Cara began, and then seeing how badly she had put it, joined his laughter. 'Tea at our house will make up for the back-handed invitation . . .'

'Can't beat their cook for scones an' chocolate cake,' took up Tom. He looked through the window to position the sun and check the time. 'Clear the decks for tea, girl,' he yelled as if he were speaking down a voice tube in heavy seas.

'Can I help?' Lance offered.

'No, you stay put and talk to Uncle Tom. I'm used to being ordered about.' Cara disappeared into the cubby-hole. The kettle was simmering on the gas ring. There was no hot water system in the shack and she had already refilled the kettle several times for the wash. She made the tea, collected a tin tray, laid three mugs out and a bottle

45

of milk she had found on her arrival by the plank. A bowl of sugar, some spoons and a tin of 'hard tack', as her uncle called it, swiftly completed the preliminaries. She 'cleared the decks' on a corner of the heavy table, pulled up a stool, and waited for the tea to draw in the pot. Her uncle liked his tea strong.

She sat quietly at the table like a well-mannered child listening to the men talking fishing. Then she poured out the tea and handed the mug to Tom the way she knew he liked it. 'Milk and sugar?' she asked Lance.

'Please,' he said looking at her with big open eyes. 'You look like a charming little girl playing at mummies and daddies with two frightful old men in boots.'

'Speak for yerself,' growled Tom.

'I'm not playing,' she said very seriously handing him the open tin of biscuits, 'I'm stoking up two rugged salts so that they'll stay warm and won't starve in their lifting of the lobster pots.' And then she added, 'What's happened to Janet?'

'She went up to Scotland with her mother for the rest of the season's shoot. I'm joining them next week.'

'Why didn't you go up with her?'

'I wasn't sure I wanted to get trapped.'

'*I* am trapped,' Cara said with an odd little catch in her throat, 'and I can tell you, don't. It's . . . it's . . .' she searched for the right word ' . . . inhibiting. It's no fun being a lobster in a lobster pot.'

'I've met Tinling,' Tom said following his own train of thought. 'Bloomin' rich.'

'Bloomin' rich,' Lance repeated with a chuckle. 'Not much fun being a lobster about to be boiled alive, but nice to be rich. Think of all the lobsters one can set free with the money.'

'Is that what you'd do with it?' Cara asked nibbling at a biscuit and wishing she weren't trapped when they were on the brink of war. She filled up the mugs with more tea.

'Cigarette?' Lance held out the cardboard packet as he had on the Club verandah to Janet.

46

'I don't smoke.'

'Mind if I do?'

'Go ahead. I like the smell, which is just as well with Uncle Tom – What on earth's that?' For the first time she noticed a large square box on the table.

'A bloomin' gas-mask,' Tom grunted, 'up for grabs for everyone, men, women, children and babies. Delivered by the bloomin' ARP this afternoon.'

'Good Lord, has it really come to that? I haven't been listening to the news.' Lance pulled the box towards him and drew out a hideous-looking rubber affair with celluloid visor and snout, straps over head. 'Want to try it on, Miss Thornton?'

'I expect we've got ours at home – nine of them to include the garden boy. Father will turn pea-green at the sight. He was gassed in the trenches, poor lamb.'

'Poor lamb, yer say? More like a chargin' pink hippo,' grouched Tom. 'Fiery Brig-Gen and lets you know it, and don't forget to "sir" him, sonny, unless yer wants to be thrown out t'morrow before yer has time for a knock-up.'

'You haven't said what you'd do with riches besides letting lobsters out of lobster pots.' Cara succinctly switched the conversation from the subject of her uncle's *bête noire*.

'Do up some property in the United Provinces. Derelict at the moment. Lovely position on a Ganges tributary called the Pila Nadi. Stands for Yellow Stream.'

'I know that much. My father was in India. He will enjoy meeting you and talking about it. Will three o'clock be all right? We'll get in some tennis before tea. You drive through Christchurch, turn left at the crossroads and go on over Tuckton Bridge. Left again down Wick Lane, and there we are, Wick House. See you tomorrow, Uncle. Mind you pop in for some fresh scones and your favourite cake!'

Lance got to his feet and saw Cara to the steps. He stood watching her run lightly down to the polished Wolseley and start up the engine without over-choking or revving unduly, which one person in particular had an unfortunate habit of doing.

'Very competent young lady, your niece,' he said back on the 'deck' with Tom.

'Competent, yer say? She's a bloody good bit more than that. She's a bloomin' angel about the house. It'll be a bloomin' lucky man who wins *her* heart!'

'"The Angel in the House,"' Lance quoted softly, '"He meets, by heavenly chance express, The destined maid . . . *Par la grâce infinie, Dieu les mit au monde ensemble.*"'

The main entrance to Wick House was through the conservatory. Lance, in long white flannels, a Calcutta 'Slap' (for Saturday) Club blazer, and carrying his racket, seeing no bell, opened the low-handled glass door and walked up the wet, square-tiled path bordered with tropical flowers on tiered shelves. A tall palm bent its height against a top pane next to a mimosa tree in flower. Dripping ferns lower down mixed with powerfully scented stately lilies and exotically coloured orchids. He sniffed the air and felt the film of sweat coming over his skin, a not unpleasant sensation he knew so well in the heat of monsoon time in Calcutta.

At the other end of the conservatory was an oak door with brass knob-handle, and letter-box. On the floor was a brass surround containing a brush mat. Obediently he acceded to its demands and wiped the damp from the soles of his tennis shoes upon its rough surface. Lots of brass and elbow work in this household. Lance mentally compared the elder Thornton brother's abode with the younger's entrance plank and one upstairs brass bell. Bell? He searched for it and found it hidden by a frond of cascading blue plumbago. He gave it a good blast.

There was a pause, a scurry of feet, and Cara opened the door. Today she wore a sleeveless tennis dress with narrow yellow belt, ankle socks to match and heavily blancoed tennis shoes obviously overdone by Fred the batman. Her hair was all over the place.

'Come in,' she said pushing it back off her face, 'you'll have to wait a minute; we're on gas parade! Do take a chair.' She left him in the hall and went through to the drawing-room leaving the door open. Lance looked about him.

The hall was typical of hundreds in the country. Heads on walls: black-buck, ghural, chital, nilghai, chinkara, barasingh, he noted, and a stately Highland stag such as the Tinlings must at this very moment be stalking. A huge snarling tiger's glassy-eyed head with ears flattened, mouth open showing curving mauve tongue and sharp fangs, was set up over the stairwell. There were panther skins tacked to the panelled walls of the wide polished mahogany stairs, a bearskin on the half-landing, swords, lances, two elephant-foot umbrella stands, pictures of regimental groups, *syces* standing by horses' heads, Baluchi rugs on the floor – the whole gamut of *koi-hai*'s nostalgic past.

Hearing barked words of command Lance moved to the door and there before him saw a remarkable sight. A sandy-haired and red-moustached choleric old gentleman was inspecting a row of household personnel of various ages, sizes and dress standing to attention and wearing gas-masks. Tom's 'Brig-Gen' brother (as he must be) was passing down the line adjusting angles and straps on heads, while muffled voices gasped and protested. Lance of course did not know them at the time, but they were Cook, Rosie, Ford, Mr and Mrs Field, the garden boy, Mrs Thornton, Cara, Bobby and Susan Langley who was for the practice wearing the Brigadier's gas-mask.

'Masks off!' commanded Charles Thornton, and pink-faced they did so, the 'boy's' terrified mouth slack, his slanted eyes bewildered. Cara and Susan dissolved into giggles.

'Gas warfare is no laughing matter, Carissa,' her father sternly reproved.

'No, of course not, Father. I'm sorry.' She looked repentant, whereupon the domestics dispersed, Cook visibly puffed, Rosie giving Lance a dimpled smile as she passed.

'Please come in, sir.' Ford in squeaky boots led the way from the hall into the room.

'Thank you, Fred,' Lance said in a voice which carried.

'*Fred*?' the Brigadier bellowed. 'Who called my batman "Fred"? His name is *Ford*!'

'I stand corrected, sir.' Lance made a mental note he'd have something to say to Tom about that . . .

'This is Mr Gardner, Father. He's come to take Captain Brownlow's place at tennis.' The older and the younger man shook hands, and Cara introduced Lance to her mother and Susan.

'Gard*i*ner, did you say?' Charles, who had become slightly hard of hearing, queried.

'No sir – *Gardner*.'

'Ha! Famous name in India. Gardner's Horse, Indian Cavalry.'

'My great-grandfather raised the Horse in 1809.'

'Interesting. Most interesting.' Brigadier Thornton glared at Lance speculatively while searching his memory. 'You following the tradition?'

'No, sir, though a keen Saturday soldier.'

'Glad to hear it with another bloody war about to burst. What unit?'

'Auxiliary Battery, Calcutta.'

'Jutney Gunners! In their way as famous as Gardner's Horse. You must be Scottish?'

'Half sir, my mother's from Dundee, hence the connection with jute.'

'Hummn.'

'Ready for tennis?' Bobby impatiently interrupted the interrogation.

'Will renew the conversation over tea . . .' Charles

Thornton collected the discarded gas-masks and put each back in its named box. He tut-tutted at the indiscipline. Masks should be kept by one's side in case of emergency. Each individual was responsible for his or her own, and here they had left them in a heap in the drawing-room. If he hadn't taken the trouble to mark them, someone would breathe the garden boy's lamentable breath!

'Pa likes to hold forth on Indian affairs. 'Fraid I'm woefully ignorant.' Bobby led the way out of the French window to the tennis court.

'So am I.' Susan measured the net with hers and Cara's rackets. 'Up a few inches, Cara; bit more; that's about right. Gardner's Horse sounds romantic.'

'Thereby *does* lie a romantic story, as well as an exciting and exotic one,' Lance vouchsafed. 'Sleeman's written some of the exploits down in his *Recollections*; they're also in Tod.'

'I suggest you play with Susan. Spin?' Bobby organized.

'OK. Rough so it is. Would you like to serve, Miss Langley?'

'I can tell you Bobby and Cara make a formidable pair when on form,' warned Susan.

'Unfortunately I'm not.' Lance knocked some balls over the net and proceeded to do some practice serves, all the lassitude of his loose-knit figure vanishing into a spring of energy on the court. 'I've been playing golf all summer. You'll have to be kind to me.'

That he was out of practice could be seen when the balls flew over the back net and had to be retrieved by the grinning garden boy, but when accurate, it was not difficult to see that his overhead smashes would be unreturnable.

As the game progressed with the 'well dones' and the 'bad lucks' coming thick and fast, Lance was soon on Christian name terms with the company. Predictably, with Susan not so strong a player as Cara, she and Lance lost the first set by which time they were called in to tea.

There Lance was plied with pertinent questions from

his host about which public school he'd been to (he hadn't; he'd been to a grammar school in Dundee as a day boy), where he lived in Calcutta, and so on, all of which he answered amicably with the amused look on his face Cara had come to expect. He was also plied by his hostess with scones and rich chocolate cake. At the rate the former were going he hoped they had a reserve in the kitchen for Tom, whom, while playing tennis, he had observed rolling up the path to the back door. At one point he managed to talk to Doreen Thornton pouring out the tea on his left. He asked her about her impressions on India to Charles's impatience, who believed the only impression his wife made on anything was one of muddle.

'When was your Battery raised?' Charles cut his wife's voice off.

'1883 I believe, sir. Originally the Naval Artillery Volunteers, manning port defences and coast batteries. "Gallop" guns in those days.'

'What field guns do you have?'

'When I first joined we were still using the fifteen-pounder BLs—'

'Strewth! Obsolete. Dating from the Boer War, though we utilized them in the last.'

'They kept them on in India to use up the large stock of ammunition.'

'Cheese-paring as usual.'

'Exactly, sir! I'm glad to say we are now equipped with six-inch howitzers.'

'Been called out on emergency recently?'

'Once or twice on civil disturbance and communal riots – "aid to civil power" they call it. Last year we manned the guns at Diamond Harbour and provided guards at Budge Budge. On our winter manoeuvres we joined up with the Cossipore Field Brigade.'

'Used to be hundred per cent European Club recruiting. Same now?'

'Pretty strict still, sir, though some Armenians and

52

Anglo-Indians have been allowed in the trade. Damned difficult for any of them to get into the Jute-wallahs.' Lance smiled, a smile his host did not at that moment appreciate.

'Your mother has talent' – he approached Cara on their return to the tennis courts – 'those paintings of Moghul ruins she did in India are charming.'

'She was delighted to show them to you. No one takes much notice of her hobby in this household.'

'So I have noticed.'

'You made a hit with the Brigadier,' Susan said.

'That I am not too sure about,' Lance replied.

'Why? What do you mean?'

'You had better read Sleeman,' Lance said mysteriously. 'There are shades and shades . . . besides which jute is "trade", bottom of the list of box-wallahs; not even commerce!' Neither the girls nor Bobby had any idea what he was talking about. He walked over to his side of the court purposefully and promptly served an ace at Cara.

'That was great fun.' Cara came up to the net at the end of the third set which Lance and Susan had marginally won after losing the first two.

'I shall have to leave.' Lance glanced at his watch. 'I've enjoyed it enormously. Thank you for asking me.'

'Are you going lobster potting tonight?'

'Yes; with dear old Uncle Tom.'

'Let's have a return match tomorrow,' Susan suggested. 'We were just about getting into our stride, weren't we, Lance?'

'Yes . . . do come again,' Cara found herself having to add.

That night she searched along her father's shelves for Sleeman, found a tome, and took it to bed with her.

CHAPTER 4

After the second day of hard hitting tennis, Bobby suggested that Lance should join a picnic party of Yacht Club members on the morrow to Lulworth in Dorset. His car would be useful for giving lifts. As before, good-naturedly, Lance agreed. Cara kept silent during this conversation. She felt she was being pitchforked into a situation she would prefer to avoid. She did not want to go on meeting the dark-bronzed man who looked more handsome than ever in tennis flannels. She did not want to come face to face daily with the man who belonged to Janet. She may have started the ball rolling in the first place by asking him to tennis, but either Susan or Bobby or Fate were taking over from her – and she seemed powerless to stop *them* or *it*.

With Bobby driving Doreen, Cara and Susan squashed in his Austin 7, they did not see Lance until the picnickers foregathered off the main road to park, and he disgorged from his Lancia with four others. The party of some fifteen all told carrying picnic baskets and bathing gear set off in a straggle to walk the mile along a lane, skirt round a field, over a stile, and down a narrow sandy path to the pebbly beach. As they had expected, they had the small bay to themselves.

It was a sunny day, though not a hot one, the sea breeze ruffling up with wisps of white the choppy green and purple waves in the cove. Even so most of the party disappeared behind rocks to change. They re-emerged to walk gingerly down towards the sea on tender white feet, and brave the water. Doreen Thornton wandered

54

off on her own with her pad to sketch from a higher vantage point.

'Not bathing?' Lance came over to sit on a wall above Cara who was with Susan and another girl combining the lunches in the lee of the shelter. She laid out a tablecloth, placed a pile of sandwiches on a round tray, hard-boiled eggs, tomatoes and lettuce on another, and positioned bakelite cups and plates round.

'Too busy,' she said without looking up, 'what about you?'

'Too cold. I'm a tropical beast.'

'Do you never swim in England?'

'I have done, but it takes a heat wave to get me in!'

'I read a bit about your great-grandfather a couple of nights ago.'

'Great fellow, wasn't he?'

'Sleeman describes him as a "tall, commanding figure with handsome countenance, military air, and striking appearance"'. She remembered the exact words because they were so descriptive of *him*.

'How clever of you to memorize it. As well, he had brains and humour — often bawdy in keeping with the times — and he was as brave as a lion in battle. He could easily have been killed on a dozen occasions. Instead he lived to go back to his beloved Dilmilee.'

'What a strange name. Who was she? Oh, here come the hungry gang. Tell me more after lunch . . .'

Later, when the baskets had been packed up and most of the rest of the party had gone off to explore the ruins of Lulworth Castle round the headland, and Doreen was filling in her morning sketch with water-colours from her paint-box, Lance and Cara sat on the shelving beach looking down at the sea. She took off her *espadrilles*, hitched up her skirt to between her knees, and with her smooth golden legs before her, flexed her slim feet. Lance threw down the crumpled jacket with its leather-patched elbows, and with rolled-up shirt sleeves lounged back on an elbow, cigarette in hand. She noticed how, compared to some dark men who had legs and arms like gorillas, he was comparatively fine-haired.

'Well,' she said, 'tell me about . . . Dilmilee was it?'

'*Dil* means "heart"; *milee* is from the root *milna* to meet. Hence "hearts meeting" or "meeting of hearts". There are two love stories, but I'll only bore you with one. You asked for it! Lieutenant-Colonel William Gardner came from a well-connected Anglo-Irish family. He was the nephew of Baron Gardner of Uttoxeter, which title went into abeyance when the 3rd Baron died. Incidentally I'm in line to claim the barony, as could one or two others of our poverty-stricken clan in India did we have the means to go into litigation. To cut the story short, in 1795 Her Highness Princess Mah Manzil-ool-Nissa, the beautiful daughter of the Nawab of Cambay and soon to be the adopted daughter of the Moghul Emperor of Delhi, Akbar Shah, due to a coup in her country on the death of her father, was imprisoned with her mother, escaped by boat to Surat, and sought refuge with the British Governor of nearby Bombay. Got it?'

'Sort of! Go on.'

'William Gardner, conveniently to hand, was ordered to take the Princess into safe custody. One day, whilst living in the *zenana* quarters, she evaded the eunuch bodyguards and slipped away to the durbar hall in a bid to see what her benefactor looked like. William was in conference in the room and excessively bored with the proceedings. Most daringly for a girl in her position, she peeped at him through the folds of a curtain – and loved the "fair god" on sight. He for his part glimpsed the "slim brown hand and the most beautiful black eyes in the world" and fell instantly in love with his "dark Princess". She was fourteen years old, he twenty-four. Despite every opposition, every difficulty – different language, race, religion – he demanded her hand in marriage, and for nearly forty years they loved each other devotedly. They lived happily together through the many anxieties, terrible dangers and grim adventures of those times of inter-warring in India when William was a soldier of fortune under the Mahratta Holkar chief's banner. Some years later he founded and commanded his own Horse. When William died, the Begum Nissa (as she was known) died a few days later, it was said of a broken heart.'

'True love . . .' Cara murmured, eyes on the horizon where blue sky and turquoise sea met. 'Such things don't happen in this country, not even any more in India, I imagine.'

'You'd be surprised. Arranged marriages can be very successful. If the four parents have chosen well, when the bride and groom see each other for the first time on their marriage night, they can fall in love and remain faithful all their lives.'

Cara turned to Lance. 'You have inherited your great-grandmother's black eyes – *when* you condescend to expose them.'

'A terrible habit I developed in the strong sunlight.' He put out his cigarette on a stone, buried it, and lay back on the beach stuffing his jacket behind his head. 'I should wear dark glasses; but don't you find it off-putting talking to a person whose eyes you cannot see behind the disguise? Personally I rather like to watch the reaction to my cryptic remarks. On reflection I am not sure that likening my eyes to a woman's soft ones is a compliment to my manly ego.'

'What happened?' Cara smiled.

'I told you. They lived hazardously but richly and happily ever after. The Emperor Akbar Shah bestowed on the Begum a huge grant of land containing 365 villages in a remote reach in the fertile Gangetic basin, perfect for the growing of jute and indigo crops. There, by a bubbling spring of pure water, William built a fine mansion for his Princess and named it the "Chashma Shahi", the Spring Imperial. It had rooms all round the outside sheltered by deep verandahs, an inner pavilion designed for the ladies in purdah by a hidden garden full of bright flowers, fountains splashing cool water and golden swings.'

'This is the place you hope one day to restore?'

57

'Not *hope* to. *Shall!*'

'My father once told me that no person of British blood was allowed to own land in India.'

'That is so. This is an exceptional case. The Imperial Shah gave the land to the Begum, and her heirs are permitted to hold the inheritance in the name of Gardner. I came into the small remaining part of the estate, on which the palace is situated, through my father who was the last Gardner to live there; my mother rescued him in old age from the ruins.'

'What happened to the rest?'

'After my grandfather James Gardner's death, it was dissipated by the extravagant living of his wife, Mulka, a royal princess of Delhi, the sister of the Queen of Oudh.'

'Yes?'

'Too involved to explain on a summer's day' – Lance's eyes were shut – 'except to say they ran away together . . . You see what a mixture I am, of the House of Timur and Genghis Khan from my grandmother Mulka; the Moghul dynasty and Arab slave traders from the House of Cambay of my great-grandmother Nissa; Irish, Dutch and American connections from the noble English family of William Gardner just to lay it on thick – and proud of every drop of blood! I've talked far too much about myself. Tell me about yourself.' Lance opened his eyes and turned his head on his jacket to look at Cara's profile with its straight small nose, the shine of her tumbling hair forming a halo in the sun.

'There is nothing to tell,' she said. 'I love my mother and my father and my brother and Uncle Tom, not to mention Susan, Rosie and all the rest. I have never been anywhere, done anything. Simply Christchurch and the harbour with its boats, the river, the sea.'

'You don't need to go anywhere when you have all that on your doorstep.'

'You need to go somewhere if only to have something to compare it with.'

'Wise answer. In India it is crowded, noisy, smelly and

black with flies. There is appalling poverty such as you cannot imagine until you have seen it, and dire disease that can strike the strongest down in a day. Stay where you are you . . . ' He broke off, the words 'you lovely healthy innocent' in his mind; he did not voice them. Instead he said, 'May I ask you a personal question?'

'You may,' she put out a hand on the stones to lean back and look at his face behind her shoulder, 'but I won't guarantee to answer!'

'You love many people, you say. That means you have a big heart. Have you ever been in love?'

'No,' she said sitting up straight again to hide her blush, 'and I've arrived at twenty. Isn't that terrible? Isn't that cause for going out somewhere and finding it?' She did not need to ask him in her turn the same question, for he patently was in love with Janet. They were probably this leave planning their marriage, perhaps soon in India. It was so easy for those with plenty of money to fly hither and thither these days, not only Prime Ministers to Berlin to try and save the world from having to wear hideous gas-masks. The crisis was as bad as ever. There were crowds standing in Whitehall, silent crowds the night through in Downing Street. It was frightening and despairing having to watch Europe sliding down a glassy slope into war and be helpless to stop it, or do anything about it, except slash London's parks gay with flowers to make muddy slit trenches. There was nothing her family could do about it but turn the basement billiard-room into an air-raid shelter, stack stores down there, and drape the windows black in mourning for Europe about to be plunged into a dark abyss . . .

'Come on, Cara. We've got to dress up to hear Tovarich this evening,' Bobby interrupted Cara's sombre thoughts. Together they fetched their mother from her rock, collected their picnic things, and with Susan made their way up the sandy path to the stile.

Cara did not say goodbye to Lance. She left him there lying on the beach, his head resting on his folded jacket, his eyes half-shut. She looked back from the stile, after which the beach was hidden from her sight, and saw that he was still lying in the same position facing the sea. She thought he must have fallen asleep.

She sat with her mother as if stunned in the back of Bobby's small car, half-listening to the chatter of her brother and Susan.

'Not well, sweetie?' Her mother put a sympathetic hand on her daughter's knee. 'I saw you weren't bathing. Time of month?'

'Yes, mother.'

'You needn't come to the concert if you don't want to.'

'I do want to.'

'Good.'

Once on the main Wareham road Bobby put his foot down flat on the floorboard. He looked at the speedometer and saw it barely touched thirty miles an hour.

'Just as well you asked Lance if he'd like to come tomorrow or we'd never reach Exeter.' He addressed Susan beside him, and then over his shoulder, 'Mother, we're barely moving. I declare you must have put on weight!'

'I can quite see your problem, dear,' Doreen said chirpily thinking how pleased her art master would be with her painting which had gone rather well.

'What's that? Who's asked Lance where?' Cara sat up.

'Sue invited him to stay. Bit too much for this bus is three with luggage.'

'Besides,' took up Susan, 'it'll save you having to catch a train at Crewkerne on the way back when Bobby and I veer off to the Squadron.'

'You seem to have got it all worked out to your advantage without so much as asking me.' Cara's voice sounded disgruntled.

'Not entirely, old thing,' her brother shouted over the rattle of his car. 'Must be pretty dull for a chap like that in Mudeford with only Uncle Tom for company.'

'But . . . I don't understand . . . he was going to Scotland.'

'He said he could fit it in before. Only a couple of days.'

'I thought he wanted to fish. I think you're both using him.'

'Maybe a bit,' laughed Susan. 'We all get on so well together it seemed a good idea. I think he's terrific!'

'Steady, Sue.' Bobby grinned over the steering wheel. 'Let's make an early start – picnic breakfast en route. I'll ring the Ship Inn tonight to fix timings, and I propose we stay in convoy in case the old banger decides to conk out. You girls can ring the changes in the cars to keep Lance company.'

'What'll Father say?'

'I'll square him,' said Bobby.

But it didn't square Brigadier Thornton. 'Staying in convoy' was not sufficient information. He wanted a great deal more detail of the two days and nights they proposed to be away at the invitation of Mr and Mrs Langley. In fact when he had found out on the family's return from the picnic that there was a new plan to include Mr Gardner on the tour, Charles Thornton stayed up late to question his son in his study when he came in.

'Don't altogether trust that fella, y'know, mixed blood, what, what,' he came straight to the point.

'Really? I had no idea.'

'The great-grandfather married an Indian, grandfather ditto, which makes the father three-quarters native.'

'So what? His mother is Scottish; that brings him back to a quarter.' Bobby treated the subject as a bit of a joke.

'Exactly. Four annas. Screwy lot. Mercenary. Out for what they can get. This one latched himself onto you and Carissa fairly rapidly.'

'Not at all, Father. There's been no "latching on" about it.' Bobby showed his annoyance. 'The boot is on the other foot. *We've* done all the latching. You'd never guess he wasn't English, public school—'

61

'Grammar school — I asked him,' Charles stopped his son. Grammar school boys he considered were unfit escorts for his daughter. In his eyes there were five 'top' schools: Eton, Harrow, Marlborough, Winchester, Rugby — all the rest were seconds, the grammars further down the list.

'Public school *accent, if* you'll allow, Father, was what I was about to say.' Bobby gritted his teeth at the stupidity of the feeble old so-and-so. 'It might ease your mind to know that he's engaged to the Tinling girl.'

'That I confess I did not know. Thank God for that!'

'Why?'

'Carissa is susceptible.'

'Father, honestly . . . she has more sense than to get tied to a man who is as good as married. To allay any fears you may have on her behalf,' Bobby went on tongue in cheek, 'I'll watch him like a hawk in case he attempts to climb into my little sister's window one night.'

'Enough of your damned levity, Robert. Enough!' barked Charles. 'I demand to know your programme.'

Bobby spelled it out. 'First night we'll be snug under the Langleys' parental roof; the second evening we plan to start back from Exeter after a day at the exhibition, stay at a pub en route so that I can arrive at the Squadron in reasonable time next morning; I think I mentioned that Susan is coming to our farewell ball? We'll see them off from the pub. Should be with you by tea-time, anyway in daylight.'

'What do Susan's parents say to her going to the Air Force Ball unchaperoned?' grumbled Charles, unable to fault the arrangements that would safeguard his daughter's chastity.

'They trust me, Father.' And, excessively irritated, without further ado, Bobby removed himself from the study.

It was a long drive in those days from Christchurch to Exeter on the winding main roads through Bournemouth and round Poole harbour to Dorchester and on to join the A30, though there was little traffic, that was until they arrived on the outskirts of the city. Here, later, they found themselves jammed in bumper to bumper with cars on their way to or from the exhibition of the decade. Gear boxes ground, clutches burnt out and broke down, bonnets steamed, helping hands pushed cars out of the way onto the side of the road.

At first Susan drove with Lance, Bobby taking Cara.

'Don't tell Father or Mother' — Bobby looked in the mirror at the Lancia following (the Austin led for fear it would break down and have to be towed, but nothing more untoward happened than a puncture; the wheel was quickly whipped off and replaced with the spare by the men) — 'but we want you to know we're privately engaged.'

'*What?* Oh! Bobby, darling, I'm thrilled, absolutely thrilled! What could be nicer than you and my best friend.' Cara hugged him.

'Oi there or you'll have us in the ditch.' Bobby clamped onto the small wheel. 'Better not mention it to Lance either. Don't want it to get round.'

'No, of course not.'

'Can't get married for ages so there's no point in blowing it. If there's war we're going to bloody well get spliced at the first opportunity. We're both fatalists. If I prang, I prang!'

'Don't talk like that, Bobby, please don't, Bobby . . .'

The cloud that had loured over them menacingly that summer, and would not go away and became darker than ever in September, continued to hover overhead in looming depression as ranting speeches poured out from Germany. One moment they were allowed to glimpse a patch of blue; the next moment a blacker shadow obliterated hope. How would Chamberlain be able to make an agreement with a yo-yo madman like that? *Oh God*, thought Cara sitting next to Bobby driving down the near-empty road at a spanking forty miles an hour, Susan waving cheerfully behind them, *oh God*, don't let there be a war; don't let Bobby be killed in the air . . . *don't let Lance* . . . The Territorials were on standby for immediate call up; he was Auxiliary. India was safe, though. Japan was an ally. China was an ally. Russia would stay out of it, and probably America, isolationists as they were over the wide ocean. She, Cara, had believed that if Hitler invaded Austria – brave Austria where the British loved to ski – that would be the moment of truth. Surely, she had thought, they could not abandon Austria to the Nazis? But they had. And now Czechoslovakia. The most popular show in London was *The Fleet's Lit Up*, hugely funny. The lights were still on . . . for how much longer? Why can't we have peace? Oh God don't let there be war . . .

They had stopped for their picnic of hard-boiled eggs and marmalade sandwiches – surely the most delicious of English breakfasts when hungry after an early start – washed down with coffee hot from a thermos, and now they stopped for a pub lunch, and Cara kissed her friend warmly in the privacy of the ladies'.

'Hush, Cara,' Susan's blue eyes sparkled, 'we don't want my parents to guess. They'd *smother* us! They love Bobby. I'm so happy, so lucky . . . the Squadron won't go to Egypt if there's war. The whole posting will be cancelled.'

'There won't be war, Sue, darling. There *can't* be war, not now that you and Bobby . . . ' Oh God, don't let there be war. Please, dear God, don't let there be war.

Susan sat in the Austin beside Bobby and they led the way on through Chard and Honiton, Lance and Cara following obediently slowly in the comfort of the Lancia's deep seats and independent front-wheel springing.

They were both quiet, Cara resting her head on the door lintel and watching the shadows and light of hedges and trees flicker past like a slow-moving film. Lance appeared disinclined to talk, and she felt no need to break the silence as she would have with most men. She thought he looked dispirited; that strange mouth hard and straight. Brown hands on the wheel, slim with well-formed dark half-moons clearly defined. Half-moons. 'Moon of my delight'. 'Heart's meeting'. 'Meeting of hearts'. Had Dilmilee had such distinctive half-moons a hundred years ago? Had the exquisitely beautiful (according to Tod) Mulka possessed those slim distinctive hands? Cara saw Lance stifle a half-yawn.

'Are you tired,' she said from where her head rested, 'or merely bored?'

'I am never bored,' he said. 'Life is too short to let boredom in. When there is nothing else to do one can always watch the miracle of a bird's flight. In any case it would be unpardonable of me to be bored when a fair maid sits beside me resting her head so charmingly in my carriage! No, I am not bored and neither am I tired, but going at this doleful pace I get a bit somnolent.'

'It's the beer!'

'Not only the beer. I did not sleep much last night.'

'Oh? I'm sorry. I imagine the beds in the Old Ship Inn are pretty awful.'

'Pretty awful is about right! Passable when lying athwart. My thoughts kept me awake backed by the booming of a sea of guns against the rocks of life in an attempt to destroy humanity. I thought that was rather good so I turned on the light and wrote a very bad poem on the theme.'

'Recite it.'

'Not on your fanny!'

He was a poet, and a lover of nature. Oh God, don't let there be war. 'If you are sleepy, perhaps I could drive? I would like to try out a Lancia.'

'But of course! How stupid of me not to have thought of it first.' Lance was suddenly awake. He brought the car to a standstill on the verge, leapt out and came round and opened her door. The Austin disappeared ahead. Cara slid across into the driving seat, her wide-skirted cotton dress disarrayed round her. She tucked it neatly in and felt for the pedals she could barely reach.

'Have to push the seat forwards; I'll show you how.' Lance got into the passenger seat. She adjusted hers, tested the gear in neutral, found the hand-brake down beside her, and started off. She drove slowly at first to get the feel of the car, and then more quickly, with a spurt catching up Bobby and Susan who appeared to have been unconscious of their absence. The Austin bounced along on its narrow wheels, Cara taking her foot off the Lancia's accelerator well ahead so as to not brake, gently gliding into their shadowing position. Lance and Cara exchanged glances and laughed.

'Oblivious,' he said, 'never missed us. Good for a tease.'

'Lovely,' she said. 'Lovely car to drive. Did I scare you?'

'Certainly not. I have complete confidence in your ability to do anything. I remarked to your uncle when you drove away from his shack that you were a most competent young lady, and you are.'

'Thank you,' she said simply, and wondered at herself. With anyone else she would have denied being competent, or perhaps said, 'Oh, I don't know . . .' rather crossly. Now she asked: 'What did Uncle Tom say to that?'

'He said you were an angel in the house.'

'Dear old Uncle Tom!'

They lapsed into silence, Cara concentrating on the traffic building up near Exeter. She followed the Austin to the Langleys' home by a round-about route Susan was taking in order to avoid the exhibition exits, the tents of which they could see over the rises. Now it was Lance's turn to rest his head on the lintel, though he did not doze. Indeed his eyes were wide open, and she was conscious of his turning sideways to study her profile. Yet, again, in no way did the gaze make her feel embarrassed or self-conscious. She had never felt so at ease at close quarters when alone with a new acquaintance before – as if with an old friend or a relative. Instead of blushing or staring fixedly ahead and wishing he wouldn't look at her, she turned quite naturally to glance at him, catching his eye and smiling before turning her eyes back to the road. His relaxed self-confidence in some strange way included her, enveloped her, gave her an assurance new to her, almost a feeling of elation. She *was* attractive – at least when with *him*! Did he make all women feel the same? Sophisticated Janet must feel even more glamorous when in his presence. A few more days and he would have gone to her. Oh God, don't let there be war . . .

The two cars, one behind the other, swept up the drive to the Langleys' four-bedroomed detached house in the village of Ide. The front door burst open, scattering barking spaniels, the Langley parents following, wide smiles on faces.

'Have you heard?' they rushed, embracing Susan and Cara, Mrs Langley placing a loud smack on Bobby's cheek much to his astonishment. Had they guessed about Susan and him? Who could possibly have let the cat out of the bag when it had come about only yesterday evening in the conservatory of Wick House? Susan introduced them to Lance.

'Heard? No we haven't heard anything; heard what?'

'*Peace in our time!*'

'What, when, who . . .?'

'The Prime Minister. He returned by air today all smiles waving a bit of paper!'

No war! Oh thank God for no war. Peace in our time. Unbelievable unloading; lightness, happiness; celebration champagne; bubbles of joy with Mr and Mrs Langley, Susan and Bobby, Cara and the dark stranger from India.

CHAPTER 5

'Looks like rain.' Lance examined a sky filled with scudding clouds. 'If it does we're in for a mud bath. No need to lock the car; nothing worth pinching. Anyone can come back and take refuge.'

'Plenty of people about to push,' Bobby expressed cheerfully.

'If I get lost I shall never be able to locate the car.' Susan looked doubtfully at the long rows.

The AA official had directed them into No. 4 car park in a huge area on a slope where were parked hundreds of other cars, black roofs shining in serried ranks in nearby fields.

'Row D. Here, I'll tell you what.' Lance dived into the Lancia and retrieved a cloth from under the seat. He proceeded to search for a stick.

'Should have brought the Club burgee!' Bobby helped tie the contraption onto the wing mirror.

It was a longish walk to the exhibition park of tents and pavilions, fair-grounds and shop-booths interspersed by an 'H' of main walkways from which branched innumerable lesser paths. They queued at one of the turnstiles to buy their tickets and then stood examining the glossy programme by which time the tower clock, a replica of Big Ben, read twelve noon.

'What about making for the main hall from where we can find our bearings and decide what we want to see next,' Bobby suggested.

'Good idea,' Lance agreed, 'there's one hell of a crowd. If we get separated, what time do you want to rendezvous?'

'I should say five at the latest, preferably four. The exhibition goes on half the night but even so there'll be a queue to get out at dusk, and after picking up our gear we've got a longish drive ahead.'

'Right, four o'clock it is.'

'I shall stick to Bobby like a leech. I know I couldn't find the car on my own,' wailed Susan who was determined she had no bump of location.

'What about you? Could you find the Lancia, competent Cara?' Lance's eyes narrowed at her.

'I probably could, but I don't like crowds and don't want to have to do so.'

'Then I suggest you stick to *me* like a leech,' he invited, leading the way to the big tent.

Inside was an assortment of agricultural equipment down the ages, from the first wooden implement unearthed in Britain to the latest modern machines.

'That ancient plough looks mightily like the bullock-drawn affair still used in India,' Cara heard Lance say, the men going on to discuss new mechanical land techniques while the girls took more interest in the history.

'For goodness sake let's have some fun at the fair,' demanded Susan an hour later when she and Cara had had more than enough.

'Kid's stuff next,' Bobby condescendingly agreed.

Here in the fun-fair the crowds were at their thickest and they had to queue for everything including an exhilarating ride clinging onto the great dipper, their screams of thrill added to the others, tears in their eyes from the wind blow. Tears of joy and relief – 'peace in our time!'

When Lance and Cara disgorged after a second round, Bobby and Susan were nowhere to be seen.

'No good trying to find them in this mill.' Lance stood for a few moments looking about him over everyone's heads. 'Where now, Cara? Lead on! I feel like a boy let out of school; that ride took years off my life.'

'Put years on mine,' Cara laughed. 'What about the

ghost train?' She saw the letters written up in bright lights not far away. Lights were being switched on all over the exhibition as the clouds darkened and there was a rumble of thunder overhead.

'Come on.' Lance took her hand and shouldered the way ahead through the crowd.

It was a perfectly natural, as well as a sensible thing to do in that pushing, jostling throng, but the effect it had on Cara was out of all proportion to the simplicity of the gesture. The strong, sinewy hand, clasping tightly her hot one, sent a nervous impulse up her arm. She had never experienced before anything so instantly effective. It made her jump, the shock akin to the prick of static electricity, so much so that for a second she wondered if she had indeed been struck by lightning. Whatever it was, she stumbled.

'All right?' Lance halted abruptly; she took a further step to find herself against his shoulder.

'Ye-es, sorry — a stone . . .'

'After the ghost train, shall we have a snack? All this shoving is exhausting even for me with my head above it. It must be claustrophobic for you down there in the midst of it.' His mouth twitched into his smile.

'Yes,' she said again. Since he had taken her hand she seemed incapable of saying anything else. How stupid he must think her.

They sat side by side clinging to the rail in front of them in the narrow-gauged ghost train which whistled and howled and jerked its way in the semi-dark through tunnels, over bridges and into black caverns where cobwebs brushed their laughing faces. Hung skeletons macabrely clacked loose limbs, and socket-empty lit-up skulls leered from ledges a bare foot away.

'What I must look like . . .' Cara swept a hand over her hair in the exit.

'You look deliciously abandoned.' He in his turn brushed a tickling cobweb from his mouth. 'You'll have to take my hand again if we're to get anywhere. Do you mind?'

Mind? 'Peace in our time.' Happiness with a tall man. 'How could I mind?' she said because Bobby and Lance and all of them had been reprieved from war. He took her hand then, and this time there was no shock, only the warmth of familiarity and the comfort of belonging to someone in an anonymous crowd. They sat at a rough wooden table under a thatched roof. He drank beer and she ginger-beer. They munched 'mediaeval' snacks brought by a waitress dressed in Middle Ages country clothes.

'Arr, I be a yokel wi' straw in me 'air.' Lance comically wiped the froth of beer off his mouth with the back of his hand.

'Would you like to have lived in those days?'

'Not much. Life must have been distinctly uncomfortable, streets ankle-deep in mire, freezing houses. When I'm not being horribly active, I like my comforts. No point in wasting effort being uncomfortable.'

That's him all over, thought Cara. Leisurely stance, deceptively sleepy look, a body that could burst into steely activity. 'Do you mind if we go down Fisherman's Row?' he asked. 'I'd like to look at some tackle.'

Cara nodded. Why did he always ask her if she *minded*? She did not mind anything with him. He was very polite and considerate, almost old world manners. Was that the Indian influence?

There was no need to take her hand again, and he did not do so. With the deterioration of the weather the crowds had thinned perceptibly. Lance bought the fishing tackle he wanted and they made towards the No. 4 car park exit. On the way Cara noticed a Scottish shop selling cashmere jerseys. She had long promised herself a twinset in that softest of wools, and she had the money in her purse, for Lance had insisted on paying all but the entrance fee that day though she had protested they should go Dutch as Bobby and Susan were doing.

Now she darted over to the booth, and held a yellow jumper to her chest, then tried a green set.

'Which do you think? These are my favourite colours. Blue doesn't do anything for me, and I can't wear red.'

'No, but you could wear this colour; try it,' Lance selected.

'Pink with red hair?' Cara expressed doubtfully, inspecting herself in the small mirror.

'Not pink, it's a soft rose. It suits your complexion.'

'The gentl'man has taste.' The sales woman sidled up.

'I'll have it!'

'Let me give it to you in return for the pleasure of your company.'

'No, Lance, really, but thank you.' She looked at the price and handed over the exact amount of three one pound bank notes. 'Horribly expensive,' she said, 'but my bit of luxury for "peace in our time".'

Outside the turnstile the first raindrops fell heavily, and they quickened their steps. The heavens opened and this time it was Cara who held out her hand to Lance. They fled along the gravelled path, through a wide-open gate, down a muddy field and up into another via a gap in the hedge, effortless strides taken together, side by side, hand in hand like children or lovers, young, healthy, a man and a woman.

'This way.' Lance peered through plastered hair. 'Row D; here we are, one more sprint down the line and we're there.'

Laughing and panting they arrived at the car with its rag hanging damply in the deluge. He opened the door for her.

'Thanks, get in quick yourself.' She subsided on the front seat, face dripping, he jumping in the other side.

'No one in the back yet, I see.' He twisted round.

'They'll be here soon. Sue doesn't like getting wet.'

'Are you soaked?'

'Not too bad.' She took a comb out of her bag and began to brush through her tangled hair. 'What about you?'

'Dry inside my jacket. I'd better take it off to stop it steaming.'

'Do you have a comb?'

'Good God no! What do you take me for – a smart-aleck gigolo? Wouldn't be seen dead with one in my breast pocket,' he grinned.

'All the same I think you need one,' she said firmly, and handed it to him.

'I bow to the competent lady's orders,' he expressed whimsically.

'I'll never live that down,' she said happily. Then she thought, 'Soon he'll be gone,' and her happiness vanished.

'Tired?' he asked.

'Not really. The fizz of the ginger-ale has died out of me, that's all.' She spoke with forced jollity. How observant he was. He sensed her feelings before she was barely aware of them herself. They called it being on the same wavelength – like Bobby and Susan . . .

The rear doors were wrenched open and the couple fell in exuding a smell of damp wool.

'What have you two been doing besides getting wet?' Cara asked from her seat as Lance started up the car.

'Oh, this and that,' they said vaguely. 'What did you do?'

'Oh, this and that,' Lance and Cara said.

After a hurried cup of tea at the Langleys', suitcases were dumped in boots of the respective cars. Bobby had given his sister the name of the hotel he had booked into, two double bedrooms – girls and boys – in Crewkerne, and suggested to Lance that, since in the pouring rain with headlights on it would be difficult to keep in convoy, they should aim to meet at the hotel where they would wait for one another and have a late supper together.

'You'll beat us to it easily,' were Bobby's last throw-away words before surging down the drive. In the event he was wrong. Lance and Cara never caught them up.

To begin with Lance drove with extreme caution, and only hoped Bobby ahead was doing the same on the beast of a night. The rain lashed down, rivers forming in side ditches. The slow thumping windscreen wiper was unable to clear the torrent with each sweep. The surface of the road in the continuing downpour became slippery, and the tyres of the Lancia were thin. Indeed the only trouble Lance had had with the car were punctures, of which there had been several. He hoped the old lady would behave herself and not let him down on the last days, on this day in particular. It would be a hellishly uncomfortable business changing a wheel on the dark night with traffic flashing past spraying him with water!

During the first miles Cara was able to help by reading signposts and indicating the way which she knew from previous visits to the Langleys, though without a windscreen wiper on her side she was hard put to see much, and found it clearer to look through the side window. Once they reached the A30 and were heading east in a queue which became longer with every mile that passed, she sat tensed in the front seat, deep in her own agonizing thoughts, her arms crossed and clasped round her waist as if holding herself together lest she disintegrate.

By now Cara could not deny that she had fallen hopelessly in love, and she was tormented by the knowledge that Lance would never return her love. All the elation of the day had vanished in the thought that he was bespoken to another, that his heart was already Janet's, that his liking for her, that their 'getting on so well together' could never develop into anything further. The truth she faced was that she could hardly contain herself for her longing to touch him. Somehow during the next twenty-four hours until they reached home she must find the strength to stifle the emotions that possessed her to such an extent they took over her whole body: head, heart . . . limbs.

So *this* was the much talked of 'falling in love' she had never quite believed in. It was more overwhelming and total than she had imagined; she was wild with the wish to be in the arms of the man who was driving the car. This had happened to *her* who had never been the

74

slightest bit abandoned, who had learnt through fear of her father's temper to control her own, who had been disciplined to behave beseemingly from the earliest age. She must never allow herself to hold hands with Lance again, or let him take hers, for if she did . . . she might explode. God knows what would happen!

Bobby and Susan had fallen in love over a period of time, but not she. If she thought back to her feelings when she had first seen Lance silhouetted in the doorway of the Yacht Club, she had fallen in love then and there with the look of a man who was a complete stranger. If that was 'love' it must be pure physical attraction that had hit her. But surely it was more than that? Surely it was much much more? It was a phenomenon, this falling in love at first sight, *à coup de foudre* as the French expressed it. She had never met anyone to whom it had happened, but she had read about it in romances, and again not quite believed it. Two days ago on the beach she had heard a true story: about Colonel William Gardner's sighting 'of the most beautiful black eyes in the world', and Dilmilee's glimpse of her 'fair god', which had been enough to ensure they adored one another for the rest of their lives. And this same wonderful occurrence that had happened to her, unsought and unexpected, which deserved the same happy ending, would have to be ruthlessly and for ever cut out of her heart and thrown away on the dust heap of time.

'Relax, Cara,' Lance's deep voice impinged. He believed her to be nervous, as well she might be on such a night. 'I'm going carefully. It doesn't matter how late we are as long as I get you there safely. Damn this fug, it should be compulsory for every car in this country to have a heater.' He wiped the windscreen for the umpteenth time with the cloth from under the seat and handed it to her to do the same her side.

They were third in line behind a lumbering lorry that all but came to a halt on every rise, the driver two in front darting out to have a look to see if he could pass, and darting back again with every evidence of growing impatience. On what appeared to be a straight piece of road the man decided to take the risk. He changed down, pulled out, and accelerated past the lorry, by the skin of his teeth avoiding an oncoming car looming out of the murk.

'Bloody selfish fool,' growled Lance. 'Let him kill himself if he wants to, but what about the innocent others? Should be booked for dangerous driving.'

Sobered by the sight of the narrow miss, the car immediately in front of them made no attempt to pass, and with a grinding of low gears the cortège-like queue, that stretched out of sight behind, rumbled on.

Near Honiton the storm burst overhead with deafening rolls of thunder. Brilliant flashes of lightning lit up the road like high-powered electric bulbs switched on and off. There was a particularly blinding flash ahead. Cara started to count to herself, each count said to represent a mile, but she had not got 'two' out when there was an almighty crash with the sound of splitting and cleaving, followed by cracks, snaps and breaking fractures.

'God that was close . . . ' Lance jammed on the four-wheel brakes at the same moment that he saw the lorry one ahead shudder to a slithering stop. In the abruptness of the braking Cara had just enough time to raise her clasped arms against the dashboard as she was forced out of her seat, her arms cushioning her head against the windscreen.

'Sorry about that,' Lance said putting on the hand-brake. 'You all right?'

'I think so,' she said breathlessly, feeling her wrist. Seconds later she watched the car in front of them react tardily to the lorry's braking with a violent screech of tortured tyres that caused the car to lurch across the road and end up with one wheel in the far ditch, the body of the car across half the road. 'Bloody fool,' Lance expressed for the second time in a few minutes. 'Hang on, I'm going to stop any oncoming traffic.' He leapt out and vanished, sprinting up the road. Cara got out and went over to the slewed car. She found the passengers tumbling out shaken and bruised but no one badly hurt. From behind her there was a banging of doors, and in no time a small crowd had gathered to enquire what was happening.

'I don't know,' said Cara, 'there was a blinding flash ahead and the lorry braked suddenly, the car behind going into a skid. As, thank God, no one seems to be hurt, I'm going to get out of this downpour.' This she proceeded to do, and there in the car she stayed for some considerable time before Lance returned.

'What happened?'

'A tree across the road. Enormous one. Good old English oak struck by lightning!' He heaved himself into the driving seat.

'You really *are* wet this time. Is the lorry driver hurt?'

'Suffering from shock! The ruddy great bole fell out of the blue like a ten-ton weight a couple of yards in front of him, completely blocking the road. I rang the police from a house up there.'

'What now?'

'What now. We wait for the police.'

'We'll be hours late and I'm already hungry!'

'Same here. Bobby and Susan must be miles ahead of the block.'

'Nice and dry and having a drink and tucking in I wouldn't be surprised.'

Half an hour later the police arrived to investigate. The verdict was that the road could not be cleared for a day or two. They would have to turn round; diversion notices would be set up.

There was a banging of doors and a sound of revving and reversing of cars, the Lancia joining the queue going the opposite direction to the way they wished to go. There were as yet no notices up. Cars began to peel off. Lance suggested they take the first turning right and make a detour round the back of the A30.

'Shouldn't be difficult.' Cara shone a torch over the map she found under the seat. 'At Awliscombe there's a mainish road which leads back into Honiton.'

She was feeling much better. The incident had taken her mind right off her personal predicament. It was an adventure. What a lot of chatter there would be when they met up with Bobby and Susan! She was going to enjoy the extra time alone with Lance, and think no further than the present. 'Blast.' She peered at the map as the torch flickered and went out.

'Try my lighter,' he handed it to her. 'I'm turning right.'

She flicked on the lighter but it was impossible to read the small print on the white roads with it, and there was a maze of white roads, none appearing to be mainer than the others. He handed her a box of matches. 'Want to stop and get the line of where we are?'

'No. On, on,' she said merrily. 'When we get to the main road in Awliscombe we turn right.'

But when they got to what they thought was Awliscombe (it was not marked up) there was no turn right, so they turned left, the only way they could go, and then at the first opportunity took a right turn. The road did not lead them back to Honiton. Instead it wound northwards. It became narrower and narrower, the hedges on either side higher and higher, no room for two cars to pass, which did not matter as they met no cars out on such a filthy night. The rain teemed down; the windscreen wiper did its inadequate best while exuding a smell of hot rubber, and whenever they came to a crossroad, nine times out of ten there was no signpost.

'Dunkeswell Abbey (Ruins),' Cara opened her side window to read one at last, 'what about that for the night?'

'Too damned wet and uncomfortable,' Lance growled stopping the car. Heads together they studied the map. 'We're heading for here, miles north of where we ought to be.' Lance put a bony forefinger on the word 'ruins'. He lit another match. 'We'll have to go on to Hemyock and turn east from there towards a place called Church something-or-other which should lead us south to a B road. What about that?'

'Fine,' she said, 'as long as we don't get stuck in the Blackdown Hills instead. Golly I'm hungry. Do you realize we haven't had a bite since our "mediaeval" snack?'

'My rumbling tummy realizes it, and my skin tells me I'm sopping wet and none too warm.' Lance got out a handkerchief just in time to catch a sneeze.

Two hours after they had turned off the A30 for Awliscombe they were still hopelessly lost. Cara struck another match from the dwindling box and looked at her watch. 'Nine o'clock,' she informed.

'Right,' Lance said in a business-like manner. 'No more fiddling around in the depths of the country on a night like this. The very next pub we come to we'll stop for a stoke-up and review the situation.'

Round a bend they saw fairy lights strung across a building before which dangled the inviting picture of a smiling Sun sign swinging and clattering in its frame.

CHAPTER 6

'Wait a mo'.' Lance got out of the car.

'Marvellous,' he said coming back ten minutes later, 'couldn't be nicer. They've room for us and will rustle up a meal while we're changing into dry clothes. I've rung the Red Lion at Crewkerne and spoken to Bobby; very relieved to hear we are OK. They had a pretty awful drive themselves, but are as snug as anything now. He'll ring you in the morning.' Lance pulled out the suitcases and they went into the dark entrance of the small pub situated on a crossroads in the midst of nowhere.

'Tarrable night.' The landlord watched them sign in the book and then led them up a linoleumed staircase. ''earrd on the local news 'ow there's a tree down nerr Haniton.'

'We got lost in the detour. We've been going round in circles,' Cara laughed in her relief at being out of the howling night and in the shelter of a friendly pub. She followed to a bedroom, Lance disappearing next door.

'Lounge over thar with faer. Be mar private-like than baar.'

'Thank you, that's most thoughtful,' Cara heard Lance say.

She was not as wet through as he, but she was cold, and stripping to her petticoat she was glad to find piping hot water come from the tap. She put on a beige skirt, her new twin-set, and, as if to protect herself on the first occasion of being alone with a man and unchaperoned overnight, she clasped the single string of pearls her mother had passed on to her round her neck. She wasn't sure what was going to happen. She felt excited and rather daring and not a little apprehensive. If anything 'happened' she'd probably be landed with an illegitimate baby. That would kill her parents, the disgrace ruin her life. But it *wouldn't* happen because Lance was engaged to Janet, and anyway he was a decent sort of person who wouldn't pounce at the first opportunity, and if she thought he *might* try something funny there was always that key she could turn on the inside of her door . . .

Going out of her room Cara found the layout of the passage with bathroom, and then crossed over to the lounge to hang her damp coat and skirt over a chair. Lance came in and drew up another chair over which he laid his jacket before the crackling fire which had as yet not much heat in it.

'You look very formal for a pub,' she observed eyeing his dark-blue double-breasted suit.

'Only other garment I've got with me; if I may say so, since we're making personal remarks, *you* look very nice in that skirt and the twin-set. As I thought, the rose suits you.'

'Come on, I'm famished,' she said gaily, feeling like a film star, which was one of the extraordinary effects Lance had on her. They descended the stairs and went into the bar where they were greeted with stares and nods by the few locals, who then returned to their farming talk of bad harvest, the dreadful weather, and took no more notice of them.

'Yarr table's hearr,' the landlord said and showed them over to where two plates of ham were laid out with a wilting salad leaf and a tomato on each. The polished oak table was crowded with condiments, tomato ketchup, chutney, English mustard and salad dressing. There were also hunks of home-made bread, a large slab of butter, a generous whack of cheddar and a bowl of apples.

'Super. Exactly what's needed,' Lance praised.

'Anything yarr'd like to drink?'

'Cara?'

'What about draught cider in Somerset?'

'I'll stick to whisky, with water please.'

'My father drinks whisky, his *chota* peg he calls it. It looks

81

rather bigger than *chota* to me. Why does everyone drink whisky in India?' Cara picked up knife and fork. They tucked in.

'Thirst quencher and pick-me-up after a gruelling day. A lot of them drink far more than is good for them out there, and they can't kick the habit when they retire. I limit myself to two of an evening. Those I regard as a necessary tonic.'

'Never more?'

'Hardly ever more,' he smiled at her.

'You're very disciplined.'

'Islamic tradition — I shouldn't be drinking at all.'

'Aren't you Church of England?'

'Church of Scotland. Please note the difference — but with definite Muslim tendencies.'

'And how many wives can *they* have?'

'Four at a time. Easy to divorce for more!'

'But *you* will only have one wife?'

'Only . . . one . . . wife,' he said slowly, and then added as if an afterthought, 'heart's meeting — my love.'

'Ah, Dilmilee,' she said feeling violently envious of Janet, his 'my love', his 'meeting of hearts'. The feeling left her as quickly as it had come. He was Janet's and that was that. In the meantime he was *hers*, and she was enjoying herself. The ham was delicious, and so was the bread. They chatted on easily about this and that and where on earth had they gone wrong in missing the road back to Honiton? The time flew.

'Yarr coffee and brandy's upstairs,' the landlord hovered wanting to clear the table. 'Got all yarr wants?'

'Indeed,' Cara smiled at him, 'it's good of you to have rustled up this late meal.'

'What pub's for. Help out lost travellers.' He had his little joke. 'Breakfast from seven-thirty. 'Night.'

'Good night.'

Upstairs Cara re-arranged the clothes on a chair and positioned it to one side, Lance drawing up two ancient armchairs to the fire now glowing with coals. 'I wonder what he thinks of us,' she said taking off her cardigan in the warmth of the room.

82

'Runaway pair on an illicit week-end, I shouldn't wonder, with a cock-an'-bull story about getting lost in a rainstorm.'

'Certainly not with *two* bedrooms,' Cara said primly and wished she hadn't. She felt the blush rising at the word 'bedroom' and turned her head away hoping he would not see. 'But it *is* nice, isn't it? I mean to end up in a sweet place like this while the rain is lashing down outside, the wind still howling.'

'Perfect,' he said and lit a cigarette. '*Especially* when the wind blows a great puff of soot into our faces,' he chuckled as the chimney belched black. 'Seriously, I shall look upon this rainy day and night as the highlight of my leave when I am sweltering it out in India.'

'Not the shooting in Scotland?'

'Not the shooting in Scotland.'

'Tell me about Calcutta' she asked to still the leap in her heart.

She wanted to find out all she could about his life in the short time she had left with him. She drank her coffee and he sipped his brandy, and Lance told her about Calcutta and the life a bachelor led there and how with all the hard work and hard play, the social functions with the cocktail parties, dinners and dances and the Government House balls, it was still a lonely life for a single man. He told her about the jute trade in which he was going to make his fortune so that he could restore the land that should never have been divided and sold. Jute, he told her, produced fibre, a raw material that was second only to cotton in world consumption, was low costing, and made strong bulky fabrics used for packing bags, twines, wrappings, insulating cables – it had a hundred usages. His small piece of land in the moist climate of the fertile Ganges basin of well-drained soil was perfect for the growing of it. Most jute when harvested was cropped, stripped, retted (soaked in water), hung up to dry, graded and sent to the jute mills of Calcutta or overseas to Dundee to be woven into fabric. During the recent course in Dundee they had been investigating new experiments on the *white* and *daisee* jute, with new methods of manufacture. He on his *zemindari* plantation planned to conduct the total process on the spot, from sowing of seed to the spinning and weaving. He wanted to build a factory, or factories, employ hundreds of persons.

'Am I boring you?' Lance stopped his enthusiasm for his subject to ask.

'I find it fascinating.' Cara wanted him to go on so that she could sit there, close to him, listening to his voice. 'How does your week-end soldiering fit into all this?'

'Ah, dear old Jute-wallahs! Good fun. We're all dead keen. I was telling your father they were raised as volunteers in the last century; divided up subsequently into five offshoots for port and coastal defence duties to be called up in emergencies. Each unit (Battery to us) is like a club. Frightfully sticky to get into. In our case we all have to be something to do with the jute trade, and no one can join unless unanimously balloted by the committee. One black ball and that's it!'

'Black ball . . . ?' Cara faltered.

'Yes, literally. Each vote is taken in the form of a small ivory ball placed hidden in fist into the side of a mahogany box. There are two piles of them to collect from; the blacks used to reject a candidate. Antiquated way of balloting which works excellently.'

'Don't have anything like that in our Yacht Club. Why are candidates rejected?'

'For all sorts of reasons, many of them snobbish or racial. We used to be one hundred per cent European, but some Anglo-Indians, including me,' Lance raised a dark eyebrow, 'have been allowed in recently, as have Parsees in the Bombay Battery, also Christian Koreans and some Armenians engaged in the jute trade. To a great extent we provide for ourselves, private cars for transport, trucks, camping equipment, that sort of thing.' Lance threw his cigarette stub into the fire.

'Who pays for it?'

'Comes out of jute funds,' he grinned. 'Officialdom

provides us with guns and ammunition, usually all the left-over stuff no one else will use. We are extremely proud that the Viceroy is our Honorary Colonel.'

'My, I should think so. "Anglo-Indian" doesn't seem to fit you, Lance. You're, well, so British.'

'Most of us *are* more British than the British.'

'You've never told me about the second love story. Your grandmother, wasn't it?'

'Yes. Mulka. You really want to know? Well, my great-grandfather William and his Begum Nissa were frequent visitors to Lucknow in Oudh, which, when the pomp and circumstance of Imperial Delhi declined, took on much of the glories of the old capital. There was patronage, court-liness, exquisite manners (it was said anyone from Luck-now had the best manners in the whole of Hind) and a good bit of effetism too. Nissa went there for medical treatment. She was in ill health. Their sickly elder son had died as well as a daughter and a loved grandchild, and she was grief-stricken. She and William became great friends with, and stood high in the esteem of, the King and Queen of Oudh. The Queen's sister was reputed to be, I quote, "the most celebrated native beauty in India". At any rate both she and the Queen were famed for their beauty. They were descended from the House of Timur and were nieces of the Emperor Akbar Shah and therefore related to Nissa. You may not know, Cara, that in India adopted children are as closely integrated in the family as blood children. Well, Mulka had been married to her cousin, the Emperor of Delhi's second son, but, desperately unhappy, she had fled to her sister at the court of Oudh, and a divorce was about to take place. Unfortunately, the King, who neg-lected his beautiful Queen and had become bored with his concubines, found himself enamoured of his wife's sister, and attempted to force her to enter his hareem. Mulka fled again, this time to her relative Nissa then staying in Oudh for her health. After a great deal of brouhaha – the liaison would have been classed as incest and was against Muslim law, so that it was in the interest of the King that his

85

sister-in-law should be removed from his reach — William Gardner and his Begum took Mulka back to their home in Kootgunge. There in the inner household she came face to face with James, their second son, now a widower and in his prime, said to be affectionate, honourable and upright. He was a lieutenant in Gardner's Horse, and the apple of his father's eye. Moreover he was tall and strikingly handsome! Guess what happened between these two paragons of beauty?'

'Obviously they fell in love — '

' — and ran away together.'

'Why should they have to run away if he was a widower and she divorced?'

'Because Mulka was under the protection of James's father. She had been saved from the King of Oudh's advances only to be seduced by her protector's son! It cast a slur on William's honour. He was furious, leapt onto his horse and gave chase the moment he was informed of the flight, Nissa with her tender heart and memories of their own love affair begging him not to be too hard on the couple. In the event he failed to catch up with them. James and Mulka were married, and for some time lived in the wilds of the jungle in what must have been considerable hardship to one used to palaces. However, his father eventually relented and allowed them a house on his land, and on William's death James came into the estate. James and Mulka never regretted their elopement. To them theirs was a miraculous love story. They lived in the same tremendous style as William and Nissa had, with a guard of forty men, "a merry pack" (according to old family letters) of fourteen slave girls, innumerable servants and a great many "hangers on" of complex relationships. Both princesses brought with them into their marital home their prestige, their throne of state, their jewels and their regal fan of peacock feathers to denote their royal position. Unfortunately, Mulka, perhaps because of her time of penury with James, indulged in untimely extravagances, and after James's death, when he was no longer there to restrain her, her lavish spending knew no bounds. Hence the consequent breaking up of the *zemindari* with the mortgaging and eventual selling off of the properties, and the decline into poverty of the descendants, including my father. End of second love story.'

'But your father kept a small part, and you will restore it,' Cara said starry-eyed. 'I really believe you will!'

She had, all the while he was speaking, been very conscious of him next to her in his chair in which he lounged in his relaxed way, his long legs stretched before him, feet touching the fire surround. Her arm rested along the edge of her chair, skin bare below elbow in the short-sleeved rose jersey.

'Thank you for believing in me.' Lance's voice sounded moved. 'No one else has ever said that.' He lifted a hand, and brushed a forefinger lightly upon her forearm from wrist to elbow. 'There is no doubt about it, rose suits you,' he said softly, and repeated the light caress.

Cara did not know what effect the touch had on him or why he did so except perhaps to show his appreciation for the interest she had taken in the story. All she knew was that she could bear his touch no longer. She longed to throw herself into his arms with the same intensity she had longed to embrace him in the car. Suddenly, as once again his finger touched her, she jumped to her feet with an electric shudder and stood in front of him looking down at him, staring, mesmerized.

'It's late,' she managed huskily, her voice croaking unnaturally, 'we ought to go to bed.'

'Yes,' he said standing up within inches of her before the fire, a stranger who looked at her in so odd a way she hardly recognized him, and was all of a sudden frightened. That mouth! She knew nothing about him other than what *he* had told her. He could have made it all up, or nearly all from reading Indian history, claiming relationship because he had the same name.

His eyes looking into hers were unsmiling in their intensity, the pupils black and large, his mouth hard and suppressed, his body tensed. The closeness was too much and she did what she had tried not to do all day: she launched herself into his arms blushing violently, face averted. He held her for a moment, then bent to lift her chin with a hand, and kissed her on the lips very gently. His embrace was so lovely she thought she should die, the feel of his arms about her worth dying for.

'Good night, darling,' he said holding her away from him.

'Good night,' she whispered, terribly ashamed of herself, and fled.

She did not lock the door on the inside. She would never lock the door against *him*! She undressed, put on her crêpe de Chine nightgown, and got into bed and lay there under the bedclothes – trembling. Would he come in? Did she *want* him to come in? Her emotions were so mixed that she had no idea what she wanted at that moment. She did not even know very much about what would happen if he *did* come in, only that it would be wrong, a betrayal of her upbringing, her parents horrified. She wondered if Bobby and Susan had done it, or were doing it that very night alone in the Red Lion . . . no, she did not know what she wanted at that particular moment, only that she loved him and would do anything in the world he asked of her.

A long time later she heard him scrape back his chair from the fire in the lounge and replace the fender. She heard him shut the door quietly and come across to outside her room. He stopped. Holding her breath she lay rigid and frozen barely daring to breathe. Was the door handle turning? Should she turn over and pretend to be asleep? What *should* she do . . . ?

It seemed he stood there an age before his steps moved on into his room, the door shut behind him. She did not relax. He could still come in . . . when he had undressed.

But he did not come in, and at last Cara slept.

CHAPTER 7

''Morning,' Lance said at the breakfast table. He put down his newspaper and got to his feet, the crease in his cheek apparent. 'Sleep well?'

Cara noticed his jacket was more crumpled than ever after its wetting, though his trousers looked ironed, and she remembered that he said he always put them under the mattress.

'Yes, thank you.' It was true, *once* she'd got to sleep. He had such beautiful manners, like those people of old in Lucknow. It was one of the things she loved about him. Not manners to impress, but manners that showed he cared for other people. He was as courteous to the servants as to Uncle Tom as to her mother.

'I suggest you have tea,' he advised *sotto voce*, eye on the approaching serving girl, 'the coffee's stale; warmed up.'

'Tea and toast only,' Cara ordered brightly.

'I had the full complement — excellent, except for the coffee.'

'I didn't lock the door,' she said apropos of nothing, and bit her lip the moment she'd said it.

'I know,' he grinned across the table at her.

'You . . . How?' She was taken aback.

'Happened to peep in this morning and saw you all rosy in bed with your hair spread on the pillow like Guinevere or whatever the woman's name was.'

'Oh. The Lady of Shalott. What a sunny day.' Cara, embarrassed, looked out of the small-paned window.

The telephone in the passage shrilled.

'For Miss Thornton,' the landlord shouted.

'Bobby? Thank goodness. For a ghastly moment I thought it was Father!'

'You OK, old thing?'

'Absolutely, and you?'

'Absolutely,' he laughed. 'Now look here, old girl, Sue and I are going to crack on to base. There's no point in our hanging around for you two.'

'Agreed.'

'Promise you'll beetle for home? I told Pa you'd be back for tea, or at the latest before dark and that I'd see you off on the way. I know that you are not exactly brilliant at telling white lies, but you've got to imply that we were all together at the Red Lion last night or you're going to get *me* into the most appalling hot water, my birthright cut off, I shouldn't wonder.'

'Got it, Bobby. I'll be home before dark like a good little girl and tell a load of fibs into the bargain if necessary. My love to Sue, and oh, Bobby, I suppose I shan't see you again?'

''Fraid not since you didn't turn up last night,' he teased. 'I'll ring the parents before I take off. So long, old girl, keep cracking!'

'So long, Bobby. Take care . . .'

'That was Bobby,' Cara said unnecessarily on her return to the table.

'So the whole room gathered.' Lance put down for the second time the newspaper he was reading.

'They're not waiting for us. I promised I'd be back by dark. It – it was horrid saying goodbye.'

'But not so horrid as if there hadn't been "peace in our time",' he crinkled at her.

'So what now . . . ?' she asked vaguely, not knowing whether she was coming or going, whether he called every woman he met 'darling', and kissed them goodnight wonderfully on the lips. She only knew that she was headily in love and that she would grasp at anything to go on being with him a little longer.

'What happens now is we pay the bill.' He rose.

They did so separately – 12s 6d each, which included supper and a packed lunch. He wiped the Lancia's windscreen, took the hood down, stuffed in the luggage, and the car burpled off on the clear sunny day, their hair blowing, blue sky washed of clouds above. With no trouble at all they found their way onto the B road which led across the A303 to the A30 west of Chard. At Crewkerne they passed the Red Lion, which hotel Lance declared not to be half so cosy-looking as their Sun Inn and probably a darned sight more expensive. They turned south off the A30 for Dorchester.

Following a stop Cara took over the driving while Lance studied the map. He appeared preoccupied by it and after one attempt at conversation, she relapsed into silence. Is it going to end like this, she thought, desultory conversation until with patent relief he drops me at home? Has he so soon tired of me? Did the closeness of their time together in the rain, the things said, the kiss, mean nothing? Was all love like this: up in the heights one moment, down in the depths the next, tossed up and down on a see-saw as in the latest musical hit *Jill Darling*: 'You throw me up and you throw me down, I don't know whether you even care . . . '?

Cara's grip on the steering wheel tightened in fury until her knuckles showed white. She would *not* be tossed any more, *not* used any more, idiot that she was to let herself one moment be charmed and kissed, the next moment ignored . . . trodden on . . . while he sat like a Pasha, or rather like a Moghul Prince, in the front seat, *damn* him!

'Cerne Abbas looks a nice place to stop for lunch, next turn off left,' he interrupted her furious thoughts.

She slowed down, and because the orange flicker was reluctant to rise fully, she made the hand signal out on her side.

'Where now in your ropy old car?' she said crossly.

'Where now is we find a quiet spot in which to have lunch and talk it out.'

'Oh? How well organized! Turn right, turn left, stop for lunch, talk it out. Talk *what* out? There's nothing *to* talk out. I'm fed up with being used.' The temper which hadn't exploded for a long time rose as it had in the old days before her father had battened her emotions down.

'On the contrary, far from being organized you've made me wildly disorganized. Hey, STOP! Park by that open gate, *if you please*.'

She jammed on the brakes, and reversed a yard or two to come to rest by the stubble field from where there was a signpost showing a footpath leading to the ruins of Cerne Abbey with its graceful fifteenth-century gatehouse. 'As for using you,' he went on, ignoring the fact that he'd been nearly jolted out of his seat, 'you ought to know better at your age than not to lock your door at night when alone in an hotel with an unknown man. Damned stupid thing to do. It would have served you jolly well right if I had come in and terrified the wits out of you.'

'How do you know I would have been terrified?' she said, turning to face him indignantly from the driver's seat. 'I'd have been too preoccupied fighting you tooth and nail for Janet's sake.'

'What the hell's Janet got to do with it?' he enquired icily.

'You're engaged to her, aren't you?'

'Who told you that?'

'No one *told* me. It was obvious at the Yacht Club. She was so, so, possessive and — and Bobby said she called you "darling".'

'Janet calls everyone "darling". It's the theatrical in-thing.'

'There are other people who call everyone "darling",' Cara said with a toss of her Titian head. 'Anyway, I thought she was a photographic model, not on the stage.'

'She *is* a photographic model, and they couldn't be more theatrical.'

'You haven't answered my question,' Cara glowered at him.

'About the "darling"? Last night we were in an exceptional situation.'

'You know perfectly well that wasn't my question.' Her green eyes blazed.

'If you'd let a mere male when confronted by a tigress get an answer out, no, Janet and I are not engaged. Now that we've got *that* out of the window let's get out of the ropy old car and have lunch — and continue the enlightening discussion.'

'I still can't see that there's anything to talk about,' she said with bad grace, determined not be bamboozled again.

He placed a rug on the stubble and promptly sat down without waiting for her. He looked over the field at the abbey. She joined him with the sandwiches and a bottle of beer, and knelt as far away from him as she could at the edge of the rug. She could not stop the warmth coming over her from the knowledge that he was not *yet* engaged to Janet, but she did not trust him one inch after he had so rudely castigated her for not locking herself in. What cheek! So he had *nearly* come in? Wanted, been tempted to? She handed him the open packet of sandwiches. He took one without looking at her, eyes screwed up against the sun, fine crow's-feet lining the corners.

'Of course, by now I might *conceivably* have been engaged to her if you'd not come barging in,' Lance mused aloud. 'Do you mind?'

'You are always asking me if I *mind*. Mind what? Mind that you're not engaged to Janet? I can assure you that I do not in the least mind one way or the other.'

'To spell it out; mind that I love you?'

'That?' she breathed, her temper deflated at three precious words — 'he loves me, he loves me, he loves me'. They echoed in her brain in the way 'peace in our time' had yesterday. 'No — I — do not quite . . . mind,' she ended on a whisper.

'Well, you bloody well *should*.' His face creased into the smile that made her heart turn over. 'You should mind very much indeed. I have nothing to offer you. I am stony broke at the end of my leave, and I cannot possibly marry until I have recouped my finances in Calcutta, which at the very least will take a year. Even then I can only provide my bride with the basics.'

'But you could have married wealthy Janet?'

'Naturally. She would have provided herself with more than the basics!'

'Your job sounds a pretty meagre one if at your age — well, how old are you?'

'Twenty-six, inquisitor.'

'If at the age of twenty-six you haven't saved a bean even though your firm pays your fare and your expenses . . . ' She refused to let herself melt though she did not care two hoots whether he was rich or poor.

'Why I have not been able to save is because I have been helping with my brother's education . . .' Lance said frigidly.

Cara was instantly repentant. 'I'm sorry, Lance . . . I — I didn't know . . . that was beastly of me. I haven't any money of my own,' she added in a small voice.

'I loathe talking money. I don't want your money. I want your love.' He took a swig of beer.

'You'll get fat if you drink so much beer.' She bit into a ham sandwich.

'Not in Calcutta, I won't. Too much sweat pours off one.'

'Has Janet been to India?'

'Do we *have* to talk "Janet"?'

'Yes we do — to clear the air. She wants to marry you, doesn't she?'

'So she has said, or rather her father has said.'

'What did he say?'

'That his daughter had set her heart on me and hadn't looked at another man since my last leave. He said he'd make a settlement, and not to worry about finance.'

'Sounds like bribery.' Cara edged up on the rug.

'More like a damned attractive proposition! My head

was all for it; only snag — heart. I talked it over with my mother and decided to go fishing on my own to try and sort myself out. That's when you came barging in, you wretch! You see, sweet fiery Cara,' he took her hand and played with her fingers, 'it was like this. I was a protégé of Mr Tinling; to me he was a father-figure. I first met him when I was one of the new apprentices in Dundee. He takes great interest in the young and creating jobs for them, has his own apprentice workshops in the jute industry and in his tea plantations in Assam. He's a great guy with a lot of philanthropic outlets. It was he who originally got me the job in Calcutta, and he's continued to take a personal interest in my career.'

'Poor Janet,' said Cara against his shoulder, 'she fell in love with a tall boy and could not forget him . . . '

'I could not marry Janet now if she were the last woman on earth, at least not so long as you are on it! As I said at the beginning of this conversation I have nothing to offer you but myself and an old ruin on some land that's gone to pot, but I'll work myself to the bone for you, love you, cherish you all my life if you'll wait for me . . . '

'Fair enough, though I wouldn't like you worked to the bone . . . '

'I'm not asking you if you *mind* this time; I'm asking: do you love me, Cara?'

'I said I didn't mind . . . I don't mind about anything but you and me . . . us together. I *do* love you, Lance. Oh how I love you.'

He took her in his arms on the rug and kissed her in the bright sunshine with long kisses that were not so gentle as the one on the evening before, and she returned his kisses, and learnt and felt. They gathered the remnants of the lunch and stood up, between them shaking the rug free of crumbs and folding it corner to corner, and embraced again, her head coming up to his shoulder. They got into the back seat of the car and kissed each other again and again, fresh tender kisses of a new-found love on a girl's glowing face and a man's dark mien, passion not there, or if it was on the man's part, fully restrained in so delicate and young and beautiful a thing between them.

And Lance and Cara, on that September day after the storm when the dust on the side road was laid by damp, never did get down the field to see Cerne Abbey no distance away, not even as far as the graceful fifteenth-century gatehouse, and in spite of the headiness of their embraces, their joy in finding each other, their love expressed in words over and over again, their making plans for the future, Lance saw that Cara arrived at Wick House before dark.

He dropped her outside the gate of Mr Field's lodge, and, carrying her suitcase down the drive, she walked up the exotic-scented dripping conservatory newly watered by the garden boy. She opened the front door at the same moment pips announced the news was about to begin. There they were – her parents – one on either side of the fireplace, her mother stitching at her tapestry, her father leaning forwards in his chair to listen intently to the disembodied voice.

Overweight Bugler struggled up to greet her in the doorway, lips drawn back in a smile, fat tail scything. Doreen put a finger to her mouth, while Charles grunted his acknowledgement that she had returned. They had not changed. Nothing had changed at home. She knew exactly what they had done every hour of the day she had been away. She knew exactly what they would do and say tomorrow and the next day and on and on. But *she* had changed! Utterly and completely. Something had happened to her that was so huge, that had so transformed her life, that surely her parents could not fail to observe the difference? Surely they would see the shining look, notice the heightened colour from the rasp of a blue-black chin, and perceive the lips rosy red from kisses?

Cara sat down in her accustomed chair hemmed in between her parents, and when the news was switched off and they questioned her on the trip, and she told them about the Langleys and the exhibition and, yes, there had been a bad storm that evening on the way to Crewkerne, she realized they did not see any change in her, and she knew that for the time being she must hide all her innermost feelings from them.

She knew she must play it cool and slowly, nothing said, for there was nothing concrete to say when she and Lance could not be married for at least a year, and neither parent would countenance an engagement to someone she had known for such a short time. She knew she was in for a tremendous battle with her father, the battle of her life, which she must play cleverly if not with cunning so that he was unaware it *was* out and out warfare. This she must do if she was to get her way without having to elope as James Gardner and Mulka had, if she was to avoid a complete rift with her family. She knew that in the few days left to her and Lance in Christchurch they would have to act with extreme caution, utmost tact, and watchful discretion lest the thunder boom and the light-ning strike, and their happiness tumble about their ears in a crash as great as the felling of the ancient English oak across the A30.

She knew all this, but she did not for one moment foresee, in the strength of her new-found love, that it was she herself who would be her own adversary, that *she* could be the one to break the link and betray the trust.

CHAPTER 8

The days passed as if in a dream. With every morning's awakening Cara found herself deliriously happy. It was no dream, it was the truth, reality of the most exquisite kind, first love in all its delicacy of purity and unconsummation, its all engrossment of one another, its getting-to-know, its closeness, its laughter, its surprises, its hopes and plans for the future, its pledges of faithfulness and undying love.

On the first day after their return, Lance and Cara went sailing. Together they pushed out the boat from its muddy moorings, hands touching, glances meeting. Christchurch, which Cara knew so well, she now saw with new eyes, Lance's eyes, the beauty of the day and the landscape reborn, reflected in that extra glow. The dinghy flitted up and down the channels of the harbour like a newly hatched butterfly warming its wings in the sun. When they berthed up-river and went to buy themselves cream doughnuts, because all of a sudden they found themselves ravenously hungry in the fresh air, the baker gave them extra smiles, so transparently in love was the red-headed local girl with the tall sunburnt man. Wherever they went they were consciously proud of being noticed, happy for others to see their happiness.

'I love you, my Dilmilee,' Lance said kissing Cara in the nest of the rushes where the dinghy lay hidden.

'I love you, Lance, oh, how I love you,' she said lying in the crook of his arm in the boat.

'When I have made the place habitable we will have our holidays in Kootgunge.'

'Would you want to retire in India?'

98

'Not if you don't want to,' he said kissing the top of her head.

'The Ganges basin would be hot?'

'Yes, that is why the Gardner mansion must be designed in the old style with cool inner courtyard and garden-playing fountains in which you can dabble your pretty hands, and swing on a golden swing. Plenty of rain in monsoon time. They say there is nothing more erotic than swinging in the rain soaked through!'

'I don't know much about eroticism.'

'It will give me great pleasure to teach you.' He smiled his lazy smile and tickled her neck so that she felt erotic already.

'Also I shall be too busy looking after you and our hordes of children to have time to swing on a golden swing. How many children shall we have, Lance?'

'Four? Two boys and two girls? No, no, no. *None*. I could not bear you to go through that pain, that danger.'

'I would gladly go through any pain to bear your child . . .'

'My darling; my darling . . .'

They went back to Wick House and played tennis and succeeded very well in ignoring each other at tea with the parents, so that it was even sweeter to be alone together that evening when they went to see *Anna Karenina* at the Boscombe Plaza.

'What a depressing film,' Lance stated on coming out of the cinema.

'Well, she did have a possessive and oppressive husband to spoil everything.'

'I intend to be possessive but not oppressive,' Lance declared. 'By the way you are more beautiful to me than all the Greta Garbos put together.'

'And you more handsome than all the Rudolphos,' she said tucking her hand into his arm as she had once seen Janet do.

'Can I ask Lance to lunch tomorrow, his last day here?' Cara addressed her mother at the breakfast table.

'I suppose so, dearie,' Doreen said vaguely.

'Been with the man non-stop for days; aren't you running him a bit hard?' Charles had his say.

Cara kept cool. 'I'm not really running him, Father. He's very good company.'

'I daresay. Most travelled men of the world are. I'm warning you, Carissa.'

'Warning me of what, Father?'

'Warning you not to get involved.'

An hour later she met the man she was not to get involved with at the base of Hengistbury Head and they walked the circular road with its view of the ancient Priory over the picturesque harbour, Uncle Tom's shack in Mudeford seen across the way. They scrambled up the sandy track to the Head and stood in the wind at the top admiring the scene of the river rushing past the spit and out to sea. Rocky Highcliffe lay beyond, the Isle of Wight on the skyline with the Needles standing out clearly, a steamer ploughing over to Bournemouth, another, with black smoke belching, coming from Studland Bay. In the foreground a resting fishing boat rose and dipped on the swell. The wind whipped, and Cara shivered.

'Cold?'

'A bit.'

He pulled her down into the bracken where they lay entwined, hidden from the outside world, warm in each other's arms, lost in each other's embraces and the marvel of one another, until once again time and convention called them back.

'Plans,' said Lance sitting up and pulling pieces of bracken out of Cara's hair. 'If you could come out in the spring we'd manage to scrape along financially somehow, but you'd have to go to the hills in the hot weather and that would mean separation almost straight away. I propose you come out in exactly a year's time, October 1939. How's that sound?'

'Twelve months, fifty-two weeks, three hundred and sixty-five days; it sounds unendurably long.'

'We'll write to each other every week – several times a

week. The time will fly with you getting together your trousseau and all the rest. Think of the joy when I meet you off the ship! You can stay with my friends the MacCreaths. You'll love Johnny and Joan. If you like it he'll give you away. We can be married in the old cathedral and we'll honeymoon in Assam.'

'If only Father . . . '

'If only Father what, darling?'

'If only he doesn't put difficulties in the way.'

'Even if he does that can't stop you. You'll be twenty-one by then and can do what you like.'

'You don't know Father.' She looked doubtful.

'I think you should let me speak to him, Cara. I dislike this undercover stuff.'

'Oh no,' she panicked. 'No, it's best to say nothing at this stage. Nearer the time you can write to him.'

'He'll want to know why I did not come out with it before. I am a straightforward sort of bloke and I'd prefer to have it out now, man to man, if we've got to have it out.'

'He'll say we don't know each other. That how can we possibly tell after so short a time? He'll have all the stock answers pat. He might even be rude, or have a blistering row! Don't spoil that he likes you, likes talking Indian Army with you.'

'It takes two to make a quarrel. I can soothe him by explaining my honourable intentions. When he brings out the pat answers I will entirely agree with him: of *course* we don't know each other all that well; of course we will wait, and so on. My speaking to him can't do any harm.'

'We–ll,' Cara agreed reluctantly, 'but promise me you won't say anything about when we plan to marry. I know that would cause a blast. Please, Lance.'

'All right. I'll speak to him tomorrow.'

They played golf in the afternoon, she warning him that she was a beginner.

'A very promising and beguiling beginner,' Lance said

101

on the Highcliffe Golf Course, appraising her slim figure addressing the ball in stylish stance. 'I expect you'll distract my eye in those pants.'

'They're not pants. They're a divided skirt; the latest thing for golf. Style of swing due to the pro. He's a first-rate teacher. You ought to be playing with him not me.' She watched his ball soaring away twice the length of her drive.

'I'll take over as instructor in Calcutta.' His eyes caressed her. 'You've made me so happy. You don't know, darling, how happy you've made me.'

'I do, I do. You too . . .'

They went on to make Tom 'ship-shape', Lance carrying a whisky bottle, Cara a basket of eggs, vegetables, cheese and fruit for their supper. They ran up the outside steps two at a time.

'Well, me dears, what have yer been doin' since I last saw yer?' Tom's beady blue eyes twinkled.

'Tell him, Lance.' Cara busied herself with putting the kettle on, scraping some sprouting potatoes she found under the sink, and cutting up the cabbage. She took the boiling kettle off, lit the other two gas rings with a match, and put on the vegetables. She collected a pile of washing from a corner and began to scrub it in the sink, the suds rising. With a little secret smile she watched the men. It was all so familiar, so happy, so wonderful! Could it really be under two weeks ago that she had first met him, two days later that she had first got to know him here in this deck-room? She felt as if she had known him all her life.

'I've brought tobacco, Gold Block. Hope you like it.' Lance pushed a tin over to Tom.

'Swank's shag. Thank'ee all the same,' Tom mumbled. He shoved his cap from its usual angle onto the back of his head and began to stuff his pipe from the tin. 'Help yerself to whisky,' he invited as if the bottle were his own. He poured beer for himself into a murky mug.

'Damn you, sir, for telling me the batman's name was Fred. How was I to know the extent of your wicked humour. Ruined my chances with the Brigadier-General!'

'Ha, ha, ha, so it got a rise out of the old bastard did it? So much the better, stuck-up old bugger.'

'How're the lobster pots?' Lance asked and the men were soon deep in fishing talk.

Cara, half-listening, felt weak with loving them. Two darling men; they got on so well. If only her father . . . She brushed her damp nose with an arm, rinsed away, wrung and hung out the washing on the string, put down several basins for the drips, tested the vegetables, and beat up the eggs with a fork for an omelette.

'Clear the decks!' she shouted ten minutes later, placing large chunks of omelette on three cracked plates, potatoes and cabbage waiting well-drained in their black-coated saucepans. Tom did as he was bid by sweeping with the stroke of an arm everything off half the table onto the floor.

'Uncle Tom, *really*!' Cara glared at him, plates in hand, while Lance dissolved into laughter. 'Now we've got to get down on our hands and knees and pick everything up.'

'Not till we've eaten, me hearty,' Tom leered at her unrepentantly, and began to dance the horn-pipe in his boots, feet remarkably dainty. His cap looked as if at any moment it was about to fall off though it never did. Cara used to say it was stuck on with dirt.

'Sit down and behave,' she said severely. 'I don't want the food to get cold.' Obediently Tom piled up his cushions on a box. Lance drew up the one chair, and Cara sat demurely on her stool at the head of the table dispensing vegetables from the saucepans.

'Ho, ho, ho, m'darling,' Lance chuckled, 'Mrs Gardner-to-be keeping everyone in order with a frying pan!'

'Have you told him?'

'Yer don't have to tell 'bout you and me niece. An ol' blade like me saw it comin' a mile away. So yer found out for yerself she was more than competent, did yer?'

'I did. I say, delicious omelette.'

Tom raised his mug. 'Here's to yer both.'

'Have a wee drop o' whisky.' Lance fetched another

glass and splashed a small amount in. 'To us and to Uncle Tom,' he clinked glasses with Cara.

'Ugh.' Cara swallowed a mouthful neat. 'Horrible!'

'You'll get used to it in Calcutta. Pick-me-up, remember? And I'll require you to be perky of an evening.'

'Mooin' and cooin' at the table's not decent in front of an ol' bachelor.' Tom's eyes shone.

'I'm broaching the subject of permission to marry tomorrow. How do you think your brother'll take it?'

'Never can tell with the wiley ol' devil. If yer were livin' on the spot I'll wager he'd boot yer out of the house and tell yer to go and take a running jump in the river, and do it good and proper with a ton weight. But as yer leavin' the country, he'll likely let yer off lightly. Whatever *he* says, sonny, and I can see him sayin' crappin' things behind yer back, I wish yer both the best of bloomin' luck!'

'Oh, thank you, Uncle Tom, thank you for those lovely words,' Cara said happily, jumping up to give her uncle a smacking kiss on his cheek.

Tom was, as it turned out, the only person to congratulate them.

Luncheon next day went off more smoothly than Cara had dared to hope, Lance asking the Brigadier-General's opinion on this and that and listening attentively to the long-winded replies. In fact Lance *was* genuinely interested. As has been said before, Lance Gardner was seldom one to be wholly critical. He usually managed to find something agreeable to latch onto even in a dyed-in-the-wool, puff-puffing, paroxysmal, narrow-minded British general who despised colonials, let alone a man such as himself.

Brigadier-General Charles Dunbar Thornton had everything going for him in Lance's eyes. He was Cara's father for one thing, and Lance was more than grateful to him for her birth. As well, Lance was sympathetic. He could see he had been badly bruised in the Great War. With his decorations he was an undoubtedly brave soldier, and an able one to have risen to his rank. He was now stuffy and set in his ways, but he admired him for what he had once been, and he hoped to God he wasn't going to be difficult. His own peace of mind depended on whether the Brigadier would make Cara suffer for loving him, or whether he would give them his blessing, a benediction which he doubted very much he was capable of. From the first day he had met her, Lance saw that Mrs Thornton would have no say in the matter. What worried Lance at lunch was that in a few days' time he would no longer be within reach to support Cara in whatever was coming to her.

With these concerns in his mind, Lance broached the subject when taken for a smoke into the study, and he kept to the somewhat uncommitted approach Cara had wanted.

'I have come to love your daughter, sir, and in a year or so's time I hope to be in a position to ask for her hand,' he said formally.

'Time will show; time will show, Mr Gardner.' Charles Thornton's response, given with a choleric twitch of red moustache, was as mild as Tom had foreseen.

He did not even trouble to ask Lance the date of his departure for India, nor to enquire whether the young man believed his feelings were reciprocated, which was perhaps just as well. He appeared not to want to hear more, switched off the subject the moment it had been opened, shook hands in the hall under the glassy eyes of the tiger, and turned his back on the man and the affair. It was left to Doreen limply to wave Lance good-bye from outside the conservatory as he drove off with Cara.

In Lance's room in the Old Ship Inn, Cara clung to every dwindling moment she had left. She was by now so in love she cared nought who saw them with their arms about each other, or walking hand in hand in the district. She cared nought how much the fishermen she had known since childhood winked, or how much Jess Baker gossiped with the locals about the handsome dark man in the upstairs room who had swept Miss Thornton off her feet.

She opened the black leather trunk at the foot of the bed and helped Lance pack. She knelt in front of the trunk and buried her face into his shirts to remember the cotton and viyella scent of them when he'd gone.

They sat on the sagging feather bed and talked about his immediate drive up to London to return the car and catch the night train to Dundee to say goodbye to his mother. He would not see the Tinlings. His apologies for not coming to the shoot had been sent by letter, another short one to Janet. He would soon be on his way down to London again where he and Cara would meet at Susan's.

The time ticked past far too quickly, and there were long silences when they did not talk but lay on the bed in the closest embrace they had had yet, and Cara would not have minded if he had taken her then and there, but even so was glad he did not. He was the one who kept an eye on the time, sat up first to disentangle himself, brushed his hair with his brushes before packing them in his suitcase, and turned laughing to see her still there flat out and say, my God, she looked as if he *had*! With sadness they said goodbye to the little room with a view, and bumped the trunk down the stairs and out to the car.

Cara watched Lance drive away from Christchurch quay by the bandstand; and with a lump in her throat she walked alone to the ferry and rowed herself over the river.

He took her out to a show, a meal, and to dance at the Hammersmith Palais with its banks of potted flowers where they could dance for hours to the Harry Leader Band on the French-chalked floor – and all for 2s 6d.

With his arm around her, they sat talking late into the night on the sitting-room sofa in Susan's flat.

It seemed no time later that they met at Victoria Station and saw the labelled black trunk into the luggage van, and with Lance carrying his battered suitcase in one hand, and holding her hand in the other, they walked up the platform of the boat train and found his reserved seat. He dumped the case and came out to stand on the platform and hold both her hands so tightly it hurt.

'Oh God,' he said, 'I hope the bloody train goes punctually. You won't forget me?'

'How could I? I—I will never forget you, Lance, you *must* know that.' Her chin trembled.

'You *could* – you have known me such a short time.'

'If you think I could, you could too.'

'That is one thing that for sure will not happen. Cara, don't hide anything from me. If you meet someone else promise me you won't make any decision until we've had a chance to meet again, talk again?'

'Oh, Lance, darling, don't be silly.' She had never seen him so tense, so afraid. 'Of *course* I won't meet anyone else. All I can think of is *you*. All I'll be doing is counting the days until I can come out . . . '

The whistle went. The guard, holding his green flag, came closer, banging the doors shut along the coaches. Lance put his arms round Cara and enfolded her in a bear's embrace. He kissed her with the guard waiting to shut the door a bare yard away, a laconic expression of patient tolerance on the man's face.

'Trust me, Lance . . . ' she said.

'It is just that I' – he swallowed – 'I . . . cannot contemplate life without you.' He leapt up the steps, and opened the window behind the shut door. She saw his fists clenched on the windowsill, his broad shoulders shake – a strong man moved to tears. It was wrong; strong men should not be made to cry.

The train slid away from her. She did not move nor wave, but stood stock still. She kept his face in view, tears trickling down her cheeks. His face blurred through her tears, he no longer seen, no longer with her.

She would never forget him, never, never . . .

CHAPTER 9

'Hallo,' Derek Brownlow said at the Highcliffe Golf Club on a Saturday late in October.

'Hallo. Good gracious, you playing?' Cara eyed his clubs. 'I thought you never had time away from work.'

'Finished, thank the lord. Missed the tennis season, so am taking up golf. Finding the little ball somewhat elusive.'

'You should have a lesson with the pro. He's great.'

'Maybe I will. What about a game with me?'

'I'm not sure.' She wished Susan would hurry up and come out of the ladies' room.

'Must find someone to practise with. Come on. Be a sport. Next Saturday?'

'Well. Perhaps. How did the Staff College exams go?'

'Not bad. Lived like a hermit for six months,' he smiled. 'Tough going. Two weeks hard at it.'

'Where did you take them?' He had a nice smile, no crinkle or dimple like Lance, but nice. In fact there were similarities: he was tallish, though not so tall; dark haired, though not so dark; of wider not so slender build. Skin pale and pasty-looking. Too much book work!

'Headquarters in Salisbury. Three three-hour test papers at a time. Fairly intensive to start with, then on to voluntary subjects; those are not compulsory.'

'You mean to say you add unnecessary work?'

'Certainly. Every subject gets extra marks towards a competitive vacancy. The more marks the merrier.'

'When will you hear the results?'

'Not till June. I'll be in India by then.'

'Well, good luck in prospect. See you Saturday.'

As it happened she saw him next day at Church Parade at the Priory. With her parents she rowed and walked across as usual to matins. Officers and men marched in looking spruce in their khaki uniforms with shining buckles and belts, the other ranks making a clatter in their highly polished black boots, to take up the whole of one side in the reserved chancel. They lounged and yawned in their seats and dropped their hymn books, though none too obtrusively lest the Battery Sergeant-Major had something to say afterwards. They were all very clean and young-looking with their short hair-cuts, a smell of hot blanket pervading the old building. Cara's thoughts wandered once more during Canon Ray's lengthy sermon to thinking of Lance, and how glad she was he wasn't in the Army to become cannon-fodder as these young men might now that the 'peace in our time' elation had been snuffed out.

After the service Charles Thornton asked Derek and another gunner officer in for a drink. Gunners were still mounted in 1938 and the officers looked particularly smart in khaki jacket, Sam Browne belt, breeches, and buckled Greenaway boots. They drove up in Derek's Ford to Wick House, ablaze with autumn colouring. Chrysanthemums, as yet unnipped by frost, bloomed late in the season; Michaelmas daisies in the borders displayed hues of pinky-blue and violet-mauve; yellowing leaves on the trees fluttered down like rusty rain. The copper beech by contrast remained packed into the magnificence of its height and size, massed by the shiny dark burgundy of leaves.

Cara was glad of the presence of the two officers in Wick House that day and of the subsequent invitations her father extended. Her Saturday golf encounter with Derek and her bringing him back to tea became a weekly event. Though he had no musical training and could play no instrument, he had a good ear and liked to listen to full orchestral symphonies, and he took to inviting her to concerts at The Pavilion in Bournemouth. They also went to the skating rink where they staggered round in a waltz, she holding him up to fits of giggles on her part while he remained earnestly concentrating. She found he was hopeless at ballroom dancing. He had no sense of rhythm, and danced off-beat. She often wondered how he managed to march to time with the band, which she had seen him do with perfect precision, and looking very smart, at the Barracks on parade days. He was an odd mixture. He intrigued her with his blunt aura of honesty – and he was attentive in a distant way without being at all pressing. As a platonic friend he helped to fill the gap of Lance's absence.

The first pangs of parting, when she had missed Lance more than she could have believed possible, the ache in her heart and the hollowness of life without him permeating every moment, had been ameliorated by the arrival of the missives. There had been a telegram from Calais, a phone call from Marseilles (which she had taken in the hall with the household listening in spite of which it had been heaven hearing his voice), a highly coloured postcard from Port Said, and then the first bulky letter from Calcutta followed by sometimes three in a week.

The pinpricks started with this regular flow. The letters usually arrived by early morning post, were sorted by Ford, those for the Brigadier taken into the study, those for the rest of the household 'above stairs' put by places on the breakfast table.

Charles was invariably up early, unable to sleep late from long habit of rising to ride before breakfast. Though he no longer rode, he rose just as early, went into his study, had his tea and checked the mail. Whereupon he settled down for an hour to write letters, particularly forthright, if not downright inflammatory ones, to the newspapers. He enjoyed the response these brought (the more scurrilous the better!) and positively savoured the cut and thrust of a battle of wits in his otherwise 'woman-ridden sterile life' as he expressed it. Until now he had taken no notice of the family's letters of which there were remarkably few: Cara's had been mainly from her school friends; Doreen had an occasional one from a cousin in Ireland, and there was one a fortnight from Bobby.

It was as obvious to Charles Thornton as it was to everyone else that the letters at Cara's place were from Mr Gardner. The young man had been open enough, in the enthusiastically boyish way many Indians had, to declare his love for his daughter. That was not surprising! Who wouldn't be in love with her? However he had expected the spate of letters soon to dry up. But that had not happened due to Carissa cheapening herself by encouraging the torrent. Openly she did so. Day after late autumn day she sat at the antique Sheraton escritoire in the drawing-room, which up to then she had seldom used, scratching away with a fountain-pen. He reckoned she must have acquired a load of flimsy writing paper and blue air-mail stickers with the correct stamps, for more often than not there was lying on the outgoing silver tray in the hall a letter addressed to L. D. Gardner Esq., Box No. 423, Calcutta, India. The girl was patently egging the man on.

With commendable restraint for a person with the temperament of Charles Thornton, he made no more than the odd snide remark at the breakfast table about the number of letters from India, and the odd sarcastic one in the hall about not *another* letter to post on his walk with Bugler, and had there not been one yesterday? He could not believe there was anything in it, that his daughter could be so foolish – so stupid – as to return the man's feelings. If she had, like some adolescent schoolgirl, allowed herself to be carried away by the fellow's romantic inventions, the connection would be bound to evaporate during the absence. To reply to the letters with a spate of her own so that she constantly reminded him of her, and herself of him, was, Charles came to the reluctant conclusion, due to the fact that, in spite of recently taking over the housekeeping from him and doing the shopping, she did not have enough to occupy her.

He admitted to himself that perhaps he had been wrong in expecting a high-spirited girl like his Carissa to live contentedly at home until she married. It was too late for the autumn term, but he would suggest she might attend a day secretarial course at the Bournemouth College for Young Ladies starting next January. The news from the Continent was not good. It was bloody bad. Chamberlain had been bamboozled by Hitler into believing all that balls-aching peace talk. The latter was rampaging on as much as if not more than before, threatening his neighbouring states with dire results if they refused to toe the line and give him the minerals he demanded. In the event of war Carissa would be called up to man one of the local factories, or to work on the land – either quite unsuitable occupations for a gal of her upbringing. Better have secretarial training – more lady-like. Meanwhile, with the winter evenings closing in on them, he'd order Doreen to throw a series of dinner parties. Get the young people together. Play billiards after, or send them off dancing to The Pavilion or the Bath Hotel – he'd pay. Plenty of young men glad to be invited from the Barracks, every one of them more suitable than that Gardner. Diversionary tactics often worked. If it did not, build up the steady pressure next, after which, if the trouble persisted, bring out the big guns! He was getting beyond it. Only Ford knew how beyond. He was not *against* her marrying. Far from it. He would die happier knowing she was settled with a decent chap. But Gardner . . . NEVER!

Cara jumped at the idea of the course and booked herself in for the New Year. Lance wrote enthusiastically. The secretarial training to fill in the time was a good idea. She could get a job in Calcutta and help with the finances! Theirs was going to be a true partnership in every sense of the word. He was saving, and his work was going well. Johnny MacCreath hinted at promotion – most 'juniors'

112

had to wait for that until they were thirty. Last week had been a terrific one for the Jute-wallahs. Communal riots. They'd been called out on *three* occasions!

Cara treasured the letters. She read them, answered them explicitly, tied them into neat bundles, and put them away on a shelf in her bedroom cupboard, only to take them out and look at them again in bed at night. They were written in black ink on white paper in a small handwriting. They were long and interesting, were full of affection and love, and they gave her hours of gladness, each letter re-read until engraved upon her heart. She bought a calendar which she hung on the back of her wardrobe door, and slowly at first, then more quickly, the crosses against each day grew. October, November . . .

The pinpricks also grew. They grew into rocks of pressure she could not ignore, the *sangar* battlements for the great guns building up steadily, relentlessly. Cara arranged for Rosie to bring the mail to her bedroom with her early morning tea.

'It's a lovely day, Miss.' Pink-faced, Rosie would dump the tray triumphantly down on the bedside table, ''nother letter from the gen'leman, Miss!'

To avoid further vexatious insinuations, Cara took to writing her letters in her bedroom and posting them herself. Even so, despite removing the seen evidence, she sensed the coming storm and braced herself for it. She sensed it coming by the thick wall of silence that surrounded Lance's name at Wick House. She had hoped it would not be so from her father, though she had expected it, but from her *mother* – that she had not expected. She was hurt that her mother would not talk about Lance. There were plenty of opportunities to do so when they were alone. On the occasions that she had brought his name in, invariably her mother changed the subject. Then . . .

'Carissa, it is time you and I had a serious talk.' Charles Thornton shut the study door behind his daughter on a foggy morning towards the end of November. Bugler's

113

tail thrashed on the hearth rug and then subsided. Thinking, 'Here it comes, keep it cool, Cara old thing,' Cara sank into the worn leather armchair.

'I do not care for subterfuges.' Charles stood behind his desk.

'Subterfuges, Father? What subterfuges?' she said as innocently as she was able.

'You receive letters through Rosie and are encouraging that man by writing back secretly. If that isn't subterfuge I don't know what is. *It must stop!*'

'I asked for the letters to be brought to my room because I could see they were upsetting you. I don't understand why the sight of them should. You liked Lance well enough when he was here, liked talking about India with him.'

'Liking to talk about India is one thing, anything closer is another.' The pink patches on Charles's face deepened.

'I fail to see why.'

'I warned you not to get involved.'

'I am involved.'

'May I enquire how much?'

'Very deeply. I believe he told you one day we hope to marry?'

'NO!' Charles barked. 'Gardner said he hoped to *ask for your hand*. It does not follow that *you* wish to marry him.'

'I do, Father, I do,' Cara said softly.

'Then you have lost control of your faculties. Can you not see the seriousness of the position?' Charles thumped the desk, Bugler pricking his ears interestedly.

'I can see that Lance would make an admirable husband,' Cara declared with hauteur, her colour rising.

'Good God, woman, there are so many objections to the match I hardly know where to start.'

'I can't think of *any* objections.'

'For one, the man is *not your class*.'

'Oh *really!* Not that old hat.'

'Yes, *that* old hat as you rudely observe. He is a

114

grammar school boy and a box-wallah to boot. Once a box-wallah, always a box-wallah with the mentality to match.' Charles spat out the word in a way which made it sound dirty. 'Extra to that, jute is at the bottom of the barrel, the scum of trade. Clubs won't have anything to do with 'em.'

'Well, Father, they're having Lance. The Jute-wallah's didn't black-ball him.' Cara could not help smiling at the remembrance of the small lesson Lance had given her. Her father's objections were pathetic, ridiculous, petty, outdated.

But Cara's half-smile caused Charles's temper to snap. So the wretched girl thought it was *amusing*, did she? He'd show her it wasn't funny. Bring in the big guns!

'Damn and blast it, girl, isn't it about time you took a look at what's staring you in the face?' he exploded.

'What?'

'The man is no more than a half-caste mountebank, a charlatan of the worst type!'

An acute silence followed this outburst, Cara's colour receding. From her chair she looked up wide-eyed and aghast.

'Father! How *dare* you. What a perfectly *appalling* accusation. I wouldn't have thought you were capable of such—'

'*I* wouldn't have thought you were capable of such crass blindness. Can you deny that he is a half-caste?' Charles glared at his daughter, red moustache twitching.

'I do not deny he has Indian blood. But to call him *that* . . . that is disgusting of you. That is going *too far*!' Her voice rose while Bugler's watchful eyes switched from master to mistress.

'I regard it neither perfectly appalling as you exaggerate, nor disgusting, nor is it going too far. It is the accepted word for what Gardner is.'

'Perhaps in eighteen-ninety when you were commissioned, Father. Not any more it isn't. You can't say that sort of thing nowadays without people taking offence, as

115

I most assuredly do. You make him into a mulatto, a fuzzy-wuzzy, or—or—' Cara's eyes blazed with indignation.

'Could tell on sight. Hands – shape of fingers, half-moons, always give 'em away.' Charles mumbled, surprised at the violence of his daughter's reaction, proud of her spirit despite his scorn at her stupidity. The pink patches on his face turned puce; unexpectedly he sank into his chair at the desk, his hands trembling.

'Maybe I spoke too hastily.' Charles Thornton changed his tactics. He knew he had the advantage, held all the aces. The half-caste (he could not think of the man as anything else) was on the other side of the world. His daughter had no money of her own beyond what he gave her, but his biggest trump card was that he could play upon her emotions. He knew she loved him, and from long habit wanted to please him. He continued the diatribe from his desk chair. 'Let me take back the word which has caused such offence. It is a word, I grant you, used in the days of the Honourable East India Company, since when we *koi hais* have kept it on. You would not object, I presume, to the definition "Anglo-Indian" which in olden times was used for the British who lived in the country?'

'No-o.' Cara wondered at her father's sudden mild tone. It was not like him to beat so hasty a retreat.

'Whatever term we use, it comes to the same thing: Gardner's father was twelve annas – er, for your benefit that is three-quarters Indian. Not that I have anything against the Indians or being Indian – in fact I have a considerable respect for them – it is the *mixture* which I find obnoxious, against nature, all wrong; it despoils *both*. Having never been to the country yourself, it is difficult for you to understand the complexities of the caste system, the domination by religion, the way the Eurasians are caught in the middle and are looked down on by white and black alike—'

'Lance is of aristocratic blood,' Cara interrupted;

116

'nobody could look down on him.' As far as she was concerned Lance was Scottish educated, and as British as they came, and she could not see where all this talk was leading to.

'There, to put it in the kindest terms, you have been misled, and there my second, to your way of thinking "objectionable", noun comes in. The man is a mountebank with a trumped-up story about ancestors, all of which I regret to say you have been artless enough to swallow hook, line and sinker.'

'If you are suggesting that what Lance has told me about the Princess of Cambay and his great-grandfather is untrue, I suggest you look up Sleeman's volume on your own shelves,' Cara responded cuttingly, her white face showing her disgust.

'What I am saying, Carissa, is that Gardner has twisted the facts to suit his ends. That the Colonel of Gardner's Horse married an Indian lady I will not deny, but she was not a daughter of the King of Delhi—'

'Lance never said she was. He said she was adopted.'

'Ah, there you have it. A *very* different kettle of fish,' Charles picked up triumphantly. 'The Moghul kings had dozens of wives and hundreds of concubines as well as, hrum, hrum, we'd better leave it at that. She could have been a common slave girl's offspring; she could have been anybody, and here you have an equally ambiguous tale in the next generation. To marry into the royal family of Oudh may sound to you the height of glamour, though to call it the depths of depravity would be more realistic. The Kings of Oudh were a particularly decadent lot. The one at the time we are concerned with ruled over a corrupt court. They were a debased, debauched bunch of sybarites, taking part in disgusting public displays of drum-beating orgies, and a great deal more sprees behind closed doors.'

'All this has got nothing to do—'

'I am attempting to explain, Carissa, if you would listen,' Charles continued in a contained manner, though the puceness of his blotched face showed the pressure was rising, 'that the bland tale you have been related is no innocent fairy story. Rather is it an account involving horrendous intrigues and "goings on" of incest and other unspeakable animalistic cults unimaginable to a girl brought up sheltered as you have been, subjects I hardly care to mention, but am forced to present to convince you of your unimaginable folly—'

'History of the far past, Father. What happened *then*, I repeat, has nothing to do with Lance *now*, any more than your smuggler grandfather has anything to do with you now.' Cara felt she had scored a point.

'Please do not deviate from the matter in hand,' Charles said sternly, his choleric mien deepening into purple. 'Have you never heard of *inheritance*, girl? We are talking of bad blood from the tainted Oudh dynasty. Throw-backs are prone to appear for generations, especially in cases of mixed blood. Two white-skinned persons produce a black baby. Do not think I don't know what I am talking about in this case. I have long ago studied Tod and Sleeman and a good many other historic volumes of that period. In this instance the grandfather's wife squandered their money in riotous living.'

'Lance also told me that.'

'Did Gardner tell you she took drugs, became an opium addict? Did you know addiction can be passed on from mother to foetus so that the child is born addicted? We are talking about Gardner's *father* now. Getting a bit near, eh?'

'I wish to goodness you'd call him "Lance"' Cara was irritated beyond endurance by her father's tone.

'The children of this misalliance, and *their* children,' Charles continued doggedly with his theme, hammering it in, 'went from bad to worse.'

'What bad to worse?' Cara put in automatically. None of this character bashing had anything to do with Lance, and she wished to goodness her father would stop and let her go. He had said nothing, and *could* say nothing, that would deviate her from her path with Lance.

'Breeding like flies, they became poverty-stricken, drug-ridden, thieving, crazed, diseased, reduced to becoming professional beggars, I shouldn't wonder – who knows to what depths they haven't descended? Have you stopped to think, Carissa, that some of those down-and-outs are first cousins of the man you blithely contemplate marrying?'

'Ridiculous! Too far-fetched for words. You have no proof any of them exist.'

'It is recorded that there were many descendants. For one, I heard a decade ago of a station-master at Kalka who made himself known to the Vicereine when she was passing through on her way to Simla.'

'Good for him!' Cara said rebelliously.

'We are talking about *relations*, Carissa.' Charles's patience was on the verge of breaking point. 'Poor relations in India are proverbial. They are the first to hear through the infallible source of the bazaar grapevine of the arrival into their country of a well-heeled member. I have no doubt they will, if they have not already, turn up in Calcutta pestering Gardner for money, use blackmail I wouldn't be surprised, go to every and any length—'

'Tush and nonsense.' Cara borrowed her father's favourite expression.

Her irreverent attitude, her refusal to take what he was saying seriously, infuriated Charles. He had had enough. He held himself up straight, and banged forcibly with his fist on the desk, the ink-pot jumping. Bugler sat up attentively on his haunches at the sound, while Charles let his daughter have it:

'You have allowed the whole falsification of the truth to go to your stupid little romantic head. You have been taken in by the bastard's suave looks. I'd have thought as my daughter you'd have had more sense. I am ashamed of you, and I am disappointed in you. You have been

119

conned by a man who has told you a fat lot of fallacies about his ancestry to impress you. Why does he want to impress you, do you think? Let me tell you why,' Charles shook a severe finger at his daughter, 'because he feels inferior. All Eurasians do. Take note of that, my girl; Gardner deep down will always feel inferior though he will cloak it by fabricating a background, by taking up a posturing domineering pose, by being as twisty as hell—'

'I refuse to sit here for a moment longer listening to you slandering the man I am going to marry.' Cara stood up and made for the door with what dignity she could muster, her repugnance visible in her face.

'God damn it, over my dead body you will.' Charles rose to his feet. At the same time he picked up a book off the desk and clutched it in his right hand as if intending to hurl it at her head. Bugler, at the shouted words, got up with his master and began to bark excitedly, tail wagging. 'You won't get a penny from me; I'll cut you out of my will; you bloody well deserve to sample life with a half-caste, produce a horde of throw-backs . . . live trapped by milling proverty . . .'

To the accompaniment of Bugler's barks, Cara shut the door on her father's words, and heard the thump of the book hurled in uncontrollable fury against the study wall.

The crash shook her into an awareness of the dauntingly difficult struggle that lay ahead; and she walked up the stairs to her bedroom with feet of lead.

CHAPTER 10

For all the control she had kept on herself in the study, for all that she held her head high on leaving the room, Cara was left shattered.

Upstairs she tried to collect her thoughts among the jumble of accusations thrown out against Lance. What stuck in her gullet most was the offensive term 'half-caste' mostly used to describe primitive uneducated mixed races. To have so labelled Lance, who could not be more gentlemanly, more civilized, a literary and poetic man as she had discovered from his letters, was not only erroneous, but in the worst possible taste.

Her first instinct was to sit down and write to Lance and tell him everything – they were to have no secrets from one another. In the same moment that this thought came, she knew that it was the last thing she could do. *That* word, those horrid things said, she could *never* repeat to him. If she did he would be terribly hurt, terribly insulted. Not only did she not wish him ever to know the things said, but she could never say them for the shame she felt that her *father* had said them. All she could do was to write of her father being 'difficult'. She would have to use half-truths if he questioned her as to the particulars.

Cara went to her mother who had always backed her up in her gentle ineffective way. 'Father and I had a row when you were at your painting class this morning; he said some beastly things about Lance.'

'What sort of things?' Doreen stabbed at her tapestry.

'Picked to pieces pretty well everything about him from

121

accusing him of being a half-caste with tainted blood to pointing out that he is not my *class* – how futile can you get? You liked him, Mother, didn't you?'

'Yes, I liked him, sweetie. I liked him very much. He has charming manners, a melodic speaking voice, and is thoughtful of others. I would say he is straight and genuine. I dislike the word half-caste your father uses as much as you do. Better to say he is *part* Indian. You know what your father is,' Doreen sighed.

'Lance is proud of his Moghul blood and does not attempt to hide it.' Cara's heart lifted now that she had found an ally in her mother.

'Whether what your father says about Lance's ancestors is true or not I have no way of judging, and I do not suppose that your father has either. Most people have a black sheep or two in the family . . . oh dear . . . I don't mean *black* . . . you know what I mean. *I* have some with my roots in the Irish bog!' Doreen tried to retract.

'So you agree to my marrying Lance?' Cara asked with relief.

'I did not exactly say that, dearie.' The sigh came again. 'I would be very concerned for you going out to India on your own to marry a man you had known such a short time. It would have been helpful to have met some of his family.'

'I could go and see them in Scotland,' Cara said doubtfully.

'Yes, dearie, perhaps, but that doesn't solve the problem of India with no friends the other end. He might have funny habits, Indian habits, that could upset you. It has happened not infrequently that a fiancée takes the next boat home.'

'That wouldn't happen to me.'

'Then there is the climate which is unhealthy in Calcutta, and married to a businessman you have to face that he will be there for the rest of his working life. Have you thought of that?'

'He has some property to the north.'

'In the Ganges basin . . . he told me, dearie. Hot and mosquito infested. India is a quite frightening place. The millions, the seething crowds of the cities, the dust and poverty in the countryside, the noise and heat.'

'I thought you loved it.'

'I loved it because I was basically secure with my parents.'

'Is the country so horrendous?'

'It can be horrendous, especially if you are taken ill. I don't like it. You see, I do not think he is quite *suitable* for you, dearie. You are young; if you wait you'll have plenty more offers to choose from.'

'I have chosen, Mother.'

'I wish you hadn't.' Doreen sighed deeply. 'I would prefer it not to happen. Your children, my grandchildren, would be, be . . . ' She stumbled over saying 'blacky-white'. 'You see, sweetie, my family may be bog Irish, but we are bog *white*.' Doreen attempted to make a joke of it. Her attempt could not have fallen more flat.

'Thank you for talking to me, Mother,' Cara said evenly. She returned to her room disillusioned and down-cast. Her parents were hopeless. Her mother in her own way was as narrow-minded, bigoted, rigid and as preju-diced as was her father.

Cara wrote to Lance without saying anything specific. Lance spotted the difference at once from the care-free style of before and asked what the matter was, what had gone wrong? She wrote in return about the 'difficulties being put in our way'. 'What difficulties?' he wrote back immediately, fear making his hands clammy, the ink blotching. She could not tell him. She said her father had frightened her about India. And it was true. She had nightmares about arriving on the dockside and finding not her handsome Lance to welcome her, but a monster who held her captive in the historic Black Hole of Calcutta. She had never seen a black man in her life, nor even an Indian. There *were* no such alien races living in Christchurch, nor in Bournemouth, that she had met, and she had never come across one when shopping in Knightsbridge, or Bond Street, though Susan had when doing charitable work in the Isle of Dogs. She would have to go without her parents' consent, without a trousseau, without a wedding dress in her trunk, would have to throw herself on her bridegroom's bounty for the fare. She faced a terrible dilemma. The awfulness of letting Lance down, the man she loved, who when they had been together she would have done anything for (she knew that if he were on the spot she could not resist him), or cut herself off from home for always, kill her father, inevitably ruin the last years of their lives.

'Another letter from the gen'leman, Miss. It's a lovely day!' But it wasn't a lovely day. It was foggy, or raining, or frosty December, cold in the house unless huddling over a fire in the grate, bitterly cold and damp outside. She wrote to say that she loved him, but that she did not love him *sufficiently*. It was the only thing she could think of to say that wasn't a bald lie. She began to believe it. If she still loved him as completely and utterly as she had at first, she would not be writing like this. She would not be dithering, putting the doubts and fears into his mind that had stuck to her since her row with her father like burrs from long grass; she would instead be planning ahead for October, buying summer frocks and hats in the sales, saving every penny she could out of her allowance for her ticket. Rather, she was funking it. Funking it not only because she was frightened of going to India to a man she did not know all that well, but because the seeds of doubt her father had so ably sown of heredity, of blemished blood, of poor relations, and all the rest of it, had taken root. With the persistent dampening parental reminder in a steady weight of persuasion to give up all idea of marrying Lance, the seeds grew and branched and flourished in the soggy wilderness of her isolated distress every bit as fast as the tropical plants grew in the conservatory under the garden boy's deft hands.

The letters continued to arrive, questioning, demanding

124

an explanation, begging her: 'For God's sake, Cara, come clean, tell me what has happened. Can it be you have had second thoughts because I am an Anglo-Indian? Can it be I have unwittingly said something, done something, to offend you? We said we would have no secrets between us. The torture of not knowing what is turning you from me is worse than facing the truth however agonizing, I can assure you . . .'

She wrote again the only thing she felt she could say because she could never *deny* loving him. She wrote at Christmas, a white Christmas when the sun shone on the sparkling crystals of the tennis court, and they went skating on Mudeford pond; and at Wick House they celebrated without Bobby, without Lance, but with a lot of other young people from the New Forest, from the Yacht Club, from the Barracks, particularly Derek Brownlow, who was quiet and considerate, and whom she was now seeing more than ever.

'Where do your parents live? You never mention them,' she asked, interested enough to want to find out more about her escort's background. They were standing outside The Pavilion during the interval of a concert.

'My father was killed in the war,' he answered in his flat, unemotional way. 'My mother is Canadian. Afterwards she took me back to her people.'

'How sad about your father,' she expressed with sympathy, and then on a brighter note, 'Canada didn't do much for your skating! Why didn't you join the Canadian forces?'

'My mother hoped I would. I determined to join the British Army in my father's footsteps. That's better,' he said drawing a deep breath of winter air into broad lungs, then exhaling.

He was so *serious* about even taking a deep breath it was all she could do not to laugh at him. She had watched him in the Barrack parties with the other men. The more frivolous ones were inclined to take the mickey out of him, and she saw how that could be all too easy to do.

She knew he kept well away from the boyish pranks that went on in the Mess, though she imagined he'd had to endure the baptism of fire as a subaltern as they all did. He was a loner, and though the junior officers considered him distinctly stodgy, they one and all respected him.

'I suppose you go back on leave to see your mother?' Cara suppressed her smile at the breathing exercise; she went on with her enquiries really for something to say. He never questioned *her* about her people, her likes or dislikes, and never entered into a long discussion on politics, religion, personalities or anything else. If asked a question he would answer enough to give his opinion with precise and limited exactness. End of conversation!

'I used to see her a lot. She died last year. Ah, there's the bell. We'd better go in.' They walked back towards The Pavilion.

'I'm so sorry, Derek,' she said.

'Thank you,' he replied briefly.

She wanted to touch his arm to show her sympathy, but she did not like to. He was so self-contained, so sure. But underneath the surface she felt there must be feelings of sadness, of loss for a mother who had brought him up without his father. She liked him. She liked his shyness with women, and diffidence with men. She had never met anyone else quite like him: a non-flirtatious, non-jolly-with-all-the-chaps type. In a funny way she felt sorry for him, though why she could not think. To all intents and purposes he was completely in charge of his life with the knowledge of what he wanted and where he was going. Her reason told her he was the last person to need compassion!

They resumed their seats.

'Comfy?' he said turning to her with his shy smile.

'Yes,' she said, applauding the conductor walking in for the second half.

She invited him in to Wick House on their return. 'A drink?' she offered in the drawing-room.

'Whisky, please – a small one. I have some work.'

126

'At this time of night? I thought you'd finished with work since the Staff College exam. What work?'

'Bit of experimentation. There's always work—'

'If you *make* it,' she said, pouring herself some lemon water from a glass jug. 'My father calls this *nimbu pani*.' Cara sat in her mother's chair on one side of the dying embers and sipped the boiled drink. 'In India they make it with limes. Father showed Cook how to brew it up.'

'Won't be long before I'm off.'

'Oh, yes. I'd forgotten you were going there. Are you looking forward to it?'

'Certainly.'

She looked at him sitting in her father's chair, his whisky in his hand. For all the world they could be a staid old couple sitting by the fire not saying much, though *not* similar to her parents. He had an even temper; she was well-organized. Not a bad combination! Suddenly she had a vision of the two of them in old age sitting like this, and as suddenly as the thought had come she rejected it violently and figuratively threw it into the red glow before her. *That* excluded Lance. What was happening to her?

Derek looked at his watch. 'Better be going,' and he finished his whisky in one gulp.

'Thanks for the lovely evening,' she said in the conservatory, and because she liked him and felt sorry for him in a way, and it was the accepted thing to do after a young man had spent money on taking a girl out, she looked up and kissed him on the cheek.

He did not kiss her back – but she saw the blush.

Meanwhile the loving, questioning letters from Lance continued unabated. She could only reply: 'I do not love you enough.'

'I feel I don't love you *enough*,' she repeated. 'Enough is enough,' Lance wrote back, relieved for the moment, amusement coming into the letters once more. 'What quirk of mind is this that is worrying you so? What has got into you that you use that silly word "enough"? Have you become a psychologist that you must dissect love, take it apart, cut it up into degrees? Why, for heaven's sake? Let it go freely as it has before, let it flow like our shining river Avon, carrying us joyfully along in our little boat out into the adventurous seas of the great wide oceans. Let me have no more neurotic psychoanalysing please! In any case I care not two hoots how *little* you love me. A "little" will do very nicely thank you, my Dilmilee!'

She could only repeat what she had said before, and she asked him not to pressurize her with so many letters. Hurt, he stopped writing for two weeks, and there was only one the following week when Lance in Calcutta felt the ice-band tightening around his heart. Only his friends the MacCreaths knew of his near-engagement to a girl in England, and that their plans to marry the following year seemed to have gone awry. Only they knew of his anguish and despair, Johnny covering up for him in the office when he walked in, did his work, and walked out again heavy footed like a man with a mountain upon his shoulders.

'We had perfect trust,' he said to Johnny. 'I must go back and sort it out.'

'The firm will not permit you leave so soon after your return.'

'Then I shall have to resign, borrow the money to go back. Get a job in England.'

'Jobs in England are not easy to find. The boss will not let you resign and ruin your career. Besides you are not thinking straight. Ride it out, old man.'

'I'm losing her. Why? Why? Why?'

Driven by his desperation at the distance between them when he was convinced that if only they could meet they could talk it out and resolve what was troubling her; driven by his futility in not knowing what it was that had changed her in the space of two – three – months, though he knew it must be something to do with her father, Lance essayed one more plea:

'Try not to take any notice of what your father says. He must be beside himself. If only you would go up to

128

Scotland and see my mother. I have written to her and she knows about you. Please go, Cara. You cannot go on writing as you have been writing that you love me and yet you do not love me. You *must* not unless you want to destroy me. Men have more delicate hearts than women, you know! Have you seen Uncle Tom? He knows what I am, wretched man that I am. If you have to go against your father's wishes, you have to. Women down the ages have left dearly loved fathers and homes for a greater love. It is right that they should, and you are no longer a child to be dictated to, but a woman who is soon to come of age, a woman who has the courage to take life in both hands and do what her heart dictates. The MacCreaths will welcome you. I will look after you, cherish you. We will be happy here. I love you, God how I love you. Put it back another year or two or three if you will. I will wait. Only promise me you will not thoughtlessly throw away the miracle we have between us, promise me you will not take a big step without telling me . . . '

'You have been brain-washed,' said Susan coming to stay for the New Year Territorial Ball at the Gunner Barracks to which Derek had invited them. She noted that her friend had lost weight and was more subdued than she had ever known her. 'Not only has your father's bullying reduced you to pulp, it has squashed you to such an extent you have no mind left of your own. Same as your poor mother.'

'I daresay.' Cara perked up at Susan's plain speaking. Impossible-to-answer innuendoes had become the norm about her home. 'I daresay I *have* been brain-washed and reduced to pulp, but I have a perfectly sound mind of my own which has told me, against my inclination, *not* to marry Lance Gardner.'

'That sounds too clinical for words. I'd go for my inclination every time.'

'What do *you* think about his being half-caste, as my father horridly puts it?'

'I don't have any particular racial prejudices, if that's what you're asking. If you fancy a dark skin that's all right with me. Whoever you decide to marry I'll go along with it, old thing! Why not? Paul Robeson's all the rage, and he's as black as . . . personally, if Bobby were a negro I don't think I'd have fallen for him in the first place. Now Derek—'

'What about Derek?'

'Well, he's particularly *white*-skinned, isn't he? I think he's nice. What do you think of him? One can see he's mad about you.'

'Rot! Derek couldn't be "mad" about anyone! But I like him; I like him very much. He's solid, and sort of comforting; that's quite different from . . . ' she left the sentence unfinished.

By now thoroughly run-down, Cara went to see Dr Walker at Square House, a graceful Palladian-style mansion built in 1776 facing the old Market square. He had known her since childhood; was an old family friend who came to dinner and played billiards with her father; and he had briefly met Lance. Moreover he knew India having in the last war at one period been posted to Delhi in the RAMC. He examined her, found nothing radically wrong, prescribed malt and cod liver oil to be taken daily at breakfast, and advised her very strongly *not to marry Lance Gardner*.

'Why, Dr Walker?'

'For reasons of his birth. For reasons of where he lives . . . '

They were *all* against him, all except Uncle Tom who had wished them luck. She went to make his cabin 'ship-shape'.

Uncle Tom was repairing a lobster pot, yacht cap all but obliterating the sight of one eye. 'Let 'em say what they like about the colour of his skin, he's a bloomin' fine man and that's all that matters. Yer has to make up yer own mind whether yer goin' to have him or yer family, for yer can't have *both*. Yer'll have to split with Lance

Gardner, or yer'll have to split with yer father, the bloody old bastard. He'll cut yer off without a penny for sure's sure. Never speak to yer again. Quite simple, m'dear: yer has to make up yer bloomin' mind which.'

She did make up her bloomin' mind. She had already made it up, and now she reinforced it. She had first made up her defence that she did not love Lance 'enough', and now she resolved that she did not have the strength of character to go through with marrying him against all opposition. She convinced herself she was not tough enough physically or mentally to leave home and family and friends in Christchurch and never be able to see them again, or meet in the Yacht Club and sail in the harbour, or walk on Hengistbury Head . . . never bring her children, her 'blacky-whites', to the parental home. She was not the strong determined type that ran away as Mulka had done (how easy when *with* James!) nor the courageous fourteen-year-old girl that Nissa had been when daring prejudices and opposition far greater than she had encountered to marry her 'fair god' of different skin colour, race and religion. She was not brave. She was not capable of the sort of love that could surmount every difficulty and survive. She would flounder, sink under the poverty of India, become ill, be a burden to Lance . . .

She wrote to him telling him it was 'all off'. He wrote one more letter, a short note: 'I only ask that from time to time you keep in touch. I would like to know you are well. I would like to hear how you get on with the secretarial course. A note every now and then will do . . .'

But Cara did not start the secretarial course in the January of 1939. Instead she became engaged to Derek Brownlow, who was an extremely nice, capable, intelligent, Gunner officer. He proposed on the golf course. It could not have been less romantic, and it was an enormous relief after all the emotions, all the traumas, all the feelings of guilt and self-hate that had drained her in the past few months.

131

'Will you marry me?' was all he said. 'Yes,' was all she said. He kissed her briefly, his bag of clubs clutched in his hand, and they went on playing golf.

Doreen heaved a sigh of relief. Charles took on a new lease of life, and the whole beaming household was galvanized into the preparations for a slap-up white wedding. Rosie polished everything in sight and said it was a lovely day every day regardless; Mr Field and the goofy garden boy got down to hoeing and sweeping leaves and tidying with a vengeance; Cook, humming away to herself, thought up new recipes for the reception, and Ford squeaked round the house in his ex-army boots guffawing, 'Brig won *that* battle, knew 'e would!' And Cara wrote to Lance to inform him of her forthcoming marriage in as few words as she was able. He had asked her to promise to tell him if she were to take a 'big step', and she did not want him to have the shock of hearing about it second-hand. She did not tell him Derek's name, nor who he was, nor where they were going. She wanted to put the past irrevocably behind her, and she wasn't too sure that he might not do something desperate, or be difficult, even try to stop her.

The wire came in a pile of congratulatory letters: 'Do you love him? Lance.' A reply was prepaid.

For some days she thought she would not answer. On the face of it it was a damned cheek of him. Then she thought she'd better answer or he would think she *couldn't*. All the fears and hateful contradictions came back to haunt her. All she wanted to do was to get rid of him, to never be upset again by hearing from him; she wanted him right out of her life once and for all. Her life in future was with Derek, dear, solid, safe Derek. She sent off the prepaid wire: 'I am marrying the man of my choice. Carissa.'

After that the silence was total.

In mid-March the marriage service was taken by Canon Ray in a Priory decked out with early spring flowers artistically arranged by Doreen. Charles Thornton, pouter proud, came down the aisle with his beautiful daughter on his arm, only too happy to be giving her away to the upright captain, to whom Cara earnestly made her promises with every intention of keeping them. Susan was the single bridesmaid, and Bobby flew back for the wedding.

The reception for five hundred guests was held in a marquee on the Wick House tennis court where speeches were duly made, champagne duly drunk, home-made canapés and cakes scoffed, the colourful display of crocuses under the great copper beech duly admired. It was the Christchurch wedding of the decade, the only blot on the landscape being Tom, who became distinctly maudlin, half-seas over, and had to be bodily removed by his good friend Fred who drove him with a half-crate of champagne to his shack. There the quay and the Old Ship Inn were rocked to the caterwauling of bawdy songs until at last in the early hours a heavy quiet enveloped No 1 Mudflats, so much so that Jess Baker popped over to make sure the incumbents were still breathing.

That morning, for the first time ever, Brigadier-General Charles Dunbar Thornton had to get his own early tea. He switched on the wireless in the study and heard Mr Chamberlain telling Mr Hitler in no uncertain words what he thought of his promises. Yet another crisis was upon them, tension was high, if not higher, than in the previous September. Rumania had on the day of Cara's wedding rejected the Führer's ultimatum to grant him sole use of their oil-fields, the Rumanian government appealing to King George VI to intervene.

'What does the bloody little house-painter want oil fields for except to make war?' Charles grumbled to himself slurping his tea.

The preparations for war were very apparent to his daughter mid-morning that day at a Victoria Station thronged with troop movements, soldiers packed into crowded trains on several lines.

Six months since she had seen Lance silhouetted in the Yacht Club doorway, Mrs Derek Brownlow, in her smart going-away grey suit and small becoming cloche hat, stood on the same platform where she had seen him off on the boat train. She and her husband were about to do the same journey to Marseilles, and board much the same steamer, though not to Calcutta but to Bombay. When the train drew out and they were rattling along on their way, Cara and Derek exchanged smiles and she squeezed his hand, a pleasant feeling of achievement stealing over her.

It was Susan who many years later said that Cara, though she may not have known it at that time, had married Derek so that she could be on the same continent as Lance.

PART II

Quetta Water

CHAPTER 11

With her hot face pressed against the windowpane, Cara watched the engine and the first carriages curling forward on the railway track. They were nearing the end of their journey. Ahead lay Quetta and the Staff College.

Since dawn they had slowly climbed, turning and twisting up the graded incline of the sixty-seven-mile Bolan Pass in Baluchistan, a marvel of engineering. On either side the view was blocked by barren rocky contours of heights and ravines from which the line had been blasted. The cliffs excluded any breeze. It was early June and stiflingly hot in the carriage, but Cara dared not open the window for the blast of smuts and swirling dust that would assail her did she do so.

In the further corner of the coupé, Derek lolled asleep, head against the backrest. Though he was travel-grimed, he looked as always what he was: a professional soldier, dark moustache neat, chin freshly shaven, his creased uniform trousers and khaki shirt, though black with sweat where his body touched the seat, still showing starched creases. Full of excitement at the approach to their new venue, Cara longed to exclaim and chatter. She looked wistfully at her sleeping husband but refrained from waking him. He needed the sleep after working all out up to the eleventh hour in the Station garrison of Ambala, followed by two disturbed nights in rattling trains with several changes.

As for herself she was too interested in the scenery, or rather non-scenery, to allow herself to doze, which it would be only too easy to do in the intense heat. She sipped boiled water from the thermos to keep herself awake. She had found in her first hot weather the previous year that she could tolerate the extreme temperature unlike many redheads who tended to dry up like sucked oranges and become dehydrated. She supposed she sweated more easily than they, her skin kept cool by her own damp, because her colouring was deep rather than light.

The climb that had begun in Sibi now came to Mach where the train stopped. The engine hissed and steamed and took on water as thirstily as Cara was drinking from her thermos. It started up again towards Spezand at the zenith. The only vegetation that she could see was an occasional straggly sage bush: no trees, no shade, no shelter from the blistering sun. The arid land of red-gold soil was broken occasionally by the appearance of a straggle of black goats from over a hill, the herd tended by a ragged, bare-footed small child carrying a stick. What the goats, or the child for that matter, found to live on Cara could not imagine.

She determined that when there *was* something to see at the top she would wake Derek, for there must be *something* spectacular on a 5500-feet-high plain in the middle of which was the capital Quetta, the name a variation of *kwat-kot*, the Pashtu word for 'fort'. The line from Quetta went on northwards over the Khojak Pass to Chaman where it stopped on the Afghanistan border, a mere eighty miles or so by rough track from romantic-sounding Kandahar with its old walled city. That was the way Lord Roberts of Kandahar had come in the second Afghan War. His army, 10,000 strong, had marched from Kabul to Kandahar in the Great March of 1880 when they had become 'lost to the world' for three weeks with no telegraph wires rolled out or other means of communication. The world had been electrified by the feat! The British had fought successfully at Kandahar and had come on down to Pishin in the State of Baluchistan.

The journey from Ambala to Lahore and on south-west

across the vast Sind desert had been the most exhausting and scorching one Cara had yet experienced. Their coupé was not air-conditioned, and though coolies brought fresh ice at Rohri, near the Lloyd Barrage in the green valley of the mighty Indus, to replenish the blocks in the tray on the floor under their feet (on which the one fan played) the ice melted in no time to slosh and spill each time the train rounded and leant, the puddles generally adding to the sordidness of the carriage.

With no restaurant car on the train – as there had been on the main line from Ambala to Lahore when they had descended onto a platform and walked back to have a meal, the process reversed later, the whole train being corridorless – Cara had brought food and drink with her in a large hamper. Though she had attempted to tidy up, after a series of meals there remained paper and cardboard cartons, bottles and unwashed cups and glasses to add to the look of mess as if at the aftermath of a revelry. Only there had been no revelry. There would be no revelry with Derek, not even in a little coupé all to themselves, two bed bunks made up at night, to do what they liked and when they liked behind the drawn blinds of a hot, hot nowhere. Dreamily Cara thought of the coupé as rocking on a desert sea in waves of shimmering heat, absolutely ripe . . . she was nodding off. Determinedly she woke herself up with a gulp of the earthy tasting water.

She did not mind. He was everything she had married him for: solid and predictable, reliable and even-tempered, unflustered, kindly, concerned when she'd been ill, good to be with in a crisis; and she soon discovered that in India there were plenty of those!

The first had come her way when she had been only a week in the country. On arrival Derek had been posted to the Gunner training depot in Ambala on the Grand Trunk Road 120 miles north-west of Delhi. After a day of valiantly trying to unravel the intricacies of housekeeping and servants whose language she could not understand, at the same time as checking the quartermaster's stores for 'knives, chopping, two', and '*degchies* (handleless saucepans), graded, ten', a rabid dog rushed into her quarter lathering at the mouth. It jumped, shivering and barking high-pitched, onto her twin bed on which she reclined feeling more tired than she ever had in her life. Petrified, she tumbled out and lay cowering under the bed. Rapidly Derek appeared with a pistol and shot the dog, properly messing up her new sheets and pillow cases.

Although the dog had not touched her, there had been a considerable amount of saliva about, and she had been marched off to the MO to have the first of fourteen extremely large painful injections into her stomach which had left her feeling very sore to say the least, but grateful nevertheless that she lived in an age where such antidotes existed. She was still recovering from the shock when the *khansama* cut himself badly in the outhouse kitchen on one of those 'chopping-knives, two' which she subsequently declared should be listed as: 'chopping-knives, very sharp, two'. Blood spurted on whitewashed walls; the Hindu cook waved his damaged hand in panic. She managed to jam on the semi-severed finger, and scream to the bearer to fetch the Captain-sahib. Fortunately Derek was once again to hand to deal with the emergency.

Together with an attack of dysentery, it had been a quick baptism of fire all in her first month, and Cara reckoned she had been thrown in at the deep end with unusual severity. Not so, her new friend and neighbour in the cantonment, Pammie Dangerfield, disillusioned her. Events such as she had experienced were the norm, and most of the time husbands were *not* there to cope with them. Anything and everything could happen in India, lovely things as well as dreadful things – and usually all at once.

So far the loveliest thing Cara had come across was the scenery of the foothills, and the tremendous panorama of the Himalayas viewed from Simla where she had gone in May for the rest of the hot weather to recoup from dysentery. She was determined to master the language, so that she could speak directly with the servants. In this the plump, gentle bearer, Nasrullah Khan, Derek had engaged proved a great asset as he spoke some words of English.

The wives got together in Ambala and helped one another along, particularly the new wives and those with small children who tended to worry that the slightest upset would turn into a dire illness for their offspring. They shared a *munshi* who came to their bungalows in turn several times a week to teach Urdu, and after the kitchen episode Cara enrolled in a Red Cross first-aid course.

With her buoyant interest in the country that marriage had opened up to her, so vociferous and different from the calm ways of her home town, Cara learnt fast, especially about army life, and Derek in particular. She soon saw he was one of those who never stopped working unless it was to 'play' even harder at sport. In this particular she found a soul-mate in Pammie whose husband Frank (a Gunner senior to Derek) was as ambitious in his career as was Derek.

They were lean, incredibly fit men who never relaxed. In the evenings Derek was deep in some mechanical invention to do with guns, papers with drawings and figures spread all over his desk. Tired herself, more often than not Cara gave up waiting for him and went to bed.

Though she tried not to think of the past, Cara could not help wondering at times what it would have been like to live in India with a civilian who had regular office hours. Surely it would not have been so male-intensive, so wife-excluding, so self-sufficient as military life was? She sometimes wondered why officers bothered to marry to take upon themselves the added worries of looking after family and home when they could live in a comfortable Mess, all found. Yet those going on leave were dead keen to come back with a wife! For the convenience of sex, naturally, taken when wanted and quickly over into a short night of solid sleep, but not for companionship. Companionship was out in the field with the other chaps, or in the Headquarters poring over maps. The wives were left to look to the other wives for companionship.

When after a day's work Derek came into the bungalow, handed his cap and swagger-stick to his Gunner orderly Jit Singh, kissed her in perfunctory manner, asked her how things were and went to change into riding kit or hockey shorts without waiting for her answer, Cara banished her thoughts as unworthy. The boredom that had gone with her life in Christchurch had vanished, but something else had entered that she had not experienced before, nor been prepared for: loneliness. In spite of new friends, a small social life, the grappling with the housekeeping, the tentative approach to entertaining in her new home, the classes; in spite of a household of servants who lived with their families in the compound, she was often alone, often lonely. She had known Derek would have postings where she could not follow, but she had not thought to find herself lonely when *with* him.

After six months of her marriage, the expected depressing news of war breaking out in Europe on 3 September was flashed through to HQ in Ambala, and dread for her parents assailed Cara. She felt sorry that she was not within reach in case they needed her. In her hidden disillusionment over marriage she felt she should never have left them for her own selfish reason of getting away. She sat down and wrote asking for news. What was happening in Christchurch? Had they had air-raids? What about the evacuees designated to Wick House? How were they coping? Would the domestics be called up? Was Bobby staying on in Egypt?

During the wait for the first of the war-time letters from England, Cara's loneliness grew. The pressure of training was on in the Artillery. Derek could be, and was, called out at all times of day or night. There was the raising of new regiments. There were manoeuvres when he was away for days at a time, and even *he* came back looking tired to fall into bed to catch up on sleep while she lay awake thinking of the journey out to India which had meant to be a honeymoon and hadn't been a honeymoon at all. Instead of the anticipated warm springtime cruise paid for by His Majesty, it had been vilely rough through the Mediterranean from Marseilles.

Derek, tough on land, had collapsed on the first day at sea and taken to his cabin. There was nothing the slightest bit attractive in one's newly-wed groaning on the top bunk, the vile smell of vomit permeating the cabin, particularly when you yourself were a good sailor and enjoyed the motion of the ship! Conditions had improved in the Suez Canal, but in the Red Sea, no one having warned her about the tropics, Cara had swum in the troop-ship's canvas pool on the upper deck and sun-bathed too long. She had come out with peeling red skin compounded by prickly heat, and could not bear to be touched. When they sailed through the Indian Ocean in a near-gale and her rash receded, his sea-sickness started up again!

'Bang went our honeymoon,' Cara whimsically related to Pammie on one of their more intimate talks when their husbands were away, and Cara had come over to help pack up their house. These neighbours had three dis-ruptive small boys namely Jack, David and Peter, who, according to Frank, badly needed to be sent home to prep school, but could not go because of the outbreak of war. At that moment the two eldest were climbing the highest tree in the garden, Peter following gamely. The *ayah* in charge stood under the branches looking up helplessly. It was December 1939, weather perfect, and the Danger-fields were leaving for the first of the shortened Staff College courses starting in Quetta in the New Year.

'I bet you've since made up for loss of honeymoon,' Pammie laughed heartily. She was a happy-go-lucky uninhibited person, her dress usually a bit of a mess with a button missing, hem needing to be stitched, ladder in stocking when she wore them, which was hardly ever.

'Not exactly.'

'I thought Frank would wear himself out in the first year. Some hopes! He's settled down a bit since, thank God.'

'What do you mean by "settled down"? I mean . . . how, how often?'

'Oh God, I don't know.' Pammie took a tumbler Cara had wrapped in wetted newspaper and placed it carefully in the half-full tea-chest. 'Too often.'

'I want to know. I've got nothing to compare with, having been an innocent on marriage. What *is* normal?'

'*Chacun à son goût*,' Pammie shrugged, 'I know of no normal unless it's the once-a-week-Saturday-night-get-drunk sort of stand of the downtrodden British working class. Derek performs, doesn't he?' Pammie stopped, a glass decanter in her hand. She looked speculatively at her friend.

'Yes. Of course, but . . . but . . . not so frequently. I just wondered, that's all.'

'Well, in that case you're damned lucky, Cara. Believe me t'other way round's no joke. You're bloody fortunate if he doesn't jump into bed every night. I'll change shoes with you anyday!'

'Do you enjoy it?'

'When I'm in the mood. A build-up of "not so frequently" sounds a good bet for a nice toss!' Pammie gave her hearty laugh, stuffed a pillow on top of the tea-chest, and called the hovering bearer to bring hammer and nails. There was a scream from the garden, and the two women downed tools to rush out. They found Peter rolling on the ground.

'Oh God,' groaned Pammie examining the angle of the child's arm, 'not *now* of all times.'

'I'll drive you to the hospital.' Cara ran to bring the Dangerfields' car to the door.

Cara missed Pammie and their talks (although on the occasion that Peter had broken his arm she had gained little more knowledge) and was therefore delighted to hear six months later, when she and Derek were themselves packing up for the Staff College, that Frank had done brilliantly and was staying on as an instructor thereby by-passing the rank of major and reaching Lt-Col. (local) in one jump. They would be near neighbours again. Frank was certainly an exceptional man in more ways than one, Cara now had a chuckle to herself on the train. Lieutenant-Colonel F.C. Dangerfield would never speak to her again if he ever got to hear that she knew of his prowess in the bedroom! Not that she had, nor would, repeat it to anyone, least of all to Derek.

In Simla Derek had warned her not to get into the gossipy set. 'Tittle-tattle' he called it. She hadn't. That lot mostly played bridge and she did not. She did not consider the private conversations with Pammie qualified as gossip, though they did discuss other people in the Station and speculate upon them. She wondered how Pammie would fare in her elevated position as *burrah-mem* with the considerable amount of entertainment of students and Directing Staff (DS) she would be required to do. Cara decided to have a go at pulling her together dress-wise. Pammie had a good figure if only she'd tidy herself up a bit.

Spezand stop. The train started up and gathered speed into a barren wilderness of vast plain opening out before them. The level land was surrounded by rocky bastions of mountains ascending to the sun-pulsating sky. Fantastic . . .

'Derek, Derek, wake up! We've breasted the Pass. You *must* look.' She went over to his side and sat beside him gazing out of the window at the plateau, one mountain rising nearby out of the flat base, which she discovered later was the 11,000-feet Chiltan.

Derek stretched, yawned, and got up to open the window. Hot sweet air mingling with undefined odours wafted in. He sniffed, sat down and placed his arm about his wife's shoulders.

The heat was intense in the carriage, but the air

draughting in had a promise of freshness – dry freshness as opposed to the enervating sticky heat of the monsoon areas. The morning light in the foreground had a sharpness about it Cara had not seen before, though in the distance Quetta itself lay, further north on the open plain, shrouded in a gauze of heat haze, strings of fog draped overhead. The new scene exuded a certain incitement together with an agreeable aura, though *why* Cara could not fathom when in a perfectly barren wilderness, as bare as the Bolan Pass had been, with no sign of water, no sign of cultivation in the stony soil. Why did not rather such a forbidding spectacle fill the mind with dread?

'We're going to have a great time here.' Derek drank the slight cool with relish into his lungs. 'By God I shall have to work hard to compress a two-year syllabus into five-and-a-half months. The curriculum states practically no cuts! You'll have to help me, little woman.'

'How?' She rubbed her cheek against his shoulder.

'Typing out my notes and such. We students face a tremendous challenge. Do you realize that if I pass out of here well, I'll be for the top echelons, red hat an' all? How's that for you? If I fail, back to the humdrum.'

'I used to type for Father. I think I could do that.' She warmed to know that she was to be of some use in furthering her husband's career.

'Good woman. Ha. Here comes Quetta.' He gazed into the haze, a horizontal mirage of trees and green bouncing in the heat before their eyes. 'They say it's an extraordinary place, as freezingly bitter in winter as it is diabolically hot now. Men go *pagal* and shoot themselves, other madmen swap wives. Four officers did exactly that. Played musical beds for a live-long year. Crazy. The Big Bed Scandal they called it. Frank told me.'

'Pammie wrote they'd meet us.'

'We go to Capper Road.' Derek took out some instructions from his case and examined them.

'If scandals abounded before, what will it be like now with the war expansion?' Cara wondered.

146

'God knows. Heavens, abandoned wives left behind in droves when their husbands go to the front, joined by others sent from the plains for the duration; new regiments arriving unaccompanied; WAC(I)s and ECOs. You'll have to watch your step!'

Cara had by now learnt the military jargon the officers spouted. She knew the first of the combinations (pronounced 'Wack-eyes') stood for 'Women's Auxiliary Corps, India' which consisted mostly of locally recruited married women and single girls who worked in khaki uniforms as typists, clerks and personal assistants to generals in the various headquarters. The second lot of letters stood for 'Emergency Commissioned Officers' or 'Temporary Gentlemen', war-time call-up soldiers. Pammie had written in her last letter that Quetta was crammed full of these types, huts burgeoning like mushrooms on the landscape to house the influx. The social life, Pammie wrote, even in the time they had been there, had grown from hectic to frenetic.

It all sounded to Cara exactly what was needed for her marriage to blossom. Here Derek would work as hard if not harder than before, but here in the 'frenetic' atmosphere there would be the stimulation of dances, parties, mixed tennis and golf to which she would drag Derek. Here she could help him in his work. Here she too could work hard and play hard.

In the high fresh air of Quetta she and Derek would start again.

CHAPTER 12

'Hallo! How are the boys?' Cara jumped down onto the bustling platform to embrace her friend.

'Fine. Under control when all three were at school. Not so good now in the hols!'

'Peter's arm mended?'

'Oh that. I've forgotten about it there've been so many episodes since. Welcome to the land of Quetta water.' Pammie pecked Derek on the cheek. 'Frank apologizes for his absence. Desperately busy getting ready for the next course – your course. Sudden switch of tactics.'

'Hmmn. Desert warfare,' said Derek in his spare way.

He had, like Frank and all the other soldiers, been itching to get to the front, any front. Nothing particular had occurred in India after over ten months of war in Europe other than the stepping up of the volunteer army with the training and raising of new battalions on a huge scale. Some Gunners in Ambala, in their eagerness not to miss the war, had put in for repatriation to the UK, and were now frantically trying to do a U-turn. For in July 1940, after the débâcle in North West Europe and the miracle of Dunkirk, there was only *one* front left: North Africa, where the Allies faced the Italians in the Libyan desert. All the jungle warfare studies at the Staff College were hectically being switched to desert warfare. Frank and the Directing Staff certainly had no spare time to meet old friends at Quetta station.

So it was Pammie who ushered Derek and Cara with their small luggage into the family Buick parked outside, and drove them up Lytton Road in the civil lines where the Agent to the Governor General resided in a brand-new brick mansion of stalwart appearance. The rest of the avenue was lined with corrugated iron huts, each building incongruously set in a large well-established garden.

'Temporary replacements.' Pammie started up her commentary by waving a hand in the direction of a hut. 'The whole road was destroyed in the earthquake. Hit the civil lines and the bazaar worst, cantonments second with main shopping area. Staff College was fortunate to come off best.'

'That was 1935, wasn't it? I remember reading about it at home,' Cara said from the back seat.

'That's right. Last day of May. Some forty thousand casualties. Ghastly. You'll get used to earthquakes here. Minor ones are quite frequent.'

'Five years ago. Hmmn. Taking a lot of time rebuilding,' Derek commented from his seat next to Pammie. He wished she'd keep her eye on the road instead of swivelling round to speak to Cara in that haphazard way.

'They're getting on with it gradually. A mammoth job,' Pammie informed, slowing down at a main crossroad. 'Tremendous rivalry exists between civil and military engineers as to which is the best anti-earthquake build. The RE wanted reinforced concrete, the civil brick.'

'Only being a humble Gunner I wouldn't know,' Derek said in his dry-humoured way while registering a brick building going up, 'though in loyalty to the Sappers I'd back concrete.'

'Deadlocked and unable to decide either way they reached impasse,' said Pammie brushing some wisps of damp fair hair out of her eyes, hot air from the open windows blowing through the car. Her hair was tied up at the back to keep it off her neck with what looked suspiciously like a bootlace. Most likely one of Frank's, and there would be ructions when he found it missing, the orderly getting stick, Cara's thoughts wandered. Her friend had not changed in spite of her husband's rapid promotion.

'Looks as if brick won,' Derek observed while Pammie

149

attempted to change down, the grinding gears causing him to grind his teeth.

'Not so,' Pammie gaily rattled on, 'with both civil and military firmly entrenched in their positions, the AGG came in like King Solomon, and in his wisdom ordered the making of one brick model and one concrete model house. To test them he had them put into a railway truck, and chucked the whole thing – stage-managed, mind you, with all the VIPs and red-hats watching – over a steep railway embankment; whereupon the gathering scrambled down to have a look-see.'

'Gracious,' said Cara mildly, 'which won?'

'Neither,' Pammie declared triumphantly. 'The result was a tie. Both stood up equally well to the shock. Hence, brick in the civil lines, concrete for the Army. You can see for yourselves. Cantonment area.' She pointed while driving up a wide fairway bordered by dusty pepper trees and concreted ditches. At regular intervals straight lesser roads with thoroughly British names such as Queen's Road, London Road, and Pall Mall, crossed theirs at right-angles.

'Good God. Concrete boxes. Hellish hot inside.'

'We've got one, Derek. Very nice too with all mod cons. Fans keep the temperature down a bit though I admit our student bungalow had the edge on it coolth wise. We've moved to the Directing Staff road next door to the main building. But you'll like your old one. It's the last in the row on the edge of the moon landscape with unimpeded view . . .' She chatted on non-stop.

The city in the middle of its wilderness lay like a fertile oasis in a rocky desert. There were private gardens, a park, vegetable plots, golf course with 'browns', shrubberies, green lawns, cricket pitches, avenues of trees and fields of vineyards. Some trees looked shrivelled, most lawns appeared parched, hedges drooped, though the flowers in the gardens bloomed prolifically in a variety of brilliant colours, and roses were flowering.

They ran out of traffic, bicycles the only wheeled

vehicles, and passed a string of burdened camels plodding silent footed. They climbed up almost imperceptibly from the straight cantonment roads to curve round towards the old, partially ivy-clad bastion of the Staff College opened in 1907. In all its thirty-three years of gentlemanly, leisurely, erudite courses, its weathered bricks could never have dreamed that it would overnight become a buzzing beehive cramming the brains of officers fit to be staff officers, and officers not so fit to be staff officers. Yet it had, and it did: in a few weeks of intensive teaching it spewed them out, 'Staff-trained', from the constipated sausage machine it had become.

Beyond the Staff College building the road curled on past a riding-school area to the Hanna Lake, nearly dry now (when bone dry it was used as a training area) and on up past the Hanna rest house via the Wam Kotl Pass of chikor shoot fame, to Ziarat, a small, unspoilt, hill station at 9,000 feet set in a fragrant juniper forest of stunted trees. On that day of the Brownlows' week-end arrival, more than half the military and civil personnel in Quetta were in Ziarat enjoying the coolth.

Now, short of the Staff College, Pammie turned abruptly right. Water, thought Cara; 'Welcome to the land of Quetta water', Pammie had greeted. The Biblical truth. Water made Quetta. With irrigation the impossible land blossomed; without water . . .

'Water is the key, and there doesn't seem to be any.' Cara voiced her thoughts aloud from the back seat.

'Key to more than you'd guess,' Pammie laughed. 'I'll be telling you all about it. At the moment – drought. Water from Hanna Lake is severely rationed in summer. Normally it comes gurgling down these ditches several times a week, the flow diverted in strict rotation to each garden. Lately it has been once a fortnight and recently not at all! Your *mali* will know when to expect it, and when it does come he rushes to divert it to his channels and swamp your lawn. The grass will recover, but some of the trees have had it. It's been a terribly hot summer,

151

100 degrees Fahrenheit in the shade day after day, and no blessed water . . .'

'Are there wells as we had in Ambala? I couldn't see any from the train.'

'You have a stand-pipe for domestic use in your compound. It comes from the catchment area on the road to Ziarat. Precious beyond gold. Spring water, pure cool springs that never dry up – *chashmas*.'

'I once heard that word: the *Chashma*, a royal Shah's spring—' Cara stopped abruptly. What on earth was she doing talking about the Moghul estate granted to the Gardners, a tale her father had declared was all ballyhoo?

' . . . use the bath water to water the flowers,' Pammie burbled on. 'Soapsuds are said to be good for plants; kills the black-spot on the roses. The lake water comes from the melting snows stored in the Hanna Lake which leaks like hell. Can't think why they don't cement it up. The snow water is carried from the foothills in *karezes*, man-made underground channels brought through the plains. Every now and then unmarked vertical holes are dug deep down to the depth of the channels for herdsmen and villagers to use. Ripe to disappear into when out with the hunt! One of the stories circulating is how last winter a pink-coated huntsman was found hours later seated on his horse, thoroughly stuck down one!'

'What do they hunt?' Derek pricked up his ears. He'd sent his charger and polo pony on ahead from Ambala.

'Jackals, with a bobbery pack the master of the Quetta Hounds is immoderately proud of.'

'Who's he?'

'Banker of the name of King.'

'Does Frank hunt?'

'Not any more – no time. He rides in point-to-points occasionally.'

'Do you?' asked Cara, knowing Pammie was a keen horsewoman.

'Did once in the women's event. Never again! Lethal. Just about broke my neck. The dust is so thick that unless

152

you're in the lead all the way the horse can't see the jumps. Here we are.' Pammie turned off at a house right at the end of Capper Road. On either side of the short drive flowered a carpet of small-stemmed single portulaca in shades of scarlet, rose-pink, purple, yellow and white. They revelled in the heat, tiny faces open to the sun.

'Oh how pretty!' Cara slipped out from the car. She followed Derek into the shade of the verandah where Nasrullah Khan, having come on several days ahead with the heavy sheesham crates, was waiting to greet them with a group of retainers.

'*Tikh hai*, Nasrullah?' Cara enquired.

'*Sub tikh hai*, memsahib.' Nasrullah Khan beamed all over his rotund face.

Carissa Brownlow had come a long way since her father had permitted her to plan the menus at Wick House with Cook. With fifteen months of Urdu lessons and experience of housekeeping in India behind her, she was now perfectly at home with the servants, could speak to them in their own language, and made sure that her orders were carried out properly and smoothly, for which she knew she was respected. She greeted the servants in turn with a word for each, first congratulating the spindly legged *mali* on the portulacas and thus winning his devotion. Next came the 'untouchable' *mehtar* engaged to do the lowly tasks of broom sweeping and emptying the thunderboxes; the *bhisti* who drew the water, heated it in kerosene cans over a wood fire behind the bungalow and poured it into the zinc tubs; and the all-important *khansama*. If the latter were a good cook, it made all the difference to their lives; a bad one, Cara had learnt, could be a disaster. The Brownlow memsahib would not put up long with a bad cook!

Together with the uniformed orderly Jit Singh, who had accompanied them on the journey in a servant's carriage, and was following up to the house with their heavy luggage in a couple of horse-drawn *tongas*, the complement of the newly enrolled Staff College student

153

was complete. Six servants, including the *syce*, for the old-fashioned bungalow was not one too many, and the *bhisti* and the *mehtar* were the only two who could be dispensed with in the houses with indoor plumbing. The retinue lived with their families in the compound at the back of the house in mud-plastered servants' quarters by the whitewashed cook-house. They were Cara's responsibility, a small village in itself, an extended family, and she relished the challenge of running the household on oiled wheels so that Derek could give his full concentration to his studies.

'Pretty bare of furniture, I'm afraid, but I've checked that the essentials are here, and you'll soon make it homely with your own bits and pieces if I know you. You're having lunch with us.' Pammie looked at her watch after showing Cara round the house. 'Come in about half an hour's time. Second road up, third house on left, No. 6. Frank'll be back; looking forward to seeing you. Where's Derek got to? Tell him to change out of uniform. No one wears uniform here. Slacks and an open-necked shirt.'

'Oh thank you, Pammie; you are a dear to have taken all this trouble . . .'

'You'd do the same for me.' Pammie brushed Cara's words aside. She drove off.

They washed and changed and walked up the road for lunch in the new DS Instructor's bungalow, which, in spite of what Pammie had said, was like a hot-house. Even the boys playing trains in their shrouded room appeared subdued by the heat, though their greeting of 'Aunt Cara' was enthusiastic enough.

Afterwards, when the two women were alone together over coffee, Pammie told Cara she was taking the boys up to Ziarat the following week.

'To a rondavel, and there's a swimming pool. You must come up when you're settled.'

'Rondavel?'

'Yes, those round straw huts the natives use in Africa. Someone after leave in Kenya had the bright idea of building them in the hill station as holiday homes attached to the hotel. The boys love it; dress up in war-paint as Zulus and brandish assegais.'

'You look as if you could do with the change. I notice you pecked at your food at lunch.'

'I'm having another baby.'

'*Four*. Help, Pammie. Are you pleased?'

'I wasn't to begin with. I was furious. *Through* a Dutch cap. There's Quetta water for you!'

'What do you mean? The drinking water from the catchment area?'

'Not necessarily. Any water. Irrigation water if you like from the Hanna Lake through the skin. That's the latest scandal. An orgy!'

'Tell me.' Cara was agog.

'The Indian chemist we all go to in the bazaar let it out. He's a Christian, and it went against his principles.'

'*What* went against his principles?'

'The film. It seems that not so long ago when half the Hanna Lake had dried up, there was a full moon party up there from the cantonment, gramophone playing, food, drink. The participants danced on the mud-cracked surface in their birthday suits to the strains of the latest blues.'

'I can't believe it.'

'True. Booze flowed and the party developed into undisguised sexual postures and cavortings which some idiot was fool enough to film for his own private erotic benefit. Several senior officers are said to be compromised. Horrified at what he had developed in his darkroom, the poor little chemist took the snaps straight to the AGG's and demanded a private audience. As in all good democracies he got one with the highest man in the state. Heads are about to roll at any minute, they say.'

'And they believe it's got something to do with Quetta water? Ridiculous!'

'Not so ridiculous. Look at *me*. You wait, my girl. Ordinary law-abiding people let themselves rip up here. The atmosphere is as electric on moonlight nights in summer as it is lit with static in winter. Our Commandant's wife, Mary Finlayson, who you will meet tomorrow – I've arranged a coffee party for the female newcomers to meet the Staff wives – is pregnant for the first time in twenty-five years of marriage! She's forty-seven, and they are both blushing like mad about having recently celebrated their silver wedding anniversary. The gynae at the Military Hospital is pulling out all the stops for her. Says it's a record age for the hospital. He firmly believes it has something to do with the water and is having it analysed with the idea of bottling it and posting it off to infertile couples, I shouldn't wonder. I'm telling you this so's you know that Quetta should be good for your marriage, Cara, *very* good.' Pammie ended her diatribe with a significant look.

Encouraged by her friend's news and cheerful comments on the possibilities in swinging Quetta, Cara returned to No. 51 Capper Road while Derek went off with Frank to the Staff College to meet the other 'chaps' and learn the lay-out. She found her house hermetically sealed in the blistering afternoon. *Chiks* hung from the ornate eaves over the closed glass, the clerestory windows under the double roof in the high-ceilinged old house giving the only light. Cara lay down in her underclothes on the clean sheet covering the hard hair mattress of the army bed next to Derek's. It was very quiet; only the distant sound of a pi dog interrupted the heavy silence in the intense heat of the hottest time of the day when Quetta slept – all except those madmen up there preparing for the Staff College course. Frenetic Quetta my foot, Cara's eyes closed. Drugged more like.

In a few seconds she had drifted off . . .

She woke two hours later in a muck sweat, and, putting on her cotton dressing-gown, called for Nasrullah Khan to bring tea which he did in their set of green Gwalior pottery.

'Any breakages?'

'Soup tureen; coffee-pot, memsahib.'

'Blast, I packed it so carefully. Keep pieces, Nasrullah.'

'Pieces keep for Captain-sahib to mend.'

Feeling slightly more human after sipping her tea which, even so, had brought her out into a further sweat, Cara went into the bathroom, splashed herself with cold water, and returned to the bedroom to dress. She combed out her damp hair and tied it into a pony tail off her face and neck (with a ribbon rather than a bootlace!) and, pencil and pad in hand, set forth to take stock of her new home. She noted the large cracks from the earthquake down the inside walls that had been whitewashed over but had reappeared. Outside there were larger cracks which had been properly plastered up. By day, if another severe earthquake occurred it was considered that the occupants could escape in time, but by night the old houses were declared unsafe to sleep in. Hence the odd-looking tents she had spied on arrival in each garden. They were for use when it became too cold to sleep out.

Practically everyone in Quetta slept out in the hot weather, the beds being brought into the house by day. In fact at that moment, without any orders from her, Nasrullah and the *bhisti* were carrying Derek's and her beds out to the small lawn on one side of the bungalow near to the road and away from the servants' quarters.

The bearer busied himself making up the beds and tucking in the mosquito nets all round so that no mosquito would be lurking inside at night, while Cara opened a narrow door into the Wana hut in the front garden. 'Wana' was the name of a post on the North-West Frontier where tents had been permanently strengthened against the bitter cold. It was stifling inside from the sun beating down all day on the khaki canvas roof supported on two trusses lashed over six-feet-high mud-brick walls, and tied onto a surrounding wooden stockade, thus doing away with a central pole and giving more room. The concrete floor was bare, the hut empty of furniture, but it had a fireplace with a tin-capped chimney-pipe cut through a hole, the chimney sticking up outside at a rakish angle. The whole contraption looked rather like an outsize Peter Pan house. Ah, sleeping under the fabulous stars in summer. Sleeping in winter under canvas snug with lit fire, flickering flames casting dancing shadows on the tent top. No wonder – Quetta water!

Out in the garden again, Cara found a vegetable bed where spinach sprouted, and another patch where bunches of grapes were neatly tied to stakes. For the many vineyards about there was a winery. Quetta had everything – even its own heady wine. Surely in Quetta . . .

With darkness falling in Indian suddenness over the garden, glow worms and fireflies appeared as if by magic, and Cara felt a sensation of delight creeping up her spine. Her afternoon sleep had cleared away her tiredness from the journey, and the evening brought a faint waft of air to stir the limp curtains at windows now thrown wide open. She went into the two-bedroomed bungalow, one of which Derek would use as a dressing-room with his own bathroom. There were two living-rooms. He would have to use the dining-room as a study.

Though the bungalow was short of rooms, it was big in space and had an 'old' atmosphere. The many memsahibs who had lived there before her had left their touches in the garden and house as she hoped to leave her touch: the rose bushes, an extra tree, the luxuriant creeper that possessed the south side, the useful shelves in an alcove in the drawing-room. Many wives must have been loath to leave after their two years, and she had only six months in which to enjoy it. What would Quetta bring her? She wanted to have nothing to do with flirtations let alone orgies! She wanted only one thing from Quetta, and apparently it was the one thing that Quetta was best at.

Derek came back from the Staff College and dumped a mound of papers and pamphlets on the dining-room table.

'Like Uncle Tom's shack. No room for a meal,' Cara exclaimed.

'Look what I've let myself in for.' With a grimace Derek gestured at the pile.

'I've made a list of furniture to hire.' Cara sat down and sucked her pencil. 'And we'll need to buy a carpet or two.'

'Baluchi rugs are said to be good value. I'll come down with you tomorrow and we'll choose some after visiting the bank. What do you think I've gone and done, little woman?' Derek tipped back his chair and looked past her. He seldom looked at her directly. She had wondered at his diffidence when they had been engaged, and had thought that marriage would be a cure-all for that as well. Since, she had discovered that he was incapable of looking a woman in the eye through shyness. Even his own wife.

'What have you gone and done?' She smiled fondly at his profile.

'I've bought a 1930 Chev off a chap leaving. Gave it to me for a song.'

'Do you need a car here?' She was surprised. They had not had one in Ambala where they had bicycled everywhere as most people in India seemed to do.

'*I* don't. It's for your use. Quite a trek down to the bazaar and uphill on the laden return.'

'How super! Oh Derek . . . if only . . .' she hesitated.

'If only what?' he prompted.

'Did Frank tell you Pammie is having another baby?'

'Good God! That's a bit much, isn't it?'

'*One* wouldn't be too much. I so want one; and you . . . Derek . . . well, most of the time you're too . . .'

'It was that damned gun invention in Ambala. I'd so *nearly* got the calculations right. No time for that sort of preoccupation here.'

'Boy or girl?' her eyes sparkled.

'Don't mind which, little woman, as long as it's ours.' Derek actually flushed.

They had supper of greasy mutton chops that were as tough as any goat, with sloppy cabbage (which did not augur well for Cara's culinary standards) served by Nasrullah; and later, on that brilliant star-lit first night, Cara took Derek's arm and they walked to the edge of Capper Road lined with straggly neem trees. Here, beyond their garden, abruptly, the tarmac ended. Before their feet stretched the virgin stony desert, a few tracks taking off and disappearing into the void. The shadow of the great mountainous form of Murdhar – meaning 'the dead man', and so-called for its flattish summit depicting the profile of a prone face and figure – loomed distinct in the distance. Beneath it, in the near foreground, lay a tented army camp, lights twinkling, a burst of men's laughter heard in the hush of the still night. They could see the larger mess tent, a flagpole before it, and they heard the skirl from a lone piper sounding in plaintive cadences over the evening air. And with the sound Cara felt a faint stirring of memory of something past, something once related.

'They must be Scottish,' she said. 'I wonder who they are.' She did not mean it as a query, rather was she questioning her memory, but Derek took it as one.

In the same moment that sheet lightning cut through the summer sky to light up the camp in a flash of momentary brilliance, Derek's answer came to stun her with its shock-making revelation.

'They are the Jute-wallahs,' Derek said.

CHAPTER 13

The words left Cara speechless. She felt as if she had been struck dumb by the summer lightning. But Derek, believing the name 'Jute-wallah' would have no meaning to her, began to explain as they walked back to their garden. His words 'from Calcutta'; 'Auxiliary Force, India'; 'Gunner Artillery section'; 'two Field Batteries posted here for war-time training', mostly fell upon familiar ears had he but known it.

But he did not know it. He had been totally absorbed in his Staff College cramming during the short period Lance had been in Christchurch, and he was the sort of man whose concentration was such that when working he remained oblivious to anything else. When the exams were over, and he had removed his blinkers, played golf with Cara and asked her out for the first time since he'd met her six months previously, no one mentioned Lance Gardner to him, certainly not the Thornton parents. Why should they? Mr Gardner was gone and mercifully soon finished with as far as they were concerned. Why upset the apple-cart by unnecessarily mentioning that she had that late summer fallen head over heels in love with a most unsuitable Jute-wallah?

'Who told you . . . about them?' Cara managed to get out when undressing in the bungalow.

'I met their CO at the Staff College. Frank introduced us as neighbours. Said we were near ones being the last house at the end of the road!'

'What is his name?' Cara had to lick her lips to shape the question.

161

'MacCreath. Nice chap. Frank's asked us to dinner to meet them. He has a wife staying at the Chiltan Hotel; joins her from his desert camp for week-ends. They're unaccompanied of course.'

So they *were* the same Battery! Johnny and Joan MacCreath, Lance's great friends, who were to have welcomed her in Calcutta, put her up, he given her away, her marriage to have taken place from their home . . . all so strangely far from what had actually happened; all so long ago, yet it could have been yesterday they were planning it. Then, 'I am marrying the man of my choice.'

She had to ask it. She swallowed, and found herself trembling in her flimsy chiffon nightgown over which she threw her dressing-gown. Shuffling her feet into mule slippers she walked out with Derek to the brown lawn, each bed cocooned in its mosquito net.

'Did he mention any more officers?'

'No. Why?'

'I just wondered how many there'd be, if . . . I mean at the dinner.'

'Three to a section usually. Only the OC and his wife are coming with the Commandant and his lady, so I gather.'

'I see . . .' She did not know if Lance was in the Battery. He could have been posted somewhere else. He could well have not been posted at all but categorized as 'reserved occupation' since his promotion in the business.

One of his later letters to Christchurch had been written from Cossipore where he had been sent to investigate some problem in the jute mills; another had come from Dacca, a centre of the trade. The firm could well have refused to allow him to go, though she knew he would have made one hell of a fuss at not being able to train with his men. Lance with his Gardner ancestry would pull every known string to get himself on active service.

It was not the slightest use her fussing about whether Lance was in Quetta or not. She would find out soon enough when she met the MacCreaths. She could ask discreetly about the other officers without giving anything away. They would only meet her as 'Mrs Brownlow'. Lance did not even know that much. If they remembered that Lance's girl-friend was 'Carissa', they would not connect it with the 'Cara' at the dinner party.

If Lance *were* stationed there, she *might* bump into him about the place, but it was unlikely. Quetta was a large military station with hundreds of officers. The Staff College was only a small part of it, exclusive to themselves with their own dances, their own tennis courts, swimming pool and parties. He would not come up there; Major MacCreath as OC was paying a courtesy call on the Commandant when Derek had been introduced. If she did come across Lance it would most likely be at the Club down the road nearer to the town. That was where she and Derek would meet men from the other regiments, other units. Everyone joined the Club. She was to have pushed Derek into going to the Wednesday and Saturday dances. Now, on the very day of her arrival, everything had changed. Now she wouldn't push him. He would be only too glad *not* to go. He wasn't a dancing man.

Cara lay awake for a long time that first night in Quetta after the summer lightning had ripped away the protective cloak of matrimony she had wrapped around herself. Now that the possibility of meeting Lance again had erupted she became desperate to have a baby, the best defence of all. No man would look at a woman with lust when her belly was swollen from another man's seed! No woman could abandon herself to the man she had once loved when in her watered womb a child moved. She lay on her back looking up through the mosquito net into the magical black vault with its dancing, sparkling stars and steady glowing orbs of planets, and watched them slowly moving – the earth moving. She longed to share with her husband. How could he sleep so soundly that first night under the stars with the beauty of the heavens spread out above waiting for them to lie in each other's

163

arms? Oh husbands, she thought, dear ignorant British husbands, are they all the same with their quick release, all oblivious of a wife's need for more? What are foreign husbands like, Continentals, Spaniards, dark southern men? She could not specify what 'more' was, but she knew that there was more, much, much more, for she had experienced it that night in the Sun Inn in Somerset when she would have given herself to one man, died for him, and had felt it every day in the subsequent embraces.

Now that she was no longer a virgin, now that she knew 'all about it', she felt more unconsummated than before. This night, with the remembrance of Lance brought back so strongly, she was particularly bereft upon her lonely Quetta plain, tucked into a single cot with the mosquito net shrouding her solitude.

Derek had come into her bed that night because he had been reminded of the necessity, and he too would like a child. He slipped in and he slipped out to more important things: six solid hours sleep which was all he ever allowed himself after which his brain sparkled with technical inventions which fascinated him more than any urge in his loins could, an infrequent urge he rather despised. The short sleep was vital to his well-being. Bed never before midnight, and probably later here at the Staff College. Up with the dawn to ride before breakfast.

Cara awoke when he rose on their first full day in Quetta, and was surprised to find she had slept at all. She lay watching the dawn creep with rosy fingers over the bare hillsides, and heard the pipes . . . *damn the pipes!* She clenched her fists and determined she would have that baby even if she had to fight for it. It would be the most compelling motive of her life. Surely Quetta water would not fail her?

From then on, despite her determination, the possibility that she might meet Lance became the foremost thought in Cara's mind. The remembrance of him, first put away by the animosity in Christchurch together with the removal of his vibrant presence, and firmly buried by marriage, was born again in Quetta to haunt her. Every time she forgot him in the daily business of directing her life, she was reminded when she glanced from her house and garden across to the prone outline of Murdhar, and saw the Gunner camp-tops roasting in the bouncing heat haze. The nearest shade to the camp was one of *her* trees on Capper Road! Trucks daily came over bumping down the track, swallowed and followed by clouds of dust, hot tyres screeching up onto the contour of the tarmacadamed roads like melting treacle-syrup in the sun. Bronzed Scots box-wallahs, seated therein, grinned at her as they passed, and gave the thumbs-up sign at the sight of a red-head. How nice and friendly they were. How *could* her father have as good as told her 'box-wallah' was a dirty word; worse, how could *she* have believed him? None of what her father had said mattered out here. If snobberies had once existed, no longer were there such definite class distinctions, such colour prejudices. There were Indians on the course. Captain Gupta Singh lived next door to her at No.49, his wife gracing the Staff College in her lovely saris. There were Anglo-Indians who were popular and much sought-after for dinner parties, one of them a brigadier at HQ – and they were certainly *not* called half-castes! If Lance were here with an English wife, or an Indian wife (a pang stabbed through her; but why not? Let's face it, she was married. She did not expect him to remain faithful to her memory for the rest of his life, did she?), no one would give it a second thought. All that her father had said on the subject was not only prejudiced but derisory, and she had been gormless enough in England to let herself be blown off course. And now she was left . . . and there again were the damnable pipes . . .

How could she ever get away from the remembrance when first thing in the morning she was awakened by the sound that was perhaps awakening *him*, a sound that tore at her heart, the haunting, tear-jerking, nostalgic, penetrating sound of the skirl of a pipe playing the reveille?

Derek found the summons a pleasant way to start the day. For Cara the call was an instant reminder of someone she was trying desperately to forget, to obliterate for ever.

She snatched every moment she could with Derek. She rose with him, partook of *chota hazri*, dressed in shirt, jodhpurs and chukka boots, and with khaki topi on went round to the verandah where the *syce* held the horses ready for them to mount.

'I'm so glad I learnt to ride in the New Forest,' Cara said.

'You have a good seat.' But he failed to glance at her slim figure mounted on the polo pony. His mind was already on other matters.

It was the time Cara loved best in the hot weather when the day was young, the air alive with freshness, the sun rising behind Murdhar in casting rays that had not yet gathered their burning strength, but softly caressed the parched land. Sometimes they trotted the horses, hooves clattering against the stones, straight out into the countryside using the jeep tracks to the foothills, and paused on their mounts to look down upon the Jute-wallahs' camp with Quetta beyond to the south, Chiltan further west. In the pale diamond-sharp light of early morning they were able to pick out details which diminished great distances, while closer it was as if they wore magnifying glasses, each individual pebble standing out. Everything in Quetta was greater, bigger, hotter, colder, clearer, brighter, finer, sweeter – more bitter . . .

Often they rode in the other direction: up the Ziarat road to the riding-school where they exercised the horses over the jumps, galloped them on the track, and returned by a circular route to bathe, change and breakfast together. Punctually at eight-thirty Derek rode off on his bicycle to the Staff College. When he wasn't on an all-day exercise, he came back to lunch, had a quick afternoon 'kip' on his bed in the dressing-room where he was 'not to be disturbed', after which he worked in the dining-room,

166

and when she came to, they went to the Staff College by car, he to play tennis, she to swim in the pool. Sensibly Cara did not play tennis in the hot weather. She had heard about the woman who was carried off to hospital on the day of their arrival and had died of heat stroke in spite of being packed about with ice.

Most evenings were spent working, Cara putting up on brass rings suspended from poles the curtains the *darzi* had made sitting cross-legged before his sewing-machine on their verandah. They were of thick country cotton bought in the bazaar, cool green for the living-room, cool blue for the bedrooms.

'What do you think of them?'

'Fine. In winter you'll wish they were red for warmth!'

'Floor coverings next. Will you come to the bazaar and help me choose some?'

'You go, I've got one hell of a lot to read up.'

She went alone and bought beige *dhurries* that were large enough to cover the concreted floors and give the appearance of fitted carpets, which indeed some of the wealthier 'cavalry' wives installed. All the cavalry was now mechanized, the Guides in Quetta one of the last to pat their horses farewell in a grand final parade. The dark blue and red Baluchi rugs were placed before fireplace and beside beds. With their wedding presents of ornaments out on mantelpiece, silver on sideboard, cigarette boxes and ashtrays on occasional tables, table lamps which Derek fitted with two-point plugs to suit the old bungalow's ancient wiring, pictures on walls, flowers arranged – such straggly few as were left – the Brownlows were ready to return some of the hospitality they had received, predominantly from the Dangerfields.

Cara had duly met the Commandant and his wife – and the MacCreaths. Pammie, and Mary Finlayson, were already beginning to look nicely rounded. They exuded that inner glow motherhood apparently brought once morning sickness was over, and there was much talk between them about breast-feeding versus the bottle.

167

Joan MacCreath was also nicely rounded but from comfortable middle-aged spread. On introduction Cara had looked at the couple curiously and for a flicker of a moment thought she saw a kind of recognition in the stare from the major, though the thought left her as soon as it had come. How could he possibly connect Miss Cara Thornton with Mrs Cara Brownlow? He was nice, a big, braw Scotsman with a small military moustache. She wouldn't have minded being given away by him. Mrs MacCreath was nice too, a motherly person with grown-up children. She invited her and Derek to dinner at the Chiltan Hotel.

All dinner parties were formal at that time. Derek wore a dinner jacket, Cara one of her elegant long evening dresses from her trousseau. On both occasions she guarded her tongue, and on neither occasion did she sit next to Major MacCreath with the result that she never asked if there was a Gardner in the Battery. Afterwards she argued to herself that it was a good thing she had *not* asked. They would have said, 'Oh, do you know him?' to her embarrassment even if he *wasn't* here. Fate, Quetta water – what difference did it make if he were here or not here? None, absolutely none.

'Time we gave a dinner party now the new Mugh cook's installed,' Cara announced when they had been in Quetta a month.

'Go ahead, little woman,' Derek said from the dining-room table piled with work. She had fast learnt this was his stock phrase meaning she could do as she liked as long as she didn't bother him about it. 'Go ahead,' he'd say when she urged it was time to go to bed, 'I won't be long.' She was always asleep when he did come, and he never woke her. Once she had blatantly told him to, from which open invitation he had winced and turned away in some distaste. 'Oh hell!' he exploded now. 'Damned DS. Who the blazes do they think they are? Read that.' He pushed over a foolscap that had red-inked remarks scrawled all over it.

'"You have not read the question. Scrap it and start again,"' Cara read out. '"Military Appreciations: (1) The Aim. (2) Facts Affecting. (3) Action. You have made a most serious mistake here. Killed God knows how many of your own men. Careless work. Do again." I think that's rather comic,' Cara giggled. 'What's "UTCAA" stand for?'

'Uncle Tom Cobley and All. By the time I wrote that my patience had snapped. I could not think of one more bloody name to add to the GS Staff list. My DS didn't think it amusing. No sense of humour! Gave me the going over good and proper and told me not to fool around, the twerp.'

'Who is he?'

'Horrible little man in Tanks. The syndicate calls him the "Chink". DS treat us worse than they did at the Shop . . .' Derek growled, pulled out a fresh foolscap from his folio and resignedly started again.

'I'll ask the "Chink" to dinner, that'll melt him!'

It did. The dinner party was a success, the 'Chink' and his wife making up the eight with the Dangerfields and the Gupta Singhs. Predictably Derek worked afterwards.

He was there in the bed next to hers on the dry lawn when reveille woke them next morning, but she had no idea what hour he had come. Intensely she loved sleeping out. It was incredibly lovely, always new stars to see in the firmament. The 'Chink', become human, had given her a night chart, and, as the summer drew on she became quite knowledgeable about the tropical skies. Mosquitoes hummed outside the net; a jackal voiced his mournful adagio, the pack adding a skeletal chorus nearby. The few bunches of grapes left on the fast-drying vine were the attraction! Every day the devoted little *mali* watered the fruit, the roses, and the portulaca from the tap that was only turned on at certain periods daily. It was a losing battle in the garden.

They said there was no regular rainy season in Baluchistan, but there were storms, plenty of storms: summer storms, winter storms, sandstorms, snowstorms. What had happened to the summer storms of 1940? By now Hanna Lake was bone dry all over and declared a forbidden area, used only for manoeuvres, the sound of small-arms punctuating the air. No more orgies! Heads *had* rolled, including the head of the Anglo-Indian brigadier at HQ. Pammie said Anglo-Indians were highly sexed. Was . . .? Anyway the brigadier's head did not roll for long. He was far too valuable a fighting man, and he was posted to a formation in Iraq where the Germans were expected to advance at any moment.

There was something aphrodisiacal about the moon. Cara dreamed vividly of Lance when the full moon shone on her face. She was in his arms, aching with longing; she woke to find herself chilly in the early hours and pulled up the blanket Nasrullah had placed at the foot of the bed. The next night she put another blanket over the mosquito net to shade her from the erotic demands of the moon. The moon made the great urgent waves of erogenic impulses to splash and foam and writhe upon the soft beaches of the world – and withdraw, only to form again. So women writhed under its white-hot flooding, and men went *pagal*, as mad as the *khansama* had on the last course at No. 32 Capper Road. A Staff College student had come in from a full moon night exercise to find his wife and children slaughtered with a cutting knife in a blood-spattered room. The rest of the servants had fled in terror, none raising the alarm or daring to return to see if the memsahib and the *babas* were still living. No. 32 down the road had been gutted so that no one else should have to live there. One day a brand-new concrete earthquake-proof bungalow would arise. Would the ghosts of the white-skinned wife and her children continue to flit through the old garden on moonlit nights?

Cara did not know, she only knew the moon drove her mad with desire for a tall man she had not seen for nearly two years, and she covered her bed from its light. But the moon was cunning, its power not so easily deflected. It crept round and shone again upon her face. And once more Cara dreamed of Lance, and once again she was awakened by the skirl of pipes.

The moon was on the wane when the earthquake struck and the storm burst. Derek had not come to Cara since the first night, and punctually as usual her period came to depress her. She did not go riding that morning, and by then she saw that she would not conceive in the summer while sleeping in the open near the road. Derek had all along been tentative about the neighbours seeing them from across the street, about a figurative Peeping Tom spying from the servants' quarters. She had suggested they sleep in, and blast all earthquakes; after all they had no children and only themselves to lose. But Derek was a stickler for regulations, and they continued to sleep out, Cara pinning her hope on the Wana hut. In winter; in the warmth of the open fire; under the tent-top secure from prying eyes, surely . . . ?

She was lying in bed thinking these thoughts when a roaring sound assailed her ears like the approach of an express train, only no express trains came in or out of Quetta, merely chugging slow ones. She sat up on an elbow and, incredibly, uncomprehendingly, saw the house swaying. Her bed began to shake violently, the flimsy bamboo sticks bending, the net collapsing in a heap over her so that she felt like Peter Rabbit caught in Mr McGregor's fruit cage! Extricating herself from the folds she grabbed her dressing-gown, put it on, and stood on the lawn. The earth heaved under her bare feet as if a hundred giants down there in the bowels were tearing rocks apart for the sheer hell of it. The earth shivered and shuddered and went on shaking.

Servants came running in their undress from the go-downs. They stood together with the memsahib on the grass, frightened eyes watching the house sway: to left, to right, to left, as if made out of a spindly meccano set loosely bolted together, new apertures cracking in the house walls. The sound of crashing was heard from falling furniture within. A rope lashing broke loose from the Wana hut, and in a sudden wind appearing from nowhere it rose and wriggled like a captured snake held by its tail.

To Cara it was the most alarming moment she had ever experienced. She was not so much frightened for her personal safety or that the ground might split where she stood and engulf her and the servants, as from the acutely unnerving sensation of soil heaving underfoot. If the earth gave way what was there left for mankind, dependent on it for everything? The earth, the very ground, was all man had. In England, she, in common with its millions of citizens, had taken the solid earth for granted. Man could do dreadful things, kill, bomb, plunder, rape and murder, but the earth would still be there for him to stand upon unrepentant, kneel upon in supplication. To feel it rock, to find it was *not* dependable, but as unreliable, as devious, as untrustworthy as everything else, was an experience that changed outlooks, changed values more strongly than any conversion. Cara learnt that day that the earth was vulnerable, and that in the end there was only God – or nothing.

In under three minutes it was all over. No rumbles, no more shakes, no more sudden wind, practically no damage, the lawn, except for a few surprising mounds like molehills, as flat as before. She went into the house to dress, the servants to clear up and prepare breakfast. The only one to appear to be perturbed was Nasrullah. He was shaking like a leaf, the coffee cups in his hands rattling in their saucers. He did not like Quetta, neither earthquakes in summer nor snow in winter. Bearer and memsahib looked at one another, the significant thought in their eyes that was it not time the sahib returned?

Which way had he gone? Had his mount bolted at the onslaught and thrown him? Was he lying out in the countryside, bleeding, head bashed against a stone? Had man and beast been engulfed by a split-like *kareze* opening under them as had happened to the pink-coated huntsman?

'Are you there? Are you hurt?' Captain Gupta Singh stood in the driveway.

Cara went out to join her neighbour. 'We're all right. Your wife? Oh good. But I'm worried about Derek. He's riding.'

'Moderately severe earthquake. Bazaar most likely to have copped it. Derek is safe horse-riding, I am thinking,' the Sikh soothed with a flash of white teeth. They stood on a while in the driveway chatting about the earthquake.

'What's going on? What's all the fuss about, Gupta?' There was a clatter of hooves and Derek abruptly reined-in his charger. He dismounted and handed over to the *syce*.

'An earthquake, old boy, that is all.'

'Didn't you notice?' Cara looked wonderingly at Derek.

'No. Is breakfast ready?'

'I – I think so. You felt and heard *nothing*? There was a wind . . .'

'Not a whisper. Thanks for coming over, Gupta. Phew! It's hot.' Derek took off his topi and wiped his face with a khaki handkerchief. He walked into the house with his wife.

'Where did you go?'

'Out by the Jute-wallahs' camp. Met one of them riding and we went on together. Looks like a storm brewing. Often happens after an earthquake.'

'Who was he?' Cara asked, her heart in her mouth.

'The Jute-wallah? Didn't ask his name.' Derek beckoned for Nasrullah to pull off his boots.

'What did he look like?'

'Great God, I don't know. Like everyone else, I suppose. Now be a good girl and let me get on with dressing or I'll be late.'

She went into the dining-room and poured out the coffee. There was always an anti-climax with Derek. 'A good man to be with in an emergency.' Situation defused. No histrionics. No panic. Not even interested in hearing about what to her had been a traumatic exprience. He took everything in his phlegmatic stride. Maddening – comforting. For a second she had wondered . . . but no. Even unobservant Derek would have noticed that Lance looked different from 'everyone else'!

It grew darker and darker, and later that morning Cara had to switch on the lights in the house only to have them cut out when, with a crack of cymbals, jagged vertical lightning flashed in blue fire over Murdhar, and in a reverberating thunder of drums the summer storm burst. Cara went onto the verandah and stood there, the wind catching at her skirt and blowing her hair. She watched the first heavy splodges of wet fall like oil drops onto the impenetrable dry sandy soil. With sensual delight she sniffed the unforgettable, wonderful, musty smell of rain falling on a parched land, and in a gesture of relief from tension she held out her hands to feel and catch the cup of blessed moisture.

And the rain hit the rocky mountains with a showering deluge which gushed in a turbulent flash flood over the foothills to stream into the deep *karezes*. The brown river swirled and flowed like a tidal wave into the Hanna Lake. Ditches were opened, and No. 51 Capper Road's scurrying *mali* joyfully directed the water into the dry flower beds in time to save the shady trees, the old rose bushes – the succulent vines.

CHAPTER 14

'Quetta water doesn't work for me,' Cara said to Pammie in October when there was a nip in the air though the sun was hot by day, and beds were moved into the Wana hut, and nothing had changed.

The weather was perfect for tennis and golf, one or other of which game Cara played in the afternoons with Derek, or, when Derek was too busy, with a host of new friends. Scandals abounded in the rejuvenating air. Some officers had got raging drunk in the Club and broken up the bar, their membership promptly suspended. The latest scandal on everyone's lips was that two men in the same regiment had swopped wives and were openly living with each other's in their erstwhile spouse's respective quarters. There was a frightful furore. The quartermaster was said to be wringing his hands not knowing what to do about it; neither apparently did the CO who was in a position to ask any officer who became involved in a divorce to resign his commission. But this was war-time. Nobody was *allowed* to resign; and apparently in this case there was no question of divorce!

'Give yourself a chance to let it work. You've only been here a bit over three months,' Pammie answered sensibly.

'How can it work when we hardly ever try, not even in a Wana hut snuggling down under blankets?'

'Well, my dear, you'll just have to go all out and seduce the man!'

'I can't, Pammie. I'm not that sort of person. He gives me not the slightest encouragement. Rather the reverse. I thought at one time there was something wrong with *me*. Now I think he's just not interested in sex, that's all.'

'Try getting him blind drunk.'

'I *have* tried.' Cara's voice showed her desperation. 'I dragged him to a party, ordered double whiskies for myself which I poured into his glass when he wasn't looking.'

'Well?'

'He *was* a bit drunk. I had to support him to bed where he promptly went to sleep fully dressed! I felt awful at what I'd done. He said next day he thought the booze had been doctored for a prank by some idiotic fool.' She caught Pammie's eye and they broke out laughing. 'Thank God I've got you to laugh with.' Cara wiped her eyes.

'There're too many children in the world,' Pammie consoled.

'That's all very well for you, bursting at the seams,' Cara grumbled, and proceeded to show the *darzi* they shared how to run up some decent maternity dresses for the DS's wife.

Most of Cara's mornings were taken up at mah-jong parties with the Commandant's wife Mary, with the 'Chink's' wife, or with Pammie. She enjoyed the game, liking the look and feel of the ivory pieces bought off the Chinaman who periodically visited their quarters with embroideries, jade ornaments, lacquer finger bowls and coffee sets, one of which she bought to replace their broken pot. The days passed quickly in this fashion and in the evenings when there wasn't a dinner party to go to or to give, when there wasn't a cocktail party or a dance, there were always the letters to write home.

Once a month letters arrived regularly from her mother. Doreen expressed herself better on paper than she did by the spoken word, and through them Cara came to understand more objectively her mother's dilemma and her father's character. The news from Christchurch was not good, and she worried about her parents, though not at first for Bobby.

Soon after the outbreak of war the previous year, the expected evacuees had arrived on the doorstep of Wick

House clutching packages of clothing, gas-masks over small shoulders. There were four allotted to the big house, and they caused havoc right from day one.

Not even Rosie, who tried to be kindness itself remembering the homesickness she had herself suffered when first entering domestic service, could control them. They were given a room each, yet the brother and sister insisted on getting into the same bed in Cara's old room to growls of 'incest' from Charles, who had on arrival inspected heads for nits and found lice. The two other boys in the big spare room of sprung mattresses, wet their beds with stunning regularity. The children tore up by the roots Field's prize chrysanthemums, and threw stones at the conservatory, shattering the glass, the garden boy having to be rescued gibbering with terror from the coal bunker to which he had fled. Even Cook's delectable dishes were not appreciated. 'Too fancy, mum. Tripe an' onion's wot we wants.'

Cook could take no more and removed herself lock stock and barrel to the north of England. A week later Rosie was called up to do land work in her village near Dorchester, where she married her childhood boy-friend before he set off for France. Mr and Mrs Field also left at about that time to be near their grown-up family in Cornwall. That left the goofy garden boy and Ford.

For some confusing days Doreen struggled on. Then Charles had a minor stroke and was ordered to bed by Dr Walker where the Brigadier was waited on hand and foot by Ford. Mercifully soon the evacuees were taken into care by the council together with the garden boy who had gone completely to pieces without kindly Mrs Field to look after him. He was found another foster home and was given the job of tending the garden round the ruins of the old castle. In time he became famous locally for the display of flowers he created.

Bobby was posted back from Egypt early in the war, and arrived in the middle of all this upset. He saw the impossibility of his parents coping without domestics – other than Ford – in the large dwelling, and persuaded his father to put

177

Wick House on the market. Later, after he and Susan were married from the Langley home near Exeter, the parents moved to a three-bedroomed house by St Catherine's Hill on the Salisbury road. The bottom having fallen out of the property market with the war, barely enough money was raised to pay for the small house. Bobby by then was not able to get away to help in the move, and it was Susan who, though pregnant, came to sort out the furniture, most of which excess, and all the heads and skins, was given away to the Red Cross to sell for the war effort. Cara's trunk and her escritoire were put in store.

Both Susan and Dr Walker wrote to tell Cara the local news and how beautiful old Square House with its large surgery and sunny walled garden, the seat of two family doctors for fifty years, father and son, a gracious house that had been such a feature of the High Street, had had its railings ripped away, the Adam fireplace, friezes, ceilings and doors removed, and was now a shell waiting to be demolished. The good doctor was practising from a small house in down-town Purewell.

On receipt of these letters, and since the Dunkirk pictures in the press of weary, unshaven, exhausted soldiers wrapped in blankets walking down the gangplanks and arriving defeated men in all but spirit, it came home to Cara with a vengeance that she had idiotically rushed into matrimony for nothing more than for the sake of leaving home. If she had been able to think straight at the beginning of 1939, she would have seen that conflict with Germany was inevitable and that it would bring an end to her parents' way of life. She was not a coward. She had not come to India to get away from war or to save her skin, but in the turmoil of her emotions at the time she had failed completely to consider the consequences of her act. Now, rather than playing endless useless games of mah-jong, rather than luxuriating in sport, riding, parties and dances, she wished she were in England and thoroughly involved in the war situation with her family and friends. She felt guilty that she was leading a lotus life in Quetta instead of being there, and she felt resentful.

Cara resented that it was Susan who had come to the rescue, Susan who had sorted through the possessions in Wick House, Susan who had decided what to keep and what not to keep, for her mother would have been in too much of a dither to make up her mind one way or the other. Susan wrote they had stored her trunk and her escritoire. Was that *all*? What about the old books in the bookshelves – the Sleeman and Tod? What about her father's memorabilia? What about hers and Bobby's toys in the attic for the next generation? As a daughter-in-law she was sure Susan had done her best, but it was she who *should have been there*.

Britain lay isolated in Europe, the beleagured island severely under attack from the air with terrible loss of civilian life, and threatened by an armada from the sea, Bobby in dire danger.

That night Cara dreamed of Bobby flying his Spitfire, and in one of those strange, fairly frequent, coincidences, an air-mail letter arrived from him next day.

'Somewhere in Kent'
1 October 1940.

Dear old girl,

Sorry I haven't written for ages, and if this letter is a little strange, it is from sheer exhaustion, so forgive me! We live an odd life over here. My job occupies very nearly 100 per cent of my mind and leisure. I am only writing to you now as the powers-that-be have pulled us out to rest and refit, having sent a squadron from the north to relieve us.

It must seem very far off to you in your outpost of the Empire, but here in our small island, twenty miles from enemy-occupied territory, the war is very real, too real, and the intensive fighting over Kent during July, August and September had to be experienced to be believed. My squadron of Spitfires fought in the Blitz for those three months – a lifetime – at the end of which we had accounted for seventy

179

enemy aircraft for the loss of eight pilots killed and five wounded. Not bad, eh? A nerve-wracking business, one excitement after another exacting every ounce of mental and physical effort that I possess. We got far too little sleep since we were doing night patrols as well. My squadron is young in years – the average age is only twenty-three – but by now we are all old in experience. Towards the end some of the younger members were too tired to eat. Some of my pilots cracked up temporarily . . . we were fighting two, three and sometimes four times in a day, and then at night. Most of our operations took place over the Channel, the Dover-Ramsgate area, where we ran into enemy fighters. Once we intercepted a daylight bombing raid of about sixty enemy bombers escorted by the same number of fighters. We were ten strong that day. I lost my Spitfire and baled out over Tonbridge, and one of my flight commanders brought his aircraft back with so many cannon holes in it that it was nothing short of a miracle that it flew at all.

Shortly after I baled out our base was bombed. We managed to knock down thirty or forty of the bombers. Squadrons from other stations accounted for many more. I have never seen such a sight in my life. There must have been a good 500 aircraft in the air at the same time in one mad mêlée: ack-ack – tracer – cannon shells – aircraft in flames. A Junkers bomber blew up in front of me. Our base was a mass of flames, and the countryside was a series of fires, bombed houses and burning aircraft. I have seen Hell, and do you know, old girl, we were operating from the battered base *that same evening*!!

I could go on, but enough of that. I couldn't exist without Susan. We are absurdly happy. We live not a mile from the aerodrome. Our nights (when I am there!) are usually disturbed by gunfire and bombs. I once told you we are both fatalists. It is the only way to keep going. I am glad you are out of it, old thing, and happily married to Derek, but in a way I wish you were here to experience history. It concentrates the mind wonderfully! How long will this madness go on for? Derek will be in the thick of it, I bet, after the course, also Lance wherever he is if I know his Jute-wallahs! Poor fellow; he really did fall badly for you. It is up to our generation who survive to make another war impossible. If we don't we shall go on and on inheriting this bloody affair.

A week, and I shall be back in the seat of my beloved machine. God they are superb. Susan sends love and will write. Parents seem OK, Pa better.

God bless,

Bobby.

Lost in the war-time world of England, lost in admiration for Bobby fighting in the air, Cara went out into the garden and stood looking up at the quiet sky over Murdhar. In England the sky was full of screaming aircraft and blobs of smoke, Bobby up there twisting and turning in his little Spitfire, shot at, evading, on fire, baling out . . . thank God, oh thank God he had survived the Blitz. Nothing surely could be as bad again as the Blitz.

The sound of a revved engine impinged on her reverie. Mindlessly Cara's eyes looked across to where a jeep changed down to breast Capper Road from the track. An officer was driving, an orderly sitting next to him and holding onto the door for dear life as they bumped over the hump and sped past the house. She recognized the officer instantly from the set of his head upon his shoulders. He did not look her way, and in a flash he was gone.

She stood on in her garden and watched the car turn onto the main road towards the town. She watched the dust from the jeep billowing until there was no more dust, nothing more to be seen. She stood there staring for minutes on end at where the dust had been. Then she went back into the house.

Now I have no need to pluck up courage to ask the Mac-Creaths, Cara thought. Now I have the evidence of my own eyes. Now I know the man whose love I threw away *is* here. Bobby is in his fight. Lance is racing past to his war. Derek will soon be gone. What am I doing leading this useless life without even bearing a son to replace a man killed? I am only an adjunct to Derek. I am not necessary to him. Where I ought to be is in England doing war work, keeping an eye on my parents. Where I *ought* to be is at home – waiting for Lance . . .

The shock of seeing Lance galvanized Cara into action. There was a thrift shop starting up at the corner of Chiltan Road to raise money for the troops. She offered her services and went three mornings a week. She went to the Mission Hospital, and was given the task of grinding up powders in the dispensary. She made herself generally so useful there that she was soon allowed to do VAD work in the *zenana* wing. She accepted every chance that came her way for tennis and golf, and every evening invitation whether Derek could come or not. And she herself became a part of the frenetic life, rising early to ride, working flat out, playing games hard, typing out Derek's notes, late to bed at night. But she did it for a different reason from that of most people in Quetta. She did it to banish Lance who was so tangibly near, his tall figure so incredibly dear.

In the ensuing weeks Cara saw Lance twice but managed to avoid him on both occasions. The first time he was playing tennis in a mixed doubles on the Staff College courts, which venue suprised her until she took in that he was a guest. His host was a man she had met who was on the same course as Derek, a regular, one Captain Paddy Cahill who had a reputation for wildness and womanizing. The latter's partner was a blonde, an 'abandoned woman' in every sense of the word known locally as the 'Blousy Bint', said to share her favours with quite a few. Lance was playing with a flashy looking woman with red nails, jangling earrings and chunky charm bracelet that surely must have got in the way of her strokes.

Next, Cara saw Lance at the Club dancing with the same woman in a close embrace, her taloned fingers holding him round his neck, he smiling his lazy smile down at her. Cara's reaction to the sight appalled her. That smile was *hers*, only for her! She could not *bear* to see him with another woman after all that had been said. So she *did* expect him to remain faithful to her memory all his life! Complete idiot.

Again Cara beat a hasty retreat to the Chev and home, leaving her party without excuse. None was required. People often disappeared for a time and re-appeared, some never returning the same evening.

'You're back early.' Derek looked up from his work, his eyes bloodshot with strain. 'Dance no fun?'

'I've got a headache. Rather wild lot tonight being Saturday. Paddy Cahill fell full length on top of the Blousy Bint on the dance floor. Even she didn't look too pleased about *that*! They were with another man, and a woman whose name I don't know.'

'Fast lot. Shouldn't have anything to do with Cahill if I were you.'

'Oh, why not?'

'Drinks like a fish; uses foul language and boasts about his conquests. At our last mess dinner he quite disgusted me with his vulgar horse-play. Pity. Got plenty up top if he'd care to use it – said to have sailed through his exams, instead of which he became a *cause célèbre*, and was removed from his regiment for being a bad influence on the subalterns.'

'What happened?'

'His CO banished him somewhere for a year to sober up, and subsequently, rather than have him back, packed him off here with the threat of sending him to "Grass Farms" if he didn't make good.'

'What on earth's that?'

'Term stands for the cutting of *bhoosa* fodder. Remounts or RIASC, postings which are considered a come-down after having been in a Punjab regiment, though I don't suppose Cahill would mind.'

'Why not?' she asked again.

'Money. They give more pay. He's up to his eyes in debt. Got several horses up here; hunts, rides in all the point-to-points, plays polo, gambles, never does any work . . . that's enough of that. Better let me get on with mine.'

'Come to bed, Derek; your eyes look tired.'

'Won't be long.' Derek resumed his reading.

She went over to the Wana hut and began to undress. It was chilly in there. November now. Pammie had told her it was a bitterly cold month. There had been little autumn, not as they knew it at home, though she'd heard there was a short, stunningly beautiful spring. She must tell Nasrullah to build up the fire more. He looked grey himself. He came from the lush tropical Ganges basin and was not used to cold. He had asked leave to go back home when the Captain-sahib left, and she and Derek had agreed. He would find her someone else when the time came. She'd be sorry to see Nasrullah Khan go, but an ill or unhappy servant was no good.

Cara climbed into bed and found the hot water bottle lukewarm at her feet. She listened to the howling wind tearing at the tent flaps, and thought of Lance and the blood-nailed woman – together.

The icy Khojak wind of winter swept through the Pass from Afghanistan with no windbreaks to halt or deviate it on its way across the treeless plain. She and Derek kept reasonably warm in the old bungalow by piling on clothes and stuffing rolled army blankets against doors to abate draughts. In the evenings they sat huddled round the open fire, an oil stove at their backs which oozed kerosene fumes. She poured olive oil in her bath to keep her skin from cracking. Soon it would snow. It would feel warmer when the wind dropped and it snowed – so said Pammie, her fount of information, but no help in her predicament. No one could help her over that. She could tell no one about Lance.

It was apparent to Cara now that she had seen Lance twice in the company of Paddy Cahill, the Blousy Bint, and the woman with the long red nails, that they stayed together in their foursome, good friends most likely as she and Bobby, Susan and Lance had been on the trip to Exeter, yet how dissimilar in behaviour. She and Susan had been properly circumspect about their feelings; here the two women concerned overtly flirted with the men. They were well-known types in Quetta, uninhibited, easy to get on with, sophisticated married women who had a sexy way with them and who as grass widows threw conventionality out of the window. Mostly their husbands guessed what went on in their absence. Some minded. Some did not. Some women (the Blousy Bint was said to be one) suffered from nymphomania which was regarded as a bit beyond the pale by most men – but obviously not by Captain Cahill! Cara, though she did not condone their way of life, had a sneaking envy of them. At least those wives knew what they wanted and went out and got it instead of putting on a false face and enduring interminable frustration.

What did puzzle her, though, was why Lance was involved in that set. It was so unlike the Lance she had known to trifle in dalliances, to go along with stupid school-mentality horse-play. To have become a close friend of the notorious Paddy Cahill he must have changed a great deal from the romantic man who with pride spoke of his antecedents, those royal princesses Nissa of Delhi and Mulka of Oudh, even if the stories had been a figment of his imagination, as her father believed. If she, Cara, were a betting woman she would lay a heavy wager that he had told none of the 'fast' lot about *them*!

Why was he so changed? Could it be because of the hurt she had caused him? Was *she* to blame for putting him into the arms of the red-nailed woman?

CHAPTER 15

Lance could not comprehend let alone analyse the effect of the cable in that January of 1939. Rational thought was impossible. It was a body blow that left him stunned.

He suffered alone a depth of anguish he had not known existed; nor, if he had, would he have believed himself capable of such a degree of hurt over being what was a commonplace occurrence – rejected suitor.

For twenty-four hours of blind darkness he sat hunched on a hard chair in his bachelor quarters. He neither ate nor slept nor spoke when his anxious Goanese bearer de Mello came in from time to time, but sat on, broad shoulders spasmodically heaving, the scalding tears forced from closed eyelids falling unheeded and unnoticed onto his knees. Then, as a man reeling from a physical blow, automatically he bathed, shaved, dressed and plodded grey-faced to the office.

The love he had poured out, Cara had thrown back in his teeth, conveyed in the stark words of the cable tapped out in Morse across the continents by unconcerned hands. How could it be that the girl he idolized was capable of such blatant cruelty? As he had once written to her: ' . . . men have more delicate hearts than women . . . you cannot go on writing that you love me and you do not love me unless you want to destroy me'. Underneath the open, candid exterior that he could have sworn was natural and genuine, was there hidden a vampire? Had she indeed set out to *destroy* him, with cunning first capturing him by her profession of a desire

186

she could scarcely contain, then by her letters of vacillation, then bluntly end it all in this heartless fashion?

Had he been like most men in the same position, he would have cursed and fulminated and declared she was a no-good bitch not worth one wink of lost sleep. He would have taken himself off for consolation to the courtesans of Calcutta where a comfortable mama would have seen to it he had all he needed. But Lance was not a person who could be so easily relieved. He was an emotional man of mixed blood who was only part the leathery Scot, and in silence he turned in upon himself, only once exposing his innermost feelings.

'. . . the betrayal,' he bared in confidence to Johnny MacCreath when outwardly he had recovered some balance, 'oh God, man, the bitter, bitter betrayal! I was certain she had the courage of her faith in me to wait for years if need be. I gave my whole heart in trust to her as I have never given myself before and will never do so again for the scar she has left on my soul. I *believed* her, and *in* her. She was to me the most beautiful creature on this earth, without guile, innocent of carnal knowledge. Her kisses were intoxicatingly fresh – sweetness from a pure spring. I could have taken her, but I would not do so. There was only one way between us. The way I wanted, the way I thought she wanted – as my wife, one I would have stayed faithful to all my life. Though she was unconscious of it, there was a certain aura of passion in her body, seen in her walk, glimpsed in her eyes, waiting to be roused – by *me*, Johnny, only by *me*! It makes me sick . . . another . . .' Lance shook his dark head violently as if to kill the thought. 'I told her we would be happy, incomparably, peerlessly happy. She believed it too, agreed it was there between us . . . And then, for some reason she would never fully reveal – something to do with her father – she chose to throw it all away, and in the process she has destroyed me.'

'Everyone has a freedom of choice, Lance, even such a bag as yon fickle woman. Heavens be, mon, you're not *destroyed*. Broken hearts mend quicker than broken bones. You put too high a value on her. There are plenty of other women as gud, better . . . I can think of several here in Calcutta waiting to fall into your arms, you good-for-nothing masculine god!'

How could undemonstrative, taciturn Johnny understand the unseen link that had drawn him to Cara and she to him, the mutual attraction that could not be explained in words of reason, in their case two romances of a bygone age somehow entwined in the love affair? The magic had happened before in his family, and he believed he had inherited the miracle in Cara. He had been mistaken, and yet, and yet, for all that his mind said, his heart went on telling him he had *not* been mistaken. That was what was destroying him: the conflict between what his reason told him, and what his heart told him . . .

So worried did Johnny MacCreath become as the weeks passed that at one period he became afraid for his friend's reason. It was his wife Joan who suggested a solution.

'Vee-able idea,' Johnny exclaimed, and without further ado set in motion the complicated wheels for Lance to join a small trade mission about to go into Tibet.

Tibet was in those days a closed country little known and little understood by the world that had never been there, the Chinese threat on the horizon no bigger than a small shadow over the remote state. Few foreigners had been fortunate enough to obtain permission to cross her rugged borders, and by the spring of 1939, when the snows in the high mountains had melted sufficiently to allow for easier passage, Lance, briefed by Government Intelligence (all trade missions had their reasons), was one of the few ready to go. The many arrangements he had to make diverted his mind from his personal trauma as they were meant to. He had to see that the stores, the bedding, cooking pots, kit, were prepared and made up into pack loads; and a bag of money, together with permits to enter Sikkim and the forbidden country, collected.

For the most part the map he took with him was blank, 'unsurveyed' printed across large areas, but that was immaterial to Lance. He was not an explorer or mountaineer; he would be going on the main route through Gyantse to Lhasa with a party of ten or so from various walks of life. He would tag along behind an experienced political officer and a sapper sent up to report on repairs needed for the Gyantse Agency building which, according to reports, was falling to pieces. In the party foregathering at Gangtok was a subaltern sent (he was told) like him at short notice.

The night mail took Lance from the steam-bath of Calcutta to Siliguri in the foothills of the Himalayas where already the air was more fresh. Box-wallah and subaltern disgorged with their packs from different carriages. The men, in the way of the British abroad, eyed each other for a while at a distance on the platform. Then the lanky subaltern strolled up.

'You on this mad trek?'

'Yep. Gardner is the name.' Lance held out a hand to the thin angular man who nearly matched him in height. He noted with amusement his exaggerated blond cavalry moustache.

'Paddy Cahill. On the face of it I'm going to relieve another subaltern in the platoon garrisoning the Agency; in truth I'm being sent up to the rarefied heights to cool my heels.'

Lance responded in kind to the man he gauged to be about the same age as he. 'On the face of it I'm going as representative of my jute firm. In truth I'm sent up to get over an affair of the heart.'

'Strewth. Rarefied height used to cool my thirst and your fork! Bloody boring it's going to be too: no pukka booze, no women. Plague it all.'

'Can't imagine Tibet being boring.' Lance smiled at the plain speaking.

189

'Faith, I wager the women make a bee-line for you.' Paddy's eyes flickered over Lance's good looks. 'Don't tell me you are *serious* over a skirt?'

'I was,' said Lance sombrely; 'she married somebody else.'

'Should be damned grateful to be let off the hook.' Paddy gave a cynical laugh. 'Bloody foolish to get involved in the first place, old cock. I prefer to buy my women when I want 'em. When I can afford it I may set up a mistress, in the meantime . . . found a damn good *randi-khana* in Lahore not too far from the regimental base in Jullunder. Good for a quick week-end.' He rumbled on while Lance, taking little notice, checked his baggage.

A waiting car took them up a winding road between green forests to Teesta bridge over a torrent of porridge-coloured water at the Sikkim border, where frontier guards carrying rifles scrutinized their passes before waving them on. The road ended at Gangtok, the capital of Sikkim, a town sprawling over a ridge of hills, the Residency situated on a promontory in a dramatic spot. There they found the rest of the party assembling.

The British Trade Agent, acting for the Resident then on furlough, welcomed them and introduced them all round. He ordered drinks.

'Good view in which to enjoy my last bit of liquor.' Paddy gazed at the mist-clung valley below with its surmounting grass-covered hills clothed in clumps of shrubs and conifers. He sucked appreciatively at his gin.

'I've packed a bottle of whisky. You can have a slug every now and then to keep you sane,' Lance offered.

'There's no ban on drink; merely a matter of priorities in transport. We've got a case going to the mess in the Agency.' The British Trade Agent misunderstood Paddy's remark.

'Nevertheless I shall use the opportunity to go dry, and my friend Gardner here is taking the opportunity to stay celibate. Not so me. What are Tibetan dames like?'

'Charming, grubby and scarce.' The British Trade

Agent showed in his tone of voice he did not care for the frivolous words of the Punjab Rifles officer. 'You must know the Tibetans are polygamous, several brothers sharing one wife. Better not try any funny stuff with the women or you'll end up with your throat cut. To business, gentlemen. You start the day after tomorrow. I'll arrange mounts for you.'

'I prefer shank's pony,' Lance aired.

'No one who can afford to ride walks; loss of face, y'know.' The British Trade Agent came down heavily on the young man's ignorance. 'Believe me, when you get up to the plateau you'll see how invaluable the sturdy little beasts are across country.'

Next day Lance and Paddy paid out money and were issued with Mongol mounts, shaggy animals with rounded noses, hair covering eyes like uncombed fringes. A straight-haired Bhutani bearer-cum-interpreter of the name of Pasang was engaged. Lance tested out his new boots on an afternoon stroll and wondered how he had ever thought he could walk the 180 miles to Gyantse let alone on to Lhasa. Paddy, being more used to marching, seemed to be better equipped feet-wise in a well-worn pair, and early the following morning they set off with the party in a string of pack-mules carrying food, spare clothing and equipment.

The first day's trek, said to be an easy one to acclimatize the Europeans, was a short walk to Karponang, a thousand feet above Gangtok, though by the time they had digressed up and down innumerable ridges they felt they had covered twice the allotted distance. It started to rain, and Lance, who to begin with had squelched along in his boots to soften them up, admitted defeat and looked round for his mount only to find Pasang had sailed ahead on the beast.

Wretchedly he limped on in a solid curtain of rain, the track they were on running a watercourse. When at the lunch-time stop Pasang was located, the mount returned to his master, Lance thought the worst was over, only to find himself miserably cold when seated on the hard saddle, the rain sluicing off his trilby hat and down his neck, leeches attaching themselves to any spare bit of flesh. With the pony on a loose rein picking its way up and down over the stones, visibility in the mist but a few yards, Lance had nothing to do other than to think of Cara being ravished by her husband in a warm dry bed. So much, he thought, for Johnny's diversionary tactics. For two pins he'd throw himself pony and all over the *khud*.

He began to feel better after he'd dried himself out in the *dâk* bungalow at Karponang in front of a roaring fire, and eased his blistered feet out of his boots and into the soft leather *chupplis* in his kit. With the rest of the party he tucked into a haunch of goat roasted by the *chowkidar* of the bungalow on a spit over a charcoal fire, and he found himself hungrier than he'd been since the advent of the cable. He had a tot of whisky – which Paddy stoically refused – and slept better that night than he had for months.

The next day the cavalcade set off early on the main route to Gyantse via Yatung in the Chumbi Valley. On the narrow track they met traders coming down and stopped to exchange news. They were travelling caravans carrying merchandise from China in *yakdan* trunks on yaks which could carry loads of up to 150 pounds on their wide backs.

With his feet under his thick socks well swathed in sticky plaster, Lance and Paddy walked a path treacherous with loose stones which slithered and plunged thousands of feet below into the abyss. It was tough going, wind coming short from the unaccustomed height, Paddy for once silenced of his blather, his bony face concentrating on every footstep, and each breath. They and the Sapper toiled on ahead of those less fit, the political officer bringing up the rear and encouraging the civilian stragglers. They traversed a giant rhododendron forest, the sun coming out from high clouds to shine down between the boles of deodar trees. The river they had crossed not so long ago wound its turbulent way miles below in a ravine.

That evening at Changu they spent the night in a bungalow by a natural lake of great beauty, the party taking their evening meal on the verandah. The Sapper, a keen ornithologist, watched through binoculars snow buntings preening and pecking at the edge of the shallows, and duck flighting in a whisper of beating wings.

'Look, lemmings,' Lance drew the Sapper's attention.

'Intoxicating air,' Paddy said drinking it deep into his lungs. He looked disparagingly at the whisky of the others.

'I must warn you,' the Sapper lowered his binoculars, 'the platoon stocks nothing stronger than beer.'

'No matter.' Paddy waved a hand. 'What's the mess like?'

'Small but comfortable. All are hutched in the Agency together with a doctor. One part consists of the officers' quarters, another the lines and the Agency offices. Outside you have football ground and a tennis court. Hilarious.'

'Why so?'

'The ball never seems to be on the ground, that's why,' the Sapper chuckled. 'It sails around like a child's balloon. You a polo man? Then you'll enjoy your term here. The escort have regular matches against the local pig-tailed gentlemen who learn to ride before they can walk, and believe you me they can hit a pretty hard and shrewd ball.'

Before he fell asleep that night, with a start Lance realized he had not once thought of Cara all day. The next day he did not once think of her either. He was too absorbed in placing one foot before another to breast the top of a 12,000-feet pass, the Nathu La, where the route entered Tibet proper. With the others he laid a stone offering on the cairn draped with tattered scarves which marked the frontier, and in a stiff wind they pressed on into Tibet and down to Yatung in the Chumbi Valley where the company of Punjabis were stationed. There the party were warmly entertained in the lively little mess, Paddy given his instructions for Gyantse by the subaltern he was relieving now on his way down.

The weather was set fair, and marches were extended to up to twenty miles a day. Blisters healed, muscles hardened, breath came more easily on the heights. Paddy's skin peeled under the special cream he had been issued with, and Lance, in the rare glare of the sun in thin air, grew as nut-brown as the Tibetans themselves.

They left the hills and ridges behind them and entered the wide treeless plains rimmed by vast, unnamed, unconquered mountains clothed in perpetual snow. Short grass of dwarf sedges formed a carpet underfoot muffling the clink of the ponies' hooves. Here the ponies paced tirelessly in a curious running trot that fairly ate up the miles with the least discomfort to man and beast. The sun blistered down on faces. The wind stung. The Europeans' skins became too sore to shave, Lance also growing a beard.

A night was spent at Phari Dzong in the middle of a plateau between two vast ranges of mountains, snow glistening down to 18,000 feet, the staging post lying below a small fort perched on a hill, which pimple of defiance stood four square in the midst of the mountains surrounding it.

For nine miles the party wound on foot up to the Tang La Pass, the ponies led. Here with bursting lungs they rested for a while at over 15,000 feet.

In some awe at its majesty, Lance gazed at Chomolohari, a 23,000-feet giant to one side, its glaciers translucent with blue-green light. It did not seem possible this could be the same planet where he worked in the city of Calcutta. Before him stretched the immeasurably wide high plain rimmed by mountains. Up there was greatness which put his heartbreak into proper perspective – a mere pinprick in the affairs of man. No longer did the memory

194

of Cara have the power to haunt him and hurt him. He was free from her, whole again. The range upon range of snowy mountains had restored his sanity; the icy winds had swept away his passion for one woman.

'Fantastic!' the subaltern breathed enthralled at his side.

In his relief at heartache gone, freedom restored, Lance impulsively put his hand on Paddy's shoulder and gripped it. The two men, each so diverse in character, brought together in trouble on the trek of a life-time, stood bound in an undemanding friendship, together sharing their delight in the magnificent spectacle before them.

'There are more worthwhile things in life than drink.' Lance turned to smile into Paddy's blue eyes.

'More worthwhile things than women, eh, old cock?' Paddy in his turn clapped Lance on the back. 'They say one can see Everest from behind Gyantse. I wonder if she beats this view.'

'Who do you think will be the first to stand at the top?'

'Bloody Germans I shouldn't wonder. They've been pushing hard for permission. Unless that bastard Hitler castrates the lot. That'd learn them!'

'I'll lay you a wager it'll be the British. Five pounds?'

'Taken. And I hope you win, you old sod!'

Lance left his friend at the fortress town of Gyantse by the rampant Dzong Fort, with the graceful tiered Gompa Abbey above the curve of the Nyang Ghu River. He went on with the trade mission to Lhasa where he was entertained by the abbot at the famous Potala Monastery straddling the hillside, and spied the boy Dalai Lama seated on a dais in an inner room. He sipped darkly brewed Tibetan tea strongly laced with salt and yak's butter with the monks, and did all the things visitors did, and a good many other things he had been sent to do, as well as looking into the jute trade. He returned with Pasang to Gyantse where he found Paddy hugely enjoying his monastic life and still on the water-wagon. He was greeted with the news that war had been declared in Europe.

Without further ado Lance raced down the way he had slowly ascended, Pasang riding close behind on a second pony, the small mule train following as best it could. He jog-trotted across the plains, breasted the Tang La, burst into the mess at Yatung for the night, had a brief word with the Resident, now back in Gangtok, and roared down by car to Siliguri and onto the train for Calcutta to be debriefed and report for active service with the Jute-wallahs.

'Not a hope, mon.' Johnny MacCreath was glad to see the young man excessively fit and in excellent spirits. 'Not a hope after all the leave you've had. You're the one being left to hold the fort, classed as "reserved occupation". I hope you appreciate that the boss finds you indispensable!'

'What about you?'

'Busy. In a few months' time I'm taking the lads off to train in camp.'

'Jute-wallahs training? *Me* appreciate reserved occupation? Good God, you must be crackers. What d'you think I've been doing all these years if not preparing for the emergency?'

Back to his old form Lance proceeded to pull every string he could, all of which took quite a few more months than he expected, and it was not until a year had passed that he was allowed to join Johnny's Battery under the shadow of Murdhar. To add to his pleasure at being back with his men, he found Paddy on the second Staff College short course.

'I see you're drinking like a fish again. I thought Tibet was going to be an all-time cure,' Lance said in October at the bar in the Staff College mess to which Paddy had invited him.

'Oh crap it all. Not *you* nannying as well! Life's too short, chum. War cometh to us all. Faith, we'll soon be dead. Might as well blow our money and be merry as hell.

196

Listen, I've discovered a beaut of a tart. Some bint, I can tell you.'

'Rotter. Back to your evil ways, eh? You'd better introduce me.'

That Lance had buried Cara in the deep recesses of his mind where she lay undisturbed and all but forgotten was undeniable. What he did not know was that his OC Major MacCreath and his wife had, the moment they clapped eyes on Cara at the Dangerfields' dinner party in July, known from snaps they had seen of her who she was.

Johnny and Joan, intrigued, had discussed the situation in their bedroom at the Chiltan Hotel that summer night. They agreed not to mention when Lance arrived in the autumn that his ex-fiancée was in Quetta. He was in such good form they did not think seeing her with her husband would set him back, but it just might.

Better to be on the safe side.

CHAPTER 16

'You look pleased with yourself,' Cara said in December when Derek came bursting into the bungalow and threw off his *poshteen* in the warmth of the drawing-room. These sheepskin coats were worn by the populace of the mountainous districts. Derek had bought his in the Quetta bazaar, and it now gave out a familiar pungent smell indicating that the skin had not been properly cured.

'Good news,' he exploded. 'Promoted major and posted to the 7th Armoured Division in the Middle East!'

'What are you going to do there?' Her heart missed a beat. She had known it would come, but in a flash the news changed her life. Perhaps she could go home to her parents?

'Join a Horse Gunner battery and help Wavell to beat the Eyeties – that's what I'll be doing,' he said smugly.

'Oh Derek, I'm so glad for you. Well done! Promotion and off to the beastly war all in one fell swoop, if that's what you want. Frank and the others will be green with envy. As instructor I suppose he'll stay on here?'

'For another year at least. I'm selling the horses to the "Chink". He says you can ride them from their house whenever you want.'

'What happens to me? Could you get me a passage home?'

'No way. I'm based on India and will revert here when my time's up. No, little woman, you'll have to stay put in one of the Club quarters, and wait for me to come back. It's a good healthy station for abandoned women. You can step up the war work to keep yourself occupied.'

'Yes, I can step up the war work,' Cara repeated, hoping

198

to God the Jute-wallahs would be leaving Quetta at the same time as Derek.

'The Commandant handed me my official report this morning and made me read it aloud. Couldn't have been more embarrassing.'

'Poor you. What did it say?'

'Promise you'll never repeat it?'

'I promise.'

'"This officer has worked hard and conscientiously. He must learn to show more consideration for those less gifted than he . . ." some backhanded compliment.' Derek could not hide his pleasure.

It seemed only a few weeks ago that they had set up house in the heat of summer. Now in the depths of winter they systematically began to dismantle it until there was nothing personal left, but only some new fruit trees planted in the old garden to replace those lost in the drought.

Perhaps the first euphoria of Derek's posting had worn off and the thought of what going to war meant in terms of human frailty had come to him, or perhaps it was that now he could relax in the knowledge that he had satisfactorily completed what he had set out to do to the very best of his ability. Whatever it was, Derek softened from the working dynamo he had been, and during the last week of his embarkation leave, when the Christmas festivities were at their height, he was more attentive to Cara than he had been during the whole of the course, even to spending the last night in her bed in the Wana hut. He made love to her in his diffident way, careful for her that she should not suffer his heaviness, but afterwards he did not leave her to go to his own bed as he always had before. For the first time since their honeymoon night in London before catching the boat train next morning, he stayed on and held her in his arms and talked. He talked about where he was going, the battery, and how he expected to be shortly into the fight.

'Does the thought scare you?' she asked.

'I expect I'll feel as lily-livered as everyone else when it comes to the point. It won't make any difference. I know what I've got to do and I'll do it. Just now I'm excited about the prospect – can't get there quickly enough! I've been trained up to the eyeballs for war. Every regular soldier wants his chance to get to the front.'

'It's frightening for me being left,' she said in a small voice.

'Not if you get on with what *you* have to do. You've got the move to the hut, and you'll have to pay off the servants and do the accounts and all that sort of thing. My pay will come in as usual. You've got that to play with. Play golf. Keep yourself occupied, little woman.'

She liked the feel of lying in his arms, her head on his shoulder. He smelt nice, his body fine-toned. He was an immaculately clean man and always took an evening tub however late. She fell asleep in his arms, and was awakened later before they rose when he took her again and quickly loved her. She felt no answering passion, though she felt a warmth that was enduring. And she prayed that this night would at last bring forth a child.

Derek was scheduled to leave very early in the morning, and he had told Cara he did not want her to come to the station. Together they walked over to the bungalow.

She watched him on the freezing morning put on his tropical uniform of bush jacket and long cotton trousers over his thick pyjamas and vest, khaki sweater over, *poshteen* over that – the thick fleece-lined coat would be useful for chill desert nights. He went over to the single bed upon which she sat clasping her knees in her thick *choga* dressing-gown and briefly kissed her goodbye. He placed his swagger-stick under his arm, his topi firmly on his head, and without a word turned on his heel and marched for the door. Cara went and stood in the bow window of the dining-room to watch him go.

It was still dark outside. The porch light shone on the station wagon; the driver stood stiffly at the salute beside it when Derek emerged. The car door slammed.

Jit Singh got into the front seat, pulled the door to. The engine started up . . . they were gone.

Cara went back to the dressing-room and buried her head in Derek's pillow and gave way to heartfelt sobs. She cried for Derek, who had always been kind and good to her, going off to war. She cried for her marriage. She cried for herself — left abandoned, entirely alone . . .

With the dawn Cara dried her eyes, rose, and finished the packing up of 51 Capper Road.

She did not want to go to the New Year's Eve Ball at the Staff College that night and she told Pammie so. She had just moved into her new quarters which consisted of a bedroom, a bathroom and a sitting-room in a row of new huts with connecting verandahs, a patch of garden to the fore, situated conveniently near to the Club where there was a canteen for the single women.

Although she had unpacked, she was not yet fully straight, and she still had plenty to do to get the place shipshape, as Uncle Tom would have said. She enjoyed doing it. She was the home-making type not the abandoned-wife type. She felt like a fish out of water sitting there on her own in her patch in Quetta.

Nasrullah had left in tears declaring that whenever the memsahib wanted him he would come back. She promised she would call for him if needed, gave him an excellent *chit*, and took down his address in the United Provinces. The bearer that Nasrullah Khan had got to replace him, Ghulam Haidar, was settling in well. He was scarcely older than a *chokra*, a youth with a few straggly dark whiskers. He was cleanly dressed and willing to undertake any work. The job was not an onerous one. There was little for him to do other than bring her *chota hazri*, keep the rooms clean, polish the silver she had not packed away, and do some shopping for her in the bazaar on Derek's old bicycle.

She herself could ride from the 'Chink's' house, and she had the Chev. She was in luxury, she told herself. By day she was more than busy with her job at the thrift shop, her work at the Mission Hospital in which she was becoming more and more involved, and some typing she had taken on at HQ. What to do in the evenings was no problem. The difficulty was to limit the parties. When spring came she would start up tennis and golf, and in the summer she would go up to Ziarat for a break. The time would pass until her husband came back and her married life resumed. Especially after the last night in the Wana hut with Derek, when he *had* been attentive, did she become convinced it was all her own fault. She knew now she was incapable of sexual love.

'What are you doing down there on your own?' Pammie rang for the second time that day.

'Nothing special. Getting the house straight.'

'You've got the next two years at least to get it straight. Don't be a stick-in-the-mud. Come on, Cara! You can't greet in 1941 all on your own.'

'No, really, Pammie, I'd prefer not to come. Thanks all the same.'

'That leaves me in a quandary, blast it.'

'Oh? Why?'

'I've got an extra man in the party which doesn't matter in the least for dinner. But as I'm not dancing with my big belly it means virtually we're two dancing partners short. The party'll be a damp squib with me sitting around looking like a tired queen ant, the men getting drunk at the bar.'

'Who is he?' Cara asked suspiciously. She hadn't seen Lance for getting on for two months and was more determined than ever to dodge him now that Derek had left. The Jute-wallahs were still in camp. The pipes had awakened her on her last morning in Capper Road. Down here, thank goodness, she couldn't hear them.

'No one you know. An ECO on the three months' 'junior' course under Frank.'

'Oh all right then.' Cara gave way ungraciously. 'I'll drive up after dinner and meet you in the ballroom. OK?'

'Good girl. The men are wearing uniform for once. Should be quite special. Put on your ball dress.' Pammie rang off.

She had Ghulam Haidar bring her over a tray for supper, and she dressed leisurely. It was really rather a bore. She was not interested in celebrating a war-time New Year with all the horrors it would bring. She would have much preferred to go to bed and read instead of having to go out in the frost on her own. The huts were cosy, warmer than the draughty old bungalows. Hot pipes ran their length taking off the intense cold.

From her wardrobe she selected a heavy moiré silk in a deep cherry. It had small puffed sleeves which would help to keep her warm. The low neckline was bordered with off-white lace in keeping with its Victorian style, skirt made out of yards of material flowing out from nipped-in waist. She put on her pearls and dangling earrings to match. She threw the beaver fur coat her father had given her over her shoulders, slammed the door behind her – no one in Quetta ever locked any doors – and went out onto the verandah.

The Chev was parked outside, its large grey shape shining in the moonlight. The frozen air hit her as she crunched over the crisp soil in her dainty high-heeled gold shoes, careful not to slip. By now she knew all Quetta's tricks, and she grasped the car door handle with gloved hand. Even so she felt the exhilarating prick of an electric shock, and saw her fur coat light with blue static. Certainly in Quetta one could not mope for long!

By the time Cara arrived up at the Staff College, rows and rows of cars were parked outside, and the strains of music were thumping through the brick walls. She was late. Pammie would never forgive her. The dance was already in full swing. Hastily she dropped her coat in the ladies' and made her way to the noisy ballroom resounding to music and laughter. She stood in the wide double doorway searching for the Dangerfields' party. Her eyes immediately alighted on the one person in the thronging room she did not want to meet: Lance, dancing sedately with a small woman.

Her instinct was to fly; to get her coat; jump into the Chev; run away. She turned to go . . .

'We're over here; good to see you.' Frank on the lookout

took her arm. He led her to one of the arched alcoves off the floor where those who were not dancing were lolling in chintz-covered upholstered chairs and sofas round a blazing fire.

'Hurray, here's Cara come at last to delight,' Pammie said pointedly from her deep chair. 'I think you know Captain Cahill. He and Derek were on the same course.'

'We have met.' Paddy eyed Cara appreciatively. 'Too briefly! Brownlow, I gather, has already buzzed off to war, lucky ba—, um, fella.'

'Yes, he has. Where were you posted to?'

'Local G2 appointment on the General Staff,' Paddy groaned. ''Tis just my luck. Begorra, I suppose I might as well put into practice what I'm supposed to have learnt. Like to dance?'

He led her out to the floor, held her fairly closely, and chatted non-stop.

'Your husband was damned fortunate. We who are stuck here are pea-green and champing at the bit.'

'I expect your chance will come.' Cara looked round the dance floor and was relieved to find Lance and the small woman were nowhere to be seen. 'I can't think why all you men are so dead keen to become cannon-fodder,' she said, relaxing. She smiled up at Paddy, taking him in for the first time, noticing his extreme thinness, his weatherbeaten skin and very blue eyes that reminded her a little of Uncle Tom.

'Ninety-nine per cent of the time, army life is bloody boring. When war comes we feel we've earned a bit of excitement.'

'Most people find Quetta exciting.'

'Plenty of loose women about for us bachelors, if that's what you mean.' He ogled her at close quarters. Marvellous hair and eyes. Passionate puss.

'You may as well know straight away that I may be an abandoned wife but I am no woman on the loose,' she said coolly to quench the bold look.

'Faith,' he made a grimace, 'all the best lookers are as strait-laced as Queen Victoria.'

'And this one is wearing a dress of the period to emphasize it!' She couldn't help laughing at his comic facial expression.

They talked on in the modern vein, a kind of sparring match of getting to know. He would come up against a brick wall; she wouldn't care if she never saw him again. 'Fast' type, Derek had called him. He was the sort of man who must have a woman, and made a fool of himself to get one, but would never marry. He'd end up a disappointed lonely old bachelor living in one of the London clubs and dreaming of his salad days. Still ogling women in his dotage she wouldn't be surprised. Why was it some people never grew up? She wondered what Lance saw in him. Thank God, the two weren't in the same party tonight. If she knew anything about that set, Lance had probably already left with his partner. With any luck he would not surface to return.

When the band stopped playing Paddy kissed Cara's hand in gallant fashion on the dance floor. He really was a complete idiot. He escorted her, hand under elbow, to the bar. 'Drink?' he asked.

'Horse's neck would be nice. Warm me up.'

'Come now, didn't I warm you up?'

'No, you didn't.' The foolish banter went on.

They returned, drinks in hand, to the party in the alcove, and stood on the edge of Frank and Pammie's circle. Before her, with his back to the fire, tall, incredibly loose-knit and elegant, not a couple of yards away from her, stood Lance. She felt her colour recede.

'Cara, this is Mrs Makin; her husband's out in the Khojak. And meet Captain Gardner – Mrs Brownlow.' Pammie turned away to talk to her other guests unaware of the bomb she had planted. The two stared at each other ignoring Mrs Makin, who, feeling slighted, a few moments later took herself off in a huff to powder her nose. Mrs Brownlow had not even looked at her let alone taken her extended hand. Shocking manners!

'Mrs Dangerfield mentioned your name at dinner. It meant nothing to me,' Lance said tight-lipped.

205

'It wasn't meant to mean anything to you.'

'Nor does it!'

'That's good!'

'What the hell are you doing here?'

'I might ask what the hell are you? You're supposed to be with the Jute-wallahs. I wouldn't have come if I'd known you'd be here.' Cara's colour flared.

'I'm on the three months' junior Staff College course *from* the Jute-wallahs. So you knew I was with them? If *I'd* known you were in Quetta I would have come anyway out of curiosity to have a look-see into what you'd become.'

'Curiosity killed the cat . . .' Cara said uncivilly.

'What *are* you two quarrelling about?' Paddy bounced in.

'Oh . . . nothing,' Cara said airily.

'Well, you look nicely warmed up now.' Paddy noticed Cara's heightened colour, as cherry-red as her dress.

'It's partly the fire, and partly this, this, awful man, a friend of yours, I gather.' I never dreamed of Lance in uniform, Cara thought. My God he looks magnificent. I wouldn't have fancied khaki service dress suited many, but it does him. He puts all the rest in their blues into the shade. It's not fair. Men shouldn't be allowed to be so, so, outstanding. No wonder little provincial me fell . . .

'Awful? Ha, ha, ha,' Paddy fell about laughing. 'My awful friend and I went to Tibet together. We were banished there, me in disgrace after beating up the regimental mess, he to get over a skirt . . .'

'Shut your blathering trap, damn you.' Lance interrupted the flow, the muscle in his cheek twitching angrily. Brusquely he took a silver cigarette case from his pocket, opened it, extricated one, tapped it and lit up. He looked at Cara. She did not appear any different. She did not look married – if it weren't for that bloody gold ring on her finger. He threw his cigarette into the fireplace behind him without having taken a puff. The band struck up.

'Cool it, chum. No need to be offensive. Mrs Brownlow might be wanting a cigarette. I've run out.' Paddy patted his pocket and wondered what had come over his friend's manners.

'She doesn't smoke,' Lance frowned. 'Would you like to dance, Mrs Brownlow?'

'How do you know I don't smoke? I could have taken it up . . .'

'You've met before?' Paddy began to rumble.

'Get the hell out of it, Paddy.' Lance shouldered the way to the floor, leaving Cara to follow.

'Didn't think you'd take up smoking.' He held her in his arms again after two years and three months.

'You've acquired a cigarette case. It used to be a cardboard box.'

'I'm better off than I was then. As I said, what are you doing in Quetta? I must confess you gave me the shock of my life. You look very well.'

'I had the edge on you. I saw you about once or twice . . . with some women.'

'You should have made yourself known. I'd have introduced you.' He looked down at her grimly. The conversation was the very opposite of the meaningless banter she'd had with Paddy. Every word here was barbed with double meaning. They were like pugilists, each attempting to find the tender spots. When unwittingly she had dreamed of him when sleeping out in the hot nights, she had melted in his arms. Now there was hard resentfulness, a striking out at each other.

'What did you say?' She failed to catch his last query in the din.

He raised his voice. 'I said why didn't you make yourself known?'

'I took great pains to avoid you . . . like the plague,' she shouted above the band. They collided with another couple.

'Why? Frightened I'd do something nasty?'

'No. Just frightened of the situation.'

'Well, humm, you haven't told me what you are doing here. Where's your husband?' He looked about the room over everyone else's head as if he expected her to point him out.

'Gone to the Middle East. Our house was the end one in Capper Road. I saw you driving past in a jeep.'

'As long as you are happy . . .' he said inconclusively. 'Any bairns?'

Cara shook her head silently.

'I suppose you've had to move out?'

'Yes, into the Club quarter. Where are you?'

'Hutched across the road in one of the new buildings for us "temporary gentlemen". So you've landed up an abandoned grass widow in Quetta. Who'd have thought it of little innocent Cara in Christchurch. Quite a coincidence, isn't it?'

'What is?'

'Our meeting again here.'

'I wish people wouldn't go on about abandoned women,' she avoided, 'it's been bandied to death until it's no longer a joke. There are abandoned women and abandoned women. What's happened to the one with red nails?'

'*I* abandoned her when I came to the College; decided she was not up to Staff standards.' Suddenly he smiled at her for the first time, the same smile that crinkled the corners of his eyes. They bumped into another pair.

'This is impossible,' Lance said impatiently. 'Let's find somewhere to sit out where we don't have to shout; anyway, I need another whisky.' He deposited her on the broad stairway. 'Would you like me to get you something?'

'Yes, please,' she said, for all her words feeling abandoned, 'a second horse's neck.'

He returned to her and handed her the glass. 'Hard liquor, what a change from orange squash.' He sat on the stairs a step below her and looked up at her, her rippling hair, her white neck encased in her mother's pearls so familiar to him, the soft lace setting off the dress, the small waist, the billowing skirt spread round her, one shoe peeping out.

'I still don't care for whisky. Remember when you made me drink some?'

208

'You look younger than ever,' he observed.

'That sounds too juvenile for words, you mean old thing.' The brandy loosened her tongue. She felt totally relaxed with him. She always had. She didn't care what she said.

'That was one of Bobby's expression. How is he?'

'Covered in glory, Battle of Britain boy! Seriously, it was an appalling time; still is, there are so few . . .'

Cara went on to tell Lance of Bobby's letter, and he said he'd be interested to read it. She told him of his war-time marriage to Susan, who would be having their baby soon; about the evacuees to Wick House and what had happened to her parents; about Derek and how well he'd done on the course and how proud she was of him. Particularly she enjoyed talking to Lance about home, the Yacht Club and Uncle Tom. It was like having an old family friend turn up. She told him everything except why she had broken off their engagement, everything except her true relationship with Derek. Beautifully she acted the part of the happily married wife.

They returned to their party, and the assembled gathering drank to a Happy New Year, each person wondering privately what 1941 would bring them personally, war-wise. They sang 'Auld Lang Syne' with arms crossed, Cara's hand in Lance's, and everyone kissed. She kissed him on the cheek and felt again the roughness of his skin and the tobacco-ey scent of his breath. They said good night and thanked the Dangerfields, who left immediately afterwards, Pammie large and heavy in the eighth month of her pregnancy. Paddy had disappeared with some pick-up, and Lance and Cara danced on together, not speaking, their steps matching. They could have been back on the Palais de Dance floor in Hammersmith – except for all the uniformed men in the room, except for the ring on her finger.

Though he did not hold her closely, in fact purposely held her away from his body, the physical attraction between them was immediately apparent. Lance must have felt it and was at pains to avoid it. Cara certainly felt it. She wasn't, never had been, cold with Lance. Why then was she unresponsive with Derek? She failed to understand herself. Men were men and women were women. Apparently men could physically love any woman, so why couldn't she . . .? Perhaps this dreamy floating feeling with Lance was not love at all, but lust for his tallness, for his beautiful body? With him she . . . Cara pulled herself together and began to prattle inconsequences.

'I'll drop you at your quarter,' she said after 'God Save the King' had played punctually at 2 a.m. There was work on the courses to be done that first day of January. The Chev started up obediently on the frosty night; the tyres crunched off on the short way. She drove as so often she had driven the Lancia while he sat half-sideways beside her, only this time he did not look at her. Before, he had made her feel good, happy, beautiful, wanted . . . loved. Now she thought he must look away from her in disgust.

She stopped outside his quarter in the stony desert. He did not suggest she come in, but she noted in the glim the number '36' in the long row of bachelor huts identical to her quarters, a verandah running the length in front.

'How much longer do you have?' she asked through the open window when he got out of the car.

'Mid-February.'

'Where will you be going?'

'To rejoin the Jute-wallahs, leaving for Burma probably. Well, so long, Cara.'

He walked into the hut without a backward glance. Slowly she drove off, reluctant to put the odd miles between them that separated her temporary home from his.

His 'so long, Cara' was a goodbye. He would not ask her out to a drink, to a dance. She would not see him again.

She had acted the part too well.

CHAPTER 17

It was as well that 1 January 1941 was not Cara's day for
typing at the GOC's HQ, in such a state of dither was she.

The encounter with Lance had sparked off what she had
always known would happen had he turned up again in
Christchurch. His physical attraction was such that she
would have discarded all advice and run off with him as
Mulka had run off with his grandfather James! Now, in
Quetta, all that she had felt on the day of the exhibition
and during the night at the Sun Inn returned. Then she had
not been able to prevent throwing herself at his head;
would have done anything in the world he asked of her;
had loved him to distraction. Now, as a frustrated married
woman, her passion was infinitely more difficult to control. Yet Cara was no temptress, no Jezebel. She only
wanted to see him again, to talk to him, to *be* with him a
short while longer before their ways parted for ever.

She did not sleep on that night of the ball for thinking
of the feel of his arm around her on the dance floor, for
the feel of her hand in his. On the face of it there was
nothing to stop her going to him. On the other hand there
was everything to stop her doing so! After all that had
happened between them, he could well in coldness rebuff
her. Nor was she the type of woman to go rushing into an
affair in the very week after her husband had left. She was
married, and basically she was loyal to her husband. She
had no wish to be the unfaithful wife.

The problem faced her, nagged at her, tore her all the
next day and half the following night. What should she
do? Which way to turn? If she did nothing *he* would not

seek her out. His 'so long, Cara' had made that abundantly clear. Once the Jute-wallahs left, she would *never* see him again. Surely the extraordinary coincidence that had brought them together in Quetta warranted action? Surely it could not be ignored after one brief meeting? Could they not meet as old friends as they had on the night of the ball when it had been fun to remember Cook's passion for Ford, and laugh over the 'Fred' trap Uncle Tom had laid for Lance?

Cara's innate modesty cringed at the thought of pouring out to Lance the story of her unhappiness. She would not. That was not the point. The point was how could she go on living in Quetta knowing he was only a bare mile or two up the road without making an effort to meet him again? It was no good waiting for an off-chance meeting. In the three previous months she had caught a glimpse of him only *three* times, and if she waited half that long again he would have left! If only he had suggested a meeting at the Club or with Captain Paddy Cahill it would have been something to hang on to, to look forward to. She only asked crumbs from his table: one more evening to treasure in her memory as she now treasured the New Year's Eve Ball; one more meeting to be by him, to hear his bass voice, see his slow smile spreading, the creases appearing. She did not ask for anything more.

On her second night of little sleep an idea began to form in her mind. Bobby's Battle of Britain letter. *That* was it! Lance had said he would like to read it. She would deliver it to his quarters with a covering note. If he was in she'd meet him and suggest in a friendly way they make up a party for the next Club dance. If he was *not* in, the onus would be on him. He would have to get in touch with her to return the letter.

She took most of the afternoon drafting the note: 'Dear Lance,' she wrote the first time, 'You said you would like to see Bobby's letter, so here it is. Can we meet again? Perhaps you can suggest something? Cara.' NO. It would be better to write, 'I didn't really come clean at the Ball. I am desperately unhappy and badly need a friend.' NO. That was *ghastly*.

Cara composed several versions, tore them up, eventually scribbled off one and before she had time to change her mind again drove up in the evening when she knew he'd be out at dinner in the Staff College mess. She expected there would be a bearer or someone to hand the note to.

When she got there she found no one about. It was dead quiet in the deserted arid area of the newly built huts where no grass, gardens or trees were as yet planted in the iron-hard ground. She knocked on the door of No. 36, and hearing no answer turned the handle. The door led straight into the study, small compared to her living-room. It contained an upholstered chair, hard chair by desk, bookshelves, bowl of fruit on table, rug on floor beside hearth with dying embers that needed stoking. It was tolerably warm, hot pipes such as she had in her hut running the length of the block in a primitive form of central heating. She went through to the bedroom and looked about her. Narrow black iron-framed army cot with bedclothes turned down, cover folded at foot. How did he manage in it with his length? What servant had turned it down; a shared bearer with others in the hut or did he have a Jute-wallah orderly?

There was little more in the room besides a chest of drawers which acted as a dressing table with a heavy free-standing mirror. On it were two photographs in black frames, one of his mother that she had seen before in the Old Ship Inn, hair drawn severely back into a bun. The other she hadn't seen before but recognized instantly. It was of Janet, handsome, fashionably dressed, and striking a model's exaggerated pose. Cara propped up her envelope against Mrs Gardner's frame, and in a fit of pique turned Janet's picture down on its face. Feeling thoroughly guilty at being there at all let alone having a good look round, she beat a hasty retreat.

213

Back in her own quarters she dismissed Ghulam Haidar and began to undress preparatory to taking a bath and going over to the Club for dinner. A dawning horror of what she had done came over her. Janet's picture! How petty, stupid and vile of her. Lance could well be engaged to Janet, and why not, for heaven's sake? For some idiotic reason she did not seem to be able to get it into her fat head that she, Cara, was a married woman who had burnt her boats. Yet she could not help herself feeling like a maiden wildly jealous because she had seen in her boy-friend's room a picture of another girl. It was ludicrous! And what had she said in the covering letter? Which version had she left? 'I didn't tell you about Derek' or 'I didn't come clean' or 'there is so much I haven't told you' or 'I am desperately unhappy.' Oh God, surely she hadn't written the latter? What would he think of her? In any case why had she left the letter in the bedroom? One thing was sure, he would be *furious* when he returned and saw Janet lying face downwards . . . he would think her quite mad.

She lay in her steaming bath shivering with nerves. There was no point in going over to the Club – she wouldn't be able to eat a thing. She'd go straight to bed. But she could not go to bed. She was in a lather of panic to retrieve the covering letter and reverse Janet's picture to its upright position. Her face was hot with shame for what she had done, the palms of her hands clammy with cold sweat. She looked at the clock and saw that it was still early. He would not have returned from dinner yet. The bachelors always stayed on awhile playing billiards or bridge. She'd have time to nip up, remove the covering letter, leaving only Bobby's propped up, and put back Janet. Why hadn't she thought of doing that straight away instead of dithering around and wasting time?

Cara was wearing her long padded housecoat, and without bothering to put on make-up she drew on her fur coat. She drove out to the main avenue, turned right, and at speed roared up the empty road lit at intervals by

214

old-fashioned lamp-posts. Before she came to the Staff College turning she bore left, and for the second time that evening drew up in front of hut No. 36.

Thanking her lucky stars that there were no lights on, she darted in at the verandah door and went through into the bedroom. Everything was exactly as she had left it. Hastily, with thumping heart, she re-righted Janet's picture, tore open her envelope, took out her covering note, and putting Bobby's letter on the study mantelpiece, crumpled her missive into her pocket and bolted. Shutting the hut door behind her she dashed back to the car. Thank God she'd made it! Thank God Lance hadn't seen that feeble, futile letter. Now he would never know she had been in his bedroom, never know about the stupid gesture against Janet.

Without thinking she grabbed the car door handle. What felt like a hundred volts went through her bare skin. With a yelp of pain she wrenched her hand away at the same moment as her fur coat lit up in a sheet of blue static. Holding her injured hand she dived for the seat and safety. Before she could slam the door she felt an iron grip on her arm.

'Oh no you do not.' Lance in *poshteen* over his dinner jacket pulled her retreating form out of the car. 'What the hell do you think you are doing going into my quarters without s'much as by your leave, and then come tearing out again like a demented chicken that has lost its head?'

'You saw?' She was horrified that he had watched her.

'Weaving down the path to beddie-byes. Could not believe my eyes!'

'I was leaving Bobby's letter. You said—'

'Oh no you were not,' his voice sounded cunning, 'I saw you stuff s – something into your pocket. Stealing, what? Hand it over, woman.' His grip tightened.

'No, Lance, really. Let me go . . .' She tried to shrug off his hold.

'Why sh – should I let you go?' He spoke with deliberation. 'You have come all this way to pay me a

215

visit and you are going to see me whether you like it or not,' he said illogically.

'I *didn't* come to see you. I came to leave the letter.' She had never heard him speak with such slow care. He must be, she deduced, the worse for drink and was at pains to hide it. He and Paddy Cahill had been drinking. She was not in the least frightened of him or the tourniquet grip that was adding to the pain of her hand. Her retrieval plan had misfired, and at that moment all she wanted was to get back to bathe her stinging hand. She was not even properly dressed!

'Come and have a drink at my place tomorrow after work and bring back the letter. We can have a chat about it then,' she said, hoping he would release her.

'Whose letter?'

'I *told* you. Bobby's letter. I've left it in your room. Now let me go home.' She attempted again to throw off his arm.

'Dammit, woman, NO! You have had it all your own way s – so far. Tonight I am going to have it all *my* way. S – see?' He frogmarched her to the door. 'And shut up will you making such a bloody noise. We are not su – supposed to have women here.'

'I'm *not* making a noise,' she said indignantly. 'I suppose you and Captain Cahill with Mrs red-nails whatever-her-name-is and the Blousy Bint—'

'Not at all, madam,' he said, aristocratic nose in air. He pushed her unceremoniously into the study. 'You are tho – *thor*oughly out of date. I have never entertained Mrs whatever-her-name-is *here*. I tol' you she was not up to Staff College standards. Take a seat Mrs Brownlow while I stoke the fire.' He made a bowing gesture towards the comfy chair. He threw his *poshteen* down on the desk, his bow tie left slightly askew.

'Thank you but I prefer to stand.' She noted that though his enunciation was careful and deliberate, his brain was ticking over brightly – he'd remembered telling her about Mrs . . .

'Le'me take that fur off you.' Politely he helped to remove it. 'And you can tell your ol' Uncle Lance *all* about it. Let your ravishing hair down wi' Uncle, eh? What were you after? Stealing my silver hair-brushes?'

'For the umpteenth time, Bobby's letter.' She stood defiantly by the chair waiting for her chance to get away. She'd left the ignition keys in the car.

'Then what is this?' He felt into the pockets of her fur. 'Handkerchief.' He sniffed. 'Smells nice. Ha, evidence!' Triumphantly he drew out the crumpled envelope and note.

'It's only something I wrote to go with Bobby's letter. I – I changed my mind and wished I hadn't so I came up to take it back.' She watched him smooth the note out on his thigh. 'Please don't read it, Lance. *Please* . . .'

'Why not when isht's addressed to me?' he stumbled.

'I'm – I'm ashamed of it.'

'Ashamed, eh?' he said teasingly. 'Ha, all the more reason for Uncle to read it. Well,' he relented at her blighted look, 'what about a bargain? I will chuck it on the fire if you tell what is in it.'

'I'll tell you.' She could easily modify it, make light of it.

'Promise? Oh dear, dear, dear, I forget. Cara does not keep promises . . .'

'I will . . .' and with relief Cara watched Lance throw the paper into the grate. He put some more coal and wood on the fire.

'Now, what may I get for madam since I have the pleasure of her uninvited presence? Pre – pre*sum*ably you have dined? Not that I can offer you more than a biscuit or a banana.'

'I didn't feel like eating anything.'

'Not since New Year's Eve?' He was all of a sudden penetratingly sober.

'Since New Year's Eve.'

'Much . . . mum . . . mum . . . boot,' he muttered to himself.

'Except that you can drown your sorrows in drink.'

'Sorrows? Who's talking about sorrows? Aren't we having the time of our lives in swinging old Quetta? Le'me get you a brandy . . . cold night. Th — that will wuzz your sorrows . . .' He fished around in a drinks cabinet in a corner. She was quite sure he was going to drop the glass. He was definitely drunk. She didn't want a drink.

'I'd much prefer to go. I think I should go now, Lance.' For the first time she glanced down at her painful right hand and saw it bleeding, the skin torn away on the knuckles of her palm in a nasty gash. 'What did you do with my hanky?'

'Hanky? Hanky-panky.' He fiddled in his pocket, found it, looked surprised to find it was not his, and gave it to her. 'Have a good cry,' he suggested. He splashed some brandy into a tumbler. ''Fraid the army does not reach to having goblets. What's that?' he frowned, noting the dainty handkerchief wrapped round her knuckles.

'It's nothing. I tore my hand on the car door.' She swallowed some neat brandy and put the glass down beside the fruit bowl. 'Aren't you keeping me company?'

'S — sufficient unto the day . . . been sozzled with good ol' Paddy since New Year . . . time to sober up. Work's got to be done. On wi' the work . . . on, on. Let's look.' He took her hand in his, removed the hanky, and studied her palm. His dark head was bent close to her face. Emotion and pain overtook her.

'Hey,' he noticed, 'hey, a tear; we cannot have that.' Speculatively he wiped her cheek with a forefinger. 'Must be sore, hey?'

He made her go into the bathroom with him, and with efficiency he washed the wound, dabbed it with disinfectant which stung, put on a dressing from a first-aid kit, and bandaged it up neatly.

'Quite clean. Should be fine, but you had better check at the hospital tomorrow,' he advised. Again she was astonished at his capacity to sober up completely when

218

the situation merited it. They went back into the study. Cara, on the way, was reminded of what she had done to the photo.

'Are you engaged to Janet?' she asked bluntly, standing by the fire. Her hand felt comforted by the bandage.

'Janet and I correspond. We shall discuss marriage when time comes. No point at present . . . couldn't get out here in any case. War comes first.'

'I must go, Lance.'

'Before, tell me what brought you running here in the dark like a li'l girl lost? What was in the note?'

'I did say I'd tell you, and I will, but, but, I'd prefer not to talk about it,' she said on a sob. 'Oh God, please, Lance, I don't want to talk about it.'

He looked at her straight then for the first time that evening, his eyes large and concentrating. He took his time looking at her from her head to the soft indoor shoes she was wearing, and up again, his eyes stopping at her breasts.

'You know what you're doing coming here half-undressed?' His eyes focused on a housecoat button. 'Playing with fire, *that's* what you're doing!'

'Undressed?' She looked down hurriedly and saw that one of the spaced cloth buttons that ran from throat to hem was undone, the gap showing a cushion of pink skin.

'Oh, sorry,' she said, and hastily did it up.

'You do not *need* to button it up,' Lance said, 'I like it unbuttoned – all of it. Women who come to bachelor pads at night wearing no underclothes are usually in a tearing hurry to throw their outer garment off.'

'The visit was *not* premeditated. Quite fortuitously I happened to have taken a bath when I decided to leave you Bobby's letter to read. Here it is since you don't seem to have noticed, on the mantelpiece,' she pointed.

Lance gave a sarcastic snort. 'Hardly believe . . . your story. Present a classic example of woman inviting s – seduction, one who knows all the titillating tricks of pretending *not* to. You came with the express intention of

219

sleeping with me, you bloody little witch. I may have drink taken, but I wasn't too drunk to tie a neat bandage, and I am not too drunk to undo all those bloody buttons if you won't oblige.'

She knew he would not let her go now if she made a dash for the door. Even though she had only taken one gulp of the fiery brandy it had been enough to relax her tension, as the bandage had eased her hand. She no longer wanted to go.

'You hold your drink like an aristocratic Gardner,' she said softly, slim and unresisting before him while slowly he undid the buttons, the long padded garment parting. He put his hands round her under the housecoat and stroked her smooth back, and, holding her, he kissed her neck and shoulders down to her small firm breasts. Her hands were round his neck fondling his hair, and she found herself responding with the longing she had felt on the hot summer nights on the lawn under the moon when she had dreamed of him, or in the cold nights in the Wana hut with the flickering fire playing shadows on the tent top when she had gone to sleep thinking of him. It did not matter which, summer or winter, her limbs would tremble for Lance, waves of desire sweep over her at his touch.

'I love you, Lance, I have always loved you,' she managed to say.

'By God, you'd better after what you've done.' He picked her up as if she were no weight at all and dumped her none too gently onto the bed while he disappeared into the bathroom, the light filtering into the dark bedroom through the open study door. She sat on the bed in her open gown on the thick grey Australian blanket noting with peculiar interest that it had a broad blue stripe down the middle; and she looked at the photo of Janet on the chest of drawers and was glad she would know love with Lance before he and Janet . . . A moment later he returned, dragged back the blankets, threw off his dressing-gown, and took her as she was in her open

220

housecoat, crushing her to him on the bed, his mouth hard on hers. He took her urgently, the tautness of her breasts against his chest. So tightly did he hold her that the rhythms of their heartbeats mingled in drums of double beats. Dilmilee — hearts-meeting. Did he remember too?

There was none of the gentleness she had known in him before, the tender embraces in Christchurch, the sweet courting in the bracken on Hengistbury Head, the fondling at the Old Ship Inn. Here was the dark man who had looked at her so strangely in the Sun Inn that night when he had not come into her room. Now she knew what had been in his thoughts then: naked passion that made the pupil grow huge. She wondered what it would have been like *had* he come into her room that night when she was a virgin. She did not know. But she knew it would have been as different from her wedding night as this was different from any of the times that followed. She would not have resisted Lance then, and she did not do so now. She unfolded to his volcanic male strength, and found she gloried in his roughness, gloried in being taken by a man who demanded she give her all. She felt for the first time what it was like to be aroused and drenched with desire in the convulsions that became the rocking boat of their puny bed.

For the first time she felt what it was like to respond, to love, to exult, to die a little. 'I do not love you *enough*,' she had written. 'Your enough is enough for me,' he had answered. There would never be 'enough' with Lance, never too often as Pammie had felt. She had believed she was incapable of physical love. Now she half-slept and woke to find that was not true. She *was* with Lance, only with Lance, even in a narrow, too short, hard, uncomfortable army cot in the middle of a frozen treeless desert in a room in a long series of bachelor huts where women were not supposed to come! Ah, the blessed electricity playing its magic rills upon her unsuspecting body. Ah, at last — Quetta water!

*

Lance stirred. He looked at the clock on the bedside table. 'Cara,' he said gruffly, waking the tousled woman in his arms who had given him more pleasure than any of the women he had had in all his life put together, 'you have to go or they might drum me out of College. Get some sleep in your own bed. I'll be in touch with you when I've had time to read Bobby's letter since that's what this visit is all about.'

'Truthfully, it really was what I came for.' Cara got out of bed, put on her housecoat and slipped her feet into her shoes.

'Then you got a deal more than you bargained for,' he grinned, propping his head up on an elbow and watching her don her fur coat. He noticed the bandage. 'Is your hand all right to drive?'

'I've forgotten all about it,' she laughed. She blew him a kiss, and departed in a rosy glow.

She drove herself back and let herself into her rooms. The clock on the mantelpiece read 2 a.m. She was earlier than when she had come in from the New Year's Eve Ball, yet she was worlds away from the person she had been then. She was bruised and used, abandoned and depraved, loose and tumultuous, and not only did she feel marvellous, she felt hungry! She brewed herself a cup of tea in the small back pantry room used by Ghulam Haidar by day, ate a slice of fruit cake, did her teeth, and climbed into her own comfortable bed without putting a nightgown on, a thing she had never done in her life before. She did not know what lay before her. She did not care very much. She had what she had: the imprint of a beloved man's body on her and in her and that for the moment was good enough for anyone.

CHAPTER 18

Lance rang up in mid-January. 'Time we had a morning's lie in. I can tell you I'm fed up with having to flit in the middle of the freezing night. I've got a room in the Hanna Rest House for the week-end. All right by you?'

'Marvellous,' Cara said.

She would have agreed to anything he suggested. She was by now totally in love with him in an all enveloping passion which filled her with happiness such as she had not known existed. She was heavy with love, light with love, could not have enough of him; she was with him in thought every moment throughout the working days, delirious with joy when she met him again in the evenings, devastated when for reasons of work they could not meet.

She lived for the exquisite present which obliterated the past of her marriage and attempted to obliterate the future, though in this she was not entirely successful. The three months' junior course at the Staff College had come to an end. Lance had rejoined the Jute-wallahs whose camp under Murdhar was about to be struck, destined to go with a Brigade from Quetta on active service to Burma.

There had been no question of Cara trying to hide her affair with Lance, though she was discreet enough when visiting his hut, leaving the car at the end of the block and coming in the back way, and she always dismissed Ghulam Haidar early to his servant's quarters when Lance was to join her at the Club. The whole of inquisitive Quetta saw them dining *à deux*, saw that they had no eyes for anyone else in the room, saw them dancing exclusively together. That they were 'madly' in love was accepted with a shrug of

223

shoulders as just another Quetta scandal of a married woman going the whole hog once her husband's back was turned, though more than a few disapproved of such blatantness when the unfortunate cuckold had recently left for the front. Hitting a bit below the belt, wasn't it?

Mary Finlayson, the Commandant's wife, bursting with righteous indignation in her late pregnancy, was particularly disgusted at Cara's behaviour. One January morning she had cut Cara dead at the thrift shop for all to see. There were plenty of elements in Quetta, especially in the more senior army and civil echelons, who held to the same rectitudes as Cara's parents, and did she but know it, many found the fact that Mrs Brownlow was disporting with an Anglo-Indian thoroughly distasteful.

Though Cara had been hurt at the slight when on her morning shift in the thrift shop, and showed it in a blush, it made no dent in her passion for Lance. He had awakened her to plunge her into the consummation of the instant attraction that had first drawn her eyes to him in the Christchurch Yacht Club. Here, in frenetic Quetta, she had met her fate in the man who was her first love, the man she now saw she had been crazy to turn down.

They did not always make love. They rode and played golf when the weather permitted, and one evening they went to the cinema near the shopping centre known by the troops as the 'flea pit'. It may not have harboured fleas any more (Lance said it was too cold for them to survive!) but it was surely the most draughty wooden building ever built, the oil stoves down the aisle making little difference. On the freezing mid-winter night, Lance and Cara sat enthralled for four hours on a hard seat watching Vivien Leigh and Clark Gable in *Gone with the Wind*. It became an endurance test for the audience, sweaters piled under coats, legs wrapped in rugs, hot water bottles on laps.

In February they booked again into the Hanna Rest House. This time it was for their last week-end together. Cara picked Lance up in the Chev and drove him past the ice-bound Hanna Lake where skaters were sporting on the same spot where not so long ago others had romped naked. The skating women were dressed in slacks and jackets, the men muffled up in balaclavas, scarves and greatcoats, and wearing any skates they could lay hands on, even to pairs screwed onto their army boots. The car went on up the Ziarat road into a snowstorm, the windscreen wiper grinding heavily to and fro, Lance turning on the front seat to catch Cara's eye, without a word spoken both remembering the stormy drive from Exeter. Their skis, made by Uberois in Sialkot of heavy hickory, leather straps binding the boots, stuck out of the open rear window, snow drifting in and settling on the back seat. Hanna bungalow was always fully booked at week-ends, and the dining room on that Friday evening was crammed with couples, none of whom they knew, though it would have made no difference had they been acquainted.

That night, when the snow continued to fall, heavily blanketing the countryside into a new, less stark, landscape, they went to sleep to the dampened sound of its soft landing on the tin roof, the fire in the open hearth flaring up and flickering down; and Cara loved Lance differently in the urgency she felt at their near parting. She loved him less abandonedly, but more intensely and deeply than she had done before. She thought he recognized the change but was not sure. There were a lot of things she was not sure about. Lance was not the open man she had known in Christchurch. At times he appeared withdrawn, his expression often preoccupied. And he had never once used endearments.

The next day they spent skiing on the slopes of Zirgund. The sun was warm and blinding on the fresh snow, not a breath of wind on the air. Cara was the more experienced having been out in Austria twice with Bobby before the war while Lance had skied only as a schoolboy one hard winter outside Dundee. Fit and young they fell and picked themselves up laughing, plodded up the slopes on skis, and swooshed out of control down the piste with a crowd of others. All Quetta it seemed was out enjoying themselves on the slopes, all Quetta was busy buying or borrowing skis and waxing them with heated candle stubs, the older experts grandly demonstrating the merits of the telemark turn in deep snow, knees bent low, heels well up. Children raced past on home-made toboggans. War had never seemed further away.

Once more, the pair breakfasted in their room, Cara in her housecoat, Lance sitting up in bed with a sweater on. Indulgently he watched her buttering the toast for him and pouring out his coffee.

'Thirsty work,' he said his face crinkling when she came over to hand him his cup. She sat down on the bed, cradling her cup in her hands.

'So you really are off this week? Oh Lance, how shall I live without you?'

The expression on his face changed suddenly, the smile gone. 'You managed very well before,' he said coldly.

She felt his tone like a stab from a steel blade. Up till now she had blinkered herself from all else but their physical togetherness. They had not talked about the future, nor made any plans. He had not asked her about Derek, and she had never vouchsafed any information. Details of her husband's sexual inadequacies in defence of her behaviour would be odious and superfluous. She was glad he had never questioned her about her marriage. But, could it be he believed it was a *success*? She was hurt by his apparent indifference to the subject, by his never expressing what he felt for her in endearments, never even talking about Janet whose photograph remained on his chest of drawers. She herself had again and again expressed her love for him in words. Not once had he responded in kind, not even in the most passionate moments.

'What'll you be in the Brigade?' She changed the subject, the steel blade in her heart.

'Staff Captain dealing with A and Q matters, but wait! When the dear guns begin to bark I'll be there with the Battery in the midst of it.'

'You men are all alike: thirsting for blood.'

226

'I should bloody well think so after all that training.'

They dressed leisurely, and drove up to the catchment area, a large tract of land guarded by fencing and barbed wire, where only those who asked for special permits were allowed in on foot on condition they obeyed the rules of no picnicking or smoking to pollute the pure water that came from springs miles up. Cara showed the passes she had obtained from the political officer in Lytton Road, and they were allowed in. They walked along a narrow sluice wall containing the reservoir, to a water channel, and onto a snowy path under fir trees draped in mantles of white. Every now and then there was a muffled thump in the woods, a blob of snow falling onto the ground. The path twisted and turned up the hillside following the blue-grey stream that bubbled and tumbled over big rocks.

'The political officer said the spring is called the Chashma Bogra. You once told me about your spring, the Chashma . . . ?' she tried to remember.

'"The Chashma Shahi" for Spring Imperial, property in Kootgunge bestowed on Nissa, plus 365 villages as part of the dowry!'

'Will you go back there?' she asked thinking it was the first time he had mentioned his derelict inheritance since she had met him again, land her father had dismissed as 'pure fallacy'. In Christchurch days Lance had called her his Dilmilee. Not any more. Dilmilee had been a pure virgin . . .

'When I get leave. There's much to be done. I'd started when the war came to interrupt.' He walked on ahead.

She followed. 'On the ruins, or on the land? I'd love to see it,' she added so quietly she wondered if he'd heard when he did not respond but strode forward in rapid strides. 'Oh God, Lance, don't cut me out . . . promise to call me if you're wounded or anything . . .'

He stopped on the path and waited for her to catch him up and pulled her towards him. He held her with a fierceness she did not understand. He stood there a long while crushing her to him, holding her head to his shoulder, his eyes on the pure spring water. The warmth of his body

227

through heavy clothes, the very fastness of his rigid embrace, was so exquisite she wished she could die then and there in the moment. She wished he would never let her go.

'You've only got to ask me,' she whispered, 'you know I'd come . . .'

'I know nothing,' he said releasing her and abruptly turning to lead downhill. 'I know absolutely bloody *nothing*,' he said again ahead of her, his head thrown back to the sky, the words wrung out of him. She recognized the anguish in his voice but she could not help him for she did not fully understand when he would not talk it out. In the old days they had talked about everything; now that they were physically one, he said nothing.

'Do you love me?' she asked on their last night, desperate that he should say something. Her hands ran from his black hair down to the muscles of his thighs. 'Please, please know, you *must* know . . . I can never forget you, not after . . . all this . . .'

'I've heard those words before,' he said gruffly; and he stopped her talking by placing his mouth over hers.

Why did he not speak the words? Why did he not say, 'I do not want Janet, I want you.' Why not, 'I love you' – just once? Why not, 'When you get a divorce we will be married'? She saw only too clearly why on that last night when he took her body but would not give her his heart: he had trusted her once, and she had killed his trust.

Now the tables were turned, and Cara felt she deserved every inch of the steel turning in her heart. Now it was *she* who loved him unreservedly. Was physical love from him alone 'enough' for her? No, but she saw it would have to be enough after the damage she had done.

'You may call it active service but you are not going into war in Burma,' she said with false bravado to hide the pain she felt at parting when on their way back she dropped him for the last time at his quarters.

'Maybe not, but it's a warlike situation. I don't trust the Japs.'

'Will you write?'

'There won't be time. Besides, I'd have thought you'd had enough letters from me in the past,' he said, bitterness in his voice.

'Lance, please . . .' she tried again.

'So long, Cara.' He slammed the car door on her words, and once again without a backward glance disappeared into No. 36 hut.

She went down to Quetta station the next morning and stood by the window in the waiting room, a shadowy figure where no one from outside could see her for the grime on the pane. The troop train rested, hissing impatiently, and Johnny MacCreath (his wife had long since left the Chiltan Hotel and was back in Calcutta) and Paddy Cahill were talking together by the end carriages. She saw Lance, very fine in his green uniform and jungle hat, his broad breast bare of medals, striding up the platform to join them followed by an orderly. She knew intimately every inch of his body from the boxing blemish over one eyebrow, to the four vaccination marks on upper left arm, down to the appendix scar on stomach. The lone piper marched up and down the platform playing his pipes, the last strangled sounds expiring in a groan when he prepared to board the train. Never again would she hear the pipes from the camp float across the plain, though many times would she dream she had heard them in the early mornings.

Movement officials saluted, and slowly the long train drew out. Dry-eyed Cara watched it go, the second time she had seen Lance off by train. In London, they had both shed tears at their parting though both held high hopes; now, in her desolation that she meant no more to him than a woman to bed, that she had no link with him, that she might never see him again, Cara hugged to herself the one thing she had left: the blessing of her secret knowledge. Thank God. Oh thank God . . . Quetta water.

Of all the war-time scandals that abounded in Quetta, the one that aroused the most resentment was the blatant case of the red-headed Brownlow woman. Just why, in comparison with the naked Hanna Lake scandal, and the foursome wife-swapping scandal, not to mention the Big Bed scandal, Carissa Brownlow's behaviour caused such ire, it is hard to understand. What at first apparently got the community on the raw was the rapidity of her unfaithfulness to her likeable, hard-working, soldierly husband. He had left for the Middle East front on Boxing Day and her affair with Gardner started up on first introduction at the Staff College New Year's Eve Ball, according to Mrs Makin who had been in the Dangerfields' party – *under* a week later! It was a bit much for even Quetta to swallow for a wife to fall into bed with a complete stranger within hours of meeting him – again according to dependable Mrs Makin whose husband was commanding the camp out in the windy Khojak.

To add insult to profligacy, by April the slim-figured Brownlow woman was seen to be unquestionably pregnant. Fingers were counted: three months. Mrs Brownlow was not ashamed. She told everyone her baby was due in late September. More fingers counted. Horrors! The baby could be either husband's or lover's. As if that was not enough there was worse to come. Within days of her Anglo-Indian paramour's departure, the now notorious Mrs Brownlow was living with the most disreputable rake in Quetta – one Captain Paddy Cahill. And not only that, Cahill and Gardner were close friends, and at one period had gone around together with two well-known Quetta tarts. The amoral woman had invited the friend in the moment the ECO left and they *continued to live together in her pregnant state*. The baby to be born (poor little mongrel) could equally be *his*! Time would show if it was born 'late'. The package had been tied up as neatly as the undeniably beautiful Mrs Brownlow was herself dressed, tied up that was to pass as her poor deluded husband's.

'I suppose you know that the whole of Quetta is talking about you,' Pammie stated cheerfully when she brought her baby daughter down to see Cara. 'I can't help it, it makes me giggle. You were so puritanical and proper in Ambala. Now look at you!'

'I still am. *You* started it by inviting Lance to the Ball, and then making me go. But for that act of yours we might never have come face to face. It was lighting a powder keg.'

'How was I to know you'd once been engaged? Anyway why did you break it off if you fancied him so?'

'My parents were dead against him, and I was very susceptible to their influence. Derek asked me to marry him. I did, and I became a disappointed woman, that's all.'

'Some all. I know your marriage difficulties. Even so—'

'Pammie, dear, don't think I am trying to condone my actions, but truly I hadn't realized how bad it was until I met Lance again. Derek is, well, a bit juvenile that way, rather like a little boy. He, he . . . I had to *fight* to get him to . . . There's no point in talking about it.'

'Will you go back to him?'

'I couldn't now. Oh, Pammie, I'm so in love with Lance.'

'Has he asked you to get a divorce?'

'No. He hasn't said anything about our relationship. He's not writing, and of course I shan't tell him about the baby.'

'That sounds pretty negative. Come clean. Whose *is* it?'

'Your guess is as good as mine.'

'What do you mean?'

'I mean my last period was over before Derek left.'

'And you didn't have another?'

'No.'

'Well, my dear,' Pammie picked up the stirring baby from the Moses basket and put the pink bundle to her breast, 'what does it matter? A baby is a baby is a baby.'

'Exactly. I'm so thrilled. You'll have to show me how to look after it.'

'With pleasure, godmama!'

'I was going to ask about that. Mightn't Frank have second thoughts now that I'm . . .'

'Quetta's scarlet woman?' Pammie threw back her head and gave her raucous laugh. 'He's not quite such an ogre as all that. He knows that Derek is as good as impotent—'

'No, Pammie. That's overdoing it a bit.'

231

'"As good as", I said. Frank says he's heard of cases like Derek's before, men who have the mechanics but not the want nor the will, and that you could get an annulment on the strength of it if you like to wash your dirty linen in public. Of course it would be frightful for Derek.'

'It would, and I would never dream of it. How's Mrs Finlayson's baby boy?' Cara abruptly changed the distasteful subject.

'Fine. Idiotic woman to have cut you dead. I can tell you her endless labour shook me rigid coming two days before I went in to have mine. Can't think why the MO didn't perform a Caesarean right at the start. Anyway, thank God they managed to save both mother and child in the end and thus preserve the Commandant's sanity. She's got a starchy white nanny looking after the son and heir; won't have black hands touching her baby – there's gross racism for you.'

'Odious woman. Might your Seti know of a good ayah for me? And did I tell you I'm having the baby in the Mission Hospital? They have a couple of private rooms in the *zenana* wing.'

'That's daft! What do you want to go there for in the middle of the bazaar buzzing with flies? Frightfully unhygienic. Noisy too; besides you'll have to *pay*.'

'I know, but I want to go. No one down there has ever given the slightest hint that they don't approve of me. I appreciate their love for the sinner! The *zenana* doctor is a lady missionary which appeals to me too, and if you're going to have a baby in India why not let it be born into an Indian atmosphere?'

'Mr Gardner's influence?'

'Not at all. My own inclination.' Cara tossed her head.

Soon after this conversation, on Ghulam Haidar's Friday off, a dewy-eyed Cara held the Dangerfields' little baby daughter, named after her, at the Garrison Church's font. On her return from the christening party in the Staff College Hall, at which in her position as godmother and guest of the senior instructor, Colonel Frank Dangerfield, even Mrs

Finlayson had to acknowledge her presence with a frosty nod, Cara found a letter and a cable stuffed under the door of her hut, which event precipitated the scandal with Paddy.

Her immediate reaction was that the cable must be from Lance. The letter she saw was from her father which was unusual. Normally he only wrote at Christmas and for her birthday. Her mother did all the writing. Hurriedly she slit the envelope open, glancing as she did so at the dates. Letter and cable were four weeks apart, and now she saw that the cable was also from Christchurch. Strange that they should arrive on the same day, but then war-time civilian mail, as opposed to military signals for anything really important, was all over the place. She started to read, first one and then the other.

The sudden roaring in her ears presaged either a dust storm or an earthquake, and by now an old hand at both these, Cara instinctively looked up at the central hanging light to see if it were moving, in which case she would bolt for the door. Not only did the flex sway wildly but the ceiling swirled above her, the walls of the room following suit in a vortex worse than any upheaval she had yet experienced. It turned her with the walls, engulfed her into a black hole, the floor coming up to hit her. Heavily she fell.

Mercifully soon, Paddy, calling to take her out to dinner at the Club, found her conscious but deathly white lying on the *dhurrie* with the missives clutched in her hand. He lifted her onto the sofa, and rang for the families' MO. Whilst waiting for the doctor to arrive, he knelt beside her and with warm hands massaged her frozen feet. He read the letter and the long cable.

The first, from Brigadier Thornton, held the stark news that Bobby had been shot down in his aircraft and killed over France. Her father thought it better to write rather than Cara should receive the terrible news by cable. The second was from Dr Walker. The house in St Catherine's Hill had received a direct hit from a German plane dropping its bombs at random as it scuttled for the Channel and base. The three occupants of the house, Cara's parents and Ford, had been killed instantly. The dog had been found unhurt. Bugler was with him.

The MO arrived, gave Cara a bromide, and ordered her to bed.

'The baby?' Her eyes were huge in her white face.

'So far so good. Better take it quietly for a while. No going to work. Have you anyone here living in?'

'I'll look after her,' said Paddy. That night he slept on the sofa.

After work the next day he came to see her bearing flowers and grapes, and found her up in her housecoat but drained and desolate. He put his arm around her and asked her to tell him about her family. He sat on the sofa with her and she told him everything. She told him how she loved Bobby, of their sailing, and other things they had done together as children; she told him about her parents, and how sweet and vague her mother had been, and how although her father was a stern and difficult man she had loved and admired him. She told him how she had made the biggest mistake of her life in breaking off with Lance . . .

Cara poured it all out, in her sadness and distress, to Paddy, Lance's good friend and companion in Tibet and Quetta, a man who drank too much, was liable to beat up a Mess or a Club, a man who womanized a great deal, and had once said that if he ever had enough money he'd set up a mistress. He was a man who knew the names of all the 'damned best brothels' in the north of India, particularly in Lahore; he was permanently in debt; he played brilliant polo and rode to hounds with dangerous disregard for his neck.

Paddy Cahill chain-smoked, used bad language, was rude to his superiors – he called Frank Dangerfield, his instructor at the Staff College, 'a bloody man-eating tiger'; the Commandant 'that old sod'; and Mary Finlayson 'an ancient addled bitch'. He was often the worse for drink, and more often still 'fed up to the bloody tits'. He was content to buy his women 'for a quick poke' when he felt like it; he did not believe in marriage or sloppy 'one pure love'; he hated work, did not trouble to use his good brain, and openly declared he had cheated over his Staff College exams. This most idiosyncratic, objectionable and contradictory man, who was amusing, irreverent, bawdy, abrasive, full of charm, fastidious and insouciant, and the very bane of his superior officers' lives, cradled Cara in his arms when she wept bitterly that she had ever left England and her parents, smoothed her hair off her hot face, listened patiently, comforted and all but moved into the hut. No wonder Quetta's eyes bulged.

They bulged even more when Cara's baby was born in the Mission Hospital on 30 September of that year 1941, a small, fair-skinned girl with dark hair who could belong to either of her two lovers, but was registered as Major Brownlow RA's to whom an official cable with the glad tidings was automatically sent from HQ. Eyes continued to bulge when the affair between Mrs Brownlow and Captain Cahill went on directly after the birth, the two of them seen dancing energetically at the Club every single Wednesday and Saturday!

For a short while longer after the birth of Cara's baby the frenetic life of gaiety, entertainments, dance, sport, tittle-tattle with bridge and mah-jong mornings, went on in Quetta, until suddenly, with the horrific news of the attack on Pearl Harbor on 7 December, and the subsequent disaster of the sinking of the *Repulse* and the *Prince of Wales* in Malayan waters, they were all 'brought up by their bloody boot straps', as Paddy expressed it. General Sir Claud Auchinleck took over. He swept the boards clean when Japan invaded Burma, and India became first line of defence. Orders galore were issued, among them that mufti was to be put away, dinner jackets banished in moth-balls. Uniform was to be worn all the time, 'blues' at dances. Some officers – fresh from the front and much envied – sported bright new ribbons on chests.

Disasters piled up: the troops in Hong Kong fought bravely every inch of the way until the hugely outnumbered garrison was forced to surrender after a last ditch fight at

Christmastide in one corner of Victoria Island. In the February of 1942 Singapore fell, thousands killed, thousands more men, women and children harried into PoW and internment camps. In the same month in the Middle East, General Rommel, leading the Germans in their counterattack, recaptured Benghazi, relentlessly pushed back the British, and with heavy armour stormed, bombed and surrounded Tobruk.

'Tobruk's fallen, and I don't know if Derek's there.' Cara looked up at Paddy from feeding Geraldine, with worried eyes. He was excessively thin; he was sweaty, grubby, eyelashes dust laden, hair whitened, and he came into her drawing-room direct from an exercise out in the Khojak.

'God's teeth I'm exhausted. I need a bath.'

'Go ahead. Help yourself to a clean towel. I'll fetch you a drink.'

Training in desert warfare had been greatly stepped up, for which the bleak reaches of the Khojak were ideal. New units disgorged onto Quetta's railway station; trained units left. Dozens more temporary huts filled the landscape.

'When did you last hear from him?' Paddy returned from the bathroom wearing only a towel round his waist and rubbing his wet hair with another. With a pang Cara noticed how his hair curled like Bobby's. She kissed him affectionately and handed him a double whisky.

'About six weeks ago. A scribble. He'd been in the thick of it. Did you hear from Lance again in Rangoon?'

'No, and I don't expect to. With Rangoon taken the exit from the country has turned into a flipping flood; bloody useless military forces in full retreat before the grinning Nips. For your information, I'm off to stem the tide.'

'What? Oh no, Paddy, not you too. No, no, *no*. When? Where?' Agitatedly Cara put the baby down in the cot.

'Yes, yes, *yes*, hurrah! Soon and Imphal. 'Bout time too. Should've been the first to go in being bloody dispensable.'

'You're not to say that, Paddy, you're not dispensable,' she pleaded, her eyes following his restless pacing figure.

'Thank you angel-child for those kind words, and shed a tear over the grave for a lost effing bachelor.'

'Oh shut up, Paddy! When you've left who is going to keep me informed about Lance?'

'I'll keep an eye for him coming out of the jungle and let you know since the good-looking bugger won't write to you direct, more fool he.'

'Hardly *that* epithet.' Cara had to laugh.

'Faith! Powers-that-be have made a proper balls-up this time, training us in open desert warfare then launching us into the impenetrable jungle . . .' Paddy grumbled on.

Another farewell on Quetta station, Cara and Paddy seen hugging. More raised eyebrows.

'Take care, Paddy,' she waved. 'Oh God, Paddy, *please* take care . . .'

CHAPTER 19

Pammie was the next to join the ranks of grass widows. Somehow she managed to squeeze her family into a three-roomed hut not far from Cara. It was an anxious time for her left with her young children while Frank joined the Staff of General Montgomery commanding the Eighth Army, and it was a continuing anxious time for Cara with no news of Derek's whereabouts in the desert, no news of Lance in the retreat through Burma, terrible reports of slaughter and privation coming in from the fleeing refugees.

During that hot weather of 1942, the two friends and their five children, their two *ayahs* and bearers, took a house up in Ziarat, wonderfully cool after the burning plain below. Theirs was one of the ugly corrugated-iron bunga-lows that were built higgledy-piggledy over the hillside above the valley. There they swam and dived in the small swimming pool, and went for long walks on the soft meandering paths cut through the stunted juniper forests of hot pungent scent. Little Carissa at eighteen months, and Geraldine at under a year, with chortles and screams of delight were pushed and bumped along in an ancient fold-ing pram by Jack, David and Peter.

Refreshed, they returned to Quetta, and there was a letter from Derek. He had been pulled out from the fighting for some rest and recuperation in a Cairo filled with men in khaki shorts, every hospital stuffed with wounded. Cara, relieved to hear from him, wrote back sending him a snap of Geraldine in a pram in Ziarat. She told him nothing of her personal problems. War was not a time she would distress a soldier at the front by asking for a divorce. There was still no news of Lance via Paddy. The latter had written from Imphal that he had been to the most advanced 'back-water' hospital (mostly tented, though there were some decrepit huts) where he had seen men staggering back, some crawling on hands and knees, some carried by emaciated companions, four hundred soldiers in a week, all in shocking condition.

Commodities and personnel that were of vital necessity (Paddy wrote with a good few expletives thrown in), from food to medicaments, clothing, doctors and nurses, were in desperately short supply. If he had not seen it with his own eyes he would not have believed the British capable of such a holy mess. The ill and wounded were being evacuated as soon as possible to the base hospitals to keep the bloody place from becoming a total shambles.

It was a typical Paddy letter, and it did not augur well for Lance and the Jute-wallahs. Cara's anxiety grew to fever pitch as the summer of 1942 turned to short autumn, and Quetta was cut off by unprecedented flooding of the Indus. The railway line below the Bolan Pass was carried away, roads left under water. The Indus River became a torrent miles wide over the green flatland. The water carried everything before it. Villagers with their homes and flocks were swept down, the people's livelihood destroyed. The floods left Quetta high and dry and cut off all except by air. Small aircraft landing on the brown-packed RAF strip out at Samungli brought in the mail and any VIPs.

Inevitably there were shortages; stores and food of all kinds ran out. Those who liked their Napoleon brandy had to buy locally made Indian 'Tiger' brand. To make the spirit less lethal the oily surface was sucked off by the Europeans through a straw to a depth of an inch, spat out, and replaced with sherry. In the cold months, mixed with ginger wine, it fairly coursed warmth through the veins! Coal ran out and Ghulam Haidar ordered the sweeper to make *golis*, rolled balls of coal dust and dung, to keep Cara's fireplace filled.

At last there came another letter from Paddy in Imphal. Cara rushed round with it to Pammie's quarters.

'Lance is out of Burma,' she panted. 'Paddy's seen him. Thank God he's safe!'

'Hang on, old thing. Where is he?'

'Evacuated to hospital, Paddy doesn't seem to know where.' Cara scanned the letter again. 'He says he was such a scarecrow he hardly recognized him . . . going to discharge himself *ek dam* and go to his property. Typical. Pammie, I have to go to him. Will you look after Geraldine with ayah?'

'Of course, but you *can't* go – the floods, have you forgotten? No one is allowed to leave unless it's on urgent military business, you know that. You'll be stopped at the station if you try.'

'I'll wangle it somehow.'

'Don't be an ass. You can't get through *physically*. The breaches. The new Commandant had to fly up unaccompanied in one of those civilian Dragonflies.'

'There are boats. I'll get into one with the populace. I'll find a way. Can you manage without Ghulam Haidar? I'd better have him with me if only to help row,' Cara replied buoyantly. Lance who had come back from the jaws of death was ill and needed her!

'I suppose you know *where* to go?' Pammie looked at her friend doubtfully.

'Hardly,' laughed Cara blithely, 'the property is at Koot-gunge somewhere beyond Aligarh on a tributary of the Ganges. That should be enough.'

'You really are the most terrible abandoned wife I've ever met. Will you stop at nothing? No wonder you've got yourself a bad name, you dotty old thing. When do you propose going?'

'As soon as I can get onto a train.'

'I wish you wouldn't. You could be swept away in the floods; you could run into Gandhi's civil disobedience disturbances in Rhori. They're said to be on the rampage, open rebellion broken out according to the local news station, and taking advantage of the flood chaos. Hundreds of people are reported murdered on the roads every week, half of them set on fire. Trains are derailed – Lord, I don't know

240

how you can contemplate leaving your daughter,' Pammie fussed.

'I could be run over by a bus! Not to worry. I'll be back.'

Pammie gave up. She saw that nothing she could say was going to stop Cara from going to Lance. And it didn't.

She wangled her ticket on the train by saying she was a nurse. (True, she had her certificate from the Mission Hospital to show she'd passed her VAD exams, not to mention her Ambala Red Cross card.) She was urgently needed in the hospital in Kootgunge to replace staff going to the Burma front in the emergency, the latter a bald-faced lie.

'Kootgunge?' the busy movement control officer asked tentatively, not wanting to display his ignorance of such a place.

'That's right,' said Cara with a winning smile, 'near Aligarh.'

'Ah yes,' he'd heard of that one. Without further ado, he stamped her pass.

She set off on her private campaign dressed for the part in WAC(I) uniform borrowed off a friend, minus the badges. It consisted of khaki trousers and shirt with sleeves rolled up, socks and sensible flat-heeled shoes. She tied her bright hair up in a green scarf bandeau. Over her shoulder she carried a bulging canvas army satchel, which contained as well as passport, purse and picnic, a good many medicaments given her by the Mission Hospital who once again asked no questions and raised no eyebrows when she said she was going to nurse 'a friend', but sent her off with their blessing. She parked the Chev at the station in a spot away from the normal traffic but convenient to pick up on return, and with Ghulam Haidar following carrying his *dhurrie*-rolled bedding, and a coolie following *him* with her suitcase and bedding roll, she marched with determined step onto the platform.

Over two years since she had come up it with Derek, Cara went down the lengthy twisting Bolan Pass, this time in no comfortable coupé for two, but squeezed into a packed carriage. In snatches she slept with cricked neck

241

overnight. Dawn brought the train to a halt on the brink of the floods, the line ending in mud.

The sight of the devastation was heightened by the sun rising blood red over what had once been land growing crops, sheets of water shining into the distance, some way away a terrifying tumultuous river roaring past. Tops of houses could be glimpsed isolated in deep water where trees, with stark branches from which gibbering monkeys chattered nervously and brown crows perched precariously, stood out of the water like remnants from a typhoon.

'Military personnel only.' An officer stood by a line of army trucks barring her way. 'There'll be a bus along presently.' He pointed to where a crowd waited by the roadside.

Cara and Ghulam Haidar joined the queue. She sat on her bedding roll and watched the young bearer get out the spirit lamp, pump it up and boil water. Nothing had touched her lips since leaving Quetta fourteen hours before, and her breakfast with Ghulam Haidar of a hard-boiled egg and buttered sandwich washed down with Nescafé, tasted delicious. Though she faced what she knew was the most primitive and difficult journey of her life, she remained elated rather than daunted. Soon she would be seeing Lance again!

The first bus filled up, and hours passed before another came and they could board it to be crammed in with other travellers. She was the only white person. Men, women, children, babies, bundles and livestock took up every inch of space inside, a great many more on the roof and hanging onto the door. The elderly broken-sprung bus bounced and careered from one hump and pothole to the other in a pall of dust and heat for twenty miles over a dirt track that had never been a road, but had been formed out of the countryside by a succession of truck and bus wheels since the disaster. It led through a narrowing spit of land with floods encroaching on either side. The bus stopped at isolated villages. In one a great many people were about waving banners and beating drums, 'Quit India' signs bold on walls. No one in the bus appeared to bear her a grudge. Indeed every time the bus lurched and she, perched on her *bistra* for a

242

seat, was in danger of flying off, they laughed gustily and helped to hold the memsahib down.

By this period Cara had progressed from kitchen Urdu to speaking it fluently from talking to the patients in the Mission Hospital, country people such as these. Seeing them under a different adversity from illness, she admired them all the more for their resilience in the calamity that had overtaken them, many of them having been left homeless. She admired them for the way they shared what little they had left in their extreme destitution. Whole families stayed determinedly together, the more able caring for the very young and the very old.

Stiff, sweaty and weary after six bumpy hours, Cara climbed down from the bus and walked with the crowd towards the torrent of the Indus proper. Here, with feet squelching on the flooded banks, the natives rushed for one or another of the country boats plying to and fro over the turgid water. Much of Cara's elation at being on her way to Lance had by now left her, and once packed into a small vessel with some fifteen fearful souls plus panicking livestock, the boat in imminent danger of upsetting on this the most hazardous part of the journey so far, the remainder of her exuberance vanished.

She looked at Ghulam Haidar for reassurance, but saw none there, and was forced herself to find a smile and nod. Ashen-faced with fear under his brown, Ghulam Haidar sat cowering in the bottom of the boat, a shawl over his head. He shivered for the whole terrifying two hours of the passage.

'I am afraid of *pani*, memsahib. I cannot swim.' His eyes rolled and all but disappeared into his skull.

'You should have told me, Ghulam,' she said remorsefully, 'I would not have asked you to come. The boat will not sink I am thinking. These men know what they are about.'

Brave words for his ears. Cara prayed that the four crew *did* know what they were doing as they guided, rather than paddled, the craft which careered at a mad rate downstream once they were in the main current. Branches, planks of

243

wood, furniture, drowned oxen and goats swirled past perilously near, even the bloated form of a white-clad body, heightening the dread of those holding on for dear life in the boat. At last they were out of the main current, the men paddling furiously in shallow water to make up for some of the way they had lost.

More than thankful though Cara and Ghulam Haidar were to find themselves on dry land over the other side, their difficulties were by no means over. They appeared to be stranded with no sign of public transport. The straggling group that had been in the boat with them wandered off towards Rohri, a railhead several miles away.

'Memsahib, wait. I find *tonga*. It is not good for lady to walk on road in night-time.'

Glad not to have to struggle on with her suitcase, Cara obediently waited. Darkness descended in a few minutes over the waterlogged land. She brewed the water in her bottle to make herself a mug of coffee, and hungrily finished the morning's sandwiches. She sat on alone in the dark knowing that sooner or later trustworthy Ghulam Haidar who had braved the water for her, would come. She was not afraid. The likelihood of a white woman being molested was remote. Yet in Rhori on the horizon she could hear the drums banging, and up the road from her there was a crowd waving banners with shouts of '*Gandhi ki jai, Gandhi ki jai*, Victory to Gandhi!'

She was puzzling over the enigma that made India safe for the white sahibs when there were demonstrations and riots against their presence with many policemen killed, police stations attacked and burnt, murders of Indians committed – so much for non-violence – when she heard the jingle of bells announcing the approach of a *tonga*, a faint orange lamp seen bobbing on the track before the clop of hooves could be heard. The driver took Cara past more demonstrations, 'Do or Die' slogans waved, straight to a rest camp in Rohri set up by the military for travellers. At last she could lie down and sleep.

Next day she boarded a train for Delhi where she spent

another night, and then caught another train south to Aligarh. There she asked the way to Kootgunge. Faces stayed blank. Nobody had heard of it.

'Somewhere not far from the Ganges River,' did not sound too hopeful, but it was all she could think of.

'Ha! Holy Ganga,' vouchsafed a resourceful station master who went to fetch a map. He traced the river with a finger. No Kootgunge was marked on it. A crowd gathered talking and gesticulating, all trying to help. Someone pushed a shy man forwards.

'The memsahib should go to Solah. Kootgunge lies beyond.' He hung his head.

'How can I get to Solah?'

'There is a bus, memsahib.'

Another long wait; another bumpy ride over a secondary country road in a rickety bus. By now, after three days and nights of travelling, tiredness had caught up with Cara, and with it near-panic set in. Ghulam Haidar spread himself in the half-empty bus and slept, and she wished she could do the same instead of her mind racing with doubts and fears. What was she doing here far away from the white man's India? What whim had brought her to this isolated country district? Had her father been right and the Chashma Shahi *was* imaginary? How much further would she have to travel before she discovered the truth?

'Kootgunge?' she asked wearily in the late afternoon when the bus arrived at Solah, a small provincial town.

'Kootgunge,' the driver pointed eastwards, 'bus stop here.'

They hired a taxi and later a *tonga* and travelled a good distance onwards, following a wide canal, every now and then a glimpse of the water caught through dark *topes* of trees. With each mile Cara became more certain that they were on the road to nowhere. She had let herself in for a wild goose chase and dragged poor faithful Ghulam Haidar along with her. The road they travelled in the horse-drawn vehicle was desolate and lonely, barren fields on one side, not even a bullock cart in sight, few signs of human life.

'Kootgunge.' The *tonga*-wallah brought his skinny nag to a halt in a village that was little more than a hamlet. Villagers came out from their huts to stare, their extreme poverty apparent.

'Ask someone if they can direct us to the Chashma Shahi,' Cara ordered Ghulam Haidar. She watched a girl in a grubby sari come near. For a moment the girl stood staring, finger in mouth, then she reached into the *tonga* and felt the texture of her khaki trousers, and Cara realized that the child had never seen a white woman before. A *chokra* in rags climbed up beside the driver.

'They say Chashma Shahi too difficult to find in dark. The *chokra* will show way,' Ghulam informed. He started up an argument with the *tonga*-wallah who was demanding double the fare for going on.

'Agree to anything he asks, only make him get going. *Jaldi, jaldi, karo.*' Cara's heart leapt. The driver responded by whipping his nag into a reluctant trot. This was Kootgunge, and they knew the name 'Chashma Shahi'! The place was *not* a myth. But would Lance be there? Cara's heart sank almost as soon as it had leapt. He could well be still in hospital in which case all this journeying had been for nothing and she would never find him. She would draw the line at chasing round all the hospitals in India for him. She would give up, and, tail between legs, do that difficult journey in reverse . . .

'I do not like this place, memsahib,' Ghulam Haidar expressed gloomily from his seat across from hers. He felt his isolation as a Muslim. 'This Hindu village, very, very poor, no *dâk* bungalow for memsahib to stay night.'

Even though Ghulam's words accentuated her fears, a prickle of excitement went hand in hand with Cara's apprehension on the last stage of her journey as the third day turned once more to night. Soon it would be over; soon she would know if what Lance had told her was true, whether there was a grant of land that the Emperor Akbar Shah had bestowed on the Begum Gardner, his adopted daughter Nissa, this the very place where the Colonel of the Horse had built a palace for his beloved Dilmilee. Soon she would know if there was a mansion where his son James and the Princess Mulka had lived after his death. Fearfully yet eagerly Cara sat forwards in her seat, eyes in the gloaming searching the road for the first sighting.

With the *chokra* indicating the way, the *tonga* turned off the canal road and made its way up a dust track covered with dried grass, loose stones, and pockmarked with rises and dips. The pony subsided into a walk, the vehicle lurching. To one side lay a thick jungle of trees narrowing the path, on the other appeared a slow-running river which the *chokra* informed in a piping voice was the Pila Nadi, a tributary of the Ganges. Another plus. Cara's heartbeats quickened. Lance had once mentioned the yellow stream!

Rapidly the sun sank over the trees, the moon rising to flood the path with ghostly light. The scene reminded Cara of stories she had read of the Mutiny where British soldiers had marched along paths in jungles like this only to run into an ambush, a volley of fire from the dark *topes* felling them. She could feel fear creeping up her spine, and she regretted having come on in the dark, wished she had stayed in the *dâk* bungalow in Solah until morning.

Yet if she could swallow her fear, the scenery before her was enchanting, the moonlight lighting up the path in the silent, tranquil night. They came to another clue, another plus, to what must once have been massive wrought-iron portals, what was left of them thrown open, half-hidden by undergrowth, one gate lying unhinged, a creeper entangled with the ornate pattern.

Now, when she saw the gates, Cara knew it was true, every word of Lance's story. A hundred years and more had passed since the Gardners had lived here and Mulka, the widow, had squandererd the inheritance to let it come to this pass, the land sold and divided up. The approach was like opening the casement to where the sleeping beauty of fairy-tale legend lay, though it became more like a fortress than a palace as the path progressed down between high dry banks which presumably had once contained a moat, the way narrowing through the remains of a massive studded gate. The drive widened to curve round in an opening free of trees, and came to an end in a large forecourt.

The *tonga*-wallah drew up his pony. Cara sat on in her seat staring in utter amazement.

Before her lay a vast, wide ruin, in pink sandstone. What had once been slender minarets soaring into the air on the rambling corners now stood, broken off, stark-snapped silhouettes against the sky. Two storeys high originally, many parts of the building had crumbled leaving great state rooms open to the heavens. The beautiful intricate parapet at the top with its dozens of graceful cupolas was left only in part, and in fragments at that.

Cara got out of the *tonga* and looked around at the cleared area where must once have been lawns and sunken gardens. Some bougainvillea shrubs gave flowering colour, a few straggly roses were left, a broken statue here, an intact stone bench there. Tall and rusting, thin lamps lined the square. Before the main entrance rose broad steps to a colonnaded porch with domed roof, and from a window on one side a flicker of yellow light could be seen through a screen. An old man appeared on the doorstep. He peered short-sightedly at the *tonga*.

'*Taihro*.' Cara ordered the driver to wait. She walked towards the steps, her heart thumping wildly.

'Is this the Chashma Shahi?' she asked the man.

'*Han*.' The retainer gazed curiously at the person's travel-worn appearance, the shirt and trousers, not sure what to make of it. '*Han*, memsahib.' He slowly recognized a woman and a white face.

'Is the Captain-sahib here?'

'Captain-sahib? *Nahin*.' The white pugried head shook. 'Memsahib has come to wrong place.'

'Who are you?'

'The *chowkidar*, memsahib.'

248

'Are you alone? Who do you work for?'

'Why does the memsahib ask?' he countered, eyes flickering past her to Ghulam Haidar standing bemused, eyes fastened on the building.

'I was told this place belonged to a Captain-sahib by the name of—'

'This be abode of Nawab of Kootgunge,' the *chowkidar* interrupted with annoyance.

'Where is he?'

'He is within,' the man allowed reluctantly, by now thoroughly suspicious of her intentions.

'Will you kindly ask the Nawab if he knows the whereabouts of the Captain-sahib of same address, maybe living in another house?'

'I will enquire.' The *chowkidar* backed up the steps and disappeared into the building, half-closing the door behind him. If she waited he might return and bar her entrance. The Nawab was an old man living like a hermit in the ruins and refusing to see anyone, no doubt. She *had* to see him to ask about Lance or all was lost, the anti-climax total. She'd come all this way to find the place existed but no one had heard of Lance! So perhaps after all it wasn't true? He had *taken* the place name to put his made-up story of family into it. She felt like bursting into tears with frustration and exhaustion. She would make one more effort. She pushed open the door and walked inside.

Cara stepped into a lofty entrance hall beyond which she glimpsed the shadow of a great marbled central room, broken staircase ending in thin air, what once must have been a huge dome now open to the sky. It was cool in the entrance hall after the sticky heat outside which had scarcely abated with the setting sun. Looking up from where she stood she saw gaps in the roof, doves resting on the exposed stonework, swallows' nests tightly clustered under a projecting eave. There was a sound of rustling feathers and a flapping of wings. An owl perhaps? She hoped there were no bats flying about.

Picking her steps between droppings, Cara followed the

retreating back of the *chowkidar* leading down a long dark corridor, musty with damp, the glimmer of a light coming from under a door at the far end. Ahead of her the caretaker opened the door and went in.

'*Hazoor* . . .' Cara heard him say.

'*Kaun hai?*' a cracked voice asked impatiently.

'*Ek tonga-wallah agaya, Hazoor* . . .' the *chowkidar* explained. Without further ado Cara slipped into the room. She stopped abruptly on the threshold.

Before her lay a picture that she could never in her wildest imaginings have dreamed up. It was a scene seldom, if ever, seen by a white woman, a scene reminiscent of another age, another century. The room was a large, semi-circular one that had been restored to its original glory. There was no electricity, but two fabulous chandeliers reflecting red, green and blue crystal hung overhead. The light came from clutches of candles, their flickering shadows lighting up glass and ornately plastered pastel ceiling. Faded flowering drapes hung on the walls, and on one side of the room, where there was a balcony recess, the drapes were rolled up like blinds into sausages to reveal exquisitely worked screens hewn out of a single marble piece, screens of such extreme delicacy they looked to be a tracery of lace. It was through these that the light came which Cara had seen from outside. The marbled floor was covered with rugs, and the room was full of heavy dark furniture. Dominating the private chamber was an outsize divan not a foot off the floor, and strewn with cushions. Over it was draped a canopy reminiscent of a throne room. On the bed, dressed only in *pājāma* bottoms, bare-footed and bare-chested, sprawled the Nawab.

'*Jao, jao*, away from here,' the Nawab said imperiously in Urdu, darkly scowling at the alien figure in the doorway. The *chowkidar* turned to see Cara behind him, and with lifted hand as if to push her out, approached menacingly. Cara stood her ground. She took a deep breath.

'GO AWAY!' the man on the bed, gazing at her angrily from black hollow eyes, exclaimed testily.

'No fear,' she said, brushing aside the *chowkidar* and removing her headscarf. She shook her hair free from the folds and allowed it to ripple down loose to her shoulders. 'No fear, after spending three days and nights travelling here through flood and heaven knows what else. And just look at you. Why aren't you in hospital?'

'I di-di-discharged myself.' The Nawab's teeth chattered, his eyes glowing with fever. 'Bloody gorgon of a matron . . . what do you want?'

'I've come to nurse you. And in case you think I don't know what I'm about, I'll let you know that I am qualified to do so.'

'D-d-don't want nursing. G-g-go away! Be be-be-better in . . . the morning. Comes on . . . evening.'

'What did they give you in hospital?'

'What's it matter?'

'Come on – tell me.'

'Emertine. Had amoebic dysentery.'

'Nothing for malaria?'

'D-d-didn't need it.'

'Well, you look to me as if you need it now.' Cara fished around in her satchel. Resignedly Lance shut his eyes when she came over to him purposefully with thermometer in hand and thrust it into his mouth.

With a quiver of a smile playing on her lips, she took up his wrist to time his pulse.

CHAPTER 20

The first thing Cara did after invading the palace un-announced and unwanted was to start Lance with a maximum dose of anti-malarial tablets. She told tired Ghulam Haidar to make himself as comfortable as he could in the least leaky part of the palace, and herself returned to the main room where Lance lay dozing. Letting down the *chiks* in the recess balcony, she made a small room for herself, and undid her bedding roll. With a sigh of fulfilment Cara lay down, and in a few seconds was asleep.

She was roused later in the night by Lance's delirious ramblings. Wakened out of deep sleep in the pitch dark, for a moment she found herself disorientated, and had no idea where she was. Then, scrabbling, she found the matches on the floor beside her and lit a candle.

' ... let me get to them ... bodies lying ... wet holes ... bullets splintering ... oh God, the *whine* ...' Lance sat up and blocked his ears with his hands against the fearful noise, his face distorted. 'Quick ... must get to them ... my fault ... *get* there! Go man ... go ...' he struggled out of bed.

'It's all right, Lance. You're safe in the Chashma Shahi.' Cara was at his side restraining him. 'You must rest,' she soothed, 'it's Cara with you.' She made him lie back, bewilderment at her presence showing in his glitter-ing eyes, his body burning with fever.

She could not find her way about in the eerie tomb-like darkness with only a guttering candle for light, the plop of falling masonry and the hoot of an owl disturbing the clinging silence, but she found a tin of water in an adjoining cobwebby bathroom where rats skedaddled, and she sponged down his face and chest. Familiar with his body as she was, she was shocked by the loss of weight. She gave him some more tablets and stayed with him until he slept.

It was the same the next night, his ravings waking her. Only now she was ready with a basin of water, a boiled drink, and clean linen. The theme kept on recurring: ' . . . should've saved more . . . no food . . . oh God, my men are starving! Johnny . . . face gone . . . bloody machine-gun fire . . . up to you to get 'em back . . . pull together man . . . take command!' The sweat poured off him, and she dried him with a towel and put a fresh sheet under him, throwing into a corner the sodden *chaddar*.

He cried again, shivering with cold. 'It's all right, Lance,' Cara pulled a *resai* up despite the warm night, 'you're here at home, in the Chashma Shahi; it's over now, and you're back; your men are back.' She smoothed his pillows. She saw it all in his strangled words. The full 900-mile withdrawal through Burma that took the Jute-wallahs three months, fighting until their ammunition ran out, then chased, ambushed, starved out by the persistent, well-trained, jungle-wise Japanese, and they, the Jute-wallahs, had been so thoroughly trained in desert warfare! Johnny MacCreath's terrible end. Bodies left in blood-spattered muddy pools.

Day after day, week after week, the ever-lessening remnants fought on, each section told to get back on their own as best they could, Lance leading the Jute-wallahs. They struggled through the hostile, steaming, leech-ridden jungle, half-starved, riddled by sickness, followed and shot at all the way. Somehow he shepherded back what was left of his unit to be deloused and deleeched with thousands of others. They were packed off to different hospitals where they were received by overworked nurses with terrible cases of those seriously

253

wounded on their hands. It was understandable how Lance, suffering only dysentery and debility, had discharged himself at the first possible moment.

'It's all right, Lance, you're home; it's all over now. You did not let them down. You brought them back . . .'

And Cara did indeed invade the old *mahal*. She and Ghulam Haidar teamed up against the ancient *chowkidar*, who had been feeding the Nawab on scruffy *chappattis* and scraps of fly-blown mutton cooked in a dungeon that passed for a kitchen. The beautiful marbled room Lance had restored was virtually the only one in the mansion that was habitable, but on searching round she and Ghulam Haidar found two rooms that were sound and weatherproof. After scrubbing and cleaning them, therein the bearer proceeded to set up his kitchen quarters. They found table and tea-chests and some mendable pieces of furniture, and soon there was a bustle and a hammering about the place that made Lance laugh. 'Huh, a woman shattering my peace!' he teased.

The *gup*, in the way of India, quickly got round that a memsahib with servant had arrived at the Chashma Shahi. Various villagers turned up and squatted outside the great ruins more out of curiosity than anything else. Life in Kootgunge was uneventful unless the Gunga Mai burst her banks and there was disaster, and the visit of their Nawab returned ill from the war followed by a white woman was an event indeed.

Thus those first days, while Lance lay weak in bed sleeping a great deal of the time, and opening his eyes in hidden amazement when Cara came to his side to give him his medicine or sit by him while he drank the broth she had made out of the mutton that was too tough to chew, a succession of vendors came to the entrance. Some arrived on foot carrying baskets of eggs, rice, fruit and vegetables on their heads, others came by horse-drawn *ekka* containing live chickens, and a goat for milking. A bullock cart rumbled up on solid wheels bringing wood for the heating of water in kerosene tins, and charcoal for cooking on. Cara left Ghulam Haidar to haggle with the salesman over the payment which she ordered should be fair, though not the exorbitant sums at first demanded. The Nawab was to be seen to be a generous man but not a foolish one – and, by custom, Ghulam Haidar received his cut.

She had got things running fairly satisfactorily; Lance was improving daily and was no longer delirious at nights, but what would happen when she left? She could not stay for more than two weeks, at most three weeks away including the journey. It would not be fair on Pammie to be away longer. If Lance was left to the old *chowkidar*'s cooking, he would most likely have a relapse of dysentery. No one from the village would be any better, and she could not leave Ghulam Haidar behind; she could never do that journey in reverse on her own.

She was still wrestling with the problem that evening when she sat on Lance's divan as usual and took his temperature.

'Normal.' She flicked the thermometer down and put it in its jam-jar doused with TCP.

'Disgusting smell,' Lance spat. 'I'm getting up.' He extended an exploratory toe from under the sheet.

'Not for twenty-four hours.'

'You can't stop me.'

'Look here,' she said firmly, 'you may think you're going to recover just like that once the fever has left you, but you're not. You only have to look into the mirror to see what a wreck of a man you are! *Listen* to me' – she would have none of his attempted interruption – 'I've nursed those ill with dysentery in the Mission Hospital. After a course of injections the patient is supposed to rest for three weeks due to the strain Emertine makes on the heart. Instead, you walk out of hospital against orders and promptly collapse with malaria. More strain on the heart. Unless you are mad enough deliberately to want to drive yourself into becoming a semi-invalid and

255

never get back to your beloved Jute-wallahs, give yourself the chance to make a complete recovery.'

'Nanny! Bossy-boots nurse! As bad as that gorgon matron.' Lance with bad grace lay back on the cushions. The truth was he felt lousy, horribly weak, his mouth like dried straw, his head buzzing. He had no appetite, and could just about get to the bathroom and back, and that was all. *Au fond* he was only too glad to be waited on by the naïve girl he had fallen in love with in Christchurch, the delicious but unhappy woman who had lived with him in Quetta, one who had developed since then into a driving force, perfectly capable of standing on her own two feet. What had so changed her in the time since he had last seen her?

'You're different, more mature, quite motherly,' Lance observed, his eyes like slits upon her. It was the following evening, and she allowed him to dress in the Muslim clothes he kept in a trunk and used only in the Chashma Shahi. They sat at a round table by the marble screens, Ghulam Haidar serving them a meal of boiled chicken in white sauce, rice, green vegetables, and stewed fruit to follow with egg custard Cara had baked by placing glowing charcoals on the lid of a *degchie*.

'I feel motherly,' she said eyes soft in the candlelight. 'Motherly' was another stage in their relationship: girl-friend, mistress, nurse . . . would she ever be his wife?

'Memsahib!' A familiar figure stood salaaming in the doorway, round face wreathed in smiles.

'Nasrullah Khan,' Cara gasped to see the Muslim servant, 'how did you know . . . how did you get here? I would not have thought it possible!'

'Bazaar news, memsahib. My familee live this side of Solah. No distance.'

'Have you been in work?'

'No, memsahib.' He wobbled his head sadly. 'Times are hard in district.'

Cara did not hesitate. 'The Nawab-sahib wishes you to serve him and look after the *mahal* when he is away . . .'

'Look here. Don't I have any say in the matter? Who is he anyway?' Lance asked sourly.

'My old bearer.' Cara turned to Lance. 'Soon I must go; you'll find him invaluable. Try him out, and if you've got an ounce of sense you'll hang onto him permanently and get his family along to do the caretaking.'

'Willingly I work for the Nawab-sahib.' Nasrullah Khan salaamed deeply to Lance. 'It is honour to serve the son of the old Nawab who married the teaching lady from Scotland.'

'See, he knows it all . . .'

'Good God, what am I supposed to say?' Lance lounged back in his chair with a smirk on his thin face. 'The palace is supposed to be a quiet spot. Since you arrived it's become more like a railway station! *Thik hai.*' He dismissed Nasrullah Khan with a 'you may carry on' grand wave of the hand.

Five minutes later, the bearer, now dressed in a clean white *achkhan*, came in with two mugs of coffee. He deposited them on a side table by their sofa chairs, and proceeded to clear the table swiftly and deftly.

Cara smiled at his retreating figure. 'Dear Nasrullah Khan, how he hated the cold of Quetta! He positively shrivelled up in it. Whether in camp or moving house, there he was within minutes of arrival establishing order out of chaos. By the way you need a tray and some proper kitchen equipment.'

'I know. All in good time. Priority one was to get this room restored so that I could stay here. Like it?'

'Love it! It's beautiful – the shape, the chandeliers, the screens . . .'

'India suits you. You appreciate the people; that's because you've bothered to learn the language properly. Most memsahibs don't get further than kitchen Urdu.'

'Everything about the country interests me.' Cara turned her head away from him to watch a myriad of moths fluttering round the candle on the table, attracted by its light as she felt attracted.

'So you've bequeathed your bearer for when you go. "Soon", you said. What's the hurry? Your husband is in North Africa, isn't he?'

'He is, or rather was the last time I heard from him. I — I have certain commitments . . .' she dodged. She longed to tell him about Geraldine, but how could she? Instead she talked about Paddy. 'He's a darling,' she said, 'wonderful to me after I heard about my parents and Bobby. It was a most dreadful shock . . . all on the same day.' She still could not bear to dwell on it.

'He mentioned it when we met briefly on my way out. I'm so sorry about that, Cara, very sorry. Bobby was a grand fellow. Poor Susan.'

'I hear from her from time to time. She's seeing to the business side, not that there's anything to see to. The parents left nothing — hadn't even insured the new house. Did you know she had a son the month after Bobby was reported killed? Another Robert.'

'That's good.' Lance took out his cigarette case from the recess of his dress, drew the candle towards him and lit up. 'Do you hear from Uncle Tom?'

'Can you imagine him writing? Never!'

'Sensible chap,' Lance said dourly, inhaling.

'When you're fit will you be going back to Burma?'

'Certainly. The Japs are gathering round Imphal like hungry jackals, eyes on the lush riches of India. Our turn now. We'll beat the hell out of them and chase them all the way down to Rangoon. The Jute-wallahs are out for revenge.'

'They're saying in Quetta that masses of Indian PoWs have gone over to the other side — National Liberation Army or something. There were demonstrations and "Quit India" signs in Rohri where I boarded the train over the floods. Can Gandhi really want India to be under the Japanese?'

'Floods? What floods?'

'Didn't you hear me telling you that first evening? No? I suppose you were too feverish to take it in. When you

258

ordered me in no uncertain terms to go away, I said nothing would *induce* me to after crossing the flooded Indus in a tiny boat where the railway line was breached.'

'Well I never,' said Lance looking at her open-eyed. 'It used to be "competent Cara". Now we must tack on "courageous Cara".'

'Come,' Lance said a few days later, 'I'll give you a conducted tour.' He led her round the outside of the ruin, indicating the rooms to be rebuilt, the marble staircases to lead up to a galleried mezzanine, above which the massive central dome would be restored. He told her how he planned modern plumbing, and how they would have their own generator plant for electricity, the chandeliers lit with low-wattage bulbs to look like candles.

They went through broken cloisters to the very heart of the building, walking almost on tiptoe so dangerous were some walls. Here were the old *zenana* quarters, a secluded and peaceful area before a large neglected open space of broken basins and rampant blue convolvulus creeper, a space which had once been the pride of Nissa who had tended a border of medicinal herbs herself. Cara was entranced. She gazed about her with shining eyes: the fountains had played, the swings swung, the laughter of Nissa's fourteen slave girls tinkled. She had always known it was true!

' . . . one day my wife will enjoy it,' Lance was saying. 'Here in the shaded garden it will be as cool as cool. Traditionally the women wear loose Indian clothes in the heat. *You* should wear Asiatic dress and do away with those restrictive waistbands.' He eyed her narrow leather belt about her small waist.

He himself looked every inch the Nawab in his thinness, long nose accentuated, his silk, high-buttoned *achkhan* of small collar with flowing vents on either side of skirt giving freedom of movement, as did his loose cotton *silwar*. In his delicate condition he wore a beige *lubuda* thrown across his shoulders against the chill of humid evening air – an Indian shawl he had told Cara had once belonged to William. Who did he have in mind for wife, she pondered, an Indian wife? Or was he thinking of Janet? What did he mean by *she* should wear Asiatic dress?

There were many questions that remained unanswered in the next few days when Lance, rapidly regaining his strength, took Cara further afield, first to the ruined stables at the back which had housed elephant stalls as well as the fleet of horses Colonel Gardner kept for his officers and for their visiting friends. She saw the walled garden of large propensities, now nothing but grass humps and a tangle of weeds, where William had instigated the growing of fruit and vegetables for his large household of staff and tail. Next to these fallen walls was the bath-house, a separate building still in fairly reasonable condition. It was an old-fashioned *hamām* where an underground furnace boiled water for steam. The clients were scrubbed and shampooed, then broiled, and finally massaged all over with coconut oil. And here it was that Cara was shown, bubbling out below a rock, the famous spring after which the Chashma Shahi was named.

One day Lance ordered a *tonga* and took Cara down river through miles of old jute and sugar plantations now gone to seed, a few huts standing in the fields, a few decrepit villages left, a few listless coolies in rags, living, or dying, in unspeakable conditions of poverty.

'I will restore the land for them,' Lance said; and Cara believed he would do that too.

They came to a spot where a tub was moored. The *tonga* waited while they paddled over to an island midstream where on a small knoll was situated a pavilion, arched and elegant. It lay in a superb position with views across the river over the tops of jungle trees, water lapping at the base, the little tub rolling gently at its moorings.

'I wanted to bring you here to show you where James came when he ran away with Mulka. From the dome of the Chashma Shahi one used to be able to see his pavilion. Nissa went up there to gaze upon it and shed tears because her husband and her son had fallen out. William did his best to harden his heart against his son permanently, so furious was he that James had run away with his ward. But he loved his son dearly, saw how Nissa was pining, and eventually came here by boat to visit James. James, overjoyed to see his father again, swam out to the boat and all but drowned. William relented only just in time to fish him out! I want to make the pavilion into a retreat and put a plaque on it in James and Mulka's memory. It would be a good place for two people to come to when they want to be alone,' Lance said. And he took Cara into his arms.

The only other living creature who saw Lance and Cara embracing was a brilliantly feathered jungle peacock startled on his wanderings in search of seed. With a great deal of pouting of feathers, and a great clatter of wings, he flew over their heads to roost with indignant beady eye in a nearby tree.

'Oh dear,' said Cara sublimely, 'we must have stolen his favourite stamping ground.'

'I am feeling better,' Lance said that night 'candle in hand' when Cara was about to bed down on the *charpoy* Ghulam Haidar had found for her in the first days and placed by the marble screens.

Lance drew Cara onto the Nawab's divan – and blew out the candle.

Now it was different again. Now they lived exclusively in the present and knew a blessed relief from tension. Now there was tenderness and gentleness and gratitude, and a roundness of love, the magical innocence of the old Christchurch days mingling with the passion of Quetta, together with the joy of being in each other's arms once more, she having battled her way down to the Chashma Shahi, he having come up through the dangers of war.

261

Now she knew that she meant far far more to him than merely a woman to bed.

'We must have a talk,' he said at breakfast.

'I thought we were talking.' She looked at him with her heart in her eyes.

'I mean seriously.'

'Oh?' She noticed the grim set of his lips.

'I can see that you have to go back to Quetta – your quarter is there; your husband's pay goes there, your war work is there. I am no ruddy use to you until this war is finished, the Japs beaten. To put it bluntly, what are you going to do when it *is* over? Are you going back to your husband, or are you going to throw in your lot with me? I know it is a hypothetical question as both I and your husband may be killed, and you may end up with neither of us. I think we ought to get it straight.' His dark eyes looked hard.

'Whatever happens I cannot go on with Derek.'

'So,' Lance said, his voice kept very neutral, 'the understanding between us is that you will get a divorce?'

'Yes,' she said in a small voice, and added, 'I don't think it would be possible when he's on active service.'

'I said *when the war is over*,' Lance threw out angrily, a muscle in his cheek working. 'The man is fighting. The whole thing stinks behind his back.'

'Yes,' she said once more, her face averted.

'I don't trust you not to rat on me again once my back is turned.' He glared at her, all his illness, all the hurt he had suffered in war and at her hands reflected in his gaunt looks and hollow deep-set eyes.

'I did what I did, Lance,' Cara was stung to answer forcibly. 'What I did is done. It is in the past and I cannot undo it. I have to – and you have to – live with it. You have to believe me when I say I cannot resume with him.' She wanted to say how she had made a terrible mistake in marrying Derek, how he had been constantly preoccupied with work, how it wasn't as bad as it sounded because they had barely lived together as man and wife. But what was the point in saying it? To try and justify herelf? That she would not do; she would *not* discuss Derek with him. As well, she wanted to tell him about Geraldine. But that was impossible. It would blatantly point out how soon she had come into his arms after being in Derek's. It might disgust him to such an extent it would kill his love for her, and that at this moment she could not bear, not now when she had just got him back. Later, when Geraldine was older, would be the time to tell; when the war was over events would be further away and they could talk more rationally. All she could do now was to try and reassure him, to beg him to trust her, to tell him her feelings . . .

'I love you, Lance,' Cara whispered in the marbled room with its screen, drapes and chandeliers, 'I will never stop loving you . . .'

Before she left, Lance gave Cara a ring. The jewel, a ruby, was embedded in a heavily embossed petalled and flowered silver setting. It was flamboyant yet beautiful, an oriental piece of jewellery such as Cara had never seen before.

'Moghul,' Lance said. 'It belonged to Mulka.'

CHAPTER 21

Lieutenant-Colonel Derek Brownlow RA, having fought through most of the ding-dong North African campaign without a scratch, and been awarded the MC for his leadership and bravery in Tobruk, embarked with the allied forces for Sicily. He proceeded with his division to fight on up the mainland of Italy. In the January of the next year, 1944, when the forces threw themselves against the heavily defended German positions on Monte Cassino, he was severely wounded on the rocky slopes, yet, isolated, he continued to fight single-handed. He lay hidden all night sodden by the downpour. Twenty-four hours later he was discovered unconscious by the Germans and taken prisoner.

This much Cara was informed by letter from the District Headquarters in Quetta. Months later a letter arrived from the Red Cross to say that on 20 May her husband was one of nine hundred to be repatriated to the United Kingdom in exchange for an equal number of German and Italian PoWs on the seriously ill list who would never fight again. The exchange was to take place in neutral Spain, the wounded carried aboard a Swedish ship.

A second letter from District Headquarters followed the Red Cross missive some weeks after to the effect that her husband was now in hospital in England, and an immediate priority passage to the United Kingdom would be arranged for her and her child *did she wish it*.

His repatriation home in the middle of war was the one event Cara had not anticipated. Derek had said he was based on India and if anything happened he would be sent back there. It was a bewildering turn of events. Her one desperate wish was to remain in Quetta where Lance, embattled in the renewed fighting in Burma, could contact her. With drawn face she told Pammie of her decision, her friend nodding silently, compassion in her eyes. Cara sent off a telegram to Lance c/o HQ Imphal: 'Derek being repatriated UK severely wounded. Stop. Am given priority passage home. Stop. Re-affirm agreement. Stop. All my love always, Cara.'

With the battle for the retaking of Burma raging, it was not surprising Lance never received it.

Cara with Geraldine, now three years old, joined a convoy which slipped out of Bombay harbour with the least possible fuss, and set sail for the Red Sea. The ship was packed with people being repatriated for various reasons of postings or compassion. The women and children were berthed on one side, the men on the other (some of them the husbands). By now the allies were firmly back on French soil, and the soldiers on board were anxious and eager to reach that front before the war terminated.

Each cabin was packed solid with extra berths. Cara shared an old two-berther with two other wives and their children. Boat station practice was the order of the day, and at night the women slept in their petticoats, outer garments and panic bags to hand. Perhaps the most chilly announcement for the mothers came over the tannoy on departure: 'The ship will NOT, repeat NOT stop for any man, woman or child overboard' – and Geraldine was at the most uncontrollable active age! Cara devised a harness out of a cot sheet, and kept a constant grip on the reins round her small daughter throughout the journey.

Other ships joined the convoy at Suez and sailed up the Canal into the choppy eastern Mediterranean where a Royal Navy aircraft-carrier waited to escort what had by now become a huge convoy. It made a magnificent sight. Cara spent much time on deck gazing at the vast concourse of shipping on all sides. Tremendously impressive, it was also heartening to be surrounded by fellow ships in such dangerous waters. With two frigates on the flanks, corvettes and more escort vessels in other positions, a destroyer scurrying to and fro like a sheepdog guarding its flock, the convoy began its dramatic zig-zagging. The ships in formation turned in perfect unison hugging the safety of the North African coast as closely as possible, a big sweep one way, a big sweep the other, all the time keeping down to the speed of the slowest ship, one of those heavily laden small freighters whose precious cargo was the life-blood of the United Kingdom.

Now at nights it was 'darken ship', portholes closed, doors screened, smoking forbidden, troops entombed in the bowels, and just before the Straits of Gibraltar it was 'batten ship', the thick smokescreen seeping into the cabins to add to the feeling of suffocation. Orders were given to keep voices down, and the ship became a clouded pall of silence. Out in the Atlantic the German submarines lurked, waiting to pounce, enemy aircraft on the alert to attack.

But Cara's convoy encountered nothing more than a good many alarms, and after sailing into snow-lashed gales round Northern Ireland (this outside passage taken in order to avoid the dangers of the Bristol Channel) the convoy divided, half heading for Glasgow, Cara's half, after five weeks of journeying, circling round the Isle of Man and anchoring well out in the Mersey Channel. During another endless week of bitter weather, colds and coughs prevalent on board where many of the families had only tropical clothing, they waited, food running short, the bombed outline of Liverpool so near and yet so far. At last the passengers on Cara's ship were allowed to disembark, she and Geraldine entraining for London and then Southampton, the stations they passed through seething with military personnel on their way to reinforce the Second Front.

Late in the evening, Cara found a room for herself and her tired, crying, snotty-nosed child in a dingy hotel

266

where an unappetizing meal was dished up for them with bad grace. After settling Geraldine, Cara fell into bed and lay on creaking broken springs nostalgically thinking of another difficult journey which had ended so differently in the Moghul room of the Chashma Shahi, Lance sprawled on his Nawab's divan, she snug and happy on her bedding roll laid out by the marble screens.

In the morning Cara took a taxi to the Military Hospital, and with Geraldine at her side, and fear in her heart, walked the seemingly interminable dark green corridors to an officers' ward. The red-caped QUAIMNS Sister took Cara into her office and bade her sit down.

'Delighted to see you, Mrs Brownlow. Your husband's been counting the days. Knowing that you were on your way has made all the difference to his morale. He hasn't seen his little girl before, has he?'

'No, he hasn't seen her, Sister. How is he?'

'Coming along nicely. The Germans looked after him quite well in comparison to the conditions of some of our patients who were returned from Italian so-called hospitals.' The Sister pursed her lips in some disgust.

'Improving from what wound?'

'Haven't you seen a medical report?'

'There wasn't time to receive one. I was given my passage almost immediately.'

'I see. Well, Mrs Brownlow, improving from his third operation to remove the shrapnel in his spine. He was operated on first in Germany, but on repatriation his health was in an unstable condition — he suffered pneumonia after exposure in Italy — and the medical board decided to wait to build up his strength before undertaking two further lengthy and delicate operations in the hopes of restoring some use in his legs.'

'Has it, Sister?'

'Too early to tell, Mrs Brownlow. He stood up to the operations very well. This way.' She led Cara into a large old-fashioned ward.

Right at the end of the room, back to a ceiling-to-floor

window, Derek lay prone on a raised bed, white sheet turned down over blankets drawn to his neck. He turned his head and watched his wife walking down the long ward towards him, her Titian hair bouncing on her shoulders, the small child's hand in hers. A smile of pure joy spread over the invalid's pale, ravaged face.

'Hello, long time since Quetta,' Cara said, bending her face to his, 'here's Geraldine to meet you.' She lifted the child up. 'Geraldine, give . . . Daddy a kiss.'

Six months later Cara had her daughter and her husband installed into one of the bungalows on the estate that had once been the grounds of Wick House. To complete the household came Bugler, fatter and silkier than ever, collected from Dr Walker's. With her small daughter gamely trotting beside them on sturdy legs, Cara took dog and child for a blow on Hengistbury Head, and came back to get the tea, wash it up and put it away, put Geraldine to bed, read her a good night story – more often than not *The Jungle Book* – get the supper and clear that up, and later do some chores for her husband that he could not do for himself, wheel-chair bound as he was.

'How's that?' she'd say plumping up the cushions and straightening her aching back.

'Wonderful!' Derek would answer with his wry smile. 'Wonderful, little woman!'

Driven by the tide of war back to these familiar surroundings (though the great old beech was gone, Cara could identify the site of the bungalow as being on the tennis court – the court on which she had played tennis with both Lance and Derek) Cara took flowers to her parents' tomb in the family vault, flowers given her by the dotty garden boy who had beautified the castle grounds. She renewed old acquaintances, snatched a sail when Geraldine was in kindergarten, and made new friends at the Yacht Club, of which she was a life member and round which her social life – such as it was

– revolved. She listened to the war tales of England and told some of hers of India and the journey home.

Susan Thornton, her widowed sister-in-law, came to stay with young Robert, the small cousins playing together; and Cara told Susan something of Lance, and Susan told Cara of her forthcoming marriage to one of Bobby's pals, an Australian Air Force man of the name of Holroyd who owned a farm outside Sydney to which he would be retiring.

'Sounds a nice open-air sort of life in which to bring up Robert.' Cara swallowed her disappointment that once the war was over they would be going far away.

'You and I, each in our own way, has to pick up the bits and start afresh,' Susan said.

'I don't think Derek would appreciate being called "bits"!'

'Well, I'm glad you had the nous to come back to him, old thing. You'd never have forgiven yourself if you hadn't. I always liked Derek. Amazing guts, hasn't he? And he's getting better every day at manoeuvring around, isn't he?'

'Yes; you've noticed he's taken to doing the washing-up for me,' Cara said tiredly. 'He's taught himself to do practically everything from the chair.'

'I think he's wonderful with Geraldine. When she's older he'll be invaluable. Help her with her homework and all that sort of thing.'

'She adores him, and trots around after him. It's Daddy this and Daddy that all day long. He's gone right into work from his old barracks. Trust him.'

'What's that?' Susan asked Derek who was wheeling himself into the room.

'MEXE. Military Experimental Establishment. Quite secret. Absolutely up my street! Books all over the place in the little woman's drawing-room.' He looked about him at the stacks on the floor. 'Humn. Have to rig myself up with a den.'

The tempo of Cara's life concentrated on looking after

husband, child, and Uncle Tom, the last remaining member of her family, and still berthed in his shack. Her caring relationship with him resumed where it had left off in the spring of 1939, only now she took Geraldine with her when she went to wash his shirts, cook him a wholesome meal, throw away accumulated empty beer bottles, and generally make him 'ship-shape'. It was obvious to the fishermen of Mudeford who knew best the eccentric, solitary old salt, that his red-headed niece and his dark-haired great-niece were the cheer and solace of his great old age.

'How's that?' Cara would say straightening her aching back after sweeping round and tidying up in the shack. She looked at her uncle's mottled blue-red nose and thought it couldn't really get any larger without bursting.

'Marvellous!' Uncle Tom would say giving Geraldine a huge wink, 'bloomin' marvellous, that's what your mother is.'

Victory Day in Europe came and went with a great carillon of the Priory bells, and a great celebrating and dancing on Christchurch's High Street. Next, VJ Day came and went to much rejoicing. By now Cara had her new home straight, had set Derek up in a room built on for him at the back in lieu of a study, where with table and desk and low bookshelves he could manoeuvre himself round and engross himself in his gun experiments and calculations. Having mastered the art of undressing and levering his body into bed, he was free to burn the electricity late into the night to his heart's content. Cara was always asleep by the time he came into their room. She never knew what time he came to bed, and he was always up before her, wheeling himself back in to wake her with a cup of tea. Nothing had changed . . . and yet everything had changed.

There was one more thing Cara had to do, and after VJ Day at last she found time to do it. Nearly six-and-a-half years after she had sailed for India, she opened the trunk she had packed at Wick House. Time raced backwards, madly out of control, as she examined her possessions from those days: favourite books, school photographs, tennis trophies, domestic course certificate, her old-fashioned skating boots, her silver dressing-table set, a shawl her mother had knitted for her as a baby, a doll — all kinds of things that had been precious enough to keep, and were still precious.

She stopped dead, though, when she saw the letters lying on the cashmere twin-set Lance had chosen for her at the exhibition in Exeter. They lay cushioned by the soft rose as she had packed them, neatly tied together in bundles with red ribbon. Each letter was numbered, the dates near-illegible over Indian stamps. She picked up the packet addressed to 'Miss Carissa D. Thornton, Wick House, Christchurch, Hants', untied the ribbon binding them, and read the first letter. Forgetting everything else, she bundled back into the trunk all the things she had taken out except the letters. She began to read them right through; and then she re-read them.

It was the most terrible mistake to have done so.

It left her exhausted, tight-chested, and parched with unshed tears. In the process of reading them Cara fell in love all over again with Lance, with those first sweet days when she held her life's happiness in her hands. Her heart cried out in anguish for the girl she no longer was who had inspired the love letters.

Even Derek, who in his innate shyness still could scarcely look directly into his wife's eyes, noticed her drawn looks and asked concernedly if she were ill.

'Yes, I am ill,' she said, her eyes like saucers in dark rings, 'I have caught an infection from sorting out that old trunk I unpacked.'

'Dust carries germs,' he said, 'hope it's not 'flu. Interesting. I must ask Dr Walker how long 'flu bugs can live. Go to bed, little woman; have a rest. Geraldine and I will manage, won't we, little one?'

Inactivity was the worst advice, and she did not go to bed. She carried on as women down the ages have carried

271

on when their hearts are breaking. Thankful for domestic chores she carried on in the worst mental agony she had yet experienced. She learnt what Lance had gone through when he read her final letter before the war.

Her pain felt like that of a hopeless living body skewered through its guts and lying in a deep dark trap with no hope of rescue, no hope of reprieve, longing to die. For some days she had not been quite sane, warped with her wistfulness for those pre-war days with Lance, with her grief at having lost him then through her own fault. She had little recollection of what she did during that time though she must have gone automatically about her business of cleaning, washing, cooking, looking after child and husband. But with the ensuing days and weeks, the grief, the agony, the remorse, the longing for Lance, did not lessen, and in desperation she wrote to him via his old Tinling firm in Calcutta, saying nothing much, but asking how he was, asking how he had come through the war.

When she had first arrived in England and saw Derek's condition, she had written to Lance c/o HQ in Imphal, the only military address he had given her. She did not know if previously he had received her telegram saying she was coming to England to see Derek in hospital, and she did not know if he had received her subsequent letter explaining that she must stay. 'It has to be "goodbye". I have messed up your life twice and you had best forget me for I do nothing but hurt you,' she had written.

For months no answering letter came to her present one, and by the time it did, she had somewhat recovered her equilibrium. Nevertheless the regular, familiar writing in black ink on white paper, exactly the same as before, unbalanced her to such an extent it was some time before she could steady her trembling hands sufficiently to slit open the envelope. He was well. He had survived the romp down Burma and Malaya more or less in one piece; he had been returned to civilian duties at the end of the war in the Far East. He was back with his firm and well up the ladder, and he was soon to be married.

Cara had no wish to start up a correspondence again, but she could not restrain from asking more. His answering letter came back promptly:

Dear Carissa,

Since you ask, yes, it is Janet, and no, I have not seen her again, in fact not since that summer in Christchurch. It is perfectly possible to become engaged without meeting, you know! Had I been able to obtain a passage earlier (the back-log of people trying to get home after the war is enormous, shipping terribly short) we would have been married ere now. Her father has bought me a partnership with the firm which opens up great possibilities. I am on several other boards. I await my marriage impatiently, deeply grateful to Janet for her quite remarkable loyalty to me all through.

Best wishes,
Yours,
Lance.

P.S. I shall be obliged if you would return the ring.

In its way the postscript was as starkly brutal to Cara as her cable had been to Lance in 1939. And the final silence that followed now was as equally total as it had been then.

There was no more to be said, no more letters to be written. Cara had finally burnt her boats. She knew exactly what Lance would do with the riches that would come with his marriage, and though it took a long time for her to become reconciled to the thought of Janet as the Begum of Kootgunge, in the end Cara was generous enough to wish them well in the Chashma Shahi.

PART III

Moghul Water

CHAPTER 22

'Good Lord, if it isn't Lance Gardner! What are you about?' Pammie Dangerfield took in the red tabs and the DSO ribbon next to the Burma Star with others on the breast of his bush-shirt. They met face to face in the lofty foyer of the Maidens Hotel in Old Delhi, Pammie flanked by four restless children. It was late September in the year war ended, but the temperature had scarcely cooled, the *punkah* overhead slowly stirring the tepid air.

'Fighting red tape and trying to get myself disentangled from army and hospitals.' Lance saluted the untidily dressed woman with the shiny face who looked as if she were at the end of her tether. His mind recalled. 'I was so sorry to hear of your husband's death. I admired him greatly. Please accept my deep sympathy.'

'Very kind of you,' Pammie replied stoically. 'I expect you knew that Frank stayed on Monty's staff for the Second Front and was killed in Northern Europe? He's left me in a hole. You're not the only one fighting officialdom.'

'Oh? How's that?'

'Damned bureaucrats are doing their best to force repatriation to the UK. I refuse to go. Peter, come here at once! For goodness sake shut them up, can't you, Jack?' She ordered her eldest son to stop her youngest chasing a small girl round the plush chairs and causing a rumpus in the otherwise sedate hotel. '*Cara*, come to Mummy.'

Perceptibly Lance jumped. '*Cara*'. He'd had no news of her since . . . typical of the woman to disappear. Other wartime letters had caught up with him – several from Janet. 'Whatever happened to Cara?' he asked laconically.

277

'Didn't you hear?' Pammie looked at him with her tired eyes. She felt sorry for him. She could see he was in pain. His wrist was held in a neat sling, left hand heavily bandaged. 'I know she wrote to you before leaving Quetta – oh, ages ago. She's in England with Derek and . . .'

'Yes, yes, that's what I thought.' Lance cut Pammie off. He did not want to hear one more word. He'd suspected all along that Cara would go back to her husband. So she'd written to tell him that she'd altered her mind had she? Well, he hadn't got the letter. The lady panther didn't change her spots! Once done, easy to do again. Though in an emotional moment he had given her Mulka's ring, even at the time he had been sceptical of her protestations of everlasting fidelity. Those great green eyes were by no means as candid as they appeared. He'd kept his reserve to such an extent that now, with his suspicions confirmed that she'd done another bunk, he was neither surprised nor hurt. Instead, the matter was of indifference to him. He was glad he'd lived with her in Quetta and in Kootgunge, where he'd let sentiment run away with him rather, due to being under par. She was worth possessing – a rather special body that fitted his – but she was not worth marrying. There was a weakness in her emotional make-up somewhere that allowed her to shilly-shally between one man and another. In marriage you'd never know who she was going off with next – poor bloody husband!

'Where will you go if not to the UK?' Lance deliberately switched his thoughts to more worthwhile channels.

'Canada. I have a brother in Vancouver who's expecting us. The boys need a father figure to control them.' She looked distractedly at David who was sliding down the banisters behind open double doors. With a whoop and a yell he fell off at the end. The other children had disappeared into the lift. 'If I'm forced to go to the UK first, I know I'll have one hell of a time extracting myself – probably made to pay the fare on, which I can ill afford. All I ask is that I be sent east-about instead of west-about. Why not? There are more passages available to Hong Kong than the other way round, and yet . . . the *trouble* trying to convince the powers-that-be . . .' Words failed her.

'Stick to your guns.' Lance could not help but admire the Amazon widow who knew her own mind. 'Wear them down!'

'And you? Your hand . . . ?'

'Not too bad. A couple of fingers gone. I told the MO I didn't care what it looked like as long as they plastered up the remains so that I can grasp a golf club. I've got one or two things to settle, then de-mob. Remember the Jute-wallah Battery in Quetta? They're being disbanded. Sad after all this time and their sterling work in Burma, but white units won't be needed when Indians take over. Well, I must be going. So long. Good luck with the eastern passage.'

Leaving the foyer, Lance walked down the steps under the high *porte-cochère*. From above he heard the children's excited voices, and looking up saw the three Dangerfield boys with the little girl called Cara in tow, walking along the parapet of the porch. For a moment he stood looking up aghast at the small figures. Then with a roar he ordered them to come down to the foyer. There was an immediate drum of feet as the boys recognized military authority and scampered for the French windows leading to the safety of the landing.

With a smile Lance placed his swagger-stick under his arm and walked down the drive to the gate entrance where was situated a post office on the main road. The cable he sent was addressed to Miss Janet Tinling in Brockenhurst, and it read as follows: 'Suggest you arrange quiet wedding December. Will wire date of arrival UK soonest. Love Lance.'

He felt relieved by what he had done. The past was over with its heart-searing entanglement. Should never have been. He ought to have married Janet in 1938. By now they would have had a lively brood like the Dangerfields'. Dear faithful Janet. She was thirty-seven, and she had never deviated from him since their first meeting in Scotland where her father had taken him under his wing into the jute trade. Physical passion had gone out of the window for him. There was nothing like an aching hand to stifle desire! Janet was not the passionate type. Too tall and languid; thin-lipped and thin-featured in her handsome way. Instead of passion there was devotion. He would be proud to have her as his wife, and she at last would have her tenacity rewarded. He'd suggested a quiet wedding as being more suitable to their years, his tastes, and the fact that her mother had died recently. Mr Tinling, he gathered, was now a frail widower with a muscular wasting disease that seemed to have been brought on from a fall when a bull chased him on the Angus estate. Janet, the only child, apparently had coped with her mother's death and her father's illness. She was a great woman – talented too. *She* had never let down anybody, least of all him. All through the war he had received her informative letters addressed via the firm. He could always rely on a letter from her to be there, pleasantly written, concerned, showing her affection.

Though Lance truly believed in that autumn of 1945 in Delhi that he left passion behind and was now entering into a kind of 'arranged marriage' that was eminently suitable, he had not discarded one all-abiding passion: the rebuilding of his inheritance.

In one way, with the dust of war yet to settle, with the political upheaval towards Independence rolling on its inevitable way, it would not seem to be a propitious moment to start burrowing away into ancient archives about lands that were hedged around with age-old laws of ownership. As it turned out, it was a very *good* moment in which to start the search before the rush for land began in a great upheaval of communities.

The decision taken to marry a wealthy woman came as a pleasant bonus when Lance found he only had to mention the name 'Tinling' for the banks to lend him the money he needed for his plans. He was proud of being not beholden to anyone in this matter. He was a *Zemindar*, that most illustrious and important position, a traditional landowner in his own right. But even so, when putting up his first bid for a few *bigahs* (each *bigah* approximately half an acre) adjoining the Chashma Shahi, Lance came up against an entanglement of red tape in the dusty land grant offices of Delhi that by contrast diluted military red tape into an anaemic shade of pink!

'The Colonel-sahib is a British subject, is he not?' The steel-bespectacled *babu* looked up at Lance from his stool through fogged lenses, his gnarled finger finding the Nawab's name in a battered file.

'An exception was made to the rule of *bilayati* ownership in our case a century and more ago. The lands were bestowed in perpetuity upon the Begum Gardner, adopted daughter of the Emperor Akbar Shah, and her heirs and successors.' Lance let him have the lot for good measure.

The *babu*, unimpressed, waggled his hoary finger at Lance. 'Indian citizenship, no problem. British citizenship, I tell you sir, *every* problem!'

Rather than go through the hurdle of attempting to explain his birthright each time he bid for land or sought permission to build and develop, Lance determined to gain Indian citizenship. Surprisingly, in those early post-war days, the positive result came through from the Indian Home Department in weeks rather than months. There was no problem. The problem lay for those in the mile-long winding queue round and round the adjoining block, of Anglo-Indians panicking to obtain *British* passports.

A sort of chaotic efficiency reigned that autumn when Lance stepped up the process of putting his house in order. Delhi reeled from the effects of years of war, from demobilizing the largest volunteer army in the world, from vociferous clamour for this and that. Loyalties were divided. Some wanted affairs to go on under the impartial Raj as they had for hundreds of years; others (called traitors or freedom fighters according to the point of view) had invited the Japanese in rather than have the British stay. It was a city pregnant with new factions, new aspirations, new nationalism. Mahatma Gandhi's peaceful demonstrations spilled over into flames. There were beatings by police, murders between sects, and the 'Quit India' signs that Cara had seen in Rohri during the floods three years previously grew in spidery markings on every wall. Few Indians grasped at that time that many British, with so much of their life-blood spilled in Europe and Asia, had grown weary of being told they were not wanted. Few grasped that by now the British were as eager to get out as the Indian politicians were to see them go, and that the only thing that kept them on for less than two years longer was a decent wish to hand over with dignity to a stable government the greatest democratic power the east had ever known, a power united by the Raj from Moghul days.

If anyone voiced these thoughts they fell upon deaf ears. Time had nearly run out for the British. Indian patience *had* run out.

But in the midst of it, the Nawab of Kootgunge was fast coming into his own.

'What are my orders?' Lance enquired of his fiancée on the Tilbury dockside. He kissed her, avoiding her red lips in case he smudged them, stood looking at her, admiring her slim legs ending in high-heeled crocodile-skin shoes, crocodile bag to match, her heavy cloth coat swirling round her.

'Your only orders, darling,' Janet laughed, 'are to be in church on time a week today! You don't have to worry about a thing, I've had a super time arranging it all. Like the new look?' She pirouetted prettily for him. 'We women, after the shortages of war, are all out for the longer extravagant line.'

'Suits you,' he said truthfully. The bulkiness hid her thinness. She had always starved herself for the sake of her career. He noticed the slightly lighter shade of hair under the fur-trimmed hat, and her Dresden-smooth complexion, She whisked him away in her father's chauffeured Rolls Royce to the West End.

'I suppose I'm allowed to buy the wedding ring?' He sat back luxuriously against the grey cushions. 'In the meanwhile I've got this,' he said feeling in his pocket for the blue velvet case from Hamiltons of Calcutta that had cost him a packet and with which he could have bought quite a few *bigahs*!

'Oh, darling, how absolutely sweet of you. It's lovely.' She displayed the sapphire and diamond ring on a manicured finger, holding out her hand for him to admire, thrilled to be with him again, overjoyed that at last they were to be married, He was better-looking even than she remembered: assured, aristocratic in his tanned way. He would make a marvellous model with that casual arrogance. How superbly tall he was. He was the only man she had ever met who made her feel smallish.

'Like a whisky?' Janet said swivelling round in her seat and pressing a panel in the car, a drinks cabinet revealing itself.

'Wouldn't mind.' Lance twiddled his thumbs comically over an imaginary magnate's stomach.

'Glad to see your *thumb* works,' she said pointedly. She poured the whisky from a decanter, added ice, and handed it to him. She mixed herself a gin and vermouth. 'How is the hand. Is it sore?' Lance put a match to her Turkish cigarette, held in a tortoise-shell holder, and then lit one for himself. She averted her eyes. The car purred on.

'Not really. A bit stiff, but I can hold a golf club. I hope it does not offend you?' He glanced ruefully at the stumps and the damaged fingers that had been stitched together to make one whole.

'You never wrote me what happened.' She looked out of the window. It *did* offend her. It flawed him. He was no longer a perfect specimen. She had not expected his wound to look so ugly. 'Perhaps you should go to a Harley Street man and get it tidied up?'

'I don't think so. The military surgeon in Delhi knew what he was about.'

'You could wear a glove for the wedding, a grey French kid one.'

'Isn't that too posh for a suit?'

'You're not wearing a suit. You're wearing morning dress. The man's coming to fit you later today.'

'Where?'

'At the Ritz. We've booked you and your family in. As our guests of course. Pa and I thought it would be a nice treat for them.'

'Isn't that overdoing it a bit?' It began to seep through to Lance that theirs was to be no quiet wedding but the full works. Hell! Oh, well, it was the bride's day. If that was what she wanted, he'd go along with it.

Lance learned more on the drive through heavy traffic, the bombed parts of the East End shocking to see. It turned out that since the accident on the Angus estate that had set in motion his muscular disability, Janet's father stayed in London, and barely left the Park Lane Hotel suite where he now lived with a day and night nurse in attendance. He had sold his yacht long since, had handed over to Janet the houses in the New Forest and Jersey, and a great deal of money as well. He proposed giving Lance the Scottish estate and the means to run it. The lawyer was coming in tomorrow to tie it all up together with a new will in which Mr Tinling was leaving 'the residue' to be divided equally between daughter and son-in-law.

'You're not to argue with Pa about it,' Janet stipulated, 'that's how he wants it. He regards you like a son, and he wants you to take the financial burden off me. I'm afraid you're going to find him terribly changed . . .'

The week was filled with fittings, the signing of documents in Mr Tinling's suite, and increasingly hectic pre-wedding parties to meet Janet's friends. Lance greeted the small band of Gardners from Scotland. They appeared somewhat awed by the Ritz except for Lance's brother-in-law Mac, who, as left-wing as Lance remembered him, clapped the footmen on the back and told them not to allow themselves to be 'stooges of the capitalists'.

On the wedding morning, Lance, his brother Ian, and Mac, were supplied with outsize favours, while his mother and sister Margaret were presented with the equivalent in flower sprays – by which period Lance had had more than enough of 'going along with it'.

Nevertheless, in spite of a hangover from the stag party of the previous evening, he was well in time at the Knightsbridge church on the bleak December day. Mrs Gardner sat in the front row behind him, a neat and composed figure in a heather mixture tweed suit, brogues, and small feathered hat bought for the occasion. Her cotton-gloved hands were loosely clasped in her lap. Lance exchanged a smile with her. She was as he had always known her: severe and serene. Beside her sat Margaret, Indian-featured and defiantly hatless, Mac next to her casually dressed in jacket and open-necked shirt into which he had tucked a red scarf.

In the line behind sat the few Gardner friends who had come the long distance. There were left two empty rows behind these, after which hordes of fashionable Londoners spilled over from the left side of the church. They whispered audibly to each other; no one knelt down to say a prayer. The Gardner group sat on quietly, ignoring the noise behind them, isolated by the empty rows. The muscle in Lance's cheek began to work. That gap annoyed him intensely. He felt it an insult to his family. They were treated like pariahs by a bad-mannered, distasteful, noisy crowd, who had no respect for the sanctity of church, but had come for the 'show'.

In a determined bid to regain some good humour on this day of days, Lance winked at Ian standing next to him. He felt rewarded that the youngest brother he had scrimped and saved for was now a well-thought-of lecturer at St Andrew's.

'Here she comes.' Ian, a replica of his mother and neither so tall nor as dark as the Gardners, raised an eyebrow in acknowledgement of the wink. Lance turned fully round to watch his bride come towards him on her father's arm the length of the Holy Trinity Church aisle.

The picture he saw could have been one straight out of a fashion plate – except for Mr Tinling whom Janet was patently supporting. A nurse in a dark suit and hat lurked in the background, and there was a chair placed across the way for the frail old man. *Why* had Janet gone to these lengths?

Why not a quiet dignified wedding? Lance's eyes narrowed on his bride.

By her lack of nervousness or even bridal modesty — her veil was swept off her face — it was apparent that Janet had acted this scene a hundred times for the camera. Keeping pace with her father's halting steps she came towards Lance. She wore a beautiful long-sleeved white velvet gown trimmed with swansdown, the slim-fitting front outlining her model's figure, acres of train tumbling out at the back. Cool, poised, long-necked and gliding, she approached.

Something in the sight of the bridal procession clicked into focus in Lance's mind another such scene that had haunted him for most of 1939 and had nearly driven him mad, a vision long surmounted. Why it came back to him at that most inopportune of moments Lance never knew, unless it was something to do with his mother's thought-process transmitting itself to him. She had 'the sight', and it had happened between them before. Whatever it was, there flashed before him with electric brightness the vision of another girl in bridal white coming down the aisle towards him, a radiant girl with green eyes and tumbling red hair — *one who brushed past him into another man's arms.* For a fraction of a second Lance lost Janet and only saw Cara.

Blinking to recover, on the instant Lance turned to Janet and began to make his vows: 'I will.' 'I, Lance Delhmir Gardner, take thee . . .'

'Your hand looks awkward, sir. Would you mind tucking it into your coat, sir?' the photographer said on the steps of the church, while Janet with professional expertise tilted her head this way and that for the flashing bulbs.

'Napoleon,' Lance joked with a jollity he did not feel. The photographer's remark brought back all his dislike of the *tamasha*, as he called it. Hell, why should he hide his hand in a too-tight glove? It was an honourable wound received in war with the Jute-wallahs. He was not ashamed of it, and his bride should not be. Cara wouldn't . . . oh blast Cara . . . he'd laid her bloody spectre long ago, so why wouldn't it lie

286

down? He considered it hitting below the belt to come out and taunt him on his wedding day! He climbed into the limousine with Janet for the short drive to the Hyde Park Hotel where the upstairs wedding reception in a huge mirrored room overlooking the Park did not improve his temper.

The lazy smile of indulgence he habitually wore when he was enjoying the cavortings of his fellow men hardened into black dislike at the continuing farce.

So disgusted was he by the long rambling speech of an old friend of the Tinlings who claimed to have bathed the bride in a tub in Calcutta – a patent fib as no one other than an ayah or mother ever bathed a child in India – that he cut his own speech short. He paid tribute to Mr Tinling for his pluck and generous qualities. He revealed that he had known his wife for fifteen years, since she was twenty-two, which was not exactly tactful of him but which nevertheless Janet took with good grace so intoxicated by the event was she.

Neither was Lance's temper improved by the reading out of *double-entendre* telegram after doubtful telegram which he suspected had been invented for the occasion to raise a vulgar laugh, and as soon as he could he circulated away from Janet's court to speak with one or two men in uniform. Some of these were army residue from the war, but most were navy who traditionally wore service dress for such an occasion.

Wending his way through the crowd, Lance found his womenfolk sitting at a table on their own. 'I hope we haven't let the side down too badly,' Margaret giggled, a white-gloved waiter refilling her glass.

'On the contrary, you've *raised* the tone.'

Margaret looked pleased at the compliment from the brother she adored. 'I'm enjoying myself, and Mac's having the time of his life telling the rest they ought to be ashamed of being stinking rich!'

'Delicious eats.' Mrs Gardner removed a glove and helped herself to a salmon canapé. A waiter placed some wedding cake on their table. 'We're all enjoying ourselves. Ian's well away with some pretty girls.' She indicated across the room. 'What happened to the other girl, dear?'

'What girl?' asked Margaret.

Mrs Gardner did not answer. Her pale eyes looked steadily at her eldest son.

'She married a Gunner – before the war, a regular.'

'You have been a generous son, Lance, but you must stop sending me cheques. I have all I need and can manage nicely.'

'Very well, but I hope you will come and stay with us in Scotland and India.'

'Maybe later on. I wouldn't want to intrude too soon,' she smiled gently. 'Do you think it would be rude to slip away? I don't want to have a rush for the train, and the others can join me at the station. The heat in here has given me a wee headache.'

'Of course. I'll come with you.'

Lance took her arm. Mother and son walked down the wide empty stairs together, and he saw her into a taxi. He knew the tone of the wedding had been as much anathema to her as it had been to him. He knew she could not get away quickly enough from the plush hotel of the last week; moreover he knew that she knew Janet was second best to the girl who had married the Gunner.

No one missed her going, and no one noticed the groom's re-entrance, decibels by this time at their highest, voices shouting to be heard. Lance stood alone smoking a cigarette. His wife was nowhere to be seen. A black-coated official came up and indicated the way to a changing room.

Some moments later Janet came in from an adjoining room, glamorous in a full-length mink fur. Lance finished dressing and stood at the *cheval* mirror brushing his black hair across his forehead.

'Hasn't it been marvellous fun, darling?' She stood behind him, her arms about his neck, smiling at their handsome reflected images; a flash from behind pronounced a photograph had been taken. 'Such fun. I just hate having to

288

go and leave all my friends, but this horrid little man in black says we must, so we must, mustn't we? The press will be full of us tomorrow. We'll have to order all the newspapers with our morning tray. The *Tatler* woman interviewed me when I was changing. She's going to write how I've set the fashion for a winter white wedding! You've enjoyed it too, haven't you, darling? I saw you talking to those men in uniform.'

'Yes, rather,' Lance lied.

'Pa insists on going down to see us off. I hope he hasn't overdone it, poor old Pa.'

Lance took Janet's hand and led her to the ornate stairs down which he had taken his mother alone, and which were now packed with a flushed mob screaming their good wishes and deluging them with rose petals. On the pavement he grasped Mr Tinling's hand, crushing it in his in the only other genuine emotion besides his affection for his mother he had felt that day. He thanked him profoundly for all he had done.

'She's yours now, son.' Mr Tinling tottered on the pavement, photograph bulbs flashing.

The day proved too much for the sick old man. 'Death of self-made multi-millionaire on daughter's wedding night. Fortune handed on.'

It was the menfolk who took the headlines. The front pages next day were splashed with Mr Tinling's last photograph shaking hands with his son-in-law.

CHAPTER 23

India was a terrible shock. Janet had left the country when she was seven and had not been back. Her childhood memories were of a spacious and cool house with shady garden, she looked after by a kindly Scottish governess who gave her her first lessons. She remembered never having to exert herself to do anything she did not feel like doing, never seeing any unpleasant sight.

The India she saw with adult eyes when she and Lance flew into Dum Dum airport in March 1946 could not have been more different from her memory of it. The heat hit her when she stepped from the plane as if from an open furnace door. Sweat trickled down between her flat breasts; her cool blue linen dress in minutes became grimed and crumpled; her silk stockings felt unbearably hot and made her legs itch, and her high-heeled soft leather shoes that were made to her exact size, unaccountably pinched.

'Thank God you're here, Lance.' 'Tiny' Beech met them with the driver in an office car.

'Why? What's going on?' Lance asked, as the car was driven off through the slums.

'Everything's going on. You name it, it's there,' Tiny laughed hollowly. 'Rapid Indianization, change-overs at every level, expansion — there's an explosion of trade to be taken advantage of. We're desperately short-staffed, and the Chief's going berserk!'

'Why don't we recruit more?'

'Not so easy to find the right people. Have to be trained up. We need specialists for the *daisee* . . .' The men talked incomprehensible shop across Janet's drooping form, while she took in with distaste turning to disgust the crowded, pitted roads packed with milling, poorly clad pedestrians. There were rickety wheeled bullock carts, the corded reins through the beasts' noses, ancient bicycles, *tongas* drawn by scraggy ponies, deformed beggars in rags – some of the forms mere trunks – fly-encrusted food stalls by hovels made of beaten-out kerosene tins, meat black with flies hanging up over foul-water open drains. The steaming putrid smells drifting in made her feel queasy, and she indicated to Lance to shut the car window; but the driver's window stayed open, his elbow protruding, his hand permanently on the horn centred in the steering wheel.

The decaying stink of vegetables, garbage, and a sweet sickly smell of cooking, continued to penetrate the car, compounded with a mixture of bad fish and curried spice. Added to this was the disgusting noise of vendors hawking, of rude clamour, shouts, and high-pitched cries in a bewildering mass of humanity all at horribly close quarters such as Janet had never been subjected to. When the car stopped in a traffic jam, which event happened frequently, dirty black hands clawed through the open window demanding *baksheesh*. There were *bodies* wrapped in white cloth lying on the roadsides! She had never seen a dead body in her life – not even those of her parents. She had not wanted to, and the nurse had said on both occasions there was no need for her to distress herself. If this was the India she had come to live in with Lance, it was horrifying. It *frightened* her. Janet shut her eyes and pressed a handkerchief to her nose.

'One of the poorest parts of Calcutta,' Lance said. He put his hand over hers. 'Don't worry, we'll soon be through; you won't have to come here again.'

'Cecelia would like to drive round and call on you this afternoon, if that is all right?' Tiny Beech enquired politely. 'Wives have a great time here.'

'What happens if the car breaks down?' Janet opened her eyes and found they had got nowhere.

'They'd help us get going again,' Lance grinned. 'The

people will always lend a helping hand if you're in a spot. I'd prefer to break down in India than anywhere else. A crowd collects quickly. It's an event.'

'There's a lot of talking,' Tiny dipped in; 'someone gets you sorted out.'

Janet could at that moment think of nothing worse than a greater crowd gathering. She shrank back in her seat when the car stalled, praying it would get going again.

'Chowringhee,' Lance announced. The driver stopped in front of a tall building on a wide street that Janet did not find much of an improvement on what they had been through. The traffic and pedestrians were as thick as ever, the honking, the dust, the fumes, the *smells*, just as appalling. 'Thanks Tiny; good of Cecilia to say she'll come. Tell them I'll be along to the office later this morning. Cheerio.'

They took a lift up to his flat on the fifth floor. Their luggage was carried by coolies up echoing back concreted stairs.

'Is *this* where we're going to live? Looks like a tenement to me . . .'

'Then welcome to the tenement building, Janet dear! Shall I carry the bride across the threshold?' Nothing could dampen Lance's pleasure at being back in India. 'As bachelor flats go this isn't a bad one, and it's very convenient for the office. Meet my bearer. A Goanese.' Lance intoduced de Mello, an elderly greyhead in white suit and plimsoles.

'Is *that* the air-conditioning?' Janet ignored de Mello, not certain whether to shake hands or not. She sailed past him into a second very large room, the bedroom, where another grimy looking machine with a box grating in the wall was making a thunderous noise.

'Oh God,' she said throwing her smart straw hat on the bed. 'Oh God, what *have* you led me to? You'll have to resign, darling, I don't think I can take it – all those hordes of smelly people.'

'They are my people.'

'Oh no, darling, not your people.' She managed a feeble

laugh. 'That was generations ago, and anyway yours were upper class.'

'Naturally it's a cultural shock at first, but you wait. You'll go to the races, to cocktail parties, dances, theatricals. There's the amateur dramatic club with a good stage where you could put on a fashion show.'

'Only one living-room?' Janet returned from the bedroom. 'Do we have to have our meals in here as *well*? How do you think I can entertain in one dingy room?'

'You can do it up. We've got running water, a fridge – what more can you want? Just you wait till I take you up country to the Chashma Shahi!'

'I don't know that I want to see it,' Janet said weakly.

'Oh come on, my dear.' Lance went over to her. 'You'll grow to like it, I'm sure you will.'

'Not in this poky flat, I won't.' She was near to tears.

'We'll move then.' He put an arm over her shoulders. 'You can choose somewhere else. I thought it better to start here where de Mello can look after everything and you won't have to cope with more servants until you've learnt a bit of the language. I'll be here with you.'

'You *won't* be here. You're leaving me right away.' Janet worked herself up into a greater state. 'I heard you tell that Mr Beech. You're going to the office – on our first day!'

'I must go. You know how I had to extend my leave because of your father. You can have a sleep or unpack our cases. De Mello will whip you up an omelette or whatever you feel like for lunch. He's an excellent cook. Boils masses of *nimbu-pani* – that's a fresh lime drink – to quench thirst—'

'I feel more like a pink gin.'

'Wouldn't advise it before sundown. Cecelia will be along presently, and this evening I'll get back early and we'll have dinner at the Turf Club. I'll introduce you to everyone. They know all about you from the fashion magazines. You'll be a sensation!' Lance did his best to boost her morale. He was sympathetic. It had been a long flight out from England. It was excessively hot. He had forgotten how suffocatingly muggy the damp climate of Calcutta was. When they were first married he would have said: 'Pull yourself together, woman; have some guts.' Not any more.

Lance had learnt a great deal in their three months of marriage. He had begun to learn on the very first day when they had been awakened in the early hours in the hotel honeymoon suite with the news that Mr Tinling had had a massive coronary. Janet, in the crisis, had collapsed with what he could only describe as an attack of nerves such as she was having now, which, if he said anything the slightest bit *zabardast*, ended with her dissolving into tears. He discovered that the same thing had happened when her mother had died, and that when her father became ill, she took to her bed.

Lance had postponed the honeymoon in Scotland, attended the funeral without his wife, coped with endless sessions in City Chambers on business affairs that involved her more than him, and he called in the doctor. He wanted to know how ill his wife was.

The going-over was thorough, heart and lungs pronounced sound, though the doctor considered Mrs Gardner was underweight, and that her 'nerves' were due to long-standing 'banting'. He recommended porridge for breakfast, milk puddings, and stout with every meal rather than gin. Janet refused to touch any of them. She continued to eat like a sparrow, and to have her gins. She did not *want* to put on weight. She would look dreadful in a photograph if she did. Neither the doctor nor Lance could move her from this stance.

Lance began to see that his wife had never faced up to anything more demanding than a camera in her life. She had been cocooned by parents and a host of 'friends' who buttered her ego in return for being invited into a moneyed circle. No one had ever said anything unpleasant to her, no one had even criticized her. On her marriage she automatically expected her husband to take on the role of shielding her, but he did not want that. He wanted a partnership, a woman who would take her share and pull her weight.

He saw that in spite of her confidence in front of the camera she had little in herself or her ability to cope when things did not go smoothly. He believed she had intelligence and a good bit more character than she would allow. He thought to 'toughen her up' both physically and mentally in Scotland once she had got over the shock of her father's death. He made her put on flat shoes and go walking the moors with him, and he tried some straight speaking. He found neither process worked. She had such high insteps that she could not wear low-heeled shoes comfortably! Tough talking did not stiffen her into the indignation of standing up for herself: it reduced her to rubble.

After some tearful outbursts, Lance changed his tactics. He became very undemanding. He believed that once he got her to India, she would change and grow. He was convinced that India would be her salvation.

In India, moneyed though their lives would be, she would learn to live within the sights and sounds of death and starvation and grinding poverty seen on the streets. She could no longer turn a blind eye on how the 'other half' lived, and he believed it would develop compassion in the place of fear. He did not envisage her going out to work amongst the poor – few other than doctors, nurses and missionaries were conditioned to do that – but he expected her to give parties and dress shows to raise money for charities, become an enthusiastic committee member, help in the many ways she could with her wealth behind her, and particularly Lance hoped she would be his help-meet in turning the Chashma Shahi into a successful venture. Above all he wanted her to be happy in India, love it as he did, be proud that their offspring were Gardners.

Now after her initial reaction he saw that it would take longer than he had envisaged. It might take years for Janet to adjust, to feel at home in India – learn to be a wife as he admitted he had to learn to be a husband. They had plenty of time to learn. They had the rest of their lives before them.

He was not sure he pleased her. She had little warmth to give out, or if she had warmth he had not yet found the means of releasing it. She was an awkward bed-mate to handle, with her bony length not too comfortable a one! She tended to curl up in the foetal position in the crook of his arm, pretending to be small if not a baby. He told her he liked her tall, admired her figure, wanted to see and feel her limbs long and straight. She attempted to comply, but always she ended nestling in, knees digging into his rib cage or stomach. Instead of staying with her, he found himself increasingly turning away to sleep on his side the rest of the night through. He tried to work out how he should help her in this particular, for it irked him that one who had fallen in love with his tallness and his figure could not be made happier than she appeared when love was consummated.

He often wondered in the night, when he turned on his side to get away from the discomfort of his wife's knees, how William and Nissa had fared on their marriage divan, how James and Mulka? Indians were generally very physical people, both men and women passionate, uninhibited by northern European standards. Nissa had been a virgin of fourteen years when she came to the marriage bed, though she must have been wise in the instruction of love-making through her hand-women. She would have known how to please her 'fair god', and how to obtain pleasure herself! That those two had been physically in love all their lives there was no doubt. And the same applied to James and Mulka. Both had been married previously when they met at the Chashma Shahi: he a widower, she divorced from the Emperor's son. They too had fused together with a passion that had lasted their life-time.

What it took Lance a long time to work out was that immature love in the figment of a beholder as in this respect, does not necessarily make for satisfactory physical love. Indeed in Janet's case her *idée fixe* of Lance as *her* god had grown in imagination to such lengths over the years of waiting, that no reality was likely to live up to it, her romantic vision bound to find disappointment. She had to grow in a maturity more in keeping with her age, to develop something deeper to take the place of fantasies. And what it took

Lance even longer to find out was that his wife was by no means as frail as she looked physically, nor as delicate as she appeared to be psychologically.

But what Lance did find out presently in Calcutta was that Janet, propped by wealth, had no *need* to come to terms with India. Had she been in the position of nearly all the other box-wallah wives in Calcutta she would either have had a complete nervous collapse and been invalided home or she would have, like most, swallowed, endured, found things that she liked doing about the place, and in the end declared that those times had been the best in her life. Janet neither had a nervous breakdown, nor 'endured', but she *did* take action to ameliorate her position, and Lance learnt that the words 'I can't stand it' were synonymous with a change.

'I can't stand it,' Janet said when they had been in the flat about a month. She threw herself onto the bed while Lance was about to change into white tuxedo and black tie. 'I can't stand this horrid little stuffy place one moment longer! I feel suffocated by it. I'm going, and I'm not coming back.'

'Fine. Where are we off to?' Lance asked whimsically from the bathroom door, his face lathered, razor in hand for his second shave of the day. 'Tell me my fate!'

'At the Saturday races Tiny Beech mentioned a house going in Garden Reach. I went to see it when you were away in Assam. The garden stretches down to the Hooghli. There's a bit of a breeze off the river.'

'Can you cope with the extra servants?'

'De Mello will cope. I've been giving him more money. He'll do anything I ask.'

'Good. Let's go ahead.' He was not going to be drawn into saying he did not approve of servants being overpaid and spoiling the market for others.

'It's for your health too, darling,' her voice pleaded.

'Of course. I shall enjoy the breezes as much as you.' Lance made a mental note that he'd keep the Chowringhee flat on for when Janet was in the hills. Garden Reach was all

297

very pleasant but it was a hell of a way from his office. However, he thought it a good idea to branch out. Anything to make her like Calcutta better.

It did—temporarily, but it also precipitated a clash. Lance was working all out in the office, and he left the packing-up of their personal effects to her. She went through his desk and found a missive from Cara.

'So you *do* write to her,' she confronted him.

'I do not. If you want the details, I asked her to send a ring back. The note came separately from the registered parcel which was waiting for me in the office when we arrived. You've read the note? It was nice of her to wish us well, wasn't it?'

'When did you give her the ring?'

'What's it matter? Ages ago.'

'I can't understand why you wanted it back unless it was particularly valuable. May I ask where it is now?'

'In the bank.' He had every intention of giving it to his wife—*in time*, perhaps on the birth of their first child. When he had unpacked it in the office and seen the ruby again, it breathed of Cara. A veil of their time together in the Chashma Shahi had floated around him like the mists rising over Indian fields at twilight. He had put the ring straight into the safe deposit with the letters. He had intended to destroy Cara's pre-war letters when he had cleared out his desk prior to going to England to marry Janet. He found he could not burn them. Thank God he had not left *those* in his desk!

'So you gave her a valuable ring when you were broke in Christchurch at the end of your leave? That sounds highly improbable,' Janet nagged on.

Lance would not be drawn.

'Does Carissa have children?' Janet tried another tack.

'She may have for all I know. Why do you bring the subject up? I told you she married Brownlow, a Gunner, before the war.'

'You did not tell me you were *engaged*. If you gave her a ring you must have been officially engaged.'

'The ring is old – of sentimental family value. She should have sent it back to me when she changed her mind.' Lance was thinking of the second time.

'She turned you down in Christchurch?'

'Turned me down *flat*,' Lance said, his eyes like flints. 'Now that's enough of that, please.'

'All the same, darling, I can't think why you waited all this time to ask for the ring back. Why didn't you ask for it back *then* . . . ?'

Lance maintained a stubborn silence, his jaw set. If she liked to think he'd given Cara the ring in the first place, let her; anything else would be treading on dangerous ground . . .

'I still don't understand; if you haven't been in touch since those days, why did you suddenly ask—?'

'What happened, Janet, was that she wrote after the war to find out if I'd survived. I wrote back saying I had, that you and I were to be married, and I asked for the ring; it seemed a good opportunity. It's all long finished and done with, Janet dear. It's got nothing to do with us.'

And with that Janet had to be satisfied. But the name Cara had been mooted after eight years, and there it stayed with a slight question-mark in Janet's sharp brain. The ring business with an exchange of post-war letters did not seem to quite tie up. Why *now* unless it was an heirloom, or something, and he wanted it back to give to *her*. But he had not given it to her – not that she wanted something Carissa had worn in Christchurch anyway – he had not even *showed* it to her on their arrival, or mentioned it before putting it away.

The large crates arrived by ship up the Hooghli carrying the newly marrieds' wedding presents of books, silver, pictures, small pieces of furniture, and trunks of Janet's clothes. Galvanized, she unpacked in the Garden Reach house, and filled it with fitted carpets and furniture bought at great expense in Calcutta. The house was delightful; she could breathe down there where it was degrees cooler outside than in the city. Inside she had the latest air-conditioning installed in living-rooms and bedrooms.

When everything was in order, as English-looking as Janet could make an Indian-built house in an Indian setting, the Gardners threw a house-warming party with dinner and dancing. They invited a mixed crowd of couples from the firm, Indian Civil Service officers and their wives, political officers, judges, army and naval men, shipping magnates, box-wallahs. It was a huge success. Invitations returning the hospitality poured in. Janet was launched, and Lance arranged for her to have her own car with Sikh driver so that she could in comfort, and independently, go about her social life.

A set, if not rigid, routine ensued for her of women's mah-jong morning sessions, shopping in the big stores, luncheon, an afternoon siesta, bridge at tea-time, and on to cocktails, dinners, dances, amateur theatricals. Often Lance changed in the flat and they met at the dinner party to which they were bidden, and drove home together to Garden Reach in the glorious Indian star nights of black velvet sky, moon so bright one could read by the light.

Sometimes Janet was more responsive in bed; sometimes she seemed almost happy.

'Do you love me, darling?' she said.

'I love you,' he said and meant it.

'Really and truly?'

'Really and truly.'

'Only me?'

'Only you. Who else? The Gardners make faithful husbands!'

He bought a well-trained quiet horse hoping to encourage her to ride with him in the coolth of the early morning. But she would not. She would not rise early, preferring a tray in bed; she was as frightened of horses as she had been of sailing in her father's yacht.

She shivered and shook with an attack of malaria in the stifling, long build-up to the monsoon, when clouds banked up over the Hooghli in an unbearable pressure, her fever rising and falling, her head buzzing with quinine.

The monsoon burst. No one who had not seen it before could believe it possible. Janet certainly couldn't. With a crash the clouds emptied, pouring rain in a force as solid as the curtains of a vast waterfall, the rain pounding down for days on end. The first relief at the release was tremendous, but it did not last long. Green mould grew overnight on Janet's dainty shoes, prickly heat tormented her, the humidity became intolerable. Scores of horrible-looking insects appeared on the walls, and crept in under doors. Toads in the garden croaked in gleeful unison; frogs hopped and drowned on the verandahs, and lay squashed in thousands on roads. A multitude of mosquitoes pinged round her net, two-inch-long cockroaches scuttled at night scenting out food, cantharides blister flies bit, and the stink bug beetle when stepped upon gave out its foul smell.

'I can't bear it; I can't bear it!' Janet lay on her bed.

'Nobody is asking you to bear it. If we hadn't had all this air-conditioning installed you'd have been in the hills long since. Cecelia went up to Simla six weeks ago.'

'How was I to know the air-conditioning doesn't work effectively in the rains? *You* never told me.'

'I'll make arrangements for you to go to Simla as soon as possible.'

'I'm not fit to travel. I'll never get there on my own. The rail journey will *kill* me!'

'I'll take you myself in an air-conditioned coupé.'

'I *hate* this country; it's horrendous and loathsome and . . . it'll be no better up there. What shall I do there all alone for three months?'

'Is nothing right?' Lance's voice hardened at the 'hate India'. 'You will not be alone in Simla. Half Calcutta is there . . . Cecelia and all your mah-jong and bridge pals. You'll feel better up there at once, the air is so fresh. You cannot *fail* to enjoy the sight of the snow-capped Himalayas.'

But in his heart Lance wondered.

CHAPTER 24

Janet wrote to Lance from Simla to tell him she was not feeling at *all* well. She was having morning sickness! The baby was due to be born in March the next year.

Lance was overjoyed. He went ahead with his plans for leave in the hill station in September, and at the beginning of October he brought Janet down to Delhi where after a night at the Maidens Hotel he hired a Mercedes with an experienced driver recommended by Cox and Kings for the journey to Kootgunge. They started early to beat the heat of day, Janet feeling rotten, with difficulty rising to dress in the hotel room.

On the other hand Lance was full of pleasurable expectation to be at last showing his wife the land of his ancestors. He sat beside the driver on the long haul down the Grand Trunk Road to Aligarh, where they turned off for Solah.

'*Asti, asti.*' He slowed the driver on the secondary road pock-marked from the actions of countless bullock-carts' wheels. It was very hot in the car even though at the rear by Janet whirred a battery-worked fan.

'What an awfully long way,' Janet's voice came over plaintively from the back seat. She had stopped feeling sick, but she was tired and sweat-soaked after several hours' driving. 'I wish we hadn't come, darling. You know how I *hate* the congestion of traffic, the filthy dust covering everything. Phew!' She wiped her face with a handkerchief soaked in eau-de-Cologne.

'You said you were longing to see the Chashma Shahi, and it's your only chance before the baby is born.'

'I know I did, darling, but I had no idea it was *this* far off the beaten track.'

'Not really far in the length and breadth of the sub-continent! Another hour or so and we'll be there. Would you like a stop?'

'No. Let's get on with it. The sooner we get this horrid drive over the better.'

Lance did not reply. She would get over her pet. He so wanted her to like it. She had quite liked Simla! He'd had a word with the gynaecologist who'd said there was no reason why she shouldn't have a perfectly normal pregnancy, but that delivery might be difficult with her small hips. A Caesarean section might be necessary. He had not told Mrs Gardner as she was of a nervous disposition and would worry. Lance kept it quiet too. That would all be gone into later with the specialist in Calcutta.

The stretch of road they were now traversing lay in the true *mofussil*, deep country by a gently flowing canal with high banks, great imli with their huge leaves and some neem trees centuries old lining the route. Lance's heartbeats quickened as always as he neared his ancestral land. At Kootgunge he saw the people out lining the road, the *gup* having got round.

'*This* is Kootgunge? Oh dear, what a mean little village, so primitive. No, don't stop, darling. *Please* don't stop, Lance; I don't want to stop here,' her voice rose.

As Lance's eagerness increased, Janet's pessimism grew. They did not stop, but the speed of the Mercedes was reduced to a crawl as they bounced and bumped over the towpath, the tall mango *topes* excluding the burning mid-day sun to one side, the Pila Nadi open and serenely flowing on the other.

'One day there will be gates here,' Lance indicated. 'The old ones have been taken to the village forge to be reno-vated, new sections made.'

The Mercedes gathered speed, and swept on through the narrow gap of the elephant gate into the open forecourt.

'Here we are!' Lance expressed cheerfully, praying his

wife would not condemn the decrepit building on sight. 'Try to reserve judgement, Janet dear. There's everything to be done still.'

If Cara had been amazed at her first sighting of the pale crumbling ruin in the eerie moonlight, Janet was aghast at the stark reality of the vast, burning red, sandstone wreck revealed in the glare of the noonday sun. Like Cara her eyes became fixed upon the first human who appeared in the entrance of the deserted building.

'Who is he?' She swallowed, watching a plump *pugried* figure in white servant's uniform hurry down the steps towards them.

'Nasrullah Khan. My major-domo – a Muslim. How is it, Nasrullah? *Sab tikh hai?*' he greeted.

'Salaam Nawab-sahib, salaam memsahib.' Nasrullah knelt on the ground and bent over Lance's feet. He rose to make a lesser obeisance to Janet. He led into the mansion, he and Lance talking rapidly in Urdu.

Finding it clean, cool, and this part restored with the entrance dome diffusing soft light from high clerestory windows, the mosaic floor in shades of blue, yellow and orange prettily depicting flowered Moghul patterns, Janet's spirits rose. Lance took her arm and they walked the length of the long corridor furnished with carved sandalwood chests giving out an aromatic perfume.

'The restoration stops here, but we've got two very comfortable rooms to live in.' Lance showed Janet into the semi-circular living-room, the Nawab's divan, strewn with silk cushions, now used as a low sofa. He led on into the room next door, newly restored, of the equivalent shape and size as the first, with the same bay-recesses of exquisite marble screens. It was barely furnished: a cane table, some chairs, but there were twin beds, each wide and low, with mosquito nets in place.

'It's nice. I like the decor.' Janet looked up at the roof painted in a deep blue scattered with stars.

''Fraid we have no electricity, nor any running water as yet. The dressing-room and bathroom are still to be done up. This is what it was like before.' Lance opened an inner door.

'Never mind,' Janet said generously after peering into a dark concreted room with yellowing walls and no window, but a tumbledown outer door for the sweeper.

'Pink marble with central bath? What do you think? I want you to design it. You really like it?' Lance hugged her boisterously.

'Careful, darling,' she laughed, pleased.

Nasrullah Khan served them a light lunch in the room where Cara had surprised the Nawab on his couch, after which Janet went for a rest, the bedroom darkened by *kuss-kuss* grass blinds let down over the screens. The last sound Janet heard before drifting off on the still, hot, early October afternoon when man and beast slept in the shade, was the *bhisti* sluicing down the *kuss-kuss tatties* on the verandah outside with water, the sweet scent of the roots drifting through. For the first time since she had arrived in India, Janet glimpsed that she might be able to make a go of it. Lance was quite a personage – that servant kneeling at his feet! His palatial home would be fun to do up. It was remote maybe, but it was peaceful and quiet after the noise of Calcutta. She was with his child in a cool boudoir of sweet scent with a restful *trompe l'oeil* sky ceiling . . .

Later, Lance came to waken her. Startled from sleep she believed him to be a bearer.

'Don't you recognize your husband?' Amused he went to pull up the blinds.

'*Darling!*' She sat up. 'What *are* you wearing that fancy dress for?'

'Not fancy – Muslim dress. I always wear it here. After all I *am* Nawab of Kootgunge.'

'I'm not sure I like it, those funny trousers.' Janet got out of bed and put on a clean dress. 'It makes you look a teeny weeny bit *too* Indian.'

'I have told you before, I *am* Indian.'

'And I've told you before that's all long ago.'

'No, Janet. I mean *now*. I have dual nationality. Here I'm

Indian, in Scotland I'm British. If we have a son I hope he'll go into the Indian Army, the old Gardner's Corps of Irregular Horse, now the 2nd Royal Lancers. What do you think of that for an idea!'

In the late afternoon they went for a stroll around the premises, Lance showing Janet the old bath-house, the spring, and the elephant tank which he proposed to turn into a swimming pool. But he did not take her through the ruins into the innermost wreck of the *zenana* quarters. The walls were too dangerous there, badly needing to be shored up. He would let her take no risks.

By the marble screens sifting the evening air, they sat with drinks in hand, whisky as usual for Lance, gin as usual for Janet – several pink gins.

'Should you?' he said, affection and concern for her condition showing in his black eyes.

'The doctor didn't say *not* to. He said whatever I fancy. I fancy my gin. No harm in that, added to which I feel quite peckish for me. Let's have supper right away.'

A hissing Petromax lamp, which smelt of kerosene, stood on the table by the screen where they dined, every now and then Nasrullah giving it a pump to keep it going. He served them cold soup, roast partridge and sliced mangoes to follow, arranged as in the days of John Company in an artistic pattern on a huge platter.

'Delicious. So refreshing.' Janet helped herself to more slices.

'Should you?' Lance said for the second time that evening.

'He's a good cook. How did you find him?' They lit up over coffee, Janet puffing daintily from her tortoise-shell holder.

'Actually—' Lance abruptly stopped himself. He had not anticipated that one! He started again. 'Actually, he was recommended. His home lies near, that's why he all but kisses my feet as his Nawab. He has not sufficient authority though. I'm disappointed to find the slow progress of the re-roofing. I shall have to employ a clerk of works or some such; I simply haven't the time to supervise from Calcutta.'

'You need an agent, darling.'

'Exactly. I plan to turn the east end of the palace into offices. The man could live in the bath-house *pro tem*.'

'Good idea. I think you should get on with finding someone. What's it like here in winter?'

'Bitterly cold,' Lance teased, 'All these draughty screens!'

'That'll be a change. Well, I'm off to beddie-byes,' she yawned.

Janet found Nasrullah Khan turning down the beds, and in her pleasant frame of mind she praised him for the dinner. 'Where did you learn to cook?' she asked.

'The memsahib taught make bread-sauce and bread-crumbs with partridge.'

'Which memsahib was that?'

'Brownlow memsahib.'

'Oh? Where did you work for her?' Janet wondered; but Brownlow was not an uncommon name.

'Ambala, memsahib. After, I go Quetta.'

'When Quetta?' Janet picked up sharply.

'I leave in winter *panch sāl* ago.' Nasrullah Khan held up one hand. 'Quetta very cold. The memsahib stay Quetta after the Major-sahib leave for war. Lady give good *chitti*.'

'You say the Brownlow memsahib gave *chitti* to come to work with the Nawab?'

'*Han, han,*' Nasrullah said nervously at the questioning in English which he spoke indifferently. He understood her with difficulty – the Brownlow memsahib had always spoken to him in Urdu. He was worried that he might have said too much and that the Nawab might be angry with him. He slipped out of the room before he could be questioned further.

'Ask for my bath to be poured,' Janet called as he left. Puzzled by the conversation, she soaped herself absent-mindedly in the dingy bathroom barely lit by a candle. She tried the bath water in the tub. It was boiling hot. She poured in the half tin of cold water and, still preoccupied by what the bearer had said, got into the tub and sat down. Of course there could be other Mrs Brownlows, the wife of a major, who had been to Ambala and then went to Quetta. She knew that Ambala was a Gunner centre, and when they were talking about the ring Lance had mentioned that Carissa had married a Gunner of the name of Brownlow. She ought to have asked Nasrullah if the memsahib had red hair. That would have settled it! If it *was* Carissa, she had been in Quetta at the same time as Lance. She did not like the idea of that *one little bit*. She herself had corresponded with Lance in Quetta. She knew the exact dates he had arrived in October and left the following February five years ago as the bearer had said. The grass widow that Carissa was then, if it was Carissa, had the audacity to plant her ex-bearer onto Lance at the Chashma Shahi. Why, if not that they were as thick as thieves?

The more Janet thought about it while soaking in the bath, the more she convinced herself that it *was* Carissa Brownlow, and the crosser it made her: to think that Lance had hidden from her that he'd met the woman in India. Why hadn't he asked for the ring back *then*?

When Janet got out of the bath she found her skin a bright red and she was sweating with the heat. If there'd been a tap she'd have run more cold — damn and blast all primitive houses. By now in a thorough state she lay on the bed flapping the sheet over her to cool herself. It was into this scene that Lance walked whistling, pleased with the way things were going, pleased with his wife and with the world.

'I want to talk to you.' Janet flapped the sheet over herself.

'I'm all for talks,' Lance replied jovially.

'I gather that Nasrullah was Carissa's bearer,' her voice accused.

'Oh?' Lance said evenly. 'How did that revelation come about?'

'It came about when I praised him for his cooking. He said the Brownlow memsahib had taught him in Ambala and that he had gone with them to Quetta. You happened to drop that her husband was a Gunner of that name.'

308

'So I did. Well, well, well, quite the little detective.' Lance remained calm. 'So what if our paths did cross in Quetta? What if her bearer did come to work here? As I believe I said once before, it has nothing to do with us.'

Janet sat up indignantly. 'You deliberately hid it from me, just as you deliberately hid the ring and the letter. Why should you do that unless you felt guilty about it? I suspect you had a rip-roaring affair in Quetta!' The accusation tumbled off the tip of her tongue not because she believed it, but because she had worked herself up into a passion of indignation, and she said the first thing that entered her head.

Lance kept his temper. 'I repeat, whom I met when and where and what I did during the war years before our engagement or marriage is nothing to do with us now. In any case because a bachelor takes on a bearer who once worked for a woman he knew, you don't have to jump to every sort of tortuous conclusion. Be reasonable, Janet.'

'I *am* being reasonable,' she said, furious at his sang-froid. 'It's *you* that is not being reasonable. It would have been reasonable to have told me that you'd met her again; that you had written for the ring. But no, you hide it, and I find out by mistake, and, and, naturally it is very upsetting . . . and I don't feel very well.' She lay back on the pillow.

He was unsympathetic. 'Your own fault. You've worked yourself up into a lather.'

'There wasn't enough cold water in the beastly bathroom . . . Oh, I *hate* everything about this country, the people, the rotten plumbing . . . I mean *non* plumbing—'

'Stop it, Janet; you must take care of yourself now.'

'*Now?* I knew it! It is the child that counts with you, not *me*. I've always known you don't love me. You never make real love; you're always thinking of that, that, Carissa; you compare me unfavourably with her . . .' She sobbed.

'Nonsense, absolute nonsense.' He noted her flushed face and hot sweating limbs that looked as if they'd been broiled. 'Hang on,' he said, 'I'll get some water.'

He fetched it himself, put a towel under her, and sponged

her down on the bed as Cara had sponged him down when his fever had broken and the sweat had poured from him. He disliked the whole unnecessary conversation, for of course there was more than a grain of truth in Janet's accusations, even to the fact that he could not always banish the remembrance of Cara from his marriage bed. He was not angry with Nasrullah Khan for having let slip that the Brownlow mem had taught him some recipes; at least the bearer had refrained from saying that the same memsahib had come *here*! If Janet discovered that, it would be a hard one for him to explain away, though why she should be so jealous of what went on in a man's life before marriage, he failed to comprehend. He supposed that Cara, the golden out-of-doors sailing girl of pre-war days, had become Janet's *bête noire*, one she could never forgive for snatching him away in 1938. If it had been Mrs Whatever-her-name-was who'd been Nasrullah's previous memsahib, he knew very well Janet would not have turned a hair.

Sponging her down, before him lay her figure as white-skinned as a ghost, the stomach showing a slight round-ness, the waist broadened: their child. A sense of guilt overtook Lance. He was to blame for his wife's present upset.

'Janet,' he said, his voice filled with gentleness, 'truly you must forget Carissa as I have forgotten her. She means nothing to me. We have not been in touch since she sent back the ring, as I told you. Our lives are miles apart. She has hers in England with her husband serving, and a whole lot of children for all I know or care. We have our life here in India together with *our* children to come; that is all that matters, Janet dear,' he soothed, stroking her forehead. He sat on by her until her eyes closed.

Lance undressed quietly and lay uncovered in his native *pājāmas* on the bed next to Janet's. It had been a long day, but he did not sleep immediately. He lay listening to his wife's breathing with its little whimpers, and to the night sounds. He was happy in spite of the stupid upset, happy to be in the Chashma Shahi with his wife and unborn child; he felt the spirits of his ancestors about him, friendly and caring, heard in the quiet the busy bustling noisy household as it was then with all the dozens of servants, the military force guarding the elephant gate, the serving girls, and all the rest. His father, Alastair, had been born in the Chashma Shahi in 1845, 101 years ago, and had spent his life here in the decaying splendour until his wife (Lance's mother) had taken him to Dundee. Alastair, adhering to the custom for the high-born of those bygone days, had never done any work, too proud to degrade himself. He must have listened night after night to the jungle sounds his eldest son was listening to now. There! The familiar 'rasp' and 'saw' of a panther. That, the low 'ah-ungh' of a tiger. He had seen the pug marks of a large tiger in the sandy path by the elephant tank where he had taken Janet in the late afternoon, but he had refrained from drawing her attention to it, just as he had refrained from telling her he had killed a deadly little krait in their bathroom before dinner, and had nearly killed the *bhisti* for not plugging the exit water hole with finer chicken wire. Janet would not exactly appreciate that there were snakes in the bathroom, and tigers on the prowl outside her verandah!

He listened to the lapping of the river, vital for his farming prospects. The Pila Nadi, a tributary of the Ganges, would never completely dry up to beset him with the problems other less watered parts had, when, with a poor monsoon, drought conditions quickly prevailed. But on the other hand the river could flood – ah, there was the fiendish brain-fever bird busy at its nightly crescendo – how it had driven him mad when he had malaria – and there the high wail of a jackal. He hoped the shriek would not waken Janet. It rather reminded him of the cry of a baby . . .

Lance was dropping off to sleep when he heard his wife stir, feel for the torch, and get up to go to the bathroom. She was there some time. He lay on, awake.

'Are you all right?' he asked when she came back.

'Yes,' she said. 'I had a bit of a tummy pain, but I can't do anything.'

Lance slept. He was awakened in the pitch dark by the sound of a groan.

He opened an eye and saw the light under the bathroom door. He lit the candle by his bedside and went in. The smell that greeted him was overpowering. Janet sat on the thunderbox deathly white, purging.

'I'm going to be sick as well,' she gasped, looking desperately round. He rushed for the empty kerosene tin and held her while she retched.

'I expect it's the mangoes,' he said more calmly than he felt, 'they are a well-known aperient. Idiot that I am, I shouldn't have let you have that second helping.'

He waited by her awhile and then helped her back to bed, and went into the living-room to get some white mixture which had morphine in it that he kept handy for stomach upsets.

'Here, drink this.' He held out the spoon. He tucked the sheet in round her and went off to rouse the sweeper in the servants' quarters right at the rear of the palace.

By the time he got back Janet was in the bathroom again, the candle guttering on the uneven floor beside her. 'I'm in agony.' She writhed on the commode. '*Do* something, Lance, for God's sake help me.' She got up to walk round the broken concreted floor in her bare feet, bent double, clutching her stomach. She went back to the seat.

But Lance had seen. With horror he took in the stain on her flimsy chiffon nightgown.

CHAPTER 25

'Fetch Nasrullah Khan! *Jaldi, jaldi*,' Lance yelled at the somnolent *mehtar* waiting by the outside door. 'You cannot go in; the memsahib is ill. Hurry!'

'*Ji han, Hazoor.*' The man scuttled away.

Lance heard the scream and rushed back to the bathroom. Full alert in war was an exigency he knew how to cope with. In this emergency he had no idea how to cope. My God, what should he do when the nearest hospital, at Solah, was thirty miles away?

He was not a man to panic, but in this unfamiliar situation Lance was as near to panicking as he had ever been. The screams came again, followed by a long drawn-out groan. He found her as before on the 'throne', clutching the edge, all but toppling over.

'Don't leave me, don't leave me. Don't go away! I'm doing blood. I can feel it. I'm bleeding to death,' Janet sobbed. She screamed again when the pain came on. She was terrified, eyes wild,.

'I *must* leave you to get help. I'll be back in a moment. I promise. Do you know anything about what to do? Shouldn't you be lying down to try and prevent . . . wouldn't that help . . . ?'

She was beyond reasoning. She screamed as the pains gripped her, and in between she sat bent double, sobbing.

Nasrullah Khan stood in the door of the bedroom buttoning up his *achkhan*, his *pugri* askew.

'It is the memsahib,' Lance said ashen-faced, 'she is with child – the *baba* comes. Is there doctor in Kootgunge?'

313

'*Nahin*, Nawab-sahib, no *hakim*. *Dhai* in my village, very good woman, *bahut achcha*.'

'Then go! Get her! Take the driver and car and bring her back, *ek dam. Jaldi*. Hurry.'

He went back to Janet half-fainting in the bathroom. She no longer screamed. He carried her onto the bed and tore up a sheet to stop the haemorrhaging. Janet lay writhing, and Lance was sure she was dying. He ordered water to be boiled, and he covered her with a blanket.

After what seemed an eternity Nasrullah ushered the *dhai* in, a bent old woman in a sari that had once been white, a smell of wood smoke and dung strong about her person. He called for the driver, and in the doorway – for he dared not leave Janet – he ordered the man to drive hell-for-leather to Solah and bring back a doctor. Sixty miles there and back. How long would that take? He had considered bundling Janet into the Mercedes, but on second thoughts believed the bumpy drive would only exacerbate her condition.

Back in the room Lance saw the *dhai* bending over Janet. 'Wash your hands.' He ordered her into the bathroom and showed her the *chalumchi* and soap. 'Use this towel, understand?' The woman took no notice of him but lifted the lid of the thunder-box and peered inside, ghoulishly fishing around with a stick.

'The Nawab-sahib can tell the *mehtar* to remove,' she croaked, and went obediently to wash at the basin.

'Can you save the child?' Lance stood before her grimfaced.

'The *baba* is gone. The Nawab should have called the *dhai* sooner. The deed is done in there,' she cackled horribly, pointing to the closet.

'God damn you!' Lance cursed. He followed her into the bedroom and watched helplessly while she examined Janet. She called for the hot water, and took some items out of a dirty bundle.

'Who is she? She smells. Take her away. I don't want

314

her to touch me,' Janet moaned from her prone position on the bed.

Lance knelt by his wife's head. 'She is the midwife. She will help you. You must let her. There is no one else.' He watched the woman pour some mixture into a cup Nasrullah Khan had brought. The bearer hovered with rolling eyes in the doorway.

'What is it?' Lance demanded.

'Ergot, sahib,' the woman mumbled between toothless gums.

'It is good, Nawab-sahib,' Nasrullah Khan nodded from his position. '*Dawai* stop bleeding.'

'Take it, Janet. *Take it*,' he insisted when she turned away, 'it will help you.' He lifted her head and pressed the cup to her mouth while the *dhai* fiddled around with hot water.

Next, the old crone coated her hands with pungent oil and without further ado pulled up Janet's soiled nightgown and began to massage her stomach, first squeezing down and across, then when satisfied the womb was empty, in sweeping upward strokes, forcing the womb back. Her strokes were rhythmic, sure and firm, small brown hands working. At last Janet relaxed. She lay quietly, yielding to the touch, her face as white as the pillow.

Exhausted and rent, she was no longer in pain. The bleeding stopped. The *dhai* turned her over, and began to massage her back, steadily moving down to legs and feet, then turning her over again she went back to the stomach, by which time Janet was asleep, a faint flush on her cheeks.

Light filtered through the screens. Birds stirred in the branches, a troupe of *langur* monkeys chattered and cavorted on the giant peepul tree across the forecourt. A peafowl shrieked and preened, displaying his feathers on the open driveway, and the koël brain-fever bird piped its maddeningly rising scale, higher and higher, over and over again. 'I can't bear it! I can't bear it! I can't bear it!' it seemed to Lance to say in Janet's hysterical tones.

315

The *dhai* left well-pleased with her night's earnings, and Lance went out into the fresh morning air and watched the domes and broken minarets of his palace tipped red by the early sun, and thanked God that Janet lived. He pondered on how nature could one moment be so vile, the next so incomparably beautiful.

Ruthlessly Janet played upon Lance's remorse that he had taken his pregnant wife on the long bumpy roads to remote Kootgunge with no doctor within reach, and only a village *dhai* untrained in hygiene or modern methods for assistance.

'That filthy crone did her best to kill me,' she said at Garden Reach.

'On the contrary, I believe she saved your life with the coagulant,' Lance responded, tight-lipped.

Though the Calcutta doctor administered injections of the new penicillin which cleared up a slight infection, Janet pleaded illness, headaches and continual tiredness. She refused all invitations and demanded that Lance come straight home from the office, which he did, giving up golf and tennis. She went on and on about her miscarriage, sensing victory. Her new ambition became as much of an *idée fixe* as her desire to marry Lance had once been: a little more ill-health on her part and he would contemplate retiring! One thing was certain. She could never *never* go back to the Chashma Shahi after that nightmare night. She shuddered every time she thought of the dingy, squalid, noisome bathroom, or the cold, sharp stars gloating overhead in their dark blue hardness on the ceiling, while she writhed in agony on the bed.

Lance's patience snapped one evening, the burden of his wife demanding constant attention on top of his office work, and the local unrest of a *hartal*, a religious strike called by the Muslims, telling. 'The doctor advises the best way for recovery is to start a family again – all in good time of course. You were pretty fit when the baby was on the way.'

316

'What?' Janet's blue eyes looked at Lance in astonished hurt. 'You surely don't expect me to go through *that* again?'

'God forbid. No reason why you should. No gin, no mangoes, and no hot baths next time!' He tried to bring some light relief into their relationship.

'I *couldn't* put myself into that position again – not here. I am amazed you can even contemplate it . . . it isn't fair to ask me . . . in England . . . perhaps. I shall never forget what I've been through, never forget Nasrullah Khan looking at me when I was half-naked—'

'So you noticed him in the doorway? I thought you were beyond noticing.'

'Don't be sarcastic, Lance. You know this country doesn't suit me. I only ask you to think about retiring. Think how we could have a family in Scotland, the winters spent in Jersey . . . the children running healthy on the sandy beaches. All I ask is that you *think* about it, darling.'

There was slaughter in Calcutta in that year of 1946 which had started out so full of hope for Lance and Janet and ended in such disappointment. A Muslim was reported killed, then a Hindu in a tit for tat vendetta, and in a matter of hours the rival communities were out in the streets accusing each other of foul deeds, rioting factions screaming their slogans, black flags flown over Muslim houses. They filled the streets in packed crowds, advancing in waves of hate and fury upon one another until dispersed by the police hitting out with long brass-bound *lathis*.

The terror escalated. With terrible vengeance the factions attacked, using every conceivable weapon. Men, women and children were killed; there were lootings, burnings, thousands left wandering lost and homeless. There were executions held on Hooghli Bridge in a macabre massacre before the police could get there; there were secret murders and reprisals for murders, three hundred dead reported in one night. Europeans were told to go to the aid of those lying wounded on the streets at their peril. The police could not vouch for their safety if they stopped in their cars. Rotting corpses piled up in the streets — five thousand said to be killed.

Lance did go out on the streets to do what he could; he saw uglier wounds than any panga cuts Burma tribesmen had made in war. Janet saw none. She shut her eyes and blocked her ears to the sights and sounds and written words of killing, and did not go out beyond the boundaries of their property. Waited on by de Mello, she sat in the warm winter sunshine in her colourful garden reading light romantic novelettes. The only exercise she took was to wander every now and then over the green lawns down to the Hooghly River where with longing akin to a disease she watched the steamers sailing out to sea. 'Home' became an obsession; but she would not give up Lance. Lance must be made to give up India.

One day as usual she walked down to the end of her garden. Idly she was watching the laden merchant vessels low in the water, and the patched-sail dhows, when her eye was caught by some objects floating past. They looked like the *mussacks* the *bhisti* used to water the *kuss-kuss tatties* over the verandahs in the hot weather, or were they blown-up buffalo skins that were sometimes used as rafts by the natives? One drifted nearer, followed by more, bobbing . . .

The nearest object bumped gently into the wooden pier upon which she was standing, and Janet saw with horrified disbelief that it was a human torso. In sickened abhorrence she stood staring, unable to avert her shocked gaze. She gaped at the grotesque decapitated body, hands tied behind back, a half-naked corpse that had floated and sunk, and became bloated to float on the surface once more. There were several cadavers clustering by the pier as if gathering together in a macabre dance near the haven of shore, fronds of flesh flowing in the water. Here were bodies tired of being carried up-river with the tide,

318

then washed down, only to be carried up again to Hooghli Bridge of the massacre, endlessly up and down, drifting. A vulture flapped in and perched on the one nearest to Janet. With a sidelong look at her presence it began pecking, tearing, red neck gorging . . . Others gathered.

Obscene repugnance. With her hands to her mouth, Janet ran up to the house. Gasping she fell upon her bed, her face pressed into the pillow.

'I can't bear it! I can't bear it!' She attacked Lance when he arrived home late and tired after a full meeting with government officials in the emergency. 'I can't stand it here another moment. I hate and loathe the foul, dirty, bestial, inhuman country. How can you call yourself Indian, think of yourself as an Indian? How can you, can you, *can* you?' she screamed pounding him with her fists on his chest. 'It's too much, all too much. It's final. I'm leaving and I'll never return to this cruel barbarous country . . .'

Lance stared at his wife, his face taut and grim, all colour drained, his mouth thin and set. 'If you have not one ounce of compassion or humanity in your make-up to give a thought for those unfortunates caught up in these terrible events, if all you can think of is your own pampered comforts, you had better go. I had hoped the sufferings of India might have changed you. I see nothing will take you out of your egotistical spoilt self, and all I have to say to you now is that I am *glad* our child did not live to have a mother like you. All I can say to you is, *good riddance*.'

Without another word Lance turned on his heel and left her. For once Janet was astonished into silence, indignant enough not to burst into sobs. No one had ever turned on her in such a manner. No one had *ever* attacked her in the despicable way her own husband had!

Within a week, Mrs Lance Delhmir Gardner had caught the next steamer home.

Admiral Lord Mountbatten of Burma took over in February 1947 as India's last Viceroy. The process of handing over was rushed through in the next five months with what to some seemed unseemly haste, many declaring more time should have been given to the sorting of problems; others, like Lance, glad to see Independence come sooner than expected. But Lance was dead against Partition. Indeed he resented it, had always been utterly opposed to Mr Jinnah's dream of a separate Muslim State. He disliked intensely the idea of a split. The British had unified India and now it was being undone. He was of Muslim descent with a *zemindari* estate on what would be Indian soil. He could not move from his ancestral home. There were thousands if not millions like him: Muslims with land in what would be India; Hindus with land in what would be Pakistan. He agreed with Gandhi that India should remain one strong united whole. He was convinced the Viceroy was making a terrible mistake in agreeing to divide ... and then the tragedy of the great exodus came:

The massacres on the roads, on the trains, in the fields, in the villages, killings of the same relentless brutality and disregard for age or sex as in Calcutta the year before, only now, in the Punjab, it was on a huge scale compared to then.

But Lance was fortunate. In the remote district of Kootgunge further south in the United Provinces, all remained peaceful. The Muslims who had lived in the area for generations continued to live there in safety, Nasrullah Khan and Ghulam Haidar (roped in by the former to serve the Nawab) among them.

Whenever he could get away from Calcutta, Lance went up to supervise his Indian clerk of works, and to sign documents for the purchase of more land, each *bigah* painstakingly bought. To get the people to move off the impoverished neglected fields, and away from their broken-down mud huts, Lance gave substantial advantages. He offered them new housing in a village complex he was building adjacent to the old Kootgunge. Here he planned a clinic, a sub-post office, a school, playing fields – and he offered the people work with good wages on the estate.

The progress was irritatingly slow to a man of Lance's

drive. He was anxious to get on with the ploughing and the seeding, anxious to start the building of factory and outhouses. As a jute farmer he planned to conduct the whole cycle from the sowing to the making of the cords, employing hundreds. He had bought a flat-bottomed old paddle boat that was being converted. One day it would be anchored in the Pila Nadi waiting to be loaded with his merchandise and on its way to the Ganges for the long haul down to Calcutta. He looked forward with pleasure to doing the whole stretch himself on the inaugural trip.

Shortly after Partition, Lance went up to Delhi to sort out yet another land problem. At Maidens Hotel – where else! – he ran into Paddy Cahill in the bar. They had not met since the end of the war.

'You look all steamed up, old cock,' Paddy said over their whisky.

'I sure am, Paddy. My wife's left me, and I've taken on more work than I can cope with.'

'Faith, more fool you for being such a crass idiot as to get married in the first place. As for too much work – easy . . . delegate it!'

'Huh! Brilliant . . . heard of that before. What about you?'

'Sent in my papers.'

'Good God. Surely they'll take you on into British Service?'

'Fed up to the back teeth with the bloody army, and no such "surely" about it. As far as the War Office is concerned we're a load of natives who don't understand pukka British troops.'

'What have you been doing since Burma?'

'Back to regimental duties. Bloody boring. Enough to make anyone send in their papers. Then, regiment split in two. Cor what a balls-up! The Muslims had to guard their fellow Hindus. Took every ounce of ingenuity I can tell you to get the Sikh element away without us all being murdered.'

'And did you?'

'I did an' all. Can you imagine the brave Sikhs huddled in trucks with the blinds down through Pakistan wetting their pants in fear? Daren't show their hairy faces. God what an effing awful mix-up! How does your wife that has left you compare with Cara?' Paddy wanted to talk no more of the recent events which, tough and hardened as he was, had sickened him.

'Comparisons are odious, Paddy,' Lance said with dignity. 'Janet was ill out here. Lost a baby, and she lost her nerve during the riots in Calcutta – not surprising. As soon as I can settle some things at Kootgunge I'm going to England in the hopes of getting her to come out for the winter. What she reads in the newspapers about the massacres in the Punjab won't exactly help my mission.'

'Poor bloody woman. Nervous type, eh? Can be terrific in bed!'

''Fraid that's not up for discussion,' Lance replied haughtily. 'I married her. *Bas.* My problem is I can't really afford the time to take leave, but if I don't fetch her she'll never come back. What are you going to do in civvy street?'

'Write. Had thought of settling in USA. Stony broke though . . .'

'As usual! What on earth have you found to write about? Our trip to Tibet?'

'Fiction. Scribble some fancy tale about a flipping officer based on meself, one permanently in trouble with the military authorities, one who knows all the best brothels and bints in the bloody country!'

'Sounds a good way of getting it out of your system,' Lance laughed. Paddy always acted like a tonic of unconventionality upon him. 'How far have you got with the novel?'

'Haven't. Glory man, give me a chance.'

'Hmn. Seems to me that if you're broke and you haven't written a word, you're madder than usual to think of going to the States.' Lance ordered more whisky. 'What's the point of going there until you've got something to sell? What do you think you're going to live on in the meantime? A miserly major's pension won't keep you in women and drink for a week. In America you'd end up living in some downtown slum with barely enough for the cheapest of tarts. That won't suit your epicurean tastes if I know you.'

'Dammit. Just what I've been thinking,' Paddy expressed gloomily.

'Here's an idea,' Lance threw out. 'I'll give you a damned good salary if you'll act as my agent at Koot-gunge, and I don't mind how much time you spend writing as long as you get the job rolling.'

'Strewth!' Paddy drained his glass. 'Let's go eat on it.' They made their way to a table in the dimly lit dining-room, *khidmatgars* gathering to hand out menus and flap open heavily starched table napkins onto knees. 'Where would I live?' Paddy continued the conversation once they had ordered.

'In the two rooms already restored in the Palace; fit for a Nawab I can tell you. The clerk of works is in the bath-house, and that's got to be restored—'

'No go. There won't be any bints within a hundred miles of your god-forsaken estate.'

'No, but, hmn, with the salary I propose giving you, you could afford to bring someone permanent along – your mistress, remember? The next wing in the palace is all but finished and I'd ask you to move into that and out of mine as soon as it is. Pressing points to see to are the roof, the running water project, and the electricity plant. The farm plan needs modifying . . . no good attempting to explain it here . . . need to examine it on the ground. Come and see for yourself. I'll give you a lift in the station wagon tomorrow . . .'

Paddy went with Lance. He came, he saw, and found himself hooked on the beauty and remoteness of the place, the ancient charm, the interest of work he could see growing, all in a situation ideally suited to the writing of his first rip-roaring, no-holds-barred novel.

*

A few weeks later, when it was autumn, Lance paid a lightning visit to the Chashma Shahi before flying to England. He wanted to see how Paddy was settling in. After a busy day touring the estate, discussing the plans, climbing rickety ladders to view how the pilaster work on the ornate parapets was progressing, he and Paddy sat down to a leisurely meal cooked by Nasrullah Khan and served by Ghulam Haidar who greeted Paddy as an old friend, bringing him his after-dinner drink exactly as he liked it. Lance raised an eyebrow in query.

'Knew him in Quetta with Cara. And that reminds me, I want to *parlez-vous* about her.' He lit up and settled back before the screen. He was replete with good food and excellent burgundy. This was the life for him! Work at his own pace, be his own boss. No Colonel breathing down his neck and thumping the table at him. Work here consisted of organization, supervision, encouragement — lots of *shabashes* for work well done. He knew how to get the best out of his men, and workmen were much the same. Afternoons and evenings were spent scribbling away about his escapades in the past. Only one thing was missing. But he'd soon remedy that: he had his eye on a bint in Solah!

'I have no intention of *parlez-vous*ing on the subject of Cara. That's all long done with. I'm going home to see my wife.'

'Point taken, old sod, but isn't it about time you came out of your hidey-hole as regards her?'

'Hidey-hole? Don't be a blithering idiot.'

'After the war I met Pammie Dangerfield—'

'So did I. Where but at—'

'Maidens Hotel!' they laughed. 'The battle-axe told me certain things about Brownlow that Cara would never herself reveal, straight and loyal as she is, bless the little darling.'

'I can assure you the last thing she was was straight with *me*.'

'Would you say that now? You can be a stubborn

324

bastard when you want to. What I'm telling you, you lunatic, is that I'm devoted to Cara, even if you're not.'

'Quite right. I'm not. So she went on to you in Quetta, did she?'

'That's a crappin' *filthy* thing to say, so it is. You ought to be ashamed of yourself, faith, an' you should.'

'Oh stop pontificating, Paddy—'

'You've got a bloody big blind spot about a girl in a million, someone who is fun to be with, honest—'

'Don't be pompous. It doesn't suit your style. Nothing you can say about Cara is of the slightest interest to me.'

'Holy Mother o' God, list will ye; I'd be obliged if you'd hear me out, you obstinate *ummuk*. She sent you a cable when she was about to leave India explaining—'

'So Pammie Dangerfield told me. I never got it. Did the widow get her brood to Canada?'

'Sure. Cut slap through red tape by sheer dogged perseverance. You can't help admiring the old bag, even though she does look like something out of a jumble sale. But I'm not goddammit letting you off the hook. Heed, you swine. Brownlow was wounded at Cassino, taken prisoner by the Germans, and was repatriated in an exchange with others. Cara had every intention of getting a divorce and returning to you.'

'Why didn't she, then? I can tell you why. She's incapable of sticking to anything. She's like a shuttlecock, a female vacillator.'

'God's truth, man. Can't you see further than your blithering nose? The circs she found him in changed all that. She stayed. She wrote to tell you of her decision.'

'Another missive I never received. Odd coincidence, isn't it?' Irritably Lance stubbed out his cigarette into a glass ashtray.

'Odd is it now? Not odd at all. You'd've done better to have told her to write to your firm rather than to Imphal in the heat of battle.'

'Could we stop talking about Cara?'

'Still ducking it?' Paddy put his feet up on the marble

table. 'I went to stay with 'em on my war leave,' he threw out airily.

'Really?'

'Yea verily.'

'Was that Christchurch? I gather her husband was stationed at the Barracks.' For once Lance sounded mildly interested. Both men lit up again.

'The husband, old sod, isn't stationed anywhere. He's in a wheel-chair.' Paddy looked at his friend from under thick fair eyelashes to see his reaction. There was none. With an air of total indifference Lance nonchalantly continued to blow rings of smoke and watch them soaring. 'He's an odd sort of man,' Paddy went on. 'Inventor. Said to be brilliant mathematically. Sort of queer twerp that prefers inventions to sex. Pretty hopeless at the latter even before his wounding, so the Pammie woman told me.'

'No children?' Lance asked, blowing out his smoke rings one by one.

'One.' Paddy could feel the sudden stillness. 'Sure now the babe was on the way when the news of Cara's parents' death came through. 'Tis true I moved into her hut for a while to keep an eye on her. Cause for another effing scandal!'

'I *thought* there was something different . . . she came down here, you may not know, after the retreat. Of course . . . that's why she had to get back . . .' Lance spoke as if to himself.

'I heard tell about the trip. That girl can do anything, so she can – even to what she's doing now. And she doesn't bloody well do it by halves either.'

'What you've told me alters nothing.'

'Blather! It's not meant to. I've told you, curse you, so that you know the truth for once instead of tying yourself up in pre-conceived knots of injury done to yourself. Brownlow is rather a decent chap under the crust. Dry sense of humour, and by God he's plucky. Life isn't easy for them, not much filthy lucre, but she's stuck to him;

326

and when I said she doesn't do things by halves, I mean she hasn't stuck by him as a *duty*. There is a kind of joy . . . her personality "radiates sunniness" as her uncle says. What stands out a mile, old sod, is that the dear girl has got on with her own married life and *made a success of it.*'

'You met Uncle Tom?' Lance looked out through the screen to the Yellow Stream and saw the Avon River flowing past.

'Sure an' how! Faith, I'll never forget how we beat up the Old Ship Inn together. Ended sleeping it off in one of his musty bunks. The old bugger's pretty feeble on his pegs. Confided to me he hopes to pass out one night in a haze of alcoholic glory, hence is stepping up the booze . . .' Paddy talked on.

Notwithstanding that he had not wanted to listen, in retrospect Lance was glad Paddy had told him about Cara. He found now that he could think of the past without rancour, and he saw too (when pondering again on his flight home the conversation with Paddy) how the barrier he had put up because of his hurt could have seeped through to Janet, how there could be truth in her accusation of the 'spectre of Cara' intervening to haunt their marriage through his own subconscious attitude.

If Cara could make a success of marriage with a husband who had never been particularly interested in the sexual side, so bloody well could he make a success of one with a wife who had never been particularly adept at it!

CHAPTER 26

Following her stormy parting from Lance in the winter of 1946/7 after the Calcutta massacres, Janet had on the advice of her lawyers sold up the Brockenhurst home and gone to live in the Tinling family house (the Angus estate had been passed on to Lance on his marriage) in the tax haven of Jersey.

Now, on a breezy autumn day, Lance after attending to some business in London, caught a train to Southampton and then the boat. He was met at St Helier's dock by his wife's chauffeur with a limousine, not Mr Tinling's Rolls Royce which had met him at Tilbury nearly two years ago when he had arrived for his wedding, but a brand-new sleek silver sports model of slimmer width in keeping with the narrow wandering roads on the forty-five-square-mile island.

The Channel Islands were a new venue for Lance, and sitting in front beside Pierre, the middle-aged French-speaking chauffeur who nevertheless was a Britisher, he regarded with interest the pretty sea scene of yachts at anchor, the picturesque Queen Elizabeth Fort across the water, and the promenade lined with white suburban houses. Along the coast were delightful views of rocky headlands rounding into long sandy beaches, coves and small fishing harbours. The effect was one of warmth in the sun, of safety, if not actual cosiness. Yes, thought Lance, a place which would nicely fit Janet. Yet not much more than two years ago it had been far from safe or cosy. The ugly German gun emplacements jutting out on every promontory were a constant reminder of what had been.

'You were here under the occupation? Must have been

grim.' Lance addressed the driver whose wife Marie (Janet had written) was the cook-housekeeper.

'*Prisonnier* in France, monsieur. My wife and children left behind. *Terrible* food problem.' He shook his head sombrely.

'Shortage of food for you also, I bet!'

'Was monsieur in *la guerre*?'

'Burma.'

'Ah. Le Forgotten Army!'

'Right in one! My wife . . . is she at home?'

'*Mais oui*. Madame awaits.'

Lance was glad to hear it. He was not sure what to expect, not at all sure what his reception would be. He lapsed into silence as the car left the coast road and purred into the southern part of the island's interior, roads lined with old hedges giving shelter from the wind. They passed big estates with large French-windowed houses beside small green fields dotted with Jersey cows swinging outsized udders.

Though Lance was relieved to hear Janet was at home waiting, the situation for him was not easy. He would have preferred to meet on neutral ground, even on the Angus estate which at least was his and which Janet had never cared for much not being a country woman who liked striding over moors. Here it was very much her territory. *Her* house and servants; *she* would do the dictating!

After a gap of six weeks when there had been a chilly silence between them, and Lance wondered if his wife was taking out divorce proceedings against him on grounds of cruelty or some such trumped-up charge after only just over a year of marriage, he had written to Janet in Brockenhurst apologizing for his outburst. He wrote that they had both been overwrought at the time, that the situation in Calcutta had been hideous, and an appalling one for her to witness. He said that he had moved back into the flat, but that he was keeping on the Garden Reach house for her whenever she felt like returning. He asked her to forgive him for the unforgiveable things he had said. And he asked her to write to him.

She had; fairly pronto! She was sorry too; her nerves, she explained, as if explanation was necessary, went all to pieces in India. She did not think she could ever contemplate returning, but it was sweet of him to keep on the house in case.

From thence their correspondence continued over the months almost in the same vein as it had been before their marriage: friendly, informative on both sides, but excluding confidences or intimacies. Lance wrote about his work, about Independence (he glossed over the horrors of Partition) and the progress at the Chashma Shahi under his ex-army friend Paddy Cahill; Janet told of her decision to sell up in England and move permanently to Jersey, a place in which she had spent her school holidays, and a place that would save her a mint of money in tax! She had many friends there; people liked to be asked to visit, and over there she could gather together a staff in keeping with the running of a big house. Most of all she liked the homely atmosphere it brought in the familiar surroundings of her childhood.

That was as far as the situation had reached on Lance's arrival, and his unease came from not knowing if he would be received as a guest and convenient escort, or as a *husband*. If he broached the subject of her returning to India with him for at least part of the cold weather, would she blow her top again and they be back to square one with he leaving her after another row, in which case he would have done better not to have come? Why *had* he bothered? Damn it, because she was his *wife*! The whole situation from his point of view could not be more unsatisfactory.

Lance took out the gold cigarette case Janet had given him, Pierre deftly handing him the car's lighter without taking his eyes off the road.

'How do you open the window of the bloody vehicle?' Lance, jaw working with tension, fiddled around with his maimed hand at the knobs on his side.

'*Voici, monsieur.*' Pierre pressed a button. Silently, the window descended. Lance drew deeply into his lungs, blew a few smoke rings out of the window, stubbed the cigarette into the ashtray to hand before he had hardly smoked it, and chucked the offending piece out of the window.

'The island looks pristine clean. I suppose I could be fined for doing that,' Lance commented wryly.

'*Peut-être*, monsieur.' Pierre's grin showed he guessed Mr Gardner was in a state. One never knew what mood Madame would be in as the staff well knew. The whole household was agog to see the estranged husband. None of them had as yet met him. Gossip in the servants' quarters was rife. They said he was an Indian, but he, Pierre, on meeting the master was not so sure. He'd get all the *bavardage* from Marie. It was a good job. They had their own cottage on the estate. Madame, though unpredictable, was not a bad mistress. She was generous to the staff (she could afford to be!) and liked to give presents to their children. Madame was fond of children – *dommage* she had none of her own.

The car turned off the road and headed up a drive leading to a large formal mansion with spacious grounds, situated some miles inland. There were well-kept paddocks and cottages dotted around, but not another house in sight. Pierre gave a slight honk on the horn as he neared, and there, on the doorstep, slim, elegant in a brilliant red dress, hair cut short and cleverly set to look casual, skin expertly made up, stood Janet.

'Welcome to Sainte Colombe, Lance,' she greeted, and placing on his shoulder a manicured hand on which flashed the sapphire and diamond engagement ring he had given her, kissed him on the cheek.

It was a graceful, perfectly executed act for the benefit of the public – in this case the servants – and it left Lance as uncertain as ever of her intentions towards him.

There was little time to speculate, for Lance Gardner found himself swept up into the social life of the wealthy inhabitants in Jersey of Janet's 'set', with whom the attractive dark husband she introduced from nowhere into their relatively small coterie became an immediate success. Before he had barely time to wash his hands and brush his hair, he was whipped off to luncheon with Janet's nearest neighbours (over two miles away), a merchant banker with wife and grown-up son and daughter who were fascinated to hear about India. Obliging in his whimsical way with answers to the direct questioning, Lance was considerably amused to hear Janet chipping in about the Garden Reach house and the Chashma Shahi which 'is being done up by us. You really *must* come out and see it one day,' not only as if she owned them, but as if she had loved every minute of living in them! Moreover, Janet told her friends that she had had to leave India because of illness, and that the doctor was doubtful if she were yet strong enough to return. Lance noted that too.

In the ensuing days two couples arrived from England to spend the week-end, and between luncheon parties, dinner parties, and a vast cocktail party at Sainte Colombe to introduce Lance to 'everyone of any importance on the island', Lance was taken around by Janet to see the sights. These ranged from the chilling miles of the underground German military hospital built at a dreadful toll with a workforce of slave labour and civilian prisoners tunnelling deeply into the hill from the Cape Verd and Meadowbank entrances, to the 'Jersey Lily' exhibition of Edwardian grace in St Helier. None of this 'gadding about', as Lance thought of it, was getting them anywhere as a married couple. Sooner or later they would have to talk, and as the days passed Lance saw that it was going to be 'later', and that entertainment and the house guests were Janet's way of putting off the moment. Why?

An indication that all was not forgiven came on the day of his arrival when she had led him upstairs in her startling red dress.

'I've put you in the dressing-room, darling,' she had said without looking at him. 'I nearly put you in one of the bigger spare bedrooms, but thought twice of it – the servants you know. We must keep up appearances,' she said awkwardly. 'I think we should, don't you, darling? Marie is excellent at

French cooking, but she's an awful little gossip; I mean, they're not to know, are they? You have your bathroom. and here's my bedroom.' She opened a through door which led into a large close-carpeted room with an old-fashioned high double bed and heavy mahogany Victorian furniture. 'Just as Pa and Ma left it. I like it that way. I can sort of relax here and forget the unpleasant world outside. Don't you think it feels nice and homely, darling?'

'Indeed I do. I'm glad you've got this place, and that you are well and happy here.' And he had gone up to her to take her in his arms and give her a proper greeting kiss.

She had backed away. 'Not now darling, we're going straight out to lunch. By the way I hope you brought a dinner jacket? Dinner tonight is at seven-thirty for eight, black tie. We've got ten minutes.' She looked at her gold watch. 'See you downstairs in a jiffy, darling.' She had shut the bedroom door on him.

'Right.' Lance washed his hands in the basin, brushed his hair before the mirror, and looked at himself in the glass. He straightened his 'Slap' tie. 'Right, my man, you're old enough to take a hint: *no more advances*. You'll have to wait for her to make the first move. You're being punished for your uncouth behaviour in Calcutta. It's all a deep-laid performance to show you can't do that sort of thing, and an apology by letter is not sufficient to mend the fences. Well, so be it; but how very stupid, how *petty* . . .' Lance stared at himself ' . . . how *funny*.' The set face reflected in the mirror relaxed into a smile. 'How very, very funny . . .' Lance descended the oak staircase laughing.

'What's funny, darling?' Janet said in the hall.

'Nothing,' he said, and taking her arm as a good husband should to impress the servants, he led her out to the car.

She called to him next morning when she heard him dressing, and he went through to her room and found her having a tray in bed. She wore a bed-jacket trimmed with swansdown soft about her well-massaged throat. The only make-up she had on was a modicum of lipstick. She looked rather pale, and rather sweet. He went up to her and kissed

333

her on the forehead. 'That's not for the servants' sake,' he said, 'that's for you.'

'What *are* you talking about, darling? Oh' – she found a piece of paper on her side table and handed it to him – 'I've written out our programme for today so's you'll know what's what.'

'Good idea,' he said glancing down the packed page – no venue for a talk today.

'Be an angel and go and entertain our guests at breakfast, will you, darling? It's all laid in the dining-room for you to help yourselves.'

He found the men engrossed behind their newspapers, the two ladies chatting, a delicious aroma of coffee permeating the room, a sideboard laden with dishes kept warm on electric heaters.

'Got everything you want? This is the life!' Lance helped himself to a kipper and sat down at the head of the table. Grandly he surveyed the others. But to himself he gave it a bare week more before the life palled and complete boredom and stagnation set in. This was the life Janet liked to live and ran so well; the office in Calcutta and the work at the Chashma Shahi was where he liked to be and was happiest. India was anathema to Janet. They were like chalk and cheese . . . and yet, and yet, there was more to it than that. They *had* to make a go of it.

The house guests left; there weren't so many parties, and Lance took to going into his wife's room to say good night. Usually she was in her dressing gown at the table fiddling with her hair, but one night he found her in bed. She patted it and made him sit down. She showed him a letter she had had some time ago inviting her to model furs at one of the large coastal hotels.

'I didn't tell you – I've kept it as a surprise. You will come and watch me, won't you, darling?' she said excitedly.

'Of course I will. When? Oh, Thursday. Terrific!'

'They give you tea and gooey-wooey cream cakes at little tables in the dining-room. It'll be such fun, won't it? Mr Weissmann, he's a famous furrier in London, did you know? Well, he heard I was here and wrote to me. They're making a splash in the press: "Nineteen thirties top model makes a come-back", that sort of thing!' Janet's eyes sparkled.

'I'm all agog!'

'Darling' – she hesitated – 'I just wondered; how long can you stay?'

'I'll stay as long as you want me to.'

'What about your work?'

'That can go hang. My wife is more important.'

'Really, darling? I didn't know you felt that way.'

'There are a lot of things I haven't said that I should've said.'

'There are some things you said that I can never forget. Horrid, horrid things—'

'I know and I'm sorry. I take them all back.'

'It's been a long time . . . Have you had – other women?' she asked coyly.

'You know I haven't. I've told you before and I tell you again, the Gardner men make faithful husbands, and I'm no exception. In war men have to stay celibate for long periods. It seems that in peace men married to women who can't live in India have to do the same! To stay sane I work flat out; dull myself into a working machine. It's been *too* long, Janet.'

'Has it, darling?' She tipped her head and looked at him coquettishly.

'Yes it bloody well has. Anyway what about you? Have you invited one of these wealthy gents I've met into your bed?'

'Lance darling, *really* don't be so vulgar. You know I couldn't . . . the servants would know. Anyway I wouldn't *dare* in case he found me cold and it was a complete flop.'

Lance put back his head and roared with laughter. 'You're always laughing at me; *I* can't see what's funny,' Janet said peevishly.

'I wasn't laughing *at* you, Janet. I was laughing at

what you *said*. You aren't cold with me. We were getting rather good at it, remember?'

'Was I?'

'Yes. You know you enjoyed it. You have a most fashionable and beautiful body and will no doubt set all those men at the show tomorrow ogling you alight with fanciful ideas.'

'There won't be any *men* – other than you of course – watching. But you *are* sweet. I've missed you, darling.'

'I've missed you too,' he said. 'I don't like being a bachelor. God, Janet dear, I've missed you. But I'm bloody well not going to get into bed with you until you want me there. Good night, my dear.' And he bent over her, and for the first time since Calcutta kissed her full on the lips.

Janet watched him go out of the room and close the door behind him. She watched with an expression on her face that was remarkably like the smile on a pussy's face after licking the cream off the milk. She lay on her parents' double bed, the bed in which she had been conceived, and in which her one great longing was to conceive again, and glowed in the knowledge that she had got Lance back. She had got him where she wanted him. She loved him. Really and truly she had adored him from the time she had met him in Dundee during his first leave from India when he was a youth of twenty-two, a wonderful physical specimen of a man any girl would be proud to show off to her friends, now doubly so in his masculine maturity. She had never deviated from her love, and she had won him in marriage. Though she knew she did not have passion as some women had it, she could say with truth she *had* known love with him in Calcutta, truly say she was not frigid any longer with Lance who had learnt patience in arousing her. In fact at that very moment she felt the want of his baby, but she would refrain from calling him, for tomorrow was a big day. Tomorrow she must not feel tired, not allow her hair to get tossed, her face perhaps a little bruised with kisses . . . But *after* the show . . . in her own good time . . .

CHAPTER 27

The imposing portals of the Hotel L'Hermitage, one of the leading hotels in Jersey, were wide open to a crowd of well-dressed, chattering, fashionable women, some of them sporting furs bought in a previous year from Mr Weissmann who effusively greeted them at the entrance by name. The show was strictly by invitation only.

Lance, head and shoulders above the ladies, walked through the crowded foyer, where a huge arrangement of autumn flowers was displayed at a strategic point, to where, on the left, the bar-room had been taken over by the furrier and his minions. Behind the glass doors were some fifty furs, insured for an enormous amount, each padlocked to a series of hangers on wheeled stands. The sound of laughter came through the door, and Lance caught a glimpse of Janet (who had come several hours ahead of him to rehearse) with three other girls, namely Sheena, Yvonne, and Ann, well-known models over from London. With them were two men in double-breasted grey suits and flashy ties, presumably the buyers from New York Janet had told him about.

Refraining from disturbing Janet or making himself known, Lance went to the long window leading out to a walkway. He looked down on an expanse of the golden sands of St Brelade's Bay, empty of all at that time of year but a man exercising his dog at the water's edge. The sea was choppy and deep blue, ruffled into feathers of white by the breeze. The colour reminded Lance of an English sea in Lulworth, aeons ago. The memory scarcely touched him or moved him. That time could have been in another world for aught it had to do with him now.

From the dining-room came the strains of a stringed orchestra tuning up, and Lance went in early to find a table to himself in a far corner. He watched, without his habitual amused look, Mr Weissmann fussily arranging his notes on a stand by the orchestra, and testing the microphone: 'Ladies and gentlemen, one, two, three, four; testing, testing.' Men? Well, Lance supposed if the Americans came in there would be three. He looked down at the cake-stand full of dainty sandwiches, and what Janet called 'gooey-wooey' cakes. Far from whetting his appetite he felt nauseated by the oozing cream of éclairs and *mille feuilles*, if not by the whole expensive set-up. If truth be told he felt like an ass in a lion's skin as the saying went, and after a week in Sainte Colombe, he wondered just how much longer he could play the game of poodle dog to Janet while being kept at arm's length on her lead.

A waitress put down a pot of china tea on the pink damask tablecloth. Lance poured himself a cup, and examined the programme which gave a run-down on the models. The name 'Janet Tinling' headed the list. The blurb told how the present company would remember her from photographs in the 'glossies' of the thirties when she had been *the* top photographic model. He could hear the ladies at the next table speculating avidly on her. What would she look like now ten to twelve years on? 'A right old hag', he heard one of them snort. Most in that hotel room were familiar with her pictures; even if they had not seen any, all recalled the name.

The show began to a background of soft music. Mr Weissmann gave a short talk on how the furs were collected, cured and made up. He then announced each model as she came in, and gave a description of the fur she was wearing. There was no catwalk, and, slinkingly, the girls moved to and fro down the main line between the centre tables to nods of approval, some women

338

making notes in their cards. Each girl's exit was followed by desultory applause.

There was a pause. Then to the strains of Cole Porter's nostalgic 'Night and Day' appeared Janet in a glorious full-length sable. There was a gasp of admiration, all eyes riveted on her. She, and the fur, looked a million dollars. She epitomized the glamour of pre-war days, and she *had not aged*! Rather did she look younger than remembered! Surely she had been dark before? If she could give such appearance of youth so could they! Tomorrow they would visit their beauty salons, and get Robert, or René, or Jean to lighten and fashion their hair in that straighter more casual cut that was so youthful. Away with longer darker permed locks!

There was the fashionable tallness of Janet Tinling accentuated by the highest of high heels in shining crocodile-leather shoes. There was the willowy look with the long swan-like neck, the square shoulders, and, when deftly she slipped off the fur to display the silk lining, the flat boyish figure as slim as a pencil. The other girls, each attractive, adept, and lean-limbed as they were, could not touch Janet Tinling for style.

Boredom was forgotten as Lance watched his wife. With immaculate footsteps placed one before the other in a line she made a dramatic entrance into the room, each time in a different and exquisite fur. Gracefully she pirouetted and turned this way and that to display the coat at hand to its best advantage, with a winning smile stopping beside a prospective customer to allow her with outstretched hand to feel and savour the soft richness of the garment. Resuming her walk she glided and gyrated, and with one last turn and flashing smile, disappeared through the door to change into yet another fur in the bar-room, the enthusiastic applause following her. Fur after fur she modelled with the other girls: mink, musquash, sable, fox, lynx, cheetah, puma, astrakhan, leopard and tiger skins ... you name them, Mr Weissmann had them.

On one occasion, wearing a beautiful three-quarter-length fox fur with hat to match, and knowing Lance was there on his own sitting in the corner, Janet made her way through the thronging tables to pivot round him with feline grace. She blew him a kiss and went on her way. As the only male audience in the room, the gesture brought the house down, and there was a burst of laughter, all eyes focused on the single man. Acclaim peeled out. Grinning hugely, Lance clapped loudly with the rest.

'Well done, Janet. Well done, my dear.' He embraced her warmly after the show. 'You were superb!'

'Do you really think so, Lance darling? Did you really enjoy it?'

'I enjoyed *you*,' he answered truthfully. 'You were streaks above the others. What about my buying a new fur for you?'

'Too late,' she laughed gaily. 'Mr Weissmann has reserved me the red fox. But I tell you what. You can buy me the hat.'

'Done!' Lance said. 'Absolutely delighted.'

Proudly she introduced him to the furrier, the two buyers, and Sheena, Yvonne and Ann, whom he congratulated heartily with well-deserved compliments. Champagne was served. 'Ve drink to Mees Tinling I tink and 'er come-back, yes? The belle of my show. I book you for next year? Your 'usband, he agree?' Mr Weissmann exuded.

People queued up to talk to Janet and congratulate her; press and reporters surrounded her; bulbs flashed. Customers crammed into the bar-room to put down their deposits with Mr Weissmann's secretary, and Lance left his wife to it and went out for a walk to the headland and back in the mauve light of slowly shifting colour on scudding clouds so different from the brilliant suddenness of an Indian sunset.

Janet's performance helped Lance to understand her aversion to the country to which he had taken her as a bride. India was the very antithesis of the sophisticated glamour of today, her home here, that stood on its own and yet was not isolated in its serene countryside, the very opposite of teeming Calcutta; while the Chashma Shahi was too remote for her taste.

On his return Lance and Janet dined with Mr Weissmann, the girls, the two buyers, and the secretary, and more champagne was drunk. Everyone kissed Janet goodbye, and with her arms full of flowers Pierre drove them home to Sainte Colombe.

And that night Janet was so excited and talked so much there was no question of the door being shut between them. When he was still doing his teeth she came into his room and sat on his bed, and he laughed and pulled her with him and said it would really be far more accommodating in her parents' double one, and he told her again how proud he was of her and what a lovely body she had and how he needed her. And she said how she needed him too and was proud of him too and everyone had said how handsome he was and he ought to have been a film star!

Janet was so over-excited that she could not stop talking while Lance made love to her, but it did not matter to either now that he had made her happy by showing how he admired her, now that she had made him happy by inviting him into her bed.

'Oh Lance,' she sighed, 'we can start again.'

'We *have* started again,' he smiled beside her.

'Yes, I know, but what I mean is we can *try* again . . . I mean, I would give anything to have a baby, *your* baby, Lance darling.'

'I'll go all out at it with pleasure to make up for lost time—'

'But not in India. I'd be frightened, I can't have a baby in India.' The panic sounded in her voice.

'You shan't. I wouldn't allow it. If it happens that way the moment you know you are pregnant you must fly back. I'll take six months' leave shortly afterwards to be with you all through. All I ask is that you come back

341

with me for the winters. I'll be with you here early summer, and we can go on to the Angus estate—'

'Only if it doesn't clash with Mr Weissmann's dates — I promised.'

'Yes, you mustn't miss that. We'll fit it in. The separations won't be too bad. We'll be together a lot.'

'Oh darling, darling Lance. You're so good to me. It's all going to work out well for us now, isn't it?' she said, flushed with love and happiness and triumph that she had had her way. Lance *very nearly* was giving up India for her. What, as he said, were a few months' separation every year?

'If only I can have a baby everything will be perfect, won't it, Lance darling?'

'Perfect,' Lance said, kissing the top of her head. He yawned. 'Try and go to sleep, my very dear and famous wife.'

He turned over on his side away from her, and slept.

Thus the pattern for the next few years was set. It says much for Janet's tenacious love for Lance, that after their reconciliation she annually screwed up enough courage to fly out to Calcutta for the winter months. Then the Garden Reach house was opened for her benefit; Goanese de Mello and the Sikh driver danced attendance, and much entertaining and race-going took place. Once a year in the hot weather Lance, true to his word, joined Janet in Jersey, usually in July, and they went on together to the Angus estate for the shooting season.

The old grey lodge, with its skeleton staff and permanent housekeeper, filled then with Janet's rich friends from the Channel Islands, and Lance's business associates. And she *did* conceive again, twice, once in Jersey, once in Calcutta from where Lance sent her straight home and arranged his long sabbatical to take place throughout her pregnancy. Alas, to their joint sadness, on both occasions, in spite of his being beside her, and with her having every medical care and rest, she miscarried, and after the second time could bear no more children.

Once India settled down after Independence, and her constitution as an independent state took effect, and most of the worst of the initial troubles in the north had subsided bar the recurring war with Pakistan over Kashmir, Lance's firm grew from being purely jute to dealing in tea, cotton, rubber and many other trading commodities.

In 1951 Jawaharlal Nehru won an overwhelming victory in the elections, and in the same year was conceived the 'five-year plan' when foreign aid accelerated economic growth. In these favourable conditions, with Nehru dominating the Congress Party, India developed rapidly in a mixed economy both in the public and private sectors, and Lance, by now an experienced businessman to his fingertips, took advantage of it, his business burgeoning to become a large consortium of firms with subsidiary companies in Australia, America and in Scotland where the old ties were kept up in Dundee. After successfully completing his term as managing director during these expanding years, when admittedly he did not see all that much of Janet except in the winter months, work curtailing his summer leave, he handed over to a fellow Indian, and himself became chairman.

He did a great deal of travelling the world on business trips on which Janet did not accompany him (she felt air-sick as well as sea-sick), first by the old 'punkah wallah' planes, and then by jet, using an executive plane for internal use which he learnt to fly himself. He had an airstrip built on the Kootgunge estate for his own convenience, and also for Janet so that she should not feel the isolation of the *mofussil*.

But Janet was never well in India. She never went there without picking up something. Once it was typhus, another time dysentery, and always the collywobbles of fear that caused her bowels to turn to water at the slightest mishap. She suffered a real terror that she might die in the country and be buried on the same day before her body had time to get cold. However happy she was to be with Lance – and they were happy in a way, she clingingly possessive, he indulgent of her idiosyncrasies – it was with a sense of release that they parted. When she waved goodbye from the steps of the plane at Dum Dum airport she was already anticipating the blessed touchdown among the green fields of Jersey, whilst he looked forward to returning to the Chowringhee flat and undivided attention to work.

At the same pace as Lance's business grew in the immediate post-war period, so did the Kootgunge venture, spurred on in the first years by Paddy's presence.

As the pink palace was taking shape with its graceful cupolas and parapets restored, as 'works' and outbuildings were rising further away, so were the fields around being ploughed with the same type of wooden plough Lance had seen at the Exeter exhibition, pulled here by patient plodding bullocks, a barefooted coolie in *dhoti* behind making encouraging clicking noises. The seeding of the jute took place from March through to June, three plants to a square foot, the harvesting from July through to October. There was a *white* jute, and a *daisee* jute which grew ten to fifteen feet high, each stalk as thick as a man's finger. Soon, unmistakably, there could be seen acre after acre of light green leaves, each leaf four to six inches long and tapering characteristically to a point.

While all this was going on, Paddy, in his spare time, wrote his 'penny dreadful', a thinly disguised self-portrait of an Indian Army officer who got into every scrape, used bad language (mostly edited out), saved kidnapped damsels on the Frontier, bashed dacoits, shot looting tribesmen, and was caught up in the horrors of thuggery – stealthy murder by strangling of unwary travellers — not to mention becoming involved with a good many *houris* on the way.

By then forty, Paddy declared he was too old to hunt for bints. He basked in the luxury of a permanent mistress he had picked up in a Solah bordello, an exotic-looking Eurasian with kohl-blackened eyes, called Lolitha, who 'knows a thing or two about the Kama Sutra, old sod'. In grand style they took up residence in a newly restored wing of the Chashma Shahi. When his first novel became a best-seller that hit the headlines with its shocking bawdiness and apocryphal adventures that rocked the establishment (the author betted the bishops read it in private) Paddy earned more than enough money to keep a *zenana*. But by then he had grown comfortable with his plump Lolitha who had lost her figure bearing their several 'natural' children, and away he went with his *bibi* to live in California.

As Janet scarcely ever came to Kootgunge, Lance found himself when there living entirely within an Indian community. He missed the fun that exploded in laughter between Paddy and him after the day's work when they settled down to drinks and dinner together by the screens. He missed the stimulation of Paddy's keen brain and sardonic humour more than he could say. And he missed the presence of friendly easy-going Lolitha and her children who whenever they saw him rushed up and tumbled about him like a lot of healthy, grubby puppies.

They were the only 'family' he had — and now they too had gone.

CHAPTER 28

Inevitably, with the passage of time Lance and Janet grew further and further apart. Her winter visits to India lapsed, as did they to Scotland. Amicably they agreed to part. There was no question of divorce. Why should they when neither of them wished to remarry? Besides, Janet liked her status as Mrs Lance Delhmir Gardner, liked talking about India to her friends, though it was an enormous relief to her not to have to screw up her courage to go there any more.

They met infrequently in Jersey to discuss financial affairs with their lawyers, but now there was no question of his using the dressing-room. Somehow when there was no longer the chance of a child, that part of their marriage faded completely. Instead Lance was given the best guest-room in the house, and Janet would throw a party to show off the dark handsome figure of her husband, more attractive than ever with greying sideburns, much speculation buzzing on the island, not to mention with the staff at Sainte Colombe, as to the actual relationship.

Inevitably too, with the years Lance was often lonely when he stopped to think in the pace of his jet-stream life. And particularly so was he when of an evening he strolled in the derelict *zenana* quarters, the only part of the palace that now remained untouched and in ruins, straggly grass and tenacious convolvulus rampaging among the broken marble basins and statues. What was the point in repairing it when his wife was not there to sit on a golden swing? What was the point when he had no children to romp in the garden and splash in the cool fountains

346

channelled direct from the pure welling of the Chashma Shahi, the Spring Imperial?

Melancholy attacked Lance in the shadows of the palace when he thought of the children he had lost — when he thought of the red-headed girl he had found and lost in England, found again in India and lost again.

A single long white envelope slithered into the letter-box of the Wick bungalow. Cara heard the clunk of the shutter and picked the letter up from the mat in the small hall. Second post; another typed official letter, as if she hadn't had enough to deal with in the first. Business, business, business; bills, lawyers, forms and more forms. Her head ached; she felt ill and drained; she was tired out mentally and physically. Once again last night she had scarcely slept.

In the kitchen Cara tossed the unwelcome letter on the table and made her mid-morning coffee. She sipped wearily, the mug held in both hands to feel the small warmth on the bitter February day. The bungalow was heated only by one radiator in the hall, and she had to watch the electricity bill . . . Her bedroom with its large picture window was like a refrigerator. Dark lowering clouds were gathering outside. It looked as if it would snow. Snow didn't lie long in Christchurch, but when it snowed, by gum it could snow!

Cara switched on the light. She looked idly at the letter and saw that it bore an Indian stamp. What the heck? She had no contacts left in India. Perhaps someone wanted information on Derek? The letter wouldn't go away so she might as well get on with reading it. She ripped the envelope up, opened the typewritten page which was folded into three, and read the official heading, her eyes leaping down the page to the signature. Oh God, not *him* to cope with on top of everything else! What did *he* want from her? Why couldn't people leave her alone? The coffee, that a moment ago had been comforting, tasted bitter in her mouth. She put the mug down on the scrubbed wooden table. At a glance her eyes took in the short letter.

25th January 1960
Gardner, Prasad, Mohan Singh & Co., (India)
Connaught Place
Delhi
India.

Dear Cara,

I feel I must write to you after all these years to express my sympathy at the loss of your husband earlier this month. As you know I never met him. I came across the full column obituary in *The Times* of London quite by accident at the Gymkhana Club. He must have been a very fine man. I certainly do not expect you to answer, especially at this sad time for you, but it would be nice if you did.

Yours,
Lance.

She sat at the table looking at the 'Lance'. The name stirred no emotion in her, made no impact – another age, another life. Thank God he *hadn't* demanded anything of her. She didn't even have to bother to answer it!

For sixteen years Cara had cooked, swept, cleaned, shopped, run the house, and looked after the daily needs Derek could not undertake for himself. She was always there, always about the place if needed, the active partner, at the same time guiding, amusing, and entertaining an energetic growing child. At the end, for six months she had devotedly nursed her husband through his last painful illness.

Geraldine, now in her nineteenth year, had stayed back from Oxford at the beginning of her second term to be with her father. With her daughter's supportive youthfulness in the house, the two close in their loss, Cara had made an enormous effort to keep going and remain composed up to and through the large military funeral

348

arranged by the Christchurch Garrison, the 'Chink', a general, attending with a good many Gunners. Afterwards Geraldine had gone back to her studies, and Cara had hoped to lock herself away in her bungalow, only wanting to be left in peace. But there had been no peace. Well-meaning friends and neighbours called continuously to see how she was and invite her out to coffee mornings and lunches. They said she needed feeding up. They said she needed taking out of herself.

She was appreciative of her friends' kindness and she went out, always to come back to the empty house, the forlorn missing of Derek, and the spate of letters, half of them business ones that must be dealt with urgently if she was not to starve before her widow's pension came through. Her solicitor informed her that the formalities might take a little time to sort out due to Major Brownlow's war wound having to be taken into consideration. She had no income of her own, and, after the expenses of Derek's last illness, there was an overdraft at the bank. Geraldine had won a scholarship to Oxford, but her allowance needed keeping up.

Cara paid a visit to her bank manager at Southbourne and arranged for the ever-increasing overdraft to be covered on the security of the bungalow. She then got ready to stay with some of her mother's cousins in Ireland, the first holiday she had had since the war. Before she left she meticulously answered all the letters of condolence. Only one was left – Lance's. She looked at it again and decided it would be churlish not to answer. Hers was as short as his: she thanked him for writing, said how clever of him to have got the address right and that No. 14 Wick Bungalow Estate was in the grounds of the old Wick House, and she sent her best wishes to Janet.

On her return from Ireland, much recovered, but still filled with a hapless feeling of depression, she found a letter from Lance waiting, this one addressed in his own handwriting. The cancellation mark on the stamp read 'Kootgunge'. The name brought a smile to Cara's lips.

Beautiful Chashma Shahi. What was it like now? Had it been fully restored by the Tinling millions? She had read in the newspapers of the old man's death on the night following his daughter's wedding. What a ghastly shock it must have been — poor Janet. What a way for Lance to start married life by having to sort out a fortune.

The handwriting was the same as ever — small, firm, even — in black ink on white paper, but when Cara unfolded the full-sized sheet, she found the engraved heading was coloured and repeated in a Persian script; rather charming. The paper was written over on both sides, and it gave out a faint aroma of sandalwood. With the graceful script, memories rushed back: the *chattri*-topped front entrance; the pink sandstone ruin that turned to red in the sunset; the broken cupolas, columns and domes, the rounded Moghul room with the exquisite bay screens; the low, wide Nawab's divan!

'I said it would be nice if you answered, and so it was. Thank you,' Cara read. 'Did you know that you quite broke my heart, not once but twice! I never seemed thereafter to collect all the pieces together, and predictably, I suppose, my marriage to Janet was never a great success. For the last nine years we have lived apart. My mother died some time ago, but my sister and brother still live in Scotland and they and their families join me when I open the Lodge. It was Paddy Cahill who told me where you are living. At the same time he gave me a straight-from-the-shoulder talk which knocked some ill-conceived ideas out of my block-head. He wrote his first novel while acting as my agent here. Please, *your* news next.'

It was such a friendly letter that Cara could not but answer it, though she wrote she had no news. ' . . . you once asked me before on the Lulworth picnic to tell you about myself — you had been relating the story of the Gardner men and their Begums — and I said compared to that there was nothing to tell. There is still nothing to tell . . .'

She heard from him again: 'When at Lulworth you said

there was nothing to tell, you added that you loved your parents, your brother, and Uncle Tom Cobley an' all! I remarked that that showed you had a large heart, and I asked if you had ever been in love.' Lance's next letter arrived air mail in record time.

'Fancy you remembering that!' she wrote back. 'I remember everything,' came the reply.

With some surprise Cara found that her spirits had lightened, a spark of interest outside herself lifting her lowness. She looked forward to receiving the next letter, whether there had been one or not during the week colouring her days. Very often the overseas mail came by second post, and she found herself hurrying back from the drab typing job she had taken on in the mornings in Boscombe to see if one had arrived. The tenor of their friendship picked up with ease; an interest between old friends but nothing more. The letters were stimulating in her dull lonely life of near-poverty, amusing small incidents about his work or the people he met making her laugh. He told her his main office had moved to Delhi which was more convenient all round, and that now he only paid occasional visits to the sub branch in Calcutta, the Chowringhee flat disposed of. To begin with she felt no alarm at the easy development of the letter contact with Lance: only pleasure. The very distance between them excluded emotion, cancelled out any threat of re-involvement.

But Lance's letters developed the relationship. Subtly they changed. Now they started, 'Cara dear,' and ended 'Lance', the 'yours' dropped. The friendly tone grew, almost imperceptibly, into something more, and Cara, as had happened once before, drew back; Lance, as had happened once before, noticed the diffidence in her replies creeping in.

Without further ado he wrote that he was coming to England on business. He hoped they could meet.

On receipt of that bombshell Cara withdrew into her shell and slammed the door. She did not want to be seen by him or to see him herself. The shock of such an encounter after so long would be too much. 'I prefer,' she wrote stiffly, 'to keep the memory of when we were young, and not to ruin that memory by meeting as we are now.' 'What has happened to the Cara who braved the flooded Indus to come to my sick-bed?' he taunted her. 'Is she so changed that she dare not look that same man in the face?'

'I am vain enough not to *want* you to see me,' she tried again. 'I am *41!* I feel like Methuselah. I am middle-aged and tired. Do not press me, Lance. Do not spoil it all. I have so enjoyed our correspondence; the interest has helped to put me on my feet after Derek's death and I am grateful. Let us leave it companionably and comfortably that way. My life is here in England with my daughter.'

'So it is to be a pen-friendship for life is it? Not on my terms, it isn't,' he wrote again. He gave her the date of his proposed flight, and insisted they must give themselves the chance to meet. 'Stop making excuses, Cara,' he wrote severely. 'Your daughter is at Oxford. You say she is of independent spirit. You must hardly ever see her! Don't try to pull the wool over my eyes for you will not succeed. I know you too well to be unsure, bemused, hurt, by your delaying tactics any more. If you *are* 41, then I must be 47. We are in the *prime* of our lives. Come on, woman: *be* your age!'

She wrote once more – back-pedalling. It was too soon; she had not recovered from bereavement; she loathed being hustled; his last letter was damned *rude*. Would he please stop pressing her. She was not going to write to him any more, so, 'Goodbye, Yours, Cara.'

That was how her last letter to Lance ended. She was determined not to write again, and she did not. He sent her one more missive from India:

'Cara, here are some facts for you to digest. We are free agents – you through your widowhood, I through my separation. Not many people are given a *third* chance! God has been good to us. I quote – as you know I am of

352

Muslim descent – *There is no God but God*. He is Absolute, and I believe He wishes us to be happy. I love you whatever life and the years have done to you. I cannot help it. I have always loved you and I always shall love you. No matter what time does to our bodies, our souls stay the same; besides, Cara of my heart, we can always draw the *tatties* and shut our eyes! I will not let you throw away unwarranted the happiness which is in our grasp for the taking. We shall meet whether you like it or not. If you are proven right, we shall meet and we shall part. If your fears prove groundless, then the earth and the heavens for eternity are ours . . .'

Trapped by the man's insistence, and his impending visit to England, Cara desperately thought of ways she could avoid Lance. She could go away again. She could visit Geraldine in Oxford – no, Geraldine was far too busy, had her own life; not welcome there for more than twenty-four hours or so! She could throw herself off Hengistbury Head. Idiot! Not she! Better to face the wretched man straight away on his arrival, and get it done with and over. Five minutes of desultory conversation while they looked warily at each other would be enough to end his foolish ideas. Sadly the meeting would put an end to the exchange of letters which had 'taken her out of herself'. All there would be left was one more polite note from each saying how much they had enjoyed the encounter . . . then – finish.

Lance did not ring Cara on his touch-down at Heathrow. He went by hired car straight to his East India United Service Club in St James's Square and wrote a postcard. On it he put the time, the date, the place of meeting. That was all. No address. No RSVP. No 'will that suit you?' He did not even sign it.

Resentfully, Cara braced herself to get the nerve-racking, useless, senseless interview over which forced her to make some fool excuse not to go to work that morning and would probably lose her her job.

CHAPTER 29

Cold with apprehension, and feeling like a foolish old woman, Cara set out for the dreaded assignment. She felt she was treading a dangerous road away from the security of her small bungalow with its tiny garden, away from the Christchurch life that she had become accustomed to, a road which, if she had any sense, she need not have taken even this far. Why then did she leave the bungalow, walk down the road towards the muddy slipway, row herself over the Avon River by Wick Ferry, and continue walking as slowly as she was able without actually halting, down the towpath? With every yard she took, her dread grew stronger. Her feet dragged, and her nervous system became as taut as an over-strung harp.

She had taken time and pains preparing for this meeting, almost, she told herself ruefully, as if she expected to die. The tension within her during the last few days had grown to such a pitch of intensity, she really felt it might kill her. Her uneven heartbeats, that had kept her awake at night, would either stop altogether, or would race into apoplexy! But no one who undressed tidy Carissa Brownlow's body in the mortuary would find a tear, a spot, or a safety-pin if *she* could help it.

She had had her hair washed and set the afternoon before in an expensive salon in Bournemouth that she could ill afford. On arrival home, hating the stiff set, she had combed the lacquer out, her locks set in a style which the maestro in the salon had said would make 'modom look younger'. She would never waste her money *there* again. In the process of combing she had noticed the new grey hairs in front among the red-gold, and had painfully tweaked them out. She had, first thing that morning, taken a bath made fragrant with Floris essence won in a raffle, had put on a becoming light-weight suit which nevertheless was a good many years old and had been shortened to fashion. Finally she smoothed up her legs the flimsy fish-net stockings Geraldine had given her for Christmas and had said were 'sexy'. Her one pair of plain court shoes, that served for every dressier occasion, finished the outfit except for the Gunner brooch she wore on her lapel. She was damned well going to show Lance where she belonged.

Just why she had taken so much trouble she was not too sure, until she decided in the boat that it was vanity: 'Vanity, vanity, all is vanity.' Which was an absurd contradiction! If she wanted the whole thing to be over in a few minutes she should have made herself look a right old bag!

Despite Geraldine's stockings, the last thing Cara felt when walking slowly down the towpath was sexy. The water in the bottom of the leaky old ferry had sloshed to and fro dirtying the hem of her skirt; she had kicked off her shoes to get a better grip on the wet floor when rowing and as a result her feet were damp, and her hair was quickly blown about by the wind into its usual curling naturalness. Tidy she may have been, but *soignée* like Janet, with every hair and eyelash in place, she would never be.

Cara was long beyond caring what she looked like. Apprehensive on outset, she was by now in a jittering funk. If only Lance's postcard had given an address she would have found out the number and rung him, better still sent a telegram to say she had some infectious disease such as typhoid or measles. She did not think 'flu would be enough to put Lance off coming to see her! But his plain postcard, stamped London SW1, had *not* given an address. He'd done it on purpose of course so that she could not duck out, drat him. She knew she had made a ghastly mistake in coming this far. The encounter was going to be a complete disaster. She had known from the beginning it would be. Two middle-aged persons confronting each other on a towpath, both horrified to see the travesties of what they had once been staring them in the face, both intent on disguising their shock and horror! He had such good manners. She knew how to contain her feelings. He would be polite. So would she.

Cara walked on, her knees trembling, her mouth dry, her eyes fixed on the ground, oblivious of the balmy spring day, the clear cerulean of the sky, the small white clouds scudding high overhead. The sun shone warm on the type of breezy day which when spent on the water wiped the pallidness left by an English winter off faces, skin whipped into glowing circulation, the sort of morning Bobby would have declared to be a perfect sailing day.

Rounding a curve on the towpath, the greensward to her left with the bandstand further on and the river on her right, Cara walked into a drift of double cherry blossom blown by the wind round her feet like pink confetti. Distracted from her inward disquiet for a moment, she looked up to view the waving laden branches lining the path; and as she did so she saw him.

He was still some little distance from her standing on the point of the harbour, the Yacht Club away on his left. He stood sideways on the path, facing the water, in silhouette as she had first seen him in the Yacht Club, then looking into the flame of the setting sun, now gazing across the shining wind-clipped river. A fleet of swans made a bee-line towards the silent form. They paddled energetically, cronking in expectation of food. They came right up to the path, the leader landing and demanding with outstretched neck and open beak, only to paddle away with the group of others in haughty disappointment that so still a shape had nothing to offer. Watching, the thought came into Cara's mind that in the little scene enacted before her, lay the truth. He and she had nothing to offer each other after so long. All Lance's written words of love were but sentimental fiction. She knew it! One could not put the clock back. With haughty disappointment they would assess each other, and, finding nothing, tack away edgily from one another as the swans were tacking away . . .

Even in the same moment that Cara was summing up

these dampening thoughts in the entrenched attitude she had steeled herself to take, she caught her breath at the very familiarity of the figure staring out over the river, the figure that as yet had not seen her. She had forgotten how intimately she knew him -- every inch of him: the set of dark head on long neck, the slant of wide shoulders, the straight military back, the so very tall upright body casually dressed in tweed jacket and grey flannels, thick-soled chukka boots on his feet. And though she could as yet not see the new lines in his face and the grey in the black, she sensed them, knew they were there.

He turned his head with an anxious furrowed look along the path and saw her walking towards him bathed in a rosy light. In wonderment he held his breath at seeing the miracle of her framed by the heavy clumps of pink blossom dangling overhead, the polished bark of the cherry tree trunks matching the dark brilliance of her hair, her skirt and jacket in pastel colour such as he liked best to see her in, her feet gliding through a drift of petals wafted by the wind, her eyes fixed on him. His gaze and her gaze locked from twenty yards and more.

Cara did not know how she walked those last few yards towards Lance for the terrible turmoil within her, the invisible thread of their glances linking them long before they met. She walked on, suffocating, each footstep placed gingerly as if she expected the earth to collapse beneath her on ground uncertain as in a Quetta earthquake. Her full skirt swung gracefully short about her long slim legs, hair blown in the wind, her mother's pearls about her neck, Gunner brooch defiant.

Lance did not shorten the distance between them by one inch, but stood stock-still waiting for her to come to him, his eyes large and dark and very wide. He looked at her in the same way he had so strangely scrutinized her once before in the Sun Inn, all those years ago when she had not locked the door against him for fear it might seem she did not trust him. Since the days in India she knew what the dark-eyed look meant with the mouth compressed into a thin line: his tension was as great as hers.

His figure blocked her path, and she stopped dead a yard from him. They stood in silence for a ticking half-minute staring at each other in an atmosphere as charged as that of an electric spring storm. Suddenly Lance's posture changed in the lightning way she knew so well. His rigidity vanished, the easy loose-knit body relaxed with the lazy half-closing of eyes while the smile spread, crinkling at the corners of eyes, the crease appearing in left cheek, the brow released – all the hallmarks that had caused her to fall in love with him in the first place.

'You're early,' he accused as if they had met yesterday instead of the last time eighteen years previously.

'The – the ferry was on my side. I – I went as slowly as I could. Anyway,' she recovered, 'who are you to talk? *You* were here before me!'

'Terribly early. If there'd been a pub handy I'd have gone in for some Dutch courage. When those bloody swans aggressively approached demanding food, I thought I would die of agitation.'

'One doesn't usually carry bread when meeting an acquaintance.'

'What an inadequate word from competent courageous Cara! "Acquaintance" makes it sound as if we have to start from the beginning.' His eyes caressed her face in the way they had in the old Christchurch days.

'And don't we?' The years fell away. She felt attractive, young. His presence had always given her confidence, uplift, and apparently the sight of him still could. With Lance . . .

'Your hand,' she noticed, 'your wounded hand.'

'I hope it does not offend you?' he asked as he had once asked Janet in the Rolls Royce.

'You wrote you had come through Burma more or less in one piece,' she said slowly. 'I wondered about the '"more or less".'

'A couple of fingers less, two others damaged by a mortar bomb on the romp to Rangoon, leaving a damned ugly stump. Hasn't worried me since they fixed it up enough to play golf to my old handicap. It worried Janet though.'

'Poor hand,' she said gently, 'poor relic of conflict, the terrible war which maimed Derek among the hundreds of thousands. *He* was so courageous. You soldiers are the courageous ones, not me! Perhaps it is a good thing to have a constant reminder: *no more wars*, please. Do you remember Bobby's last letter?'

'"It is up to those who survive to make another war impossible . . ." I wrote that I remember everything. What do you think about us having to start from the beginning?'

'No need.' She smiled up at him. 'I feel as if I know you very well indeed.'

'Thank God!' Lance said fervently. 'For my part I feel as if we had never parted. May I add that you are looking more beautiful than ever in your "middle age", as you point out, though hard to believe it.'

'*You* that does it, if you'll excuse my grammar. In my turn may I add that those grey sideburns of yours are extremely becoming,' Cara responded gaily. They started to walk towards the empty bandstand.

'I had thought of using black boot-polish, but decided you'd better know the worst straight away.' Lance kept his long stride down to her pace.

'Next confession is that I tweaked out some white hairs. Never again – too painful!'

'Tell me about . . .' they began simultaneously; they stopped, and laughed. 'Ladies first,' Lance invited, palm upwards.

Talking easily, they strolled on past the sward and the old cobwebbed mill with its ancient water-wheel, and over the small bridge along the mill stream with scarcely a glance at the Yacht Club on one side where it had all begun, or at the Priory on the other where Brigadier-General Charles Thornton's remains lay, the father who had exerted the full force of his dictatorial personality in terminating his daughter's union with the 'half-caste'. In the Castle ruins Cara talked to her friend, the gawping garden boy, whose hair was now white, and who at once remembered Lance from the Wick House days. Lance shook him by the hand, pressing in a bank note as he did so, and praised him for his well-tended beds of colourful spring flowers; and the 'boy' giggled and drooled in his show of pleasure.

'Is your passport valid?' Lance asked over lunch at the King's Arms Hotel on Castle Street.

'Yes. Why?'

'Thank God for that,' Lance said for a second time in the hour. He scrutinized the wine list, and ordered a bottle of claret. The waiter served them with roast beef. 'Can you drop everything and fly to India?'

'Heavens, you take my breath away! When? For how long?'

'As soon as you can be ready. The sooner the better. Shall we say for five weeks or so? After that comes my annual leave in Scotland.'

'All this way . . . this, this, so-called business trip. Bit brief isn't it? And the *expense* . . .' Cara gasped.

'Business trip *was* rather snatched, I'm afraid.' Lance grinned like a naughty school-boy found out. 'I justified it by doing a day's work in London before coming down here; felt strongly that if I didn't act pronto I'd land myself back to square one. Carissa can be a slippery customer! I have to get back to a board meeting in Delhi. Could you make it the day after tomorrow?'

'Five weeks or so and you'll be in Scotland. Why don't I come up there? Save all the ex—'

'Wouldn't you like to have a holiday in India? What is there to stop you if your passport is in order?'

'My boss was pretty cross when I told him I wasn't coming in this morning. I should think *that* job's gone out of the window. But, well, in any case I couldn't possibly afford . . . and I haven't got the right clothes.' She hesitated.

'Stop going on about expenses and affording and clothes,' Lance interrupted. 'No problem. I'll see to the ticket, first class. You'll have to learn to refrain from counting pennies.' He refilled their glasses.

'Pennies? More like *hundreds* of pounds. I don't believe in extravagance. Why not ordinary class?' Cara's hackles rose.

'Because I travel first, or would you prefer to sit on your own at the other end of the 'plane?'

'Don't be silly.'

'My mother would have entirely approved of your sentiments; I used to fly her out first class and she was quite distressed when she read the price on her ticket. My Scottish blood tells me I approve of your sentiments too. I certainly never squander money unnecessarily. Would you like to order a sweet?' He handed her the menu. 'So, are you coming?' he pressed.

'Just coffee for me. I'd have to ring Geraldine. Would I be able to leave her an address? I can't possibly say I'd be going off with a *man*. You make it all very awkward,' she frowned.

'I'll give you a box number . . .' With a chuckle Lance helped himself to a liberal piece from a round Stilton.

'I told you, I haven't enough summer clothes . . .'

'Chests of them where we're going . . .'

'And where is that supposed to be? Anyway I don't want to go to India at this time of year . . . frightfully hot.'

'I *live* there, Cara. Hot weather and cold weather.'

'Do you have a flat in Delhi?'

'I prefer to keep a suite of rooms in an annexe at the Oberoi Maidens . . . that's what the hotel is called nowadays. More convenient for a bachelor, I like its old-fashionedness. I remember meeting your Pammie and her brood there once. It has a swimming pool in the garden; a colourful oasis of lawns and flowers in bustling Old Delhi. Actually, after the Oberoi you'd be going on to Kootgunge. I spend a good deal of my time there now. You'll find a lot of differences in India, Cara; for instance all the big hotels are fully air-conditioned.' But Cara was no longer listening. 'Aaah.' She drew in a long breath after the word 'Kootgunge', her eyes grown soft and far away. 'Oh Lance, really? Beautiful, beautiful Chashma Shahi . . .'

She accompanied him to the station, and then caught a bus back to the end of Wick Lane. She rang Geraldine and told her she had had out of the blue an invitation from 'old friends' to visit India.

'Have a super time.' Geraldine rang off, glad she did not have to worry about her mother for a while or feel guilty that she hadn't asked her to stay in Oxford.

As for Cara locking up the bungalow and taking only one small suitcase, she felt twenty years younger, gloriously unburdened, and thoroughly abandoned.

During the whole of the encounter, which had lasted slightly under three hours, she and Lance had had no physical contact. Nor even had their hands brushed. Neither did they touch on the journey. Mr Gardner and Mrs Brownlow were not the sort to flaunt their feelings, though the air hostess who attended them, and who, attracted by their distinguished looks, watched them closely, read mystery and romance between the dark gentleman of courtly manners, and the charming red-haired woman who wore an antique ruby ring of considerable beauty. She noticed how their heads often turned from their resting places with secret gaze. And their eyes upon each other told all.

They lay on the great Nawab's divan in Lance's quarters in an upstairs wing of the palace which had been open to the skies when Cara had first come to Kootgunge. She fitted comfortably into Lance's arm, her head against his shoulder, their legs entwined – no knobbly knees! Pale moonlight shone faintly through the latticed window to give diffused light. The scent from the dampened *kuss-kuss tatties* on the roof verandah wafted cool and fragrant into the room. The air was gently turned by a large central overhanging fan gyrating in soothing swathes. It was the hottest time of the year in Kootgunge, the time before the monsoon broke, but it was not overbearingly so in the high-ceilinged room with its old-fashioned natural air-conditioning ducts in the graceful pillars, from which night air draughted and flowed to make the outsize gossamer mosquito net of pale, pale blue, billow lazily.

'Why are you crying?' Lance touched Cara's cheeks and found them wet. 'Why, when you give me the infinite pouring of pleasure I have only found with you, do you weep?' he queried when after the tumult of their love-making he drifted into the very quintessence of tenderness.

'I am crying with joy for the happiness of being with you again in the Chashma Shahi, beloved one.' Cara took up his damaged hand and brushed it with her lips.

He lay quite still on his back, the gesture touching him to his very soul. She turned to stroke the dark hair off his forehead, and raising herself she kissed his rough face all over.

'You too?' she said softly. 'Salt tears mingling.'

'Me too,' his deep voice came strangled.

'Only you have I known in love; only with you can I ever know love.' She kissed his neck and chest. 'I love you and love you and love you . . .'

'God is Good. God is Absolute. He has given us absolute perfection. All that I have is thine, my darling one, my Dil-milee, the delight of my life.'

'I have already more than enough.' Cara with shock saw the gunshot scar over the ribs . . . 'more or less in one piece'. Oh God, how close . . . oh thank God, thank God. 'My heart is bursting: there is no room for anything else.'

'There *is* more. The Begum-sahiba must have her privacy as of yore. Together we will re-build the *zenana* pavilion and you shall make the secret garden, and I will give thee a golden swing to swing upon in the rain, and the fountains will play. And there we shall live happy ever after . . .'

'The Nawab of Kootgunge will carry his Begum all exquisitely dripping to the great nuptial divan. I insist that we have this very bed transferred to the *zenana*!'

'As you wish. The Begum-sahiba must have all she desires. She only has to lift her little finger . . . stop kissing me you outrageously devastating woman, unless, that is, you want . . .'

'I want and want and want . . .'

'So much for feeling old and tired!' Lance's face creased into his winsome smile. He crushed Cara to him. He kissed her long, and then with increasing passion.

And the only sound they could hear was the drum-drumming of hearts meeting.

FINALE

1

Final entry. End of letters. End of diaries. The last minutely
subscripted page in the latter written in the spring of 1960
ended in a high note of expectancy at an imminent journey.

My mug of coffee sat stone cold on the table beside me.
The ashtray was littered with stubs. Early light filtered
round the edges of the closed velvet curtains. Absorbed in
reading, I had forgotten the drink and had scarcely moved
from the sofa all night.

Stiffly I unwound my legs from under me and stood up,
stamping one foot that had gone dead and then agonizingly
developed pins-and-needles. I limped to the mirror hanging
over the flickering red light of the electric log fire, and putting my hand up to my face, stared at myself. Big brown eyes
looked back at me above strong nose and stubborn chin,
mouth set in a tight line of disquiet. My straight hair, of
which I was inordinately proud, reflected heavy dark glossy
locks. As a child it had been plaited in two pigtails down to
my waist; for work I wore it drawn back and piled into a
knot on the top of my head in a style that suited the severity
of an academic bachelor life. However, when alone about
the flat I thought it beneficial to release it. It flowed now
freely about my shoulders softening my angular looks, bely-
ing that I was indeed mutton dressed as lamb!

Speculatively I fingered my face. Hell! Who *was* I? Why
hadn't my mother burnt those damn letters? *I* had no need
nor wish to know about her intimate past; *I* was not
interested in knowing. But that *she* had wanted me to know

was obvious. Why? Why get at me from beyond the grave? Hummn, she must have thought to dig me out of my work, out of my self-centred complacency that presumably she considered had gone on quite long enough. I on the other hand was determined work should not suffer through being diverted by what had gone on before I was born or even after I was born. My mother's affairs of the heart had nothing, absolutely *nothing* to do with me. My father was my father and always would be, the man whose name I carried and would always carry, the dear man in the wheelchair whose intellect I had inherited. He was the man who had helped me with my homework from my earliest school days, read aloud to me, selected the classics and the history books for me to study, all of which had stood me in marvellous stead in my chosen career. He had even dropped his experimental research to give more time to coach me for university exams.

I near-worshipped him. He was the one for whom I sobbed my heart out when he died – I had not wept since. He gave me my ambition to study through showing me the enjoyment and satisfaction that work brought, gave me the drive to stick at it when the goal appeared unattainable, gave me the flair to succeed. I owed *everything* to him, and would let no other usurp his memory or his rightful place, certainly not one who 'happened' to be in Quetta at the time, the lover with whom my mother had obviously taken off within a few months of my father's death, though I had as yet no proof.

Agitatedly I left the mirror and went into the kitchen to make myself some toast and boil an egg. There was a great deal I did not understand. There must be more than met the eye.

That I was personally upset was undeniable; as well I was part furious, wholly annoyed, unbelieving, and wanting to forget much of what I had read. On the other hand the professional in me, disassociating itself from any connection, looked at the saga dispassionately with objective discernment. *What* a story! Here were two people who had

365

never been entirely out of each other's thoughts since pre-war when they had met and fallen in love. Their continuing love affair was woven in with the historical romances of a well-documented family from Moghul times. The pair had met again accidentally during the war, which was not as improbable as it sounded at first read. I remember my father telling me that half the cantonment was filled with civilians called up from the sweat bath of South India. In Quetta they could be seen bicycling up to the Staff College blue with cold, heads down against a freezing Khojak gale!

Amazingly, during a lengthy period of no contact what-soever, an invisible thread continued to link the two. They had met once more, and though I had no idea what hap-pened after that since the letters and diaries had come to a full stop, and I only had box number addresses and scrawled postcards from all over the world from my mother to go on, I had read enough to know that the embers of their mutual attraction needed scarcely one catalyst to rekindle the fire.

Normally I did not allow myself to speculate. Before I could put my mother's affairs finally out of my mind I had to wait for the letter to arrive. I therefore went to the office, violet pools showing under my eyes after the sleepless night, and settled down to tackle the accumulated pile on my desk.

The letter came. As I thought: several Indian stamps; attractively coloured heading; black ink on white paper; interesting handwriting that was small and even, easy to decipher yet full of character – I knew it so well!

It was a shortish letter which started by apologizing for the stark cable: 'A dreadful shock I am afraid. I am so sorry. I was not up to telephoning you at your office; it is hard for me to write, hard to take in the dreadful finality of loss, hard to find the right words at this distance. Will you please think of coming out? That would be best. You will be very welcome. Just cable to the firm date and flight number of arrival Delhi. Yours, Lance Gardner.'

The letter disarmed me. In no way was it fatherly: 'Yours . . .' etc. I need have no fears on that score. In any case had the man wanted to claim paternity would he not have done so years ago? On the contrary, he had not even attempted to *see* me. My mind, now reassured on one score, switched from the defensive to begrudging interest. I felt cheated that I had never been invited up to Scotland. Holidays at the Lodge with my mother and wealthy benefactor would have made a nice break from work! Why had she never suggested it? I had long since had the regular summer address in Angus and believed she was staying with some of those 'old friends' from India. Surely she could not have refrained for fear of *shocking* me? Anyway, if she was so sensitive that she felt she could not tell a daughter, why had she not married and regularized the arrangement? Granted we had each gone our own ways, but this was taking independence to ridiculous lengths.

The more I puzzled over the enigma, the more I felt like accepting Lance Gardner's invitation. Out there I could see for myself. Things in the ensuing days kept on coming back to me about my mother: how well dressed she was on the occasions we *had* met, in her usual impeccable taste but surely more expensively than she could afford? How radiant she looked. With hindsight again, I saw that her regular phone calls from overseas had been guarded. She glossed over what she was doing, and asked about myself. I was only too happy to relate my successes.

Several times had I travelled to the west on business, but I had never travelled to the east. It is a pleasant idea at my age to return to one's birthplace, take a good look at oneself in perspective, and assess what life has done to one to date. By all accounts the Mission Hospital where I was born in Quetta was still functioning. I would like to see it. A short visit to India and return via Pakistan would just fit. It wouldn't do to be away too long.

I put a line across ten days in my desk diary, and went out to the nearest travel agency to book an air passage.

The ten-seater private plane circled low, the co-pilot up front talking into an intercom. My ears popped. We swayed towards a conning tower by a small airstrip. The ground rushed past. A slight bump, then firmly down, the brakes applied, the little craft turning to taxi towards the airport building.

Other aircraft squatted, dotted about on the ground, one cumbersome freight plane being unloaded. An unhurried scene confronted me in dazzling sunlight at the top of the short steps. I fished around in my bag for my sunglasses, thanked the blue-and-gold-uniformed pilot, and descended. A strong smell of spicy dust assailed my nostrils. I liked heat and always took my annual holiday on some scorching beach, and I liked the feel of it now as I stepped onto the soil hazed in mirage. That was just as well, for had I found it hostile, the series of shocks I was about to experience might have proved fatal!

First shock was the man striding from the building towards me, an exceptionally tall dark man dressed in high-buttoned, long, closely fitted coat that flared like a graceful skirt over bulky cotton trousers such as I had seen in pictures of North-West Frontier Pathans. He was hatless, a shock of grey hair brushed across a deeply furrowed forehead. The man looked haggard, lines darkly etched about the clean-shaven upper lip. I frowned and looked down, my gaze arrested by the slim brown feet fast approaching, casual in open-thonged leather shoes.

'Nawab-sahib.' The clerk at my shoulder who had been my companion on the plane touched his forehead and gave an obeisance, reverence showing in voice and gesture.

'Salaam, Aziz Ahmed.' The words were followed by more rapid Hindi. I heard the deep tones for the first time though I did not understand the meaning. The Nawab extended me a hand at the same moment that he spoke to the official. He held mine fractionally in an iron clasp that bruised. I forced my eyes, hidden from him by the dark glasses, away from his feet. Sockless Lance Gardner was an Indian: *Indian to the core*! No wonder my grandfather had put a stop to his daughter's infatuation in those far-off days. Though I have no colour prejudice myself, my generation having mixed freely with every shade of skin at school and university, I

368

could well imagine the impact this man must have made in a town like Christchurch forty years ago.

'Welcome to Kootgunge,' the voice pronounced in impeccable English. Second shock. His speech without the slightest trace of sing-song could not be more *British*! Which was he, this hybrid with one foot in two continents?

'Thank you.' I endeavoured to collect my wits.

'Come.' He indicated the way in a gesture of a hand, palm upwards that was pure courtly Indian. 'You are not at all like your mother, though I cannot really see what you are like with those revolting mirrored glasses,' the words accused.

'I am like my father,' I replied in my most haughty manner. 'He was tall and dark-haired and brown-eyed.' I took my glasses off so that he could see for himself. We looked at each other straight, eyes squinting in the glaring sun. I do not know what he thought of me, but *I* thought that he was the most prepossessing creature I had ever met though I was not going to let him know it.

'That is as it should be.' Lance Gardner's stern expression relaxed into a smile. I had a glimpse then of the 'more to it' I had come to investigate. The sheer looks, charm and strength of personality of the man in his late sixties was arresting. What must he have been like in his mid-twenties? Positively stunning! And my mother had been pretty stunning all along . . .

A servant of indeterminate age stood by a shooting brake. 'Salaam, Miss-sahib.' He looked curiously at me, and then, shading his half-look with downcast eyes, shut the door on me. As Lance Gardner started up the car, the bearer dived into the back seat.

'Ghulam Haidar remembers you as a toddler in Quetta. He took over when he was little more than a *chokra* from Nasrullah Khan, my head man in the Palace. The latter left Quetta when your father went to the front. He speaks better English than Ghulam Haidar does. You must have a word with them.'

'Oh, how nice.' I turned round to smile at the old retainer

369

whom my mother had trained, and whom I had read about in the diaries. It was he who had faithfully attended her on the journey over the flooded Indus, terrified though he was. I had no experience of how to treat Indian servants, but instinctively I felt that to show the same familiarity that is common with us all in England from whatever background would not be acceptable here where I was called 'Miss-sahib', where the caste system was as strong as ever, and where deep obeisances were made to the Nawab. (Later I was to see a villager rush out from his hut and literally prostrate himself to kiss his 'lord's' feet – this in 1980!)

We drove off leaving a cloud of dust behind, the estate car winding its way along the Pila Nadi River, another name that was familiar to me from the war-time diaries. A thick wall of jungle over the water framed an old-fashioned paddle steamer that could have been something out of the Mississippi, coolies in white loading produce.

'Jute harvest. Busy time of year.' Lance Gardner drove on. We progressed to an ornate iron gateway, two soldiers on guard coming to the ready and smartly saluting.

'You have an army?' I was so thrown by the whole set-up I could believe anything.

'Not any more,' he laughed outright, 'though in my grandfather's day there was a troop to guard the two hundred souls living here, including the Princess's fourteen slave girls! No: these are retired *sowars* I employ; allowed to wear uniforms and medals rather in the same way as commissionaires do; most are from the 2nd Lancers, the old Gardner's Horse raised by my great-grandfather, others are men who served with me in Burma. Tremendous chaps. We did up the barracks for them and their families over there by the elephant gate.' He indicated a long low brick building facing a wide grassy ditch.

By what must have been the moat soared massive wooden gates studded with spikes to keep out any invading elephant cavalry of old. 'The gate had to be almost completely rebuilt. It stays open though it has hydraulics to shut it,' Lance Gardner explained. 'No need to, thank God. Here we are a Muslim drop living in an ocean of Hindus. Don't believe all that claptrap you read in the press about being continually at each other's throats. Politics most of the time – not like that on the ground. There's a large cantonment not far from Solah. Practically all the followers are Muslim. Couldn't function without us!' The brake swerved under the gate structure on which was emblazoned in colour a winged dragon above trefoil shield of rampant lions. 'Our motto reads "*namak halal*" for "true to his salt". There you have it in a nutshell . . .' My escort, the powerful *zemindar*, talked on in an easy friendly manner.

I noticed how ably he drove the car though his left hand had but thumb and stumps. Like most of us whose hobby is fast cars, I am nervous with the run-of-the-mill driver, especially with those who chat as they go and hold the wheel with one hand! Yet though Lance Gardner drove at some pace on the uneven, meandering road, I was not uneasy sitting beside him. I knew from his last batch of letters to my mother that he had, after the war, obtained a pilot's licence. Neither would I be nervous with him at the controls in the air. The man gave out enormous confidence. He gave it to everyone he came into contact with I was sure: his servants, his workers on the estate, his friends and acquaintances – and in radiant measure I saw how he must have given it to my mother. He had lifted her from her *bonne-à-tout-faire* life in a suburban bungalow estate to all this!

Impressed enough by the physical appearance of the man at my side, and by the double-gated and guarded approach to his fastness, I was now to be dumb-struck in amazement by where he lived, a place which from the air had given the impression of being flat and disjointed.

The car swept up a loosely gravelled carriageway lined with tamarisks and punctuated by cast-iron lamp columns through a landscaped area bright with flowering shrubs and trees. Great clumps of cascading bougainvillea in every shade of red, terracotta and mauve, fronted by yellow and orange canna lilies, blazed in profusion. Flame-of-the-forest trees stood by tall palms interspersed by feathery mimosas backed by huge indigenous trees. There was a *tope* of dark mangoes, an avenue of neem and teak, a solitary peepul branching enormous pillar-rooted shade. By the edge of the drive, formal beds ranked marigolds, roses, pansies, geraniums, poinsettias. Peacocks strutted on terraces, one large bird displaying his magnificent feathers in a fan of iridescent hues of blues and greens.

I stepped out of the brake and stood staring at the building as my mother must have stared on first sighting. Then it had looked forbidding, in ruins, on a dark night during the horrors of war. Now, in a haze of brilliant sunshine it made a dreaming vision of exotic warmth.

I was no ingenue. In the States I had stayed in Hollywood-type houses, in spacious ranches, in New York apartments where no expense was spared, but I had never seen anything like this. The old two-storied Moghul mansion built by Colonel William Linneaus Gardner for his bride Her Highness the Princess Mah Munsel-ool-Nissa from the dowry of the Emperor Akbar Shah, had been exquisitely restored by their descendant Colonel Lance Delhmir Gardner, part out of the fortune left him by his father-in-law, the jute and tea magnate Mr Tinling, part from his own business acumen. Much of the original soft sandstone had been used in the reconstruction, the work executed by skilled craftsmen, most of them local, the poverty-stricken village of Kootgunge brought to life and prosperity, the sound of chisel on stone, saw on wood, vitalizing the district. No wonder the Nawab of Kootgunge was revered as a near-god, his people throwing themselves in delirious gratitude at his feet! In the way of the world over, here the craftsmen's expertise had been passed down from father to son in the age-old tradition, the artisans taking enormous pride in their work, as well they might.

One massive central onion crowned the building; its surface was glazed with shining blue and yellow tiles in contrast to the soft rose of the rest. Around and below lay lesser oriental domes and smaller still domelets besides cupolas, roof pavilions and parapets, canopied balconies, hanging verandahs, umbrella-shaped *chattris* — a whole riot of delicately worked architecture. There were tender balustrades on the roofs, deftly formed arcaded screens with beautiful friezes on the ground floors, graceful minarets on corners. Much of the central structure was embellished with leaf ornaments and palmettes, and there were elephant and peacock sculptures. Wide steps led up to the slenderly colonnaded main entrance which was topped by a Moghul *chattri* of rounded grace. I could see to one side of the front entrance the forms of the two semi-circular rooms that had been the first to be reconstructed. Above them was a flat top expanse crowded with pot plants.

'Your mother had the idea to turn the roof into a terrace for times when the sun is needed to warm.' Lance Gardner stood beside me, an expression of pain on his face. 'We often . . .' He stopped.

'Was that where . . .?' I asked hesitantly for fear of hurting him further.

He shook his head, his face ravaged, and for a long moment he stood unable to reply. 'The Chashma Shahi was built to be cool in the heat,' after a while he resumed. 'Not a corner of the *Mahal* escapes a breeze, air ducts ensuring a flow passing through to every chamber. It can therefore be really cold in winter as you will find if you are able to stay on awhile, as I hope you will. Hence your mother made a sheltered spot for winter months, as well as introducing some fireplaces for log fires. The Palace is full of your mother's ideas; her touches are everywhere, particularly—'

His words were interrupted by a cavalcade of riders trotting up the drive. A *syce* leapt out of his saddle, another came running from a side entrance, and with *pugri* ends flying held tossing manes while the riders, talking amongst themselves, dismounted. Seeing us on the steps they stopped their chatter, and walked soberly up to be introduced. There were three of them, the two young men in jodhpurs, chukka boots and open-necked shirts. Other than that they looked much the same age, they were dissimilar, one being fair and not particularly tall, the other darker and taller. The third member of the party was a slim slip of a girl in blouse and slacks. She had enormous dark eyes; her rippling hair was tied back off her face into a thick plait hanging down her back. From the colour . . .

'Geraldine, I would like you to meet William, James and Issa,' Lance Gardner said quietly.

On that morning of shocks this was the greatest shock of all.

2

'I told Aziz Ahmed I would be joining him right away in the office. Will be back to lunch. Leave you to Issa,' Lance Gardner said. Trying not to look as stunned as I felt, I watched him jump into the brake with the agility of a man half his age and drive off at speed.

'Come.' Issa used the same delicate hand gesture her father had used at the airport. She led me into the palace and through a large hallway to marble stairs that divided, a flight to the left, another to the right. Upstairs we walked along an open gallery to a suite of rooms looking over the winter terrace garden. A *chapprassi* followed with my case. He was in white uniform, the Gardner arms on blue breastplate, the end of his *pugri* stiffly fluted and starched. A small Hindu woman in a sari sidled over to stand barefoot and give me the *namaste* greeting.

'She is your *ayah*,' Issa said. 'She will look after your clothes and get you anything you need. You only have to call her. Is there something you would like, some refreshment perhaps?'

'No, no. Everything is perfect.' I took in the tastefully decorated room with bathroom and sitting-room which led out to the terrace filled with potted geraniums and fuchsias.

'Then I will leave you,' Issa said in her shy manner. 'When I have changed I will return to fetch you. In about an hour's time? Please do not try to find your way on your own. Everyone gets lost in the *Mahal* to begin with.' A small laugh tinkled.

'Yes, yes, that will be fine; in about an hour's time,' I said hurriedly, not meaning to be rude but wanting only to be left alone to straighten my thoughts out. I went to the marbled bathroom to wash and change from my tailored trouser suit to a linen dress while the *ayah* unpacked my suitcase and took my clothes away to press. I felt awkward and badly done by, my grudge against Lance growing. Why had I not guessed? Once again *why could not my mother have told me?*

I went out onto the terrace and sat on one of the upholstered swing seats and gazed at the view of trees, water, colourful shrubs, without really taking any of it in. 'You will find the palace full of your mother's touches.' How was I supposed to know what her 'touches' were when in the Wick bungalow she had never had two pennies to rub together for such luxuries as expensive matching bed covers, damask curtains, golden bathroom taps, gorgeous oriental carpets?

Restlessly I rose and went back into the sitting-room. I noted the writing paper laid out on the desk was more elaborate than that used in the last batch of letters to my mother. On those there had been some old script; now the heading was surrounded by a Moghul arch in dog's tooth design, the theme of the architecture of the building. I looked closer and saw the drawing was minutely initialled with CDG. My mother's 'touch'! I had not known she had any artistic talents. But what hit me most were the initials. At home they were CD*B*. On letters, on her will, her signature was Brownlow.

Issa came back changed into apple-green silk *shalwar* tapering into neat folds about her ankles, a long-sleeved matching *kameez* over, a flimsy *duputta* thrown round neck, the ends gracefully tossed back from her shoulders. She was extremely pretty. Unusual-looking too with her dark eyes and Titian hair. But she did not look well; her eyes were . . . With a start I realized she had been crying. Perhaps I was as much of a shock to her as she was to me. Perhaps I reminded her of her mother. I had often been told that despite my dark hair I bore a strong resemblance to my mother in shape of face and set of eyes.

'I will show you round a bit before lunch if you would like that,' she said shyly.

'How nice you look,' I said to put her at ease while my mind raced . . . crying for my mother, *our mother*. 'Is that the dress you wear every day?'

'We usually wear European dress at university. This when off work.'

'You look too young. What university?'

'I am eighteen, the twins a year older. Benares. We girls live in the women's hostel. It's good fun. I'm studying modern languages. I'm so glad you've come, because I worry about Daddy. You see . . . I have to go back this term, but how can I leave him?' Her eyes brimmed with tears.

'What about your brothers?'

'Willie's at the Agricultural College in Solah. He's mad keen on farming; and James is half-way through his training at the Officers' Military Academy and destined for a commission into the 2nd Lancers. All of us have been rather a long time away from our studies. Please. I think you should come now.'

She took me round a gallery and down more stairs and into an inner courtyard and along some cloisters through an open space – until I was thoroughly lost – to the semi-circular room which Issa explained they used when they were 'family'. It looked pretty big to me, and it was instantly recognizable from what I had read in the diaries, by the giant chandeliers sparkling and glinting in multi-colours. I smiled to myself in recognition, and went across to examine more closely the screens, each hewn out of a single slab of marble. There was no sign of the Nawab's divan upon which, in my mother's description, Lance Gardner had sprawled. Instead there were several large sofas and many comfortable chairs informally arranged.

The farther room was used as the dining-room. The

ceiling had a cleverly drawn tent-top, drapes to match in sand-coloured material on the walls. It was most effective. In the bay of the room was a round table which a *khidmat-gar* was laying for lunch, canvas Roorkee chairs arranged around in keeping with the camping decor.

'Mummee had it done in a copy of the Wana huts they have on the Frontier.' Issa whisked me off down a long corridor to the vast circular central room of the mansion directly under the dome and used only for large parties, a parquet-floored ballroom leading off it. This, she told me, was the part of the palace used for formal entertaining. We climbed endless dark stairs until we reached into the dome itself.

'I wanted you to see where Mummee and Daddy's island is. I wonder if he will ever go there again?' Her voice faltered. She opened a door in the blue and yellow tiles. I found myself on a narrow parapet enclosed by a stone balustered walk circling the dome. I followed her pointing arm to where a white pavilion stood like a dot far away among the green. 'From there one can see our dome. The pavilion is on an island in the middle of the Pila Nadi. They used to go when they came to the end of their tether and had to get away from it all! That was the place James Gardner took the Princess Mulka when they ran away. Do you know the story?'

'A little of it. I'd like to hear more.'

'I don't know what Daddy is going to do without Mummee. They . . . they were rather special, you know. They had a kind of affinity . . . everyone who saw them together remarked upon it.'

'What did your parents have to get away from in a place like this, stiff with retainers?' I asked to divert Issa who was biting her lower lip to stop its trembling. Her sorrow at the loss of her mother put me in mind of the anguish I had suffered at the time when my father died. It was all so strange. My mother had been solely mine for twenty years. Then, without my knowledge she had been the twins' and Issa's. Why had I not been told long ago? My fault perhaps for distancing myself; but that did not make me like the feeling of having been kept in the dark any the better, of being left out. I blamed Lance: why hadn't *he* insisted?

'To get away from all the work, and all the entertainment of course,' Issa replied. 'The servants whom we are *stiff* with,' she emphasized with her little laugh, 'have to be looked after with their families, and the workers and *their* families. Mummee was always at it. She had a clinic for them which she supervised . . . she was a VAD in World War II, but you know that. She and Daddy had a hospital built, schools, playing fields, a swimming pool so that the children can learn to swim and not drown in the river and village tanks, a kindergarten so the women can go out to work. They always went to the island to recover from Christmas. I don't like to think of what it will be like this year. If the guests come here it will be quite terrible without Mummee. Yet if they do not come it will be worse on our own . . .'

'Who are "they"?' We descended the stairs and went out into the garden and over to the swimming pool which evidently had once been an elephant tank. Now it was modern, blue-tiled, and tree-shaded. A boy in a *dhoti* stood by it fishing out leaves with a shrimp net.

'Our young friends, and friends of Mummee's and Daddy's and their children and grandchildren,' Issa answered my question. We settled down by the pool, a venerable bearer coming up with a beaming smile, Issa introducing Nasrullah Khan. I had a few words with him which seemed to please him. He told me in broken English he had first come into my parents' service in 1939: the 'Captain-sahib' and the 'Brownlow memsahib' he called them. That was better. For once *my* parents!

'What did the servants call your mother?' I asked Issa when the bearer had left to get drinks.

'"Begum-sahiba", or sometimes the old-fashioned "Bibi-sahiba"; that is the title for a Nawab's wife.'

I was beginning to see it: my mother another lovely Muslim princess, the Begum Sahiba who had reigned serene and supreme over her household here for twenty years, adored by the people of Kootgunge, but *wife*? I was astonished at that. It was a gloss-over of course, an illusion. Or did Issa really believe it? I listened to her talking more naturally now, less shy of me. ' . . . we go and stay with these friends in return.' I caught up with what she was saying after Nasrullah Khan had returned with a soft drink for her, a dry Martini for me which I badly needed. 'Some of them join us in Scotland. When we have a house party here Daddy says it puts him in mind of the olden days when my great-great grandparents William and Nissa had every room in the *Mahal* permanently filled with relatives and hangers-on, which in India means all the poor relations! We were fifty strong last Christmas. My brothers turned out of their rooms and camped in the bath-house. We had a great time riding and swimming. Mummee loved to ride. She and Daddy went out whenever they could in the early mornings. The boys arranged gymkhanas and *pagal* games, paperchases on horseback, and they got up a polo team. There's tennis and golf for those that want it, and the smaller children have marvellous fun running wild in the walled garden and playing sardines or hide-and-seek and inevitably getting lost in the rooms! We even keep an elephant for them to ride. She's called Mumtaz. I must show you her stable at the back.'

'Sounds a ball!'

'We have one' – she had not heard the expression and took me literally – 'on New Year's Eve, and a banquet in the domed hall on Christmas Eve. Some of the guests are relations of yours.'

'Oh, who?'

'Uncle Bobby's widow, Auntie Susan, and their son Robert.'

'Ah yes, I knew my mother stayed with them in Australia. I haven't met them since I was a child.'

'Oh you should! Robert is a very big dear. He's a pilot with Quantas. Married with three children. The whole family come. Auntie Susan brings her second husband,

Uncle Holroyd. He used to be in the Australian Air Force and knew Uncle Bobby in the war. They have two children and quite a few grandchildren. We stay with them on their farm out back of Sydney when it is our summer holidays and their winter. Robert is based on Melbourne where Mummee and Daddy knew the Governor who was once a Jute-wallah.'

'Who else besides the Thorntons and Holroyds?'

'There's the Beeches – he was in Daddy's firm; there's Auntie Pammie from Canada. Her daughter Carissa is Mummee's goddaughter, and *that* Cara comes with her Canadian husband and their children.'

'Weren't there three older Dangerfield boys?'

'Yes. They visit sometimes. Mummee says, said, she couldn't think how Auntie managed to bring them up, they were so naughty in Quetta. They're quite old now. Then there's Uncle Paddy. Christmas wouldn't be Christmas without Uncle Paddy. His *bibi* Lolitha died. She got so fat last time she came she had to have two seats booked on the plane from Los Angeles!'

'I know his books. I'd like to meet him.'

'He's interested in you and your career because he knew you as a baby. Mrs MacCreath always comes. She'd be heartbroken if she wasn't asked. She's a dear little old widow . . .' Issa prattled on.

I had one more question before we went into lunch: 'When did you come to hear about me?' I asked.

'We've always known about you.' She looked at me with wide surprised eyes. 'Mummee was always talking about you. We've been longing to meet you for years and years – our very own half-sister! It was sorrowful for you your father dying,' she expressed in her sweet manner.

'Yes; sadly he died when I was about the same age as you are now, Issa.' I finished my drink and we followed Nasrullah Khan into lunch.

That was all I wanted to know. That they, the children, had no knowledge of Quetta water! I felt as if

380

a load had been taken off my back. I felt as if my dearly loved father had been restored to me.

That first day at the Chashma Shahi turned out to be very full indeed. After lunch (the food was European. I learnt that Lance Gardner could not abide curries, which he declared burnt the stomach lining, and that he drank only fruit juice), I went to my room to rest from jet-lag, and fell into a deep sleep in the lethargy of the hottest part of the day. The shadows had begun to lengthen when William knocked on my door and asked if I would like a tour of the 'works'. I noticed his sombre looks, and once again it hit me that they were grieving for *my* mother. I said I would, and ten minutes later we were in the estate car, William at the wheel, his dark military-moustached brother beside him. Lance Gardner and I sat in the back.

On the tour, I learnt not only more about the lively intelligence of the good-looking twins and the specifics of their chosen careers, but also a great deal about jute farming. I thought I might be bored, but such was the enthusiasm of William and his father for their subject, that I found myself wanting to know more.

'You'll hear the sirens going early tomorrow. The mills start work at five-thirty every morning except Fridays,' Lance Gardner informed while taking me into a building.

'Fields are hand-weeded, thinned out by an army of well-housed, well-paid workers. The leaves are used as potherb. On the Kootgunge farms there is allowed no waste. Scottish blood!' James teased his brother.

We went to visit the retting rooms where the stems were left to soak in water for two to three weeks, then stripped and washed and hung up by grading to dry out. We moved into a factory turning out the end products of packaging bags and ropes, and on into another huge one devoted entirely to the making of prayer mats. This was what had spurred on the Kootgunge jute farming venture into an unqualified success.

'These goods are exported to oriental countries

throughout the world.' Lance Gardner held a prayer mat for me to inspect. 'The explosion came with the boom from the oil-rich Middle East nations. Sales rocketed after your mother drafted these designs taken from old drawings and mosaic paintings she found in the Palace. We have the patent. They've swept the Mohammedan world . . . cannot make enough of them. We churn out hundreds of thousands and are in the process of expanding. Her loss is infinite, not only to me, to everyone here—' he broke off gruffly.

'I miss Mummee all the time,' James said simply. He put his arm over his father's shoulders in a sweet manner of sympathy few English boys would have been seen dead doing.

'Her artistic taste must have come from *her* mother,' I mused with a finger tracing the old Moghul patterns while thinking how open and direct the young men were in their sharing of grief. 'Your Irish grandmother, Doreen Thornton, painted beautifully. Incidentally *she* was one of twins,' I revealed.

'We know.' William smiled my mother's smile at me, dark eyelashes shading green eyes, freckles marking his aristocratic nose. 'Daughter of Major-General O'Rourke who broke his neck out hunting in Ootacamund! We know about the Thorntons.'

'You have the advantage of me. I am beginning to think you *all* have the advantage of me here,' I burst out, showing my anger at the position I had been put in. I glared at Lance. *He* knew all about Quetta water, damn him!

'*You're* the one who has the advantage.' James looked at me with admiration. 'Fancy running a literary magazine. Now *that* is an achievement. Anybody can grow jute!'

Our last port of call that day, by which time the sun was lowering on the far horizon, darkness fast descending, was the Gardner mausoleum. Ringed by a linked iron chain, it rose tall above the acres of jute in the flat plain. It stood isolated, stalwart and solid, a grand three-arched gateway topped by a dome, its surface bearing the ravages of the years in old weather-pitted red-ochre stone. Near, was a mound whereunder lay a favourite elephant, and over there, by a sentinel palm tree, lay a small, and beautifully tended, cemetery.

High on a plinth was set a polished white tomb. The base was large, an extended plinth waiting for another. The setting sun bathed the grave with evening light, golden dust filtering the air, horizontal lines of still smoke verging into the sunset. The marble before me flushed into deep rose. I held my breath at the colour and the beauty of the stone in the hush of the ancient *zemandari* land, the only sound the rustling of the palm fronds in the wind. Swiftly the red globe sank, the rose faded.

And then it was dark. I found myself weeping, flanked by the comfort of three broad-shouldered Gardner men.

3

Some days later, the Nawab of Kootgunge, looking stern, uttered that one word I had come to expect. He walked ahead of me out of the drawing-room. By then I knew that coming from him, the word was a command. It was enough. I went – wondering. Anywhere else I would have at least asked, 'Where are we going?' or even, 'Why?' Instead I sensed the momentousness of the one syllable. As obediently as a respectful retainer, I followed him.

There had been time to get over my initial shock, and blocking my mind to anything further, I resolved to enjoy myself, gladly accepting the fact that far from being an only child I had nineteen-year-old twin half-brothers, and an eighteen-year-old half-sister of whom I was already proud. They were quite unlike modern western youth, though they spoke English fluently with only a trace of foreign intonation. They may have had an English mother, but they were Indian born and reared, and they had old-fashioned good manners, respect showing for their elders which I was old enough to appreciate! So when their father said, 'Come,' I went, knowing by now, as they knew, that Lance Gardner did not say 'Come' without a very good reason.

I realized that even I had fallen under his spell. Few of either sex could meet Lance Gardner and not be attracted by his strong handshake, direct gaze in the eye, and genuine niceness, a word I usually edit out, but use here for want of a better way to describe a man who had reached the top of his career without exploiting ruthless methods, and carelessly trampling over others en route.

If I had already come under Lance Gardner's mystique, I was also beginning to understand the sensitiveness and vulnerability of the man I had discovered in the letters, and to recognize his moods. From the workings of his jaw and the grim set of his mouth, I could sense that this silent progress through parts of the palace new to me was an emotional pilgrimage, and that it was costing him a great deal as we moved in and out of courtyards, and down arcaded ways. So I followed him to the most private quarters of the palace where in olden days only males of immediate kinship, or eunuchs, were permitted to enter through the guarded *deodhi* gates.

'I have not been to the *zenana* pavilion since your mother died.' Lance Gardner paused at the entrance to an innermost garden surrounded by a series of lofty rooms with jutting balconies upon which creepers clung before lattice-grilled windows. 'I thought you should see . . . I thought it right to come with you to show . . . please do not smoke here,' he managed, his face seared with emotion. He sat down heavily upon a marble bench in the open. 'Go.' He swallowed. 'Go round it all; take your time. I will wait here.'

I went into the rooms. They were dusted, clean, tidy, her scent and silver brushes upon an antique dressing-table just as my mother had left them when she went out into the garden for the last time. I paused in this most feminine of bedrooms with its flimsy blue-netting drawn back from the great Nawab's low divan, over it a draped canopy in rose satin. I looked up in delight at the rounded ceiling covered with tiny convex mirrors which glittered like silver stars.

Yellow and blue stone mosaic paintings adorned the walls between carved ivory panels. I switched on the bulbs. The effect of the mirrors reflected in the soft light was one of pure enchantment. In a gesture of genuine wonderment I gently touched the satin bedspread with my hand before progressing into the adjoining room.

Here louvred cupboards contained layers and layers of clothes wrapped in pristine white tissue paper. The clothes were entirely Muslim, the soft trouser suit style of ladies' clothing such as Issa called her *shalwar kāmeez* with *dupatta* veil. In another cupboard I found draped *pājāmas*, short saris, and on hangers numerous sparkling jewel-encrusted and brocaded waistcoats fit for a princess.

Wishing that I had seen my mother in this dress and in this setting, I went out into the garden, a dripping sequestered pool of lush greenery with beds of varied pansies and double poppies in an oasis of pink. I came upon two *malis* watering, and with pleasure sniffed the uniquely refreshing smell of moisture on hot paths and borders cooling the evening air. The angles of the high walls that surrounded the garden, together with the balconies, cast deep shadows so that all through the heat of the summer weather there was always to be found a pond of shade to sit in or work in . . . and my mother had worked much in this garden.

As the Princess Nissa had done before her Cara made a herb garden, finding her inspiration, as she had for the prayer mats, from old documents of those times. She rediscovered the herbs and their uses with which she treated her household when they fell ill, found these medicinal infusions for the simpler ailments often benefited the people of the soil who came to the clinic more than up-to-date drugs. Cara cut back, but did not cut out, the clear-blue convolvulus creeper that had grown wild, trained it to grow up the pink walls beside sweet-scented white jasmine. In another corner I found a mass of violet clematis next to riotous purple passion-flower growing beside a fig tree heavily laden with ripe magenta fruit.

I wandered on around the secret garden, its quietness

calming the upheaval that had been within me since my arrival in Kootgunge. The serenity of the old enclosed space seeped over me and I felt closer here to my mother than I had since childhood days.

Here flowed the cool water that was channelled directly from the pure spring of the Chashma Shahi, the Spring Imperial. It spouted from a figurine into an alabaster basin and cascaded splashing in glorious abandon into marbled garden pools where blue lotus lilies floated. The fountain played and sprayed, the liquid blown by the zephyr of air that ruffled into transparent curtains of bead droplets.

There came into my view the golden swing that Lance had given to Cara so that she could discover the sensuous experience of swinging in the rain, and be carried, her draperies moulding her figure, by her Nawab to the privacy of their starry room and the intimacy of the divan. I forced myself to face that this had been so. And why not, with my father dead? I had no doubt that Lance and Cara had been lovers right up to the day of their final parting, and at last I felt a glow of gladness for my mother.

'I came upon your mother sleeping – as I thought.' Lance's words came gruffly to me after I returned and had sat down on the bench by him. 'Did you know that she had a heart condition? She kept it from me, at least she said it was nothing, a mere murmur that the doctor had given her some pills for; that was all.'

'I did not know even that much.' The regret showed in my voice. 'There is so much I wish I had known.'

'But you have read the letters?'

'Yes, I have read them, and the war-time diaries.'

'You know more than I,' he said adjusting his *lubuda* which I knew had belonged to his great-grandfather William. Unashamedly he wiped away a tear with a grey Meshedi silk handkerchief. 'Altogether you know too much about me!' His eyes crinkled at the corners into deep crow's feet, the crease in the cheek appearing that my mother had described and I had not yet seen. A man of swift changes of mood, I remembered. How quickly from melancholy to amusement.

'Did you burn the letters, or have you kept them?' he went on.

'I have brought them. I neither want to burn them, nor do I wish to give them up.'

'Oh?' He sounded cautious.

'Do you have my mother's letters to you?' It was my turn to question.

'I do.'

'They are far too interesting to burn, and might be put to good use.'

'Hummn. What do you mean? The Gardners were never ones for publicity. I fail to see the particular interest. Your mother and I are not the first people to have fallen in love!'

'But don't you see, the interest is the love story of the British for India entwined in an old historical romance. I first felt the lure of India when my plane circled Delhi before landing. There below me was a modern city encompassing an ancient one of vast red walls. And when I got off, the scorched soil upon which I trod seemed already part of me. After all it *is* the land of my birth!'

'Ha!' Lance exclaimed with raised eyebrow, 'so under that professional exterior there beats a heart! I will have to think about your mother's letters. *We* need time as a family to adjust to our loss, to stabilize ourselves. Your mother has broken my heart for the third time by deserting me on the last lap. If I could get hold of her I would berate her roundly for her underhand trick,' he expressed with a gusto that I found a good sign, and then he said, his voice mellowing, 'The good that has come out of this, is that it has brought you here.'

There was a pause. I was taken aback. Had he wanted me to come before? There was another circumstance that puzzled me. 'May I ask a rather personal question?' I enquired, somewhat tartly.

'Fire away.'

'Why did you and my mother never marry? I mean, after my father died?'

'We did marry.'

'But . . .' I took a deep breath, my bitterness coming back sharply. '*Why wasn't I told?* Why didn't *you* insist?'

'Listen, Geraldine,' he said quietly. 'Listen . . . I should explain that my first wife, Janet, refused to divorce me. I was surprised though I should not have been. We had, years before, parted amicably and met from time to time. Neither of us even contemplated going through the distasteful complications of divorce in those days when it was all a put-up farce of male partner seen with a paid female stooge by a chambermaid in a hotel bedroom bringing in the morning tea! Why should we bother with that rigmarole when neither of us wanted to marry again? But all that changed when a divorce was mooted after your father's death and Janet discovered whom I wished to marry. The name Carissa was like a red rag to a bull. She blamed, with reason, your mother for coming between us in Christchurch in the first place, and causing her to wait through the war years for us to marry; she could never forget it. When it came to my asking for a divorce, all her old animosity surfaced. From originally misdoubting your mother after the war, when she found some correspondence in Calcutta and saw that we had been in touch (it was over the matter of returning a ring), she became even more suspicious, and by the time the subject of divorce came up, insanely jealous, which rapidly turned into pathological perversity. 'Over my dead body' were her flung words when I confronted her in an appalling interview in Jersey in an effort to try and sort things out sensibly, the last time I had any direct communication with her. After that her house was barred to me and letters via the solicitors failed to dent her resolve. As you probably know, in those days both parties had to consent to obtain a divorce.'

'Yes, but how did my mother take this impasse? Did you try again later when the divorce laws were relaxed, the seven-year separation, wasn't it, and later still the "quickie" divorce?'

'That is another story. When the law was changed I proposed we put proceedings in train for your mother. She flatly refused. She wouldn't hear of it. She said to leave Janet alone. The last thing she wanted was for her to be distressed all over again, to have to face once more the facts. She said that much of what had happened to upset Janet's life *was* her fault; that she *had* butted in way back in Christchurch. She said that she could see how Janet liked the status of being Mrs Lance Delhmir Gardner, and that her pregnancies not coming to fulfilment had been a tragedy for her. Your mother ended by saying, "I have so much. I have all this. I have *you*. We love one another, and we have our children. Let Janet remain your wife in name since it pleases her. It is little enough we can give her . . ." How touched I was by your mother's generosity of spirit.' Lance sighed. 'On our first acquaintance I told her she had a big heart, and over the years she proved it true many times . . . Actually, if Janet had been more amenable we would have welcomed her here to live in the *zenana* – one big happy family, she, the senior wife, exerting influence as is the custom in very many households in the country!'

'Janet died, I suppose. When was that?' I asked, ignoring this last remark, surely said as a joke? Besides it did not seem in keeping with the mother I knew to choose the role of 'mistress' when she could now at the stroke of a pen, establish the conventionality of marriage. 'I *still* fail to understand. For instance, why wasn't I told, all the more since you—' I harped back. I just could not get over it.

'At first your mother felt she could not tell you that she was living with me within a few months of your father's death. With the deep attachment between you two, she felt it might be taken as a betrayal of your father. Neither did she want you to be put off balance at that time when you were studying for your Oxford degree. Later she thought the information would be an intrusion into your way of life with your career taking off. I always felt you *should* be told and urged her to do so on one or two occasions, but it was not my business to over-press her on the subject. At that time she was rather busy having babies! Actually when she *did* try and tell you, you made it abundantly clear you did not want to know! You can be as stubborn as—' He bit back his words. But I knew he was going to say 'as I'.

'As my mother,' I put in fiercely.

'Exactly,' he said succinctly. 'She believed that you were shying off the idea of another supplanting your father, and that you could not bear the thought. And it seems she was right! Later still she felt you were not interested in her life and where she lived or whom she was with so long as you knew she was well and happy. As time passed, it seemed to both of us increasingly difficult to tell you about our long-established household.'

'True. I was caught up in my work to the exclusion of much else,' I admitted reluctantly. 'And it is true that I once stopped my mother—'

'Your mother understood very well from her own growing-up days the need to develop your own personality. The great thing was that you kept in touch. She knew she could always call upon you. But when as the years went by you seemed to have no friends outside your business ones, when you did not marry and have children of your own, she worried that you might wake up one day and find yourself terribly alone. You say you *suppose* Janet died. I must tell you that no, she did not die, nor is she dead. She is alive and well in Jersey. She is as tough physically as the proverbial old boot! Having scared the wits out of me time and time again by her illnesses in India, she has outlived your mother who was never ill, and I have no doubt will outlive me.'

'Then what . . . why . . . ?' I was now thoroughly bemused. 'Didn't you say at the beginning that you and my mother *were* married? As a matter of fact, *how*, if your wife is alive and you are not divorced?'

'No trouble,' Lance grinned, his face lightening in boyish delight at the surprise he would unfold. '*She* would

390

not give me a divorce, but *I* could obtain one. Long ago, soon after our separation, and long before I had any thought of remarrying, I took the Faith. That was when I gave up smoking. When your mother came back into the picture I approached my *maulvi*. I was requested to repeat in public three times a *talaq*, a repetition of "I divorce thee", which constitutes a final dissolution. It is all written in the Qurān. In any case I am allowed four wives by Islamic law. One at a time is enough for me! Before the twins were born, your mother and I were married in the mosque in Old Delhi. She looked wonderful in her Muslim bridal dress. I will show you photos—'

'And how did my mother feel about this?' I was astounded. I knew she had kept to her Christian faith. We had taken communion together at the Priory on one of her more recent visits home when I had come down for the weekend to join her in the bungalow. Had she had a premonition? She had handed me my birth certificate and my baptism certificate from the Quetta Garrison Church, and she had reminded me about the letters . . .

'She said she *felt* married. She said there was no need for more for her; that the solemn ritual of our being joined together in my religion was enough. I must tell you that the marriage ceremony is as legal in this country as if it had been performed by the Bishop of Calcutta. I can assure you, Geraldine, these children here are as legitimate as you are!'

What *double-entendre* lay in that last throw-away remark? I was born in wedlock under my mother's Brownlow marriage. Whether I am my father's daughter or not makes no difference to that. I did not ask Lance to explain this remark, not then nor later. I do not wish, or need, to probe further, it is enough for me to know that I have two brothers and a sister.

'In the end,' Lance was saying, 'your beloved mother and I had twenty years together. I shall ever be grateful to God for that. We were made for each other. It is *kismet*, the will of the Almighty. Nothing could alter it. If we judged wrongly in not telling you, you must forgive us. We are one family. The children need you, Issa particularly, though the boys too. They put on a brave face, but underneath there is the hurt. *I* need you. I hope you will come to love us as we love you, feel the Chashma Shahi belongs to you as much as it does to us. The *zenana* is yours if you would like it. I shall not sleep here again, but live with my sons in the outer quarters.'

'A hanger-on in an annexe provided for lonely and destitute women relatives? One of many such in Indian households!' I quipped to hide how moved I felt: they need *me*? To be loved, my sterile life transformed? With my parents gone I thought I would never be cherished again. A miracle. I find a family and with them a *zenana* in which to live that is a paradise within a paradise. How easy it would be simply to stay on. What a luxury to be waited on by Nasrullah Khan and Ghulam Haidar. And the temptation of being able to bask in the warmth of the winter sun . . .

Light footsteps approached, young voices mingling.

'Oh *here* you are,' William said. 'Issa has been working herself up into a state.'

'I couldn't find you. I thought I had lost you.' Issa, in tears, threw herself into her father's arms.

'Not lost, but found.' Lance held her and stroked her bright hair. 'I have been telling Geraldine that I hope she will make this her home.'

'We are of the same blood. All that we have we share with you . . .' Handsome James grandly struck his cavalry pose.

'Rather,' William nodded emphatically. 'You are our elder sister.'

'*Please* stay, Geraldine.' Issa came over to me and took my hand. 'I could not bear to think of Christmas without Mummee. With you here, I can bear it.'

'My dear, I will come back for Christmas, I promise you that. But now I must go,' I said gently. Her hand, trusting and childlike, was still in mine. 'Yes,' I said with a sigh. 'I must go back to my country and my work but when I am retired God willing I shall live in the *zenana* and let the sun in the garden warm my old bones; I will be the funny old

English auntie to your children, telling them tales of far off Christchurch with its rivers and boats, and of a golden sailing girl who was their grandmother who fell in love with the Nawab of Kootgunge.'

I glanced up and noticed that all of a sudden Lance looked old and ill, his shoulders drooping as if he was already in the past. And I felt desperately sorry for this man and deeply touched by the constant love he had borne my mother.

Reaching up for the pins, I shook out my tumbling hair in a gesture of release.

'That's better,' I smiled, 'that feels like home.'

'God is good, God is good,' Lance repeated fervently, his dark eyes full of emotion.

From a minaret came the call of the Muezzin to evening prayer. Lance placed his damaged hand on my shoulder, his other on Issa, and with the stalwart twins beside us we left through the *deodhi* entrance, our faces to the west – to the fount of aspirations.

Together we turned towards Mecca.

AUTHOR'S NOTE

Readers sometimes like to know how much of a historical novel is pure fiction, how much is true, and how it came about.

In this case, Lance is a fictional character, as is Carissa Thornton, but Colonel William Linneaus Gardner who raised the famous Gardner's Horse is not. Neither is his wife, the beautiful Nissa, Princess of Cambay, adopted daughter of the Emperor Akbar Shah who, in his delight at the alliance, bestowed on her and their heirs a large grant of land which included 365 villages! Equally true is it that their son James married Mulka, an Imperial Princess of Delhi and sister of the Queen of Oudh, reputed to be 'the most celebrated native beauty in India'.

This old tale of romance and adventure in Moghul India when William Gardner, a Captain in His Majesty's Service, a 'gentleman, soldier and man of pleasing address and uncommon talents', joined the banner of the Mahratta general Jaswant Rao Holkar, thus starting a life of dangers, intrigues, imprisonment and adventures galore for himself and his Begum bride, has long fascinated me. Into it I have woven a modern love story. Though I changed the district from where William and Nissa built their palace to an imaginary 'Kootgunge', those curious enough to search for it in the deep Indian *mofussil* of Uttah Pradesh, will find the Gardner mausoleum, the old bath-house, a few scattered ruins, and even some of the descendants.

The pink palace of the 'Chashma Shahi' was inspired when on a visit to India I was privileged to be invited into a princely estate barred to the public behind tall padlocked and rusting gates. I was received with great courtesy into a beautiful rambling, decaying palace, the host apologizing that all he could offer in the way of refreshment was water. To the hot and weary traveller that I was, the glass of water brought on a tray by an ancient retainer, tasted like nectar. With a zephyr of air draughting through, I sat on a faded cretonne-covered seat by exquisite screens carved from one piece of sandstone into tracery of such delicacy they looked like lace.

The opening setting of Christchurch is as I remember it from the thirties. Across Wick Ferry there lived a brigadier-general whose red-brick Victorian house (now no more) was a veritable museum of the days of the Raj. The doctor's Square House by contrast was a graceful Palladian-style stone mansion built in 1776 facing the old Market Square. It had Adam ceilings and overmantels, heavy capitals over the main doorway, and stalwart railings along its front. Nowadays a preservation order would undoubtedly have been slapped onto it, but alas, in the fifties the house was pulled down to make way for a shopping arcade. It belonged to two family doctors much loved in the district for fifty years – father and son. They were my grandfather and uncle.

The Battle of Britain letter from 'Bobby' is taken from one written to me out in India before the pilot was shot down. The Sapper keen on ornithology on his way to survey the Gyantse Agency in Tibet was my husband.

As Cara does, I followed the drum in 1940 to Quetta. Beyond our quarter where the tarmac ended, out in the barren rocky land under Murdhar, there lay the Gunner camp of the Jute-wallahs from Calcutta, the nostalgic sound of the skirl of pipes waking us at dawn. Also, as Cara does, when Baluchistan was cut off by floods, I did the perilous journey, but with my small son born in the Quetta Mission Hospital in tow, across the swollen Indus.

With the war-time influx of regiments, the shortened

Staff College courses for regulars, and the 'junior' course for emergency commissioned officers, not to mention droves of 'abandoned wives' left behind when their husbands went off to war as mine did (sensibly he left me pregnant!), the ground was ripe for intrigues and love affairs. In the high, dry, electric atmosphere, with extremes of temperature alternating from boiling summers to freezing winters, tremors and strong rolling earthquakes adding to the hazards, anything could – and did – happen. Staid people ran off with each other; the birth rate in the Military Hospital rose to record levels; and women who had been told they were irrevocably barren, miraculously produced babies.

It was all put down to the Quetta water!

GLOSSARY

Indian words written as pronounced (often badly!) by the British were scribed to the sound in a variety of different ways. Here I have used the spelling my *munshi* taught me in Kashmir in the 1930s.

achkhan high-buttoned three-quarter-length coat
asti slow
ayah child's nurse

baba baby, young child
babu office clerk
bahut achcha very good
baksheesh tip, gratuity
bas enough
Begum Mohammedan lady
bhisti water carrier
bhoosa straw, fodder
bigah approx. half an acre
Bilayati British
bistra bedding roll
box-wallah European who works in commerce or trade
bunnia money lender
burrah-mem top lady (short for *burrah-memsahib*)
burrah-sahib great man, top man

chaddar shawl, sheet
chalumchi basin
chappatti flat cake of unleavened bread
chapprassi peon, doorman

charpoy wooden framed string woven bed
chashma spring (water)
chattri graceful domed cupola tower, or memorial
chik sun-blind made of split cane
chit, chitti letter, note sent by hand
choga long warm coat worn in Gilgit districts. Often used
    by Europeans as dressing-gowns
chokra lad, boy
chota hazri 'little breakfast', i.e. early morning tea
chota peg small whisky
chowkidar night-watchman, caretaker
chuppli leather-thonged sandals worn on Frontier

dâk post
dâk bungalow posting house where travellers put up for
    the night
darzi tailor
dawai medicine
degchie handleless saucepan with lid
deodhi gate guarding the entrance to *zenana*
dhai nurse, midwife
dhurrie cotton drugget usually made in jail
duputta headscarf

ek dam at once
ekka light trap; when curtained used for ladies in purdah

go-down outhouse in compound, store room or ware-
    house
goli ball
gup bazaar rumour, gossip

hakim doctor
hamām bath
han yes
hartal Muslim religious strike
Hazoor Your Honour
houri black-eyed nymph or beauty

jaldi quick, hurry
jao go

kameez shirt, blouse
kāreze man-made underground water channels in Baluchistan
kaun hai? who is there?
khana room. *Bibi-khana* 'native' wife's room
khansama cook
khidmatgar waiter at table
khud steep mountainside, precipice
koi-hai old-timer
kuss-kuss tattie grass blind made of woven roots

langur monkey
lathi long brass-bound staff used by the police
lubuda man's shawl

mahal palace
mahseer large Indian fresh water fish
mali gardener
maulvi Mohammedan learned in theology and sacred law
mehtar sweeper, 'untouchable'
mofussil countryside
munshi teacher, scribe
mussack sheep, goat, or buffalo hide blown up to form water container or raft

nahin no
nimbu pani boiled lime drink

pagal mad
panch sāl five years
pani water
poshteen sheepskin coat with the fleece worn inside, the skin often embroidered in bright colours
pugri turban
purdah women's seclusion, literally 'behind the curtain'

resai eiderdown

sangar defensive post made of loose rocks and stone on the Frontier
shabash! well done, bravo!
shalwar Muslim ladies' trousers
shroff banker or superior money-lender as opposed to a *bunnia*
silwar men's trousers made from yards of cloth
sowar cavalryman, trooper
syce groom

taihro! wait, stop!
tamasha show, entertainment
tikh hai all right (all well?)
tonga two-wheeled horse-drawn vehicle with seats athwart
tope grove

ummuk mule

yakdan trunk made from yak hide in Tibet

zabardast powerful, strong or tough
zemindar landowner, farmer
zemindari plantation, estate, land owned by a *zemindar*
zenana women's quarters